SECONDHAND SOULS

ALSO BY CHRISTOPHER MOORE

The Serpent of Venice

Sacré Bleu

Bite Me

Fool

You Suck

A Dirty Job

The Stupidest Angel

*Fluke: or, I Know Why
the Winged Whale Sings*

*Lamb: The Gospel According to Biff,
Christ's Childhood Pal*

The Lust Lizard of Melancholy Cove

Island of the Sequined Love Nun

Bloodsucking Fiends

Coyote Blue

Practical Demonkeeping

CHRISTOPHER MOORE

SECONDHAND SOULS

WILLIAM MORROW *An Imprint of* HarperCollins*Publishers*

SECONDHAND SOULS. Copyright © 2015 by Christopher Moore. All rights reserved. Printed in the United States of America. No part of this book may be used or reproduced in any manner whatsoever without written permission except in the case of brief quotations embodied in critical articles and reviews. For information address HarperCollins Publishers, 195 Broadway, New York, NY 10007.

HarperCollins books may be purchased for educational, business, or sales promotional use. For information please e-mail the Special Markets Department at SPsales@harpercollins.com.

FIRST EDITION

Library of Congress Cataloging-in-Publication Data has been applied for.

ISBN 978-0-06-177978-7
ISBN 978-0-06-243857-7 (Barnes & Noble signed edition)
ISBN 978-0-06-243856-0 (Books-A-Million signed edition)

15 16 17 18 19   OV/RRD   10 9 8 7 6 5 4 3 2 1

In memory of Keith Bowen

SECONDHAND SOULS

PROLOGUE

(Selected from the *Great Big Book of Death*: First Edition)

1. Congratulations, you have been chosen to act as Death, it's a dirty job, but someone has to do it. It is your duty to retrieve soul vessels from the dead and dying and see them on to their next body. If you fail, Darkness will cover the world and Chaos will reign.

2. Some time ago, the Luminatus, or the Great Death, who kept balance between light and darkness, ceased to be. Since then, Forces of Darkness have been trying to rise from below. You are all that stands between them and destruction of the collective soul of humanity. Try not to screw up.

3. In order to hold off the Forces of Darkness, you will need a number two pencil and a calendar, preferably one without pictures of kitties on it. Keep it near you when you sleep.

4. Names and numbers will come to you. The number is how many days you have to retrieve the soul vessel. Do not be late. You will know the vessels by their crimson glow.

5. Don't tell anyone what you do, or the Forces of Darkness etc. etc. etc.

6. People may not see you when you are performing your Death duties, so be careful crossing the street. You are not immortal.

7. Do not seek others of your kind. Do not waver in your duties or the Forces of Darkness will destroy you and all that you care about.

8. You do not cause death, you do not prevent death, you are a servant of Destiny, not its agent. Get over yourself.

9. Do not, under any circumstances, let a soul vessel fall into the hands of those from below—because that would be bad.

PART ONE

Do not be afraid
Everyone before you has died
You cannot stay
Any more than a baby can stay forever in the womb
Leave behind all you know
All you love
Leave behind pain and suffering
This is what Death is.

—The Book of Living and Dying
(The Tibetan Book of the Dead)

DAY OF THE DEAD

It was a cool, quiet November day in San Francisco and Alphonse Rivera, a lean, dark man of fifty, sat behind the counter of his bookstore flipping through the *Great Big Book of Death*. The old-fashioned bell over the door rang and Rivera looked up as the Emperor of San Francisco, a great woolly storm cloud of a fellow, tumbled into the store followed by his faithful dogs, Bummer and Lazarus, who ruffed and frisked with urgent intensity, then darted around the store like canine Secret Service agents, clearing the site in case a sly assassin or meaty pizza lurked among the stacks.

"The names must be recorded, Inspector," the Emperor proclaimed, "lest they be forgotten!"

Rivera was not alarmed, but by habit his hand fell to his hip, where his gun used to ride. Twenty-five years a cop, the habit was part of him, but now the gun was locked in a safe in the back room. He kept an electric stun gun under the counter that in the year since he opened the store had been moved only for dusting.

"Whose names?"

"Why the names of the dead, of course, " said the Emperor. "I need a ledger."

Rivera stood up from his stool and set his reading glasses on the counter by his book. In an instant, Bummer, the Boston terrier, and Lazarus, the golden retriever, were behind the counter with him, the former standing up on his hind legs, hopeful bug eyes raised in tribute to the treat gods, a pantheon to which he was willing to promote Rivera, for a price.

"I don't have anything for you," said Rivera, feeling as if he should have somehow known to have treats handy. "You guys aren't even supposed to be in here. No dogs allowed." He pointed to the sign on the door, which not only was facing the street, but was in a language Bummer did not read, which was all of them.

Lazarus, who was seated behind his companion, panting peacefully, looked away so as not to compound Rivera's embarrassment.

"Shut up," Rivera said to the retriever. "I know he can't read. He can take my word for it that's what the sign says."

"Inspector?" The Emperor smoothed his beard and shot the lapels of his dingy tweed overcoat, composing himself to offer assistance to a citizen in need. "You know, also, that Lazarus can't talk."

"So far," said Rivera. "But he looks like he has something to say." The ex-cop sighed, reached down, and scratched Bummer between the ears.

Bummer allowed it, dropped to all fours, and chuffed. *You could have been great,* he thought, *a hero, but now I will have to sniff a mile of heady poo to wash the scent of your failure out of my nose—oh, that feels nice. Oh, very nice. You are my new best friend.*

"Inspector?"

"I'm not an inspector anymore, Your Grace."

"Yet 'inspector' is a title you've earned by good service, and it is yours forevermore."

"Forevermore," Rivera repeated with a smile. The Emperor's grandiose manner of speaking had always amused him, reminded him of some more noble, genteel time which he'd never really experienced. "I don't mind the title following me, so much, but I had hoped I'd be able to leave all the strange happenings behind with the job."

"Strange happenings?"

"You know. You were there. The creatures under the streets, the Death Merchants, the hellhounds, Charlie Asher—you don't even know what day it is and you know—"

"It's Tuesday," said the Emperor. "A good man, Charlie Asher—a brave man. Gave his life for the people of our city. He will long be missed. But I am afraid the strange happenings continue."

"No, they don't," said Rivera, with more authority than he felt. Move along. Moving along. That it was *Día de los Muertos*, the Day of the Dead, had put him on edge already, sent him to the drawer to retrieve the *Great Big Book of Death*, but he would not give weight to more reminders. *Acknowledge a nightmare and you give it power*, someone had told him. Maybe the spooky Goth girl who used to work for Charlie Asher. "You said you needed a ledger?"

"To record the names of the dead. They came to me last night, hundreds of them, telling me to write down their names so they are not forgotten."

"In a dream?" Rivera did not want to hear this. Not at all. It had been a year since all that had happened, since the *Big Book* had arrived, calling him to action, and he'd walked away. So far, so good.

"We slumbered by the restrooms at the St. Francis Yacht Club last night," said the Emperor. "The dead came across the water, floating, like the fog. They were quite insistent."

"They can be that way, can't they?" said Rivera. The Emperor was a crazy old man, a sweet, generous, and sincere lunatic. Unfortunately, in the past, many of the his insane ravings had turned out to be true, and therein lay the dread that Rivera felt rising in his chest.

"The dead speak to you as well, then, Inspector?"

"I worked homicide for fifteen years, you learn to listen."

The Emperor nodded and gave Rivera's shoulder a fatherly squeeze. "We protect the living, but evidently we are also called to *serve* the dead."

"I don't have any ledgers, but I carry some nice blank books."

Rivera led the Emperor to a shelf where he stocked cloth and leather-bound journals of various sizes. "How many of the dead will we be recording?" Something about dealing with the Emperor put you in a position of saying things that sounded less than sane.

"All of them," said the Emperor.

"Of course, then you'll need a substantial volume." Rivera handed him a sturdy leather journal with letter-sized pages.

The Emperor took the book, flipped through it, ran his hand over the cover. He looked from the book to Rivera and tears welled in his eyes. "This will be perfect."

"You'll need a pen," said Rivera.

"Pencil," said the Emperor. "A number two pencil. They were quite specific."

"The dead?" said Rivera.

Bummer ruffed, the subtext of which was: "Of course, *the dead*, you tree-bound squirrel. Haven't you been paying attention?" Rivera had still failed to produce any treats and had ceased scratching Bummer behind the ears, so fuck him.

Lazarus whined apologetically, the subtext of which was: "Sorry, he's been an insufferable dickweed since he was given the powers of a hellhound, but the old man likes him, so what are you going to do? Still, it wouldn't kill you to keep some treats behind the counter for your friends."

"Yes, the dead," said the Emperor.

Rivera nodded. "I don't stock pencils in the store, but I think I can help you out." He moved back behind the counter and opened a drawer. When the *Great Big Book of Death* had shown up in his mailbox, he'd bought the calendar and the pencils as it had instructed. He still had five of the pencils he'd purchased. He handed one to the Emperor, who took it, inspected the point, then dropped it into the inside pocket of his enormous overcoat, where Rivera was fairly sure he would never find it again.

"What do I owe you for the book?" asked the Emperor. He dug several crumpled bills from his coat pocket, but Rivera waved them off.

"It's on me. In service of the city."

"In service of the city," repeated the Emperor, then to the troops, "Gentlemen, we are off to the library to begin our list."

"How will you get the names?" asked Rivera.

"Well, obituaries, of course. And then perhaps a stop at the police station for a look at the missing persons reports. Someone there will help me, won't they?"

"I'm sure they will. I'll call ahead to the Central Station on Vallejo. But I can't help but think you've got a big task ahead of you. You said you need to record *all* of the dead. The city has been here, what, a hundred and sixty years? That's a lot of dead people."

"I misspoke, Inspector. All of the dead, but with some urgency about those who passed in the last year."

"The last year? Why?"

The Emperor shrugged. "Because they asked me to."

"I mean why the emphasis on the last year?"

"So they won't be forgotten." The Emperor scratched his great, grizzly beard as he tried to remember. "Although they said *lost,* not forgotten. So they won't be *lost* to the darkness."

Rivera felt his mouth go dry and his face drain of blood. He opened the door for the Emperor, and the ringing bell jostled his power of speech. "Good luck, then, Your Majesty. I'll call the desk at Central Station. They'll expect you."

"Many thanks." The Emperor tucked the leather book under his arm and saluted. "Onward, men!" He led the dogs out of the shop, Bummer kicking up his back feet against the carpet as if to shed himself of the dirty business that was Alphonse Rivera.

Rivera returned to his spot behind the counter and stared at the cover of the *Great Big Book of Death.* A stylized skeleton grinned gleefully back at him, the bodies of five people impaled on his bony fingers and rendered in cheerful Day of the Dead colors.

Lost to the darkness? Only the last year?

Rivera had bought the pencils and the calendar as the *Big Book* had instructed, but then he'd done absolutely nothing else with them except put them in the drawer by the cash register. And nothing bad had happened. Nothing. He'd peacefully taken an early retirement from the force, opened the bookstore, and set about reading books, drinking coffee, and watching the Giants on the little television in the shop. Nothing bad had happened at all.

Then he noticed, just below the title on the *Big Book* were the words "revised edition." Words that had not been there, he was sure, before the Emperor had come into the shop.

He pulled open the drawer, swept the pencils and office supply detritus aside, and pulled out the calendar he'd bought. Right there, in the first week of January, was a name and number, written in his handwriting. Then another, every few days to a week, until the end of the month, all in his handwriting, none of which he remembered writing.

He flipped through the pages. The entire calendar was filled. But nothing had happened. None of the ominous warnings in the *Big Book* had come to pass. He tossed the calendar back into the drawer and opened the *Great Big Book of Death* to the first page, a first page that had changed since he'd first read it.

It read: *"So, you fucked up—"*

"AHHHHHHHIEEEEEEEEEE!" A piercing shriek from right behind him.

Rivera leapt two feet into the air and bounced off the cash register as he turned to face the source of the scream, landing with his hand on his hip, his eyes wide, and his breath short.

"Santa Maria!"

A woman, wraith thin, pale as blue milk, trailing black rags like tattered shrouds, stood there—right there—not six inches away from him. She smelled of moss, earth, and smoke.

"How did you get—"

"AHHHHHHHHIEEEEEEEEEE!" Right in his face this time. He scrambled backward against the counter, leaning away from her in spine-cracking dread.

"Stop that!"

The wraith took a step back and grinned, revealing blue-black gums. "It's what I do, love. Harbinger of doom, ain't I?"

She took a deep breath as if to let loose with another scream and there was an electric sizzle as the stun gun's electrodes found purchase through her tatters. She dropped to the floor like a pile of damp rags.

2

THE RUMORS OF MY DEMISE

"You can't just shag a nun one time then dine out on it for the rest of your life," said Charlie Asher.

"You're not exactly dining out," said Audrey. She was thirty-five, pale and pretty, with a side-swoop of auburn hair and the sort of lean strength and length of limb that made you think she might do a lot of yoga. She did a lot of yoga. "You never leave the house."

She loved Charlie, but in the year they'd been together, he'd changed.

She was sitting on an Oriental rug in what had been the dining room of the huge Victorian house that was now the Three Jewels Buddhist Center. Charlie stood nearby.

"That's what I'm saying. I can't go out like this. I need to have a life, make a difference."

"You have made a difference. You saved the world. You defeated the forces of darkness in battle. You're a winner."

"I don't feel like a winner; I'm fourteen inches tall, and when I walk, my dick drags in the dirt."

"Sorry," Audrey said. "It was an emergency." She hung her head, pulled her knees up to her chin, and hid her face. He *had* changed. When she'd met him he'd been a sweet, handsome widower—a thin fellow who wore nice, secondhand suits and was desperately trying to figure out how to raise a six-year-old daughter on his own in a world gone very strange. Now he stood knee-high, had the head of a crocodile, the feet of a duck, and he wore a purple satin wizard's robe under which was slung his ten-inch schlong.

"No, it's fine, fine," Charlie said. "It was a nice thought."

"I thought you'd like it," Audrey said.

"I know. And you *did* save me. I'm not trying to be ungrateful." He attempted a reassuring smile, but his sixty-eight spiked teeth and glassy black eyes diluted the reassuring effect. He really missed having eyebrows to raise in a friendly way. He reached out to pat her arm, but the raptor talons that she'd given him for hands poked her and she pulled away. "It's a very nice unit," he added quickly. "It's just, well, not very useful. Under different circumstances, I'm sure we'd both enjoy it."

"I know, I feel like a bad genie."

"Don't tease, Audrey, it's hard enough without imagining you dressed as a genie."

They'd made love once, well, a few times, the night before he'd died, but after she'd resurrected his soul in this current body, which she'd built from spare parts and luncheon meat, they'd agreed that they would abstain from sex because it would be creepy—and because he lost consciousness whenever he got an erection—but mostly because it would be creepy.

"No, I mean I feel like you made a wish, and I granted it, but you forgot to specify the circumstances, so you were tricked."

"When did I ever wish I had this?" He gestured to his dong, which unfurled out of his robe and plopped onto the rug.

"You were pretty delirious when you were dying. I mean, you didn't explicitly *ask* for it, but you *did* go on about your regrets, most of which seemed to be about women you hadn't had sex with. So I thought—"

"I'd been poisoned. I was dying."

During his battle in the sewers below San Francisco with a trinity of ravenlike Celtic death goddesses called the Morrigan, one had raked him with her venomous claws, which eventually killed him.

"Well, I was improvising," said Audrey. "I'd just had sex for the first time in twelve years, so I may have put a bit too much emphasis on the male parts. Overcompensated."

"Like with your hair?"

"What's wrong with my hair?" She patted her swoop of hair, which approximated the shape of Hokusai's *The Great Wave*, and would have looked more in place on the runway of an avant-garde fashion show in Paris than it did anywhere in San Francisco, especially in a Buddhist center.

"Nothing's wrong with it," Charlie said. How had he blundered into talking about her hair? He was a beta male and he knew by instinct that there was no winning when it came to discussing a woman's hair. No matter where on that path you started, you were bound to stumble into a trap. Sometimes he thought he might have lost a mental step or two in the transfer of his soul to this body, even if it had been done only moments after his death. "I *love* your hair," he said, trying for the save. "But you've said yourself that you were sort of overcompensating for having your head shaved for twelve years in Tibet."

"Maybe," she said. She was going to have to let it go. For one thing, as a Buddhist nun, being vain and whiny about how her hair looked was a distinct regression in spiritual evolution; plus, she *had* trapped the man she loved in a tiny body she'd cobbled together from disparate animal parts and a good-sized block of turkey ham, and she felt responsible. This was not the first time they'd had this discussion, and she couldn't bear to extricate herself from it using a weak, *Kung Fu of the Disrespected Hairdo* move. She sighed. "I don't know how to get you into a proper body, Charlie."

So there it was, the truth as she knew it, laid out on the carpet as limp and useless as—well—you know.

Charlie's jaw (and there was a lot of it) dropped open. Before, she'd always said it might be complicated, difficult, but now . . . "When I started buying soul vessels from your and the other Death Merchants' stores, putting them into the Squirrel People, I didn't know how to do that either. I mean, I knew the ritual, but there was no text that said it would work. But it did. So maybe I can figure something out."

She didn't believe for a second she could figure it out. She'd moved souls from soul vessels into the meaty dolls she constructed, using the *p'howa of forceful projection*, thinking that she was saving them. And she'd used the *p'howa of undying* on six terminally ill old ladies, thinking she was saving their lives, when, in fact, she had simply slowed their deaths. She was a Buddhist nun who had been given the lost scrolls of the Tibetan Book of the Dead and she could do things that no on else on earth could do, but she couldn't do what Charlie wanted her to.

"The problem is the body, isn't it?" asked Charlie.

"Kind of. I mean, we know there are people out there walking around without souls, and that eventually a soul vessel will find them, they will find *it,* but what would happen to their personality if we forced your soul into someone, then they encounter their soul vessel?"

"That would probably be bad."

"Right, plus, when a soul goes into a vessel it loses its personality: the longer it's out of a body, the less personality it retains, which is good. I think that's why we learn as Buddhists that we have to let go of ego to ascend spiritually. So what if I could move your soul into someone who didn't have a soul, hasn't encountered their soul vessel yet. It might destroy their personality, or yours. I don't want to lose you again."

Charlie didn't know what to say. She was right, of course. The Squirrel People were prime examples of souls without memory of their personalities. Except for a couple, whom Audrey had moved when the soul had been fresh in the soul vessel; all of them were just goofy little meat puppets. They'd built their own little city under the porch.

"Phone," said the meat puppet Bob as he entered the room, followed by a dozen other Squirrel People Charlie's size. Bob was so called because Audrey had constructed him using a bobcat skull, which now sat on the bright red miniature beefeater uniform of a Tower of London guard. He was the only one of the Squirrel People besides Charlie who could talk; the others hissed, clicked, and mimed to get their points across, but they were all elegantly dressed in the costumes Audrey had made for them.

Bob handed the cordless handset to Audrey, who clicked the speaker button.

"Hello," she said.

A little girl's voice said, "I am become Death, destroyer of worlds!"

Audrey held the phone out for Charlie. "It's for you."

Detective Inspector Nick Cavuto, Rivera's partner on the SFPD for fifteen years, stood over the pile of pale and black that lay on the floor behind the counter of Rivera's store.

"Looks like you killed a witch," he said. "Sad," he said. "Lunch?"

He was six foot four, two hundred and sixty pounds, and took great pride in playing the old-school, tough-guy detective: wearing a fedora from the 1940s, rumpled suits, chomping on cigars he never lit, and carrying a blackjack in his back pocket that Rivera had never seen him use. In the Castro, where he lived, he was known as "Inspector Bear." Not to his face, of course.

"She's not dead," said Rivera.

"Shame. I was hoping munchkins would come sing the ding-dong song in your shop."

"She's not dead."

"We could knock off a couple of verses if you want. I'll start. You come in on 'which old witch'?"

"She's not dead."

"How long's she been out?"

"About twenty minutes, then thirty minutes, that's when I called you, then"—he checked his watch—"about fifteen minutes."

"So she came to and you rezapped her?"

"Until I could figure out what to do."

"You miss the job, don't you?" Cavuto pushed his hat back on his head and looked to Rivera for the confession. "You know, technically, you being active reserve, you can ride along with me anytime you feel like Tasing someone. Zapping random hippie chicks in your store can't be good for business. You'll have to buy lunch, of course."

When they were both on the job, Cavuto usually started talking about lunch while he was still eating breakfast.

"She's not a normal hippie chick."

"No doubt, most people are just down then right back up. That's a long time to be out from a stun gun."

Rivera shrugged. "It's her best quality, as far as I can tell."

"You're going to have to figure something out, you can't keep stunning her, I can smell burning—is that Scotch?"

"Peat, I think. Yeah. That's not from the stun gun, that's just how she smells."

"Want me to cuff her? Take her in? I can probably get a psych hold on her for the outfit alone."

"I think she might be a supernatural being," Rivera said. He rubbed his temples so he didn't have to look at Cavuto's reaction.

"Like the alleged bird woman you allegedly shot nine times before she allegedly turned into a giant raven and allegedly flew the fuck off? Like that?"

"She was going to kill Charlie Asher."

"You said she was giving him a hand job."

"This one's different."

"No hand job?"

"No, in that she's a completely different creature. This one doesn't have claws that I can see. This one just screams."

"But you're sure she's supernatural because . . . ?"

"Because when she screams my head fills with images of people dying and other horrible things. She's a supernatural being."

"*You're* a supernatural being, ya berk," said a female voice from the floor. She sat up.

Rivera and Cavuto jumped back, the latter with a slight yip.

"One of those wee soul collectors, ain't ya? Sneakin' about all invisible-like." She tossed her hair out of her face—a twig flew out onto the carpet.

"You're not from around here, are you?" said Cavuto, acting as if he hadn't just yipped in fear like a tiny frightened dog.

"AHHHHHHHHIEEEEEEEEE!"

The two jumped back farther as she climbed to her feet. Cavuto shook his head as if trying to clear a cloud from his vision.

"See?" Said Rivera.

"Do you have any ID ma'am?" asked Cavuto.

"I'm *Bean Sidhe*, ya great mortal twat! AHHHHHHHIEEEEEEEE!"

"ZZZZZT!" said the stun gun.

She fell back into a pile of rags. Cavuto had snatched the stun gun and put her down himself. He handed it back to Rivera then knelt, drew the handcuffs from his belt, and snapped them around her slight wrists.

"She's cold."

"Supernatural," said Rivera.

"She's not the only one, evidently." He took off his hat so Rivera could see his cocked eyebrow of inquisition.

"I'm not supernatural."

"I don't judge. I am not a judger. It's traumatic. I know how I felt when I got outed by surprise."

"How was that a surprise? You were marching in the Pride Parade wearing your dress blue uniform with no pants and a yellow codpiece."

"Didn't mean I was gay; *Cops without Pants* was the theme that year. You got any duct tape? That shriek is fucking spooky." Cavuto rolling with the weird, as he always had. He had the ability to deny a supernatural situation while simultaneously dealing with it in a practical way, which is why Rivera had called him in the first place.

"You're going to tape her mouth?"

"Only until I get her to St. Francis and can get them to sedate her and sign off on a psych hold. I'll say she did it herself."

"St. Francis isn't ten blocks from here. Throw her in the car, hit the lights, and you'll be there before she comes to."

"I'm not going to carry her to the car when she is perfectly capable of walking on her own, probably."

"I'll help you. It might be twenty minutes before she comes to."

"Plenty of time for you to go buy burgers down the block and bring them back."

"I'll call the order in and go pick it up."

"Curly fries. Two doubles, no tomato. You're buying."

"Inspector Cavuto, you are a huge lunch whore," said Rivera, reaching for the phone.

"*Protect and served, lunch*—SFPD motto." The big cop grinned. "But it may not be a bad idea to keep her down. I have some zip restraints in the car for her ankles. Call for burgers."

Rivera hit the burger button on speed dial and watched his ex-partner lumber out to the brown Ford sedan, which was, as usual, parked in a red zone. The big man popped the trunk and stirred around inside.

The girl from the burger place came on the line with a perky, "Polk Street Gourmet Burgers, can I help you?"

"Yeah, I'd like—"

ZZZZZT!

He barely heard the sound, just a spine-wrenching white-hot pain that started at the back of his neck and bolted to his extremities. Through the sizzling disruption of his thoughts he remembered he'd left the stun gun on the counter behind him. When he came to, Cavuto was kneeling over him.

"How long was I out?"

"Ten, maybe fifteen seconds."

Rivera rubbed the back of his head. Must have hit it on the edge of the counter when he fell. Every joint in his body hurt. He rolled to his hands and knees and looked back to where the raggedy woman had been lying.

"Gone," said Cavuto. He dangled his handcuffs in front of Rivera's eyes. They were still locked. "I heard her scream again, ran in, she was gone."

"The back door is locked," said Rivera. "Go after her."

"Not going to matter. She's gone."

"What's with all the smoke? She start a fire?"

"Nope. Just a cloud of smoke behind the counter where I guess she was standing when she zapped you."

"Oh."

"Yeah," said Cavuto. "You're going to need to call someone with more experience at this than me." He picked up the phone receiver from the floor, held it to his ear. "Yeah, did you get that order? Two double burgers, medium well, everything but tomatoes, curly fries." He looked at Rivera. "You want anything?"

3

SOMETHING ABOUT SOPHIE

Sophie Asher was seven years old. She lived in San Francisco with her aunties, Jane and Cassie, on the second floor of a building that overlooked the cable-car line in North Beach. Sophie had dark hair and blue eyes, like her mother, and an overactive imagination, like her father, although both parents were gone now, which is why she was looked after by her aunties; two widows who lived in the building, Mrs. Ling and Mrs. Korjev; as well as two enormous black hellhounds, Alvin and Mohammed, that had simply appeared in her room when she was a toddler. She liked dressing up like a princess, playing with her plastic ponies, eating Crunchy Cheese Newts, and making grandiose declarations about her power over the Underworld and her dominion over Death, which was why she was currently in a time-out in her room while Auntie Jane was frantically chattering into the phone out in the great room.

From time to time, Sophie popped her head out the door and fired off another salvo of flamboyant nonsense, because she was the Luminatus, dammit, and she *would* have the last word.

"I am become Death, destroyer of worlds!" she shouted, her passion somewhat diffused when the pink ribbon holding her pigtail caught in the door as she ducked back into her room.

"So, that's what we're dealing with here," said Jane into the phone. "She's gotten completely out of hand." Jane was tall, angular, and wore her short platinum hair sculpted into various unlikely permutations, from angry spikes to soft finger waves, all of which played counterpoint to the tailored men's suits she wore when she worked at the bank, making her appear either fiercely pretty, or frightfully confused. Right now she wore a houndstooth tweed Savile Row suit she'd inherited from Charlie, waistcoat with watch chain, and a pair of eight-inch patent-leather red pumps the same shade as her bow tie. She might have been the result of a time-travel accident where Doctor Who parts were woven into the warp with those of a robot stripper.

"She's seven," said Charlie. "Finding out that you're Death—it's hard on a kid. I was thirty-three when I thought *I* was the Luminatus, and I'm still a little traumatized."

"Tell him about the tooth fairy," said Cassie, Jane's wife. She stood barefoot by the breakfast bar in yoga pants and an oversized olive-green cotton sweater, red hair in loose, shoulder-length curls—a calm snuggle of a woman, a chamomile chaser to Jane's vodka and sarcasm shooter.

"Shhh," Jane shushed. Sophie didn't know that Jane was talking to her father, thought, in fact, that he was dead. Charlie had wanted it that way.

"She doesn't play well with others," said Jane. "I mean, since she's this magical thing, she has unrealistic expectations about other magical—uh, persons. She lost a tooth the other day—"

"Awe," said Charlie.

"Awe," said Bob, and the other Squirrel People in the room with him, who were gathered around the speakerphone like it was a storyteller's campfire, made various awe-like noises.

"Yeah, well, the tooth fairy forgot to put money under Sophie's pillow that night—"

At "tooth fairy," Sophie popped her head out the door. "I will smack that bitch up and take her bag of quarters! I will *not* be fucked with!"

Jane pointed until Sophie retreated into her room and closed the door.

"See?"

"Where did she learn that? Little kids don't talk that way."

"Sophie does. She just started talking like that."

"She didn't when I was alive. Someone had to teach her."

"Oh, so you're fine that she all of a sudden becomes Death incarnate without so much as seeing a *Sesame Street* segment about it, but a little light profanity and it's all my fault."

"I'm not saying that, I'm—"

"It's Jane's fault," said Cassie, from across the room.

"You traitorous dyke."

"See," said Cassie. "She's uncouth."

"I am couth as fuck, Cassie. Who has cash anymore? I was going to pay the kid for the tooth the next day. Sophie has unrealistic expectations."

"What do you want me to do?" Charlie asked. "I can't exactly discipline her."

"That's the point: *no one* can discipline her."

"Fear of *kitty*?" Charlie asked. When Sophie was just learning to talk, and Charlie had bought her dozens upon dozens of pets, from hamsters to goldfish to hissing cockroaches, only to find them dead a few days later, he discovered, quite by accident, that if Sophie pointed at a living thing and said the word "kitty," said thing would immediately become unliving. The first time it had happened, to a kitten, in Washington Square Park, had been a shock, but the second time, only minutes later, when Sophie had pointed at an old man and uttered the dreaded k-word, only to have him drop dead on the spot, well, it had become a problem.

"Thing is, I'm not sure she does the k-word anymore," said Jane. "I'm not sure she hasn't lost her, you know, powers."

"Why would you say that?"

Jane looked across the room to Cassie for support. The petite redhead nodded. "Tell him."

"The hellhounds are gone, Charlie. When we got up yesterday morning they were just gone. The door was still locked, everything was in its place, but they were just gone."

"So no one is protecting Sophie?"

"Not no one. Cassie and I are protecting her. I can be pretty butch, and Cassie knows that karate for the slow."

"Tai chi," said Cassie.

"That's not a fighting thing," said Charlie.

"I told her," said Cassie.

"Well, you guys need to find the goggies! And you need to find out if Sophie still has her powers. Maybe she can protect herself. She made pretty quick work of the Morrigan." Charlie had chased the raven-women into a vast underground grotto that had opened up under San Francisco, and was engaging them in battle when little Sophie showed up with Alvin and Mohammed and more or less vaporized them with a wave of her hand. Not in time, however, to save Charlie from the Morrigan's venom.

"Well, I can't have her just *kitty* someone," said Jane. "That may be the one bit of your training that stuck."

"That's not true," said Cassie. "She puts her napkin in her lap and always says please and thank you."

"Well, try it," said Charlie. "Do an experiment."

"On Mrs. Ling? Mrs. Korjev? The mailman?"

"No, of course not, not on a person. Maybe on a lab animal."

"May I remind you that most of your friends are lab animals."

"Hey!" said Bob.

"Not them," Charlie said. "I mean an animal that doesn't have a soul."

"How can I be sure of that? I mean, look at you—"

"I guess you can't," said Charlie.

"Welcome to Buddhism," said Audrey, who had moved to the corner of the room to allow space for the Squirrel People to gather around the phone.

"That's not helpful," Jane called.

"Just find the hellhounds," Charlie said. "No matter what is going on with Sophie, they'll protect her."

"And how do I do that? Put up posters with their picture. *Lost: two four-hundred pound indestructible dogs. Answer to the names Alvin and Mohammed?* Hmm?"

"It might work."

"How did you find them?"

"Find them? I couldn't get them to go away. I kept throwing biscuits in front of the number 90 Crosstown Express bus to get rid of them. But she needs them."

"She needs her daddy, Charlie. Let me tell her you're alive. I understand if you don't want her to see you, but we can tell her you're out of town. You can talk to her on the phone. Your voice is kind of the same—a little scratchier and squeakier, but close."

"No, Jane. Just keep pushing through like you have been. You guys have done a great job with Sophie."

"Thanks," Cassie said. "I always liked you, Charlie. Thanks for trusting me to be one of Sophie's mommies."

"Sure. I'll figure something out, I need to talk to someone who knows more than me. I'll call you tomorrow."

"Tomorrow," Jane said. She disconnected and looked up to see Sophie coming out of her room, a hopeful light in her eyes.

"I heard you say 'Charlie,' " she said. "Was that Daddy? Were you talking to Daddy?"

Jane went down on one knee and held her arms out to Sophie. "No, sweetie. Daddy's gone. I was just talking to someone about your daddy. Seeing if they could help us find the goggies."

"Oh," said Sophie, walking into her auntie's embrace. "I miss him."

"I know, honey," Jane said. She rested her cheek on Sophie's head and felt her heart break for the little kid for the third time that day. She blinked away tears and kissed the top of Sophie's head. "But if I've fucked up my eyeliner again you're getting another time-out."

"Come here," Cassie said, crouching down. "Come to *nice* mommy. We'll have ice cream."

Over at the Three Jewels Buddhist Center, Bob the Beefeater looked at the dead phone, then at Charlie. "Lab animals? Little harsh."

The Squirrel People nodded. It *was* a little harsh.

"Jane's a very damaged person," Charlie said with a shrug of apology.

Bob looked at the other Squirrel People in their miniature finery and mismatched spare parts. "We'll be under the porch if you need us," he said. He trudged out of the dining room. The Squirrel People fell in behind him. Those with lips pouted.

When the last of them was out of the room, Charlie looked to Audrey.

"Something's going on."

"Apparently."

"My daughter needs me."

"I know."

"We need to find her dogs."

"I know."

"But she can't see me like this."

"I can sew you a different outfit," said Audrey.

"I need a body."

"I was afraid you'd say that."

"Something's happening," Charlie said. "I need to talk to someone else in *the business*."

Mike Sullivan had worked as a painter on the Golden Gate Bridge for twelve years when he encountered his first jumper.

"Stand back or I'll jump," said the kid.

He wasn't a kid, really. He looked to be about the same age as Mike, early thirties, but the way he was clinging to the rail made him seem unsure and less grownup. Also, he was wearing a gold cardigan that was two sizes too small for him. He looked as if his grandmother had dressed him. In the dark.

Mike had been on the bridge when there had been jumpers before. They lost about one every two weeks, on average, and he'd even seen, or more frighteningly, heard a couple hit the water, but they usually went over by the pedestrian rails at the road level, not up here on top of one of the towers. This was Mike's first face-to-face, and he was trying to remember what they had taught them during the seminar.

"Wait," Mike said. "Let's talk about this."

"I don't want to talk about it. Especially not with you. What are you, a bridge painter?"

"Yeah," said Mike, defensively. It was a good job. Orangey, often cold, but good.

"I don't want to talk about my life with a guy who paints a bridge orange. All the time, over and over. What could you possibly say that would give me hope? You should be on this side of the rail with me."

"Fine, then. Maybe you can call one of those hotlines."

"I don't have a phone."

Who goes out without a phone? This guy was a complete loser. Still, if he could get closer, maybe Mike could grab him. Pull him back over the rail. He unhooked the safety line from the left side, rehooked it over the upright, then unhooked his right cable and did the same thing. They had two safety lines with big stainless-steel carabineers on the ends so one was always clipped to the bridge. Now he was within the last few feet of the top of the tower. He could walk up the cable and reach the guy in the stupid sweater. One of the guys on the crew had reached over the pedestrian railing and caught a jumper, dragged her by the collar to safety. The Parks Service had given him a medal.

"You can use my phone," Mike said. He patted his mobile, which was in a pouch attached to his belt.

"Don't touch the radio," said the sweater guy.

The maintenance crew used the radios to keep in touch, and Mike should have called in the jumper before he'd engaged him, but he'd been walking up the cable more or less on autopilot, not looking, and didn't notice the kid until he was almost to the top.

"No, no, just the phone," said Mike. He took off his leather work glove and drew the cell phone from its canvas pouch. "Look, I already have the number." He really hoped he had the number. The supervisor had made them all put the suicide hotline number in their phones one morning before shift, but that had been two years ago. Mike wasn't even sure if it was still there.

It was. He pushed the call button. "Hang on, buddy. Just hang on."

"Stay back," said the sweater guy. He let go of the rail with one hand and leaned out.

Hundreds of feet below, pedestrians were looking out over the bay, strolling, pointing, taking pictures. Hundreds of feet below that, a container ship as long as two football fields cruised under the bridge.

"Wait!" said Mike.

"Why?"

"Uh, because it hurts. They don't tell you that. It's seven hundred and fifty feet from here to the water. Believe me, I think about it every day. You hit at a hundred and seventy-five miles an hour, but it doesn't always kill you. You feel it. It hurts like hell. You're all broken up, in the cold water. I mean, I'm not sure, but—"

"Crisis hotline. This is Lily. What's your name?"

Mike held up a finger to signal for the kid to wait just a second. "I'm Mike. Sorry, they were supposed to connect me with the suicide hotline."

"Yeah, that's us. But we don't call it that because it's depressing. What can I do for you?"

"I'm not calling for me, I'm calling for this guy who needs some help. He's over the rail on the Golden Gate Bridge."

"My specialty," said Lily. "Put him on."

"Stay back," said tiny sweater guy. He let go with one hand again. Mike noticed that the kid's hands were turning purple. It was a nice day, but up here, in the wind, it was cold, and hanging on to cold steel made it worse. All the guys on the crew wore long johns under their coveralls, and gloves, even on the warmest days.

"What's his name?" asked Lily.

"What's your name?" Mike asked sweater guy.

"Geoff with a G," said sweater.

"Geoff with a G," Mike repeated into the phone.

"Tell him he doesn't have to tell people about the G," said Lily.

"She says you don't have to tell people about the G," Mike said.

"Yes I do. Yes I do. Yes I do," said Geoff with a G.

"The G is important to him," Mike said to Lily.

"Is he cute?"

"Pardon."

"What's he look like? Is he cute?"

"I don't know. He's a guy? He's going to jump off the bridge."

"Describe him."

"I don't know. He's about thirty, maybe. Glasses. Brown hair."

"Is he clean?"

Mike looked. "Yeah. To the eye."

"He sounds nice."

"She says you sound nice," Mike conveyed to Geoff.

"Tell him if he comes down, we can get together, chat about his problems, and I'll give him a blow job."

"Really?"

"The point is to get them past the crisis, Mike. Get him off the bridge."

"Okay," said Mike. To Geoff, he said. "So, Geoff, Lily here says that if you come down, the two of you can get together and chat about your problems."

"I'm done talking," said Geoff.

"Tell him the rest," said Lily. "The second part usually closes the deal."

"She says she'll give you a blow job."

"What?" said Geoff.

"I'm not saying it again," Mike said to Lily.

"Tell him I'm beautiful."

"Really?"

"Yes, fucktard, really. How are you not getting this?"

"Maybe I should just put you on speaker, and you can tell him."

"Nooooooo," wailed Geoff. He raised his free hand and swung out into space.

"She's beautiful," Mike said.

"Not again," said Geoff. "No more." He pushed off into space. No scream. Wind.

"Fuck," Mike said. He looked, then looked away. He didn't want to see him hit. He cringed and anticipated the sound. It came up from the water like a distant gunshot.

"Mike?" said Lily.

He caught his breath. He could feel his pulse rushing in his ears and the sound of people shouting below. A code blue came over his radio, signaling for everyone on the crew to stay secured in place until the captain of the bridge could assess the situation.

"He went over," Mike said into the phone.

"Balls," Lily said. "This is on you, Mike. This is not on me. If you'd given him the phone—"

"He wouldn't take it. I couldn't get close to him."

"You should have had him call me himself."

"He didn't have a phone."

"What kind of loser goes out without a phone?"

"I know," said Mike. "I was thinking the same thing."

"Well, couldn't be helped," said Lily. "You're going to lose some. I've been doing this awhile, and even with your best moves, some are going in the drink."

"Thanks," said Mike.

"You sound nice," said Lily. "Single?"

"Uh, kind of."

"Me, too. Straight?"

"Uh-huh."

"Look, I have your number. Okay if I call you?"

Mike was still shaking from Geoff's dive. "Sure."

"I'll text you mine. Call anytime."

"Okay," Mike said.

"But the blow-job thing is not automatic, Mike. That's strictly a crisis-line thing."

"Of course," Mike said.

"But not out of the question," said Lily.

"Okay. What do you do if the caller is a woman?"

"I commiserate. I can go from zero to co-miserable at the speed of dark."

"Okay."

"I know things, Mike. Many things. Terrible, dark, disturbing things."

"I should probably report in or something."

"Okay, call me, bye," said Lily.

"Bye," he said.

Mike put his phone back in the pouch then made his way to the top of the tower, hooked his safety lines on the high cables, then sat down, took off his hard hat, and ran his fingers through his hair, as if he might comb some of the strangeness out of the morning that way. He looked up at the giant aircraft warning light, sitting in its orange-painted steel cage twelve feet above his head, at the very top of the bridge, and behind it the sky began to darken as his vision started to tunnel down. He had just about fainted when out of the side of the light tower a woman's torso appeared— as solid as if a window had opened and she had peeked out, except there was no window. She was jutting right out of the metal, like a ship's figure-head, a woman in a white lace dress, her dark hair tied back, some kind of white flower pinned in her hair above her ear.

"Alone at last," she said. A dazzling smile. "We're going to need your help."

Mike stood and backed up against the rail, trying not to scream. His breath came in a whimper.

4

TRIBULATIONS OF THE MINT ONE

Nestled between the Castro and the Haight, just off the corner of Noe and Market Streets, lay Fresh Music. Behind the counter stood the owner, seven feet, two-hundred and seventy-five pounds of lean heartache, the eponymous Mister Fresh. Minty Fresh. He wore moss-green linen slacks and a white dress shirt, the sleeves flipped back on his forearms. His scalp was shaved and shone like polished walnut; his eyes were golden; his cool, which had always been there before, was missing.

Minty held Coltrane's *My Favorite Things* album cover by its edges and looked into Trane's face for a clue to the whereabouts of his cool. Behind him the vinyl disc was spinning on a machined aluminum turntable that looked like a Mars lander and weighed as much as a supermodel. He had hoped that the notes might bring him into the moment, out of a future or a past, anxiety or regret, but Gershwin's "Summertime" was skating up next on the disc and he just didn't think he could take the future-past it would evoke.

He had wept into her voice mail.

Did Trane look up from the album cover, lower his soprano sax, and say, *"That is some pathetic shit, you know that right?"* He might as well have.

He put the album cover down in the polycarbonate "now playing" stand and was stepping back to lift the tone arm when he saw the profile of a sharp-featured Hispanic man moving by the front window. Inspector Rivera. Not a thing, Rivera coming to the shop. It was cool. The last time he'd spoken to Rivera, the Underworld had manifested itself in the city in the form of horrible creatures, and chaos had nearly overcome the known world, but that was in the past, not a thing, now.

He willed a chill over himself as Rivera came in. Then—

"Oh, hell no! Get your ass right back out that door."

"Mr. Fresh," said Rivera, with a nod. "I think I need your help."

"I don't do police work," said Fresh. "I've been out of the security business for twenty years."

"I'm not police anymore. I have a bookstore over on Russian Hill."

"I don't sell books either."

"But you still sell soul vessels, don't you?" Rivera nodded to a locked, bulletproof case displaying what appeared to be a random collection of records, CDs, tapes, and even a couple of old wax cylinders.

To Minty Fresh, every object in the case glowed a dull red, as if they'd been heated in a furnace, evincing the human soul housed there, but to anyone but a Death Merchant, they looked like, well, a random collection of recorded media. Rivera knew about the Death Merchants. He'd first come to the shop with Charlie Asher when the shit had gone down, when the Death Merchants around the city had been slaughtered and their stores ransacked for soul vessels by the Morrigan—"sewer harpies," Charlie had called them. But now that Rivera was one of them, a Death Merchant, he could also see the glow. Minty had sent him the *Great Big Book of Death* himself.

Fresh said: "Y'all read the book, then, so you know you shouldn't be here, talking to me. You know what happened last time Death Merchants started talking. Just go back to your store and keep collecting the objects when they come up in your calendar, like you been doing."

"That's the thing: I haven't been collecting soul vessels at all."

"The fuck you mean, you haven't been collecting them at all?"

Minty Fresh made a motion with his hands of leveling, as if he were smoothing an imaginary tablecloth of calm over a counter constructed of contemporary freak-out. With concerted effort now, and lower register, he said, "Never?"

"I bought the date book, and a number two pencil," Rivera said, trying to accentuate the positive. He smiled. In the background, Coltrane improvised a boppy, playful riff around "Summertime" 's sweet, low-down melody. "The names and numbers showed up on the calendar, like the *Big Book* said they would? But I didn't do anything about them."

"You can't just *not* do the job. Someone *has* to do it. That's why they put it in the book, right in the beginning, right by the part about not having contact with other Death Merchants. You just ignore the *Big Book*, shit gonna get muthafuckin' freaky up in here."

"It already has," said Rivera. "That's why I'm here. A woman appeared in my shop, not exactly a human woman. A dark thing."

"The Morrigan?" Minty could still see the Morrigan's three-inch talons raking the wall of a dark subway car where she had confronted him. He shuddered.

"Different," said Rivera. "This one didn't have any bird features. She was just pale—dressed in black rags, like a shroud. I didn't see any claws."

"How you know she wasn't just a raggedy woman?"

"She disappeared. Puff of smoke, while my partner watched. Locked door. And she told me. She said she was called *Bean Sidhe*. Had a really thick brogue, I can't say it the way she did."

"*Banshee*," said Minty Fresh. "You pronounce it *banshee*."

"That makes sense," said Rivera. "She did a lot of shrieking. You've seen her, then?"

"Until ten seconds ago I thought the banshee was a myth, but I recognize the description. My ex—woman I know—did a lot of research on Celtic legends after that last—"

"Then you know what she's doing here?"

"Not being a detective like you, I can only guess, but I had to guess, I'd guess she the sound the Underworld make when you throw shit in its fan."

Rivera nodded, as if that made sense. "She *did* call herself a 'harbinger of doom.'"

"That's all I'm saying," said Minty.

"There's more," said Rivera.

"Of course there is."

So Rivera told Minty Fresh about the Emperor's quest to record the names of the dead, of his insistence that they would be forgotten, and how in the past, the kindhearted madman had been somewhat ahead of the police on supernatural goings-on in the city. When he finished he said, "So, do you think there's anything to it?"

Minty Fresh shrugged. "Probably. You broke the universe, Inspector, no tellin' how bad."

"You sound happy about that."

"Do I? Because I don't like that the universe is broken, I keep all my shit there." For the moment, he did feel a little better, because as much as he had convinced himself that he was losing his grip on his cool, here was someone who was clearly worse off than he. Then he looked at Rivera, standing there easy in his Italian suit, his lines and aspect sharp as a blade, and he realized that the cop, or the ex-cop, had *not* lost his cool. The world might be unraveling around him, but Rivera was chill as a motherfucker.

"So what do I do?"

"I'd start with doing your job."

"I'm retired—semiretired."

"I mean picking up the soul vessels."

"You think they'd still be there?"

"You had better hope they are."

"How do I find them?"

"I'd start with your date book full of names, Detective Inspector—that was your title, right?"

Some of Rivera's chill seemed to slip a bit. Rivera undid a button on his suit jacket, evidently to show that he was in action mode.

Minty smiled, a dazzling crescent moon in a night sky. "Did you just unbutton your coat so you could get to your gun?"

"Of course not, it's just a little warm in here. I carry my gun on my hip." Rivera brushed back his jacket to show the Glock.

"But you're still packing, despite your retirement?"

"*Semiretirement*. Yes, I started carrying my old backup. The banshee took my stun gun. She zapped me with it."

"So she can just appear out of nowhere and knock you out?"

"Looks that way."

"Well, good luck with that," said Fresh, feeling ever so much cooler.

"I'll call you," said Rivera. "Let you know how it goes."

"If you feel you have to."

Rivera turned as if to leave, then turned back. "Didn't you have a pizza and jazz place at Charlie Asher's building in North Beach?"

"For a while. Didn't pencil out."

"You were in it with that spooky girl from Asher's shop?"

"Also didn't pencil out."

"Sorry," said Rivera, and he seemed genuinely so. "That can be tough. I'm divorced."

"No damage can't be buffed out." said Minty. "Girl ain't nothin' but tits and sass."

Rivera nodded. "Well, good luck with that." He turned and left the shop, once again, chill as a motherfucker.

Minty Fresh shuddered, then picked up his mobile and began to scroll through his contacts, stopping on Lily's number, but before he could hit call to set in motion another humiliating surrender of his cool, the phone buzzed and the screen read *Three Jewels Buddhist Center*.

"Sheeiiiiiiit," said the Mint One, slow and dreadful, pronouncing the expletive with a long, low sustain of dread.

An iguana in a musketeer's costume ran under Minty Fresh's chair and through the beaded curtain into a butler's pantry, where Charlie Asher sat on an empty mixed nuts can.

"Nice hat," Charlie said.

The musketeer removed his hat, holding it with perfect little hands (previously raccoon paws, Charlie guessed), and bowed grandly over it.

"You're welcome," Charlie said.

The musketeer scampered on through the butler's pantry into the kitchen. Charlie looked through the swinging beads at Minty Fresh, who was sitting on an inverted dining room chair, his knees up around his elbows, putting Charlie in mind of a very large, mint-green tree frog.

"You never seen that hat before?" asked Minty.

"Every day, but it makes him feel special if you notice it."

"Ain't you sweet."

Charlie slid off his can and started through the beaded curtain.

Minty Fresh waved him off. "Ease on back there, Asher. I need to talk to you."

"Why can't you talk to me if I'm on the same side of the curtain as you?"

"Because I start looking at you, and before I know it I forget what I'm talking about, and I think maybe I should chase you away with a stick."

"Ouch." Charlie slunk back into the pantry and sat on his can. "What's on your mind?"

"You called me."

"But you showed up."

Minty Fresh hung his head, rubbed his scalp. "I'm thinking maybe us talking isn't the same now as it was before."

Charlie was happy to hear it. "So you think now that Sophie is the Luminatus, everything is over, so we don't have to worry about the rise of the Underworld?"

"No. I think that shit might already be rising. When you were collecting soul vessels, how many you think you picked up a year? On average?"

"I don't know, a couple a week. Sometimes more, sometimes less."

"Yeah, me, too. So that's about a hundred a year. And about fifty-five hundred people a year die in the city proper. So that means there must be, call it, fifty-five Death Merchants."

"That sounds about right," Charlie said. "I met the Death Merchant in

Sedona who collected my mother's vessel, he said about two a week, too."

"Right," said Minty. "So, when they all came up, when it hit the fan, we only knew a dozen Death Merchants in the city, and the Morrigan killed all but three of us. Two if we count you as dead."

"Which I don't," Charlie said.

"But you don't collect soul vessels anymore. You don't have a shop to turn them around."

"Okay, don't count me."

"And I sent your copy of the *Great Big Book of Death* to Inspector Rivera."

"Yeah. I wonder how he's doing."

"He was in my shop right before you called. A banshee appeared in his bookstore and zapped him with a stun gun."

"So, not adjusting well to retirement?"

"He hasn't collected a single soul vessel."

"None?"

The Mint One shook his head. "That's at least a hundred souls not collected, not passed on to the new owner. Plus, we don't know what happened to the souls the other dead Death Merchants were supposed to collect."

"I always assumed that when a Death Merchant died someone took his place. Audrey says the universe just takes care of the mechanics of it. Everything seeks balance."

"Audrey, the one who put you inside that little monster?"

Charlie waved his talons in the air as if to dismiss the point and realized that he might be helping to make it. "So you're saying—what are you saying?"

"Rivera said the names appeared in his date book, even though he didn't pick up the souls. What if no one has been collecting the souls of the Death Merchants who were killed? What if by defeating the Underworlders we threw things out of balance? What if the Death Merchants who were killed weren't replaced? What if there are a *thousand* souls that haven't been collected since the Morrigan rose? Maybe more. A lot of people were killed in the city at that time. What if some of them were

Death Merchants we didn't know about, and all of those souls haven't been collected?"

"I used to hear them moving under the streets, calling out, if I was late collecting just *one*," said Charlie. "When they got their hands on all the soul vessels in our shops—"

"It was a shit storm," said Minty. "Now multiply that by ten, twenty."

"So you think this banshee—?"

"I think the bitch is announcing coming attractions."

"Sssssshit," Charlie said, letting the *s* hiss out between his multitude of teeth.

"Uh-huh," said Minty. "You know where your old date book is?"

"At my apartment, I guess. I can't imagine Jane would have thrown it out."

"Call her." Minty pulled his phone from his jacket pocket.

"You'll have to help me dial." Charlie waved his talons before his face again. They were not suited for touch screens and buttons. He gave Minty Fresh the number. Cassie answered and they waited while she found Charlie's date book—a three-year calendar with only one year used when he had died.

"It's filled in for the whole year, Charlie," said Cassie over the speaker. "The latest entry is today. How can that be?" Charlie looked up at Minty Fresh and again missed having eyebrows—if he'd had them, he'd have raised one at the tall Death Merchant.

"I don't know, Cassie. I'm trying to figure it out. Let's put the book back and I'll call you as soon as I know anything. Thanks."

Minty disconnected them. "With you and Rivera, that's a couple of hundred souls uncollected right there."

"And you think it might be thousands."

"In the Bay Area alone."

"We're probably fine, all those souls and nothing has happened."

"Banshee," said Minty, holding a long finger in the air to mark his point. "She calls herself a *harbinger* of doom, Asher. You know what a harbinger is?"

"I'm really hoping it's a brand of Scotch."

"It's a messenger that tells you what is *going* to happen. With a banshee, that message is that death is coming."

Charlie shrugged. "Big Death or little death?"

Fresh shrugged, shook his head.

"Then you need to help me find a body," said Charlie.

"What?"

"That's why I called. You help me find a body, then I can help you fix whatever the banshee is warning us about."

"Like a corpse-type body?"

"Not exactly. Someone who is going to be a corpse, but before they become a corpse."

"Doesn't that describe everybody?"

"I mean *right* before they die. Like we have to be there at the moment of death."

"Are you asking me to help you kill someone, because no."

"Let me get Audrey. She'll explain."

5

THE PEOPLE UNDER THE PORCH

C höd," said Audrey. The *d* was silent, it rhymed with "foe."

"Chöd?" Minty Fresh repeated. He couldn't stop looking at the surprised comma of her hair, for which he was grateful, because it kept him from looking at Charlie, which made him uncomfortable. When Audrey came in she insisted that Charlie come out of the pantry, so now they sat at an oak table in the breakfast room of the Buddhist Center, Audrey and he on chairs, Charlie sitting on his mixed nut can atop the table.

"Chöd's the ritual I will perform to get Charlie a new body."

When Minty had first seen her in his shop, several years ago, when she was rail thin, wore no makeup, and her shaved head was still in stubble, it would have been easy to believe she was a Buddhist nun, although he remembered at the time thinking she might be a chemotherapy patient, but now, with her drag-queen hair and a girlish shape filling out jeans and a San Francisco Giants thermal, it was hard to make the leap. *This* woman had been given the secret books of the dead by a Tibetan master? How could that be? She was dating a puppet!

"She can't use the *p'howa of forceful projection* ritual that she used to put souls into the Squirrel People," said Charlie.

"There would be no way to know that there wasn't another soul in someone's body," Audrey said.

"We don't know what would happen, but at best you'd end up with two personalities battling," Charlie added.

"More likely two lunatics in one body, neither functioning," said Audrey.

"And y'all can't just use a corpse why? Your thingy of undying?"

"*P'howa*," Audrey supplied.

"Because it's not permanent," Charlie said. "You remember the old ladies who were here at the Buddhist Center when you and I first came here, the ones that were in my book but who didn't die because Audrey used the *p'howa of undying* on them?"

"Yeah, weren't they living here?"

"Well, they're all dead."

"Six months," said Audrey. "That's the longest anyone lasted."

"Really? Sorry. Why didn't you call me?"

"The *Big Book* said we weren't supposed to call you," said Charlie. "I believe you said something like, 'Don't ever call me, Asher. Ever, ever, ever.'"

Minty bowed his head and nodded. He *had* said that. He said, "But you *did* call, and there you sit, you and all your little friends are fine, a year later, not even a stain on your wizard coat, while those old ladies died in six months."

"We don't quite know how they work—the Squirrel People," Audrey said, wincing a little toward Charlie.

"It's okay," Charlie said, putting his claw out to comfort her. "I'm one of them."

Audrey put her index finger in Charlie's talon and looked into his expressionless black eyes.

"Wait," said Minty Fresh. "Y'all aren't . . . ?"

"No," said Charlie.

"No way," said Audrey.

"That would be creepy," said Charlie. "Although, did I show you this?"

He started to unbelt his robe, beneath which he appeared to be wearing an innertube wrapped around his waist.

"No!" said Minty Fresh. "I mean, yes, you showed it to me." He held up a hand to block his view of Charlie and squinted between his fingers until the croc-headed puppet person retied his wizard robe. He found it easier to cope with the sight of Charlie if he pretended he was a really complex speakerphone, but a speakerphone with an enormous peen was a peen too far.

"Mister Fresh," said Audrey, "we need you to help us find someone who will willingly vacate their body for Charlie."

Fresh pushed back on his chair as if he needed distance in order to see her. "How the hell would I find someone like that, and if I did, why the hell would they do that?"

"Well," said Charlie, "if they knew they were going to die anyway, that their soul was going to leave their body anyway, they might."

And at last Minty Fresh knew why they had called. "Y'all want me to tell you when a new name appears in my date book so you can what, go talk someone into giving up their body?"

"Yeah, and it's going to have to be the right person," said Audrey. "It's going to have to be someone who will die accidentally. If it's someone who is terminally ill, I don't know if the disease won't just continue like it did with the ladies."

Fresh shook his head. "You know the names don't come annotated with a cause of death? Just a name and the number of days we have to retrieve the soul."

"Right," said Charlie. "But Audrey can go find the person. See if they're sick. If they're the right gender. I don't think I could deal with being a woman."

"Because being a woman would be a step down from what you are now?" Minty Fresh smiled.

"Because if I woke up in the morning and saw my breasts, I'd never get out of the house," Charlie said.

"He does like breasts," said Audrey.

"Although we only had the one night together," Charlie said.

"But you were very attentive," said Audrey.

"I'm always attentive. I'm looking at them right now."

"Stop it!" Minty said. They *were* a couple. They were talking like a couple. The freaky-haired Buddha nun and the crocodile-wizard monster. It was wrong. Deeply, deeply wrong. Was he the only person on earth who had to be alone? "I can't do it. You shouldn't have called." He stood.

"You're the only one who can help," said Charlie.

"It's impossible. I have to get about finding out if the other Death Merchants in the city were replaced, if they're doing their job."

"Mr. Fresh," said Audrey, standing. "When I thought the Death Merchants were somehow imprisoning human souls, when I was trying to rescue the soul vessels from you guys, the Squirrel People helped. They fanned out all over the city. I found a few of you, but they found others on their own. They can see the glow of a soul vessel. They can move around the city in the shadows. They could help. We could help."

"No." Minty Fresh turned to leave, bent to go through the door. He'd learned his lesson about the hundred-year-old doorways in this place before. There was still a forehead-shaped dent in the woodwork above the kitchen door from when he'd stormed in here to save Charlie the first time.

Charlie jumped off the table and scampered after the big man. "Fresh, my daughter needs me! She doesn't even know I'm alive."

"Well, go see her."

"I can't go see her like this."

"She'll be fine. Kids are resilient." He didn't know anything about kids, but he'd heard people say that. "She'll understand. She's the *Big Death*."

"No she's not. She seems to have lost her—well—powers; she's just a normal kid. Her hellhounds disappeared, and *if* the Underworld is rising again, she won't have anyone to protect her."

Fresh stopped but didn't turn. "I don't mean to be critical, Asher, 'cause I know you got a lot on your mind, but that's the part of the story you lead with."

"Sorry." Charlie stood in the entry to the parlor. Audrey joined him.

"Calling you was my idea," said Audrey.

"So," said Minty, "the one thing that was supposed to end all this light versus dark, manifestation of the Underworld on earth, crazy shit that went down a year ago, *the rise of the Luminatus*, that has been undone?"

"Apparently," said Charlie.

Minty turned to them now and began to count on his fingers. "So there's a banshee loose in the city, warning of coming doom. You, Rivera, and possibly many other Death Merchants have not been collecting soul vessels for over a year, and we don't know what happened to the souls of all those who died in the city during that year. You don't even have a shop anymore to exchange the vessels if you were collecting them. And the only thing that was keeping the forces of darkness at bay has been demoted to, what, a first grader?"

"Second," said Charlie. "But she's in the advanced reading group."

"So, really, we are totally, completely fucked. And by *we*, I mean everybody."

"Pretty much," said Charlie, nodding furiously enough that his jaw flapped a little.

"Life is suffering," said Audrey, cheerfully.

Fresh nodded. "All right, then. I'll call you with the names."

"Just like that?"

"I have to collect the souls anyway. I find someone in my book is young, healthy, male, and what else?"

Charlie started to untie his robe again, "One about this size if—"

Audrey interrupted, "Just the name and address if you have it. We'll see if we can find any Death Merchants."

"Yeah, you gonna have a hard enough time convincing someone they are going to die so they need to vacate their body so the wizard lizard there can move in."

He turned to leave, then stopped and looked over his shoulder. "Oh, did I tell you that the Emperor is making a list of all of the city's dead?"

"What for?"

"No fucking idea, I just didn't want you to be the only one got to whip out a surprise." He laughed—the resigned laugh of the doomed—as he walked out.

Outside on the street he paused by the door of the great bloodred Caddy as he fished in his jacket pocket for his keys. Fog had rolled up out of the bay at sundown and was drifting in a misty wave from the south. On *this* street they had come for Charlie, the Morrigan, snaking out of the sewer grates at either end of the block, singing their taunts even as Fresh was bearing down on them in the Caddy—screeching in anger and agony as he ran them over, the claws of one raking into the metal of the Caddy's hood as she was dragged under the bumper, the other tearing at the rear fender as his tires burned across her back. The guy at the body shop said the fender looked like it had been attacked by a grizzly bear. He'd never seen anything like it. "Me either," Minty had said. "Nobody has."

He cocked his head, thinking he might have heard a female voice on the street above the jingling of his keys. Just laughter, maybe—girls out for dinner or drinks a block away on Mission Street, their voices echoing distant and diffused because of the fog. Probably.

They stared at the doorway as they listened to Minty Fresh's steps recede and the front door close behind him.

Audrey checked the clock. "I have to lead a meditation at seven. They're going to start arriving soon. You might want to get out of sight."

"I should have asked him about Lily."

"He would have brought it up if he wanted to talk about it. Why don't you go ask Bob and the others if they remember all the places they collected soul vessels? They really might be able to help."

"I don't really feel welcome down there."

"Don't be silly. They love you."

"Lately it feels like they might be plotting to kill me." Despite having been liberated from his beta-male DNA, Charlie still viewed the world with glassy-eyed suspicion, due in no small part to the fact that he had already been murdered once and hadn't cared for the experience.

"Take snacks," Audrey said. "They love snacks. There's some trail mix on the counter."

"Sure, snacks," Charlie said, heading for the kitchen. "If only Jesus had thought to take snacks with him into the lion's den."

"Jesus didn't go into the lion's den, that was Daniel."

"Well, Daniel, then. I thought you were a Buddhist."

"I am, but that doesn't make me an oblivious nitwit, too."

"Is that any way for a nun to talk?" Charlie called back, but Audrey had already headed upstairs to change. He scampered into the kitchen, grabbed a packet of trail mix off the counter, jumped down, ducked out the dog door, hopped down the back porch steps, then through the little hatch under the steps into the sanctuary of the Squirrel People.

The city under the house was a maze of mismatched found objects patched together with zip ties, silicone glue, and duct tape, all lit from above by low-voltage LED lights strung along the floor joists of the great Victorian, which kept the entire space in a state of perpetual twilight. Audrey had purchased the lights at Charlie's request, after he had watched several of the Squirrel People nearly burn the house down while trying to construct an apartment from discarded yogurt containers by candlelight.

There was no one around.

Charlie had spent very little time down here, choosing to spend his days on the upper floors of the Buddhist Center, either with Audrey or reading from the many books in the library. When he was reading he could fly away into the wildest skies of imagination, untethered to the reality that his soul was trapped in a wretched creature cobbled together from meat and bone, like us all.

Charlie entered the main passage, which was constructed entirely from automobile side windows. Once in it, he felt as if he were walking in a long, serpentine aquarium. Despite the disparate materials from which it was constructed, the Squirrel People's city had a strange symmetry, a uniformity of design that Charlie found comforting, because it was built for someone his size, yet disturbing, because it was so unlike anyplace human beings lived.

"Hey," he called. "Anyone home?"

He made his way along a street that was lined by old computer monitors, each gutted of its electronics and filled with a nest built from throw pillows and fabric scraps.

Still no one. The city had tripled in size since he'd been down here, and as he moved he encountered open, communal spaces, as well as what were clearly spaces meant to preserve privacy. The Squirrel People did not mate, as there were no two alike, no two made from the same sets of parts, but they paired off, each finding some affinity with another that Charlie could not see. The only thing they had in common beyond their size—which was chosen quite by accident when Audrey was studying to be a costume designer, long before she'd gone off to Tibet, and she had wanted to design and sew elaborate costumes without the expense of the materials for full-size models—was that each housed a human soul. The first of the Squirrel People had been little more than animated dress forms. Later, Audrey had scavenged the shops of Chinatown for animal parts, trying to give each of them a distinction, trying different parts for limbs, testing efficacy, using first fresh meat and later smoked for the protein that the soul would direct into forming a unique, living creature.

"The universe is always seeking order," Audrey had said. "The Squirrel People, how they come together, is the best example I've ever seen of that."

"Yeah, or it's black magic and creepy necromancy," Charlie had said.

She'd smacked the tip of his enormous dong with her fork, which he thought a not very Buddhist thing to do, and said so. "Buddhist monks invented kung fu, Charlie. Don't fuck with us."

"Hey, Bob!" Charlie called down the corridor. "It's Charlie, I need to talk to you."

He didn't really need to say it was Charlie, since he and Bob were the only of their kind for whom Audrey had constructed vocal cords. After Charlie, she'd found out she hadn't actually been saving souls by making the Squirrel People, but had stopped them in their karmic progression, so he had been the last.

The computer monitor street branched into a half-dozen different passageways, each constructed from a different material. Charlie ducked into one that looked to be made of plastic drainpipe, and shuffled along its length, cutting back and forth until he heard voices coming from the far end. Voices?

He slowed as he approached the end of the passageway and peeked into the wide chamber it opened upon. The Squirrel People had excavated an amphitheater here, under the house, perhaps ten feet below ground level, and it was larger than the grand parlor upstairs. He was looking down over a large group of *the people* who were surrounding a central platform that looked as if it had been constructed from an old snare drum. How could they have gotten all this stuff down here without being seen?

Bob stood on the snare drum in his bright red beefeater uniform, holding his mighty spork over his head as if it were the staff of Moses.

"Bring the head for Theeb!" he shouted.

"Bring the head for Theeb. Bring the head for Theeb." The Squirrel People chanted.

From another passage an iguana-headed fellow in a tricorner hat and a squirrel girl in a pink ball gown emerged carrying a silver tray between them. On it was the raggedly severed head of a calico cat.

"Bring the head for Theeb," they chanted.

Charlie backed into his chamber. How were they chanting? Sure, some of them were still making the clicking noises, the growls, the hisses he was used to, but *some* were chanting. They *had* voices.

He crouched and backed away until he was out of sight of the amphitheater, then he turned and scurried out of the city under the porch.

6

GHOSTS OF THE BRIDGE

A great regret of ghosts lingered on the Golden Gate Bridge. Mad as bedbugs, they slid down the cables, swam in the roadway, hung off the upright lines, whipped in the wind like tattered battle flags, dangled their feet off the anchor piers, and called into the dreams of sleeping sailors as their ships passed through the Gate. Mostly they napped, curled up in the heavy steel towers, entwined together in the cables like impassioned earthworms, tucked under an asphalt blanket snoring into the treads of a million tires a day. They drifted along the walkways, spun and buffeted by passersby, wafting along like tumbleweeds, rebounding at the shore to bounce back the other way, waves of spirits, a tide of sleeping souls, dozing until awakened by human anguish in their midst. They could sense a jumper on the bridge and gathered around to watch, to curse, to encourage, to haunt, taunt, and gibe, which is how the ghost of Concepción Argüello came to find Mike Sullivan, the bridge painter, that day.

"Oh, pardon me," she'd said. "It appears I have upset you. Of course, you need time to adjust. We'll talk another time."

She disappeared back into the steel of the tower, leaving Mike breathless and deeply, deeply freaked out. Still, when his supervisor called him down to be debriefed by the highway patrol and the captain of the bridge, Mike didn't mention the ghost, and he declined the counseling they offered. He'd done the best he could, they said, considering the circumstances. Most of the time, someone who was thinking about jumping just needed someone to say something—someone to notice them, pull them out of the vortex of despair forming in their own mind. The state patrolmen who worked the bridge on bicycles were all trained to look for and engage anyone who was alone, looking pensive, crying at the rail, and they had a great record for bringing people back from the edge, getting them to snap back into the world with just a word of kind concern. He'd done fine, he'd be fine, just take the rest of the day off, regroup, they'd told him.

Mike *had* taken the rest of the day off, and he had rested, but unfortunately, he had also shared his tale of the ghost in the beam with his girlfriend of fourteen months, Melody, who first suggested that he might have had a ministroke, because that had happened to a guy on the Internet. When he insisted that no, he had seen and heard what he had seen and heard, she responded that he needed to see a shrink, that he was emotionally unavailable, and furthermore, there were much hotter guys than him at the gym who wanted to sleep with her and she had known deep down that there was something wrong with him and that's why she'd never given up her apartment. He agreed that she was probably right about those things and that she would probably be better off if she slept with the hotter guys at the gym. He'd lost a girlfriend, but he'd gained a drawer in his dresser, a third of the clothes rod in his closet, and all three shampoo shelves in his shower, so he really wasn't all that broken up about the breakup. Once she was gone, he realized that he didn't feel any more alone than he had when she had been in the room with him, and he was a little sad that he didn't feel sadder. All in all, it had been a productive day off.

He'd been back at work for a week and was hanging in the framework under the roadway when the ghost came to him again.

"You know," she said softly, her voice reaching him before she appeared, sitting on the beam above his head, "when they were building the bridge they strung a safety net under it."

Mike caught his safety lines and tugged them to make sure they were both secure before he reacted. "Holy shit," he said.

"When a workman would fall, and he was caught by the net, he was said to have joined the 'Halfway to Hell' club. I think I am also in that club."

She had an accent but not much of one, and this time she wore a black dress with a wide lace collar. Her hair was pinned back into a bun, and again, there was a flower in her hair. He didn't know what to say, but he had been preparing himself for her to reappear, just so he wouldn't be surprised in a bad spot and end up tumbling off the bridge to his death. Hallucination or not, he'd resolved to be prepared. He said, "There's seagull shit all over these beams. You're going to mess up your dress."

"Ah, you are so gallant, but I am beyond the reach of *huano de la gaviota*."

"You are Spanish, then?"

"I was born on Spanish soil, yes, right there at the Presidio, in 1792." She pointed a delicate finger toward the San Francisco shore and the fort beyond it. "I beg your pardon, I am Concepción Argüella. My father was the governor of Alta California, commandante of the El Presidio Real de San Francisco."

"Pleased to make your acquaintance," Mike said. He didn't reach out to shake her hand, or even to kiss it (that seemed like what he should do, her being so formal and everything), but he was hanging two hundred feet over the water, and she was a good twelve feet away, and if she floated over to him, he thought he might completely lose his mind, so he sort of bowed—nodded, really. "I'm Mike Sullivan, I paint the bridge."

"Ah, I would have guessed that from your bucket of paint and your dashing coveralls," said the ghost. "May I thank you for keeping our bridge looking beautiful? We all very much appreciate it, Señor Sullivan."

"We?" Mike said. He was still trying on the idea of talking to a ghost; he wasn't ready to be gang-haunted.

"There are many here on the bridge."

"Why?" Mike asked.

"It is a place between places, and so are we, between places."

"No," said Mike. "Why are *you* here?"

She sighed, a light and ghostly sigh that was lost in the wind, and she told him.

Although I had never set foot in Spain, I was very much raised as an aristocratic Spanish lady—California was Spanish land then. I lived in the grand governor's house in the Presidio, and my mother saw to it that I was dressed in the finest fabrics and latest fashions from Madrid. I was educated in letters by the friars and nuns of the Mission, and in the ways of the world by my mother, which is to say, despite our station in the wildest reaches of the Spanish empire, I was sheltered. I spent most of my life in our house and the gardens around it, surrounded by soldiers and priests, never venturing into the settlement of Yerba Buena. But then, when I was fifteen, there came through the Golden Gate a Russian ship, their chief officer, Count Nikolai Rezanov, seeking supplies for the Russian colony of Sitka far to the north, which was starving.

My father received the count with great courtesy, and he spent many evenings at our home. My mother was intent upon showing the Russian that even in the colonies, the manners and traditions of old Spain could be maintained. Many dinners with officers and local officials and their wives were served. Even when our home was filled with guests, I could not tear my attentions from the count. He was so handsome and worldly, and he regaled us with tales of the north and Japan, where the czar had sent him as an ambassador. I was breathless in his presence, so I would retreat to the corners, but I soon found that as often as I tried to look at him from across the room, to drink him in, I found him looking back, and my heart rejoiced. I could not hide my love behind a lace fan, and he could not disguise his attentions behind courtly manners.

Finally, he passed me a note one evening when kissing my hand and I hurried away to the kitchen just to read those few precious words: "Tonight. The garden. When the moon is over Alcatraz."

He knew, somehow, that I could see the island from my bedroom window, and after the guests had left and the house was long silent, I waited, watching the moon for what seemed months, but before it was over the island, the fog spilled in through the Golden Gate like milk poured into tea, and the night sky was nothing more than a gray shroud. I could wait no longer. Still in my party dress, I went to the garden, not even stopping to take a cloak, and before the chill could settle upon me, I saw him.

"I couldn't wait," he said. "The fog—I have been here all evening."

I ran to him, then stopped, bounced upon my toes, feeling as if I might burst with excitement. He took me in his arms and kissed me. My first kiss.

In the weeks that followed I lived only for the time I could be in the presence of my beloved "Nikolasha," and he was the same for me. He made excuses to be at the fort during the day, and I made excuses to be out and about when he was there. Even a glimpse of him during the day would make my heart leap and sustain me, until evening, when I could see him again in my parents' house, and later, in the garden. Even as our love grew, though, so did the specter of time begin to loom over us. Nikolai had come to establish trade with the Spanish colony to sustain the struggling Russian settlements in the far north, but Spanish law dictated that the colonies could not trade with a foreign power. For all of his courtesy and goodwill, my father could not grant the count his request.

"And what if I were to marry your daughter?" Nikolai said one evening over dinner.

"Yes," I blurted out. "Yes, Father, yes!"

My father smiled, as did my mother, for they had not been blind to our attraction, and when my father spoke, my mother smiling in a bemused manner the whole time, I knew they had discussed this possibility before it had even occurred to Nikolai.

"I would honored to grant you my daughter's hand, but it is

not in my power to enter into a trade agreement with Russia, nor, I daresay is it yours to speak for the Czar. But if you bring me a letter of permission from the Czar, sanctioning your marriage to my Conchita, then I think I can convince the king to grant a trade agreement with your colonies. In the meantime, the people of Alta California and Mission de San Francisco, will *give*, out of Christian charity, enough supplies to sustain the people of Sitka through the winter. No trade will have taken place, no law broken. You can deliver the supplies on your return voyage to Russia to gain the Czar's permission.

Nikolai was ecstatic. Normally composed and ever so dignified, he stood and cheered, then apologized and bowed to everyone at the table individually, after which he sat down and collected himself.

I was in tears and my mother held me as I wept with joy onto her shoulder.

"I may be gone some time," Nikolai said, trying to calm himself. "Even after I reach Mother Russia's shores, I will have a long trek across Siberia to reach St. Petersburg to get the Czar's permission. It may be more than a year before I am able to return."

"I'll wait!" I said.

"The Czar will likely order I stop at the other colonies on the return voyage and the journey is too treacherous in the winter. If I miss the season, I may be two years."

"I'll wait!" I repeated.

My father smiled. "We shall all wait, Count Rezanov, as long as it takes."

"Forever," I said. "If it takes forever."

When he sailed out of the bay I felt as if my heart went with him, and I swear I could feel the tether, even as I stood on the hill above the Golden Gate and watched the mast of his ship disappear over the horizon. And I waited, after a year running to the top of the hill any time the guard announced a ship. Two years.

I spent whole days, wrapped in a cloak against the fog, staring out to sea, thinking that my presence might pull him to me. I knew he had to feel the same thing, the tether to his heart, and I would be there above the Gate so he could follow it across the ocean, home, to me.

For forty years I waited, meeting every morning with the thought of him, ending every night with prayers for him, and he never returned. Word never came. What had befallen him? Whom had he met? Had he forgotten me? I died a nun, for I would have no one else, and when he did not return, the only way to keep my father from making me marry another was to marry God. Yet I was an unfaithful wife, for I was Nikolai's and he was mine, always and forever, and there could be no other for me, not even God.

"That's the saddest story I've ever heard," said Mike, who was shivering in his safety harness, and not from the cold wind coming in the Gate. He held out his arms to her, to hold her, to comfort her.

Concepción bowed her head to hide her tears, then slipped off the beam and floated toward him.

Mike's radio crackled. "Sully! The fuck do you think you're doing?"

Mike scrambled for the mic strapped at his shoulder. "Wha, wha, wha." He whipped his head around so quickly, looking for his coworker that his hard hat nearly came off.

The radio: "I'm on the lower north tower, about a hundred feet below you. Seven o'clock."

Mike spotted him. Bernitelli, wiry little Italian guy. *Berni*, they called him, working in a window washer's lift, suspended from cables a hundred feet over the bay.

"I'm okay," Mike said into the radio. "Just shooing some gulls that were getting in fresh paint."

"You hooked in?"

"Of course."

"Then stop waving your arms around and hang on. I thought you were going to take the big dive."

"Roger that," Mike said. "Sorry."

Concepción stood right beside him, now, as solid as the bridge itself, the wind whipping her dress around her legs. Strands of her dark hair blew across her face and she wiped them back behind her ear, then reached out to touch the stream on his cheek left by a tear. He couldn't feel her hand, but at the gesture he felt a pain rise in his chest, an emptiness, and he squeezed his eyes tightly shut, then opened them. She was still there, but smiling now.

"So you never knew—you don't know what happened to him?"

She shook her head. "Perhaps he found someone else. Perhaps the Czar kept him in Russia? We would ask after him whenever a Russian ship anchored in the bay, but no one had heard of his fate. Had I been a fool, a young girl who clung forever to a broken promise? Perhaps he was pretending all along, playing on my affections to get my father to release supplies for his colonies. This is why I have come to you: to find out."

"You waited two hundred years?" He realized, even as he asked, that if you were chatting with a ghost, two hundred feet above the San Francisco Bay, you really had no right to question anyone's judgment.

"You are the first person who could hear us. Sometimes, when someone is about to jump, they can hear us, but they do not answer, and soon they are here with us. By that time, it is too late for answers."

"Then everyone who has ever jumped—they are all here? They, like you, they—"

"Not all of them, but most."

Mike tried to count in his head, about one jumper a week, since the bridge was opened, nearly eighty years ago—it was many. "That's—"

"Many," she said. "And there are others. Not only those who jump. Many others."

"Many," he repeated.

"A bridge is a place between, we are souls that are between."

"So if I can find out what happened to your count, then what, you move on?"

"One hopes," said the ghost. "One always hopes."

"One moment, please." Mike spidered his way back into a matrix of beams so he was out of sight of Bernitelli, then reached in his coveralls for his smartphone, but paused. It couldn't be this sudden: two hundred years and he simply looks something up on a search engine and resolves her mission, puts her to rest? What if her count *had* married another woman? What if he had used her, lied to her?

"Concepción, you have a modern way of speaking, do you know about the Internet?"

"Please, call me Conchita. Yes, I have heard. We hear the radios in the cars as they pass, listen to the people walking on the bridge. I think the Internet is new way people have found to be unpleasant to one another, no?"

"Something like that." He typed the count's name into a search engine, then, when it suggested he'd spelled it wrong, he hit search. In seconds, the result was back and he tried not to react as he read what the count had done, so many years ago. When she had first appeared, while he was still in shock over the sweater guy going over the rail, she had shown him pity, given him a week to prepare for her reappearance. She had warned him she was coming the second time and had only appeared to him after he was safely hooked to the bridge. She had shown him consideration. He owed her the same.

He shook his head at the phone and said, "Unfortunately, the Internet has sent me to the library to look for word of your count. It may take some time; can you come to me again, soon?"

"It takes great will to come to you like this, but I will return."

"Thank you. Give me a couple of days. I'll be working under the roadway for the next few days."

"I will find you," she said. "Until next time, thank you, Mike Sullivan." In an instant she was beside him. She kissed his cheek and was gone.

Rivera was standing in the living room of a woman named Margaret Atherton, who was eleven months dead, when he realized he wasn't invisible.

"Hold it right there, you son of a bitch, or I'll splatter you across that wall," said the old man, who had entered the room from the kitchen while Rivera was rifling through a side table drawer. Rivera fought instinct and did not reach for the Glock on his hip. Instead he looked over his shoulder to see a man, at least eighty years old, shaped like the letter *C*, pointing an enormous revolver at him.

"Wait! I'm a cop," Rivera said. "I'm a policeman, Mr. Atherton."

"What are you doing in my house?"

Rivera didn't have an answer. People weren't supposed to be able to see him when he was retrieving a soul vessel. That's what it said in the book. That's what Minty Fresh had told him. "You aren't actually invisible, it's just that people won't notice you. You can slip right into their houses when they bring in the groceries, and as long as you don't say anything to them, they won't notice you."

"That's hard to believe," Rivera had said.

"Yeah," said the big man. "That's the hard to believe part."

The old man said, "If you're a cop, let's see a badge. And you do anything sketchy I'll turn you into pink mist."

When did old people start talking like that? The old fellow was slight and frail-looking, like he might just fall apart at a touch, a man of ash, yet he held the heavy revolver with the steadiness of a bronze monument.

Rivera turned and reached slowly into his jacket pocket for his badge wallet. He'd gone back to active duty two days ago, thinking that the credentials and access would help him to track down the missing soul vessels, but he hadn't expected this—only the fifth person on his list, the first four were washouts, and already he was abusing his authority. Rivera held up the badge.

"Mr. Atherton, I'm looking into the death of your wife. I knocked and the door was open. I thought something might be wrong, so I came in to check on you."

"In the side table drawer?" The old man squinted down the sights of the big revolver.

Silent and dark as a shadow, she stepped out of the kitchen behind Atherton and touched the stun gun to his neck.

ZZZZZT!

The old man spasmed, dropped the gun, then fell and twitched in place a bit.

"AIEEEEEEEEEEE!" shrieked the banshee. Then, to Rivera, "Hello, love."

Rivera fell to a crouch as he drew the Glock and leveled it at her chest. "Back," he said. He moved to the old man and checked his pulse while keeping the Glock trained on the banshee.

"That's no way to treat someone who just rescued you."

"You didn't rescue me." Rivera moved the big Smith & Wesson away from Mr. Atherton, and shuddered. It was a .41 Magnum and would, indeed, have splattered parts of him all over the wall if the old man had shot him. "You might have killed him."

"And he might have killed you. He's fine. Catchin' a bit of a nap is all. I've your wee box o' lightning here if you need to give him another buzz." The banshee clicked the stun gun and a bolt of electricity arced between the contacts.

"Put that down. Now. And back away."

The banshee did as she was told, grinning the whole time. The old man let out a moan. Rivera knew he should call an ambulance, but wasn't sure how to explain why he was here.

"Why are you here?" Rivera asked.

"Same as I told you, puppet, harbinger of doom. Usually death, ain't it?"

"I read about your kind. You're supposed to call hauntingly in the distance—'a keening wail,' they said. You're not supposed to just appear out of nowhere zapping old people and screaming like a—"

"Like a what? Like a what, love? Say my name. Say my name."

"What doom? What death? Mine? This guy?"

"Oh, no, he'll be fine. No, the death I'm warning of is a right scary shit, innit he—a dark storm out of the Underworld, he is. You'll be wanting a much bigger weapon than that wee thing."

"It was big enough to stop one of your feathered sisters," he said.

Rivera lowered the Glock. Actually, it was smaller than the fifteen-round 9-mm Beretta he'd shot the Morrigan with when he'd been on active duty before, nearly half the weight, only ten shots, but more powerful—it was a man-stopper. What did she know about the size of a man's weapon, stupid, sooty-assed fairy anyway.

"Oh, you shot one of those bitches, and you still draw breath? Aren't you lovely?" She batted her eyelashes at him coyly. "Still, won't do for him what's coming."

"So you're not here to warn of some general rising of forces of darkness and—"

"Oh, there's those, love, to be sure. But it's the one dark one you'll be wanting to watch for—not like that winged dolt, Orcus, what came before."

Rivera hadn't seen it, the huge, winged Death that had killed so many of the Death Merchants. Charlie Asher had seen it torn apart by the Morrigan before they came for him.

"This one is worse?"

"Aye, this one won't come bashing through the front door like Orcus. This one's sneaky. Elegant."

"Elegant? So you're not part of the dark rising, you're just here to warn me, I mean, us?"

"Appears so. Unsettled souls attract a bad lot. This city of yours is a whirlwind of 'em."

"Like here, in this house?" Rivera was hoping. Maybe she could help.

"No, love, no human souls here 'cept yours and old Smokey's there."

Rivera looked down at Mr. Atherton—his shirt collar was smoking from where the stun gun had arced. He patted the ember out.

"So that's why he could see me . . ." He looked to the banshee, but she was gone, leaving behind the smell of damp moss and burning peat. Somehow she'd managed to grab his stun gun as she left.

"Fuck!" said Rivera, to no one in particular.

SHY DOOKIE AND DEATH

A study in sadness: Sophie Asher—sitting at the picnic table by the edge of the playground, away from the other kids, denied access to friends, laughter, and fun, condemned to watch from afar like some exile—was in a time-out.

He walked across the playground with something between a limp and a soft-shoe, as if there were brushes playing rhythm on a snare drum under his steps. He was tall, but not too tall, thin, but not too, dressed in different shades of soft yellow from shoe to hat, the latter a butter-colored homburg with a tiny red feather in the lemon-hued band. He sat down across from Sophie and swung his long legs in under the table.

Sophie saw him, but didn't look up from coloring her ponies. He was wearing sunglasses on an overcast day, which Aunt Cassie would explain as him protecting his retinas from UV radiation and which Aunt Jane would explain as him being a douche.

"I don't think you're allowed to be here," Sophie said. There was no gate into the playground, and he hadn't come through the building, past the nuns.

"It'll be all right," said the yellow man. His voice was friendly and he sounded Southern. "Why so sad, peanut?" He smiled, just his lower teeth showed, one of them was gold, then he matched her pout to share her sadness.

"I'm in a T.O.," said Sophie. She glared over her shoulder at *Sister Maria la Madonna con el Corpo de Cristo encima una Tortilla,* the Irish nun, who had stripped her of her recess and exiled her to this cold limbo by the fence. The nun returned her gaze with a stern, tight-lipped resolve—mime anger. The nun didn't seem to see the man in yellow at all, which likely was something else she would be stern about.

"How'd you do to get yourself in such a fix, peanut?"

"I told them I had to go home to go to the bathroom and they said no."

"You have bathrooms in the school, don't you?" He said bathrooms with an *f* instead of a *th,* which she liked and decided that's the way she would say it, too, from now on.

"It was number two," she said, putting down her crayon and really looking up at him for the first time. "I don't do number two away from home."

"So you got shy dookie. That's okay, I had that, too, when I was little. Shoot, bitches need to respect a person's habits."

"That's what I said. But they're all anti-Semites."

"Y'all lost me, peanut. This a Catholic school, right?"

"Yeah, I go here because it's by our house, but I'm a Jewess."

"You don't say?"

"And an orphan," Sophie added gravely.

"Aw, that's sad."

"And my dogs ran away."

He'd been shaking his head to the rhythm of the sadness of her story, but he stopped and looked up when she mentioned the goggies. She missed them. She didn't feel safe without them, so she was acting out, that's what Auntie Cassie would say.

The man in yellow whistled, a long, sad *oh my gracious* note. "You got shy dookie, *and* you an orphan?"

"I'm like Nemo," Sophie said, still nodding, lots of lower lip to show her tragedy.

"You don't say, you the captain of a submarine?"

"No, not that Nemo. The clown fish." Her daddy had been a huge nerd and had taught her about Captain Nemo and the *Nautilus,* but she meant the real Nemo.

"Shoot, that the saddest story I ever heard, Shy Dookie."

"That's not my name."

"That's what I'm gonna call you."

Sophie considered it for a moment. It could be her hip-hop name. Her *secret* hip-hop name. She shrugged, which meant, "Okay."

"What's your name?"

"You can just call me the Magical Negro," said the man in yellow.

"I don't think you're supposed to say that word."

"It's okay. I'm allowed."

"Some words hurt people and you're not supposed to say them. I have a word I'm not supposed to say. A really bad word."

"You do, do you? What that word?"

"I can't tell you, it's a secret."

"You got a lot of secrets."

"Yeah."

"Maybe this meeting we havin', this be our little secret."

"When a grown-up tells you it's our little secret, it means they might be up to something. You should be careful."

"You don't never be lyin', peanut. You don't never be lyin'. I do need to be careful. How long it been since you seen them dogs of yours, child?"

"This morning," she lied. It had been a week since the giant hellhounds had disappeared. "I like your hat," she said to change the subject. "It's nice. Daddy said you should always say nice things about a person's hat because it was an easy way to make them feel better."

"Why, thank you, peanut." He ran his fingers around the brim. "You miss your daddy, don't you?"

How did he know? That wasn't right. He was a stranger. She nodded, pushed out her lip, went back to coloring her ponies.

"You miss your mama, too, I'll bet."

She had never met her mama, but she missed her.

"You think they gone because of you, peanut? 'Cause of how special you are?"

She looked up at him.

"Don't look at me like that. I know. I'm special, too."

"You should be careful," Sophie said. "I need to go."

She stood and looked toward the building. The mean nun pointed for her to sit back down, but then the bell rang and the sister waved her in.

Sophie turned back to the man in yellow, held out the page she had been coloring. "Here, you can have this."

"Well, thank you, peanut." He took the drawing, then untangled from the table and stood as he looked at it. "That's very kind."

"Their names are Death, Disease, War, and Sparkle-Darkle Glitter-tits," Sophie said. "They're the four little ponies of the Apocalypse." Sophie liked saying things that shocked people, especially nuns and old people, but he wasn't shocked.

The man in yellow nodded, folded the drawing, and slipped it into his breast pocket. He looked over his sunglasses and Sophie could see for the first time that his eyes were golden-colored. "Well, y'all take care, Shy Dookie," he said.

"Bye," Sophie said. She took her handful of crayons and skipped back into school. Once in the door, she looked back to the picnic table. The man in yellow was gone.

I'm not invisible," Rivera said into the phone.

"I never said you were invisible," said Minty Fresh. "The *Big Book* never said you were invisible. It says 'people *may* not see you'. Even if you are retrieving a soul vessel, people can see you if you call attention to yourself."

"I didn't call attention to myself. The old man walked in on me —was going to shoot me."

"And the bitch just Tased him. You know, that banshee know how to party."

"I'm glad you're enjoying this, Mr. Fresh, but if I hadn't known the EMTs who arrived to take care of the old man, I'd be facing breaking and entering charges."

"Emergency operator didn't record your call, then?"

"I didn't call. The old man had one of those electronic alert medallions. I just pushed the button and they dispatched."

"Yeah, shit tend to work out like that. If our frequent phone calls don't cause the end of the world, I'll tell you about my *unified theory of irony* someday."

"I'll look forward to that. Meanwhile, that's five out of five people from my calendar who I visited and there was no evidence of a soul vessel."

"And out of five, even you would have found one. Even a blind squirrel—"

"They weren't there."

"Maybe you should try starting at the *end* of the list. Catch up on the most recent names, the people just went on your calendar. Retrieve those and work backward."

"When? I'm officially back on duty. I have real cases to work."

"Well, you put this off anymore, shit gonna get real up in here real quick. Let me call your attention to exhibit A, Inspector: motherfucking banshee Tasing motherfuckers in the privacy of their own home."

"I know. I know. But, assuming I find the soul vessels, how am I going to sell them? With my caseload, I can't open the bookstore."

"Hire someone."

"I can't afford to hire someone. I'm barely keeping the doors open working there myself, and I don't even take a salary."

"You do what you're supposed to do, collect the soul vessels, the money will come. It always does."

"That more of your unified theory?"

"Experience. I've known a dozen Death Merchants. Everyone said the same thing: as soon as you start doing it, the money comes. You are catching up, Inspector. You're not going to have time to work in your store at all. It's a bookstore. There's a multitude of bright, overeducated motherfuckers with liberal arts degrees who would be happy to come work for you, just on the outside chance someone might ask them about Milton or Postmodernism or something, just like for my record store, there's a shitload of insufferable know-it-all hipsters who will work for next to nothing for the privilege of condescending to customers about their musical knowledge. Just run an ad and hire someone."

"What about that spooky girl who used to work for Asher?" Rivera asked. "She knew all about our business. I mean, if it's all right with you, I know you two—"

"I told you, it ain't a motherfuckin' thing, Rivera."

"Sorry. Do you have her number?"

"I'll call her for you."

"That's very kind of you, Mr. Fresh."

"I do not want to, I'm doing it because she won't trust you if you try to tell her what's going on."

"Trust me? But I'm a cop."

"Seriously? You did not just say that to a black man." The Mint One disconnected.

Crisis Center. What is your name, please?"

"Kevin."

"Hi Kevin. I'm Lily. Where are you calling from, Kevin?"

"I'm on the Golden Gate Bridge. I'm going to jump."

"No, you're not."

"Yes, I am."

"Nope. Not going to happen. Not on my watch."

Now he was going to tell her his story. Lily liked to watch French movies with subtitles on her tablet while listening to *the story*. The stories were usually pretty similar, or at least it seemed that way, because they were always calling from the same chapter. The chapter where someone is thinking about jumping off a big orange bridge or walking in front of a train.

Kevin told her his story. It sounded sad. But not as sad as what poor

Audrey Tautou was going through on the screen. Lily knew there would be sad French accordion music and she tried to work an earbud from her tablet under her phone headset ear so she could feel the full weight of poor Audrey's despair . . .

Kevin paused. Lily paused her movie.

"Don't do it," she said. "There's stuff to live for. Have you tried that cereal with the chocolate inside? Not *on* it, inside the actual cereal. How about pizza under a flaming dome? That shit is tasty insanity. Fuck, Kevin, you kill yourself without trying that, you'll hate yourself even more than you do now. I'm a trained chef, Kevin. I know."

"At least it will be over."

"Oh, hell no, it won't be over. You could hit the water, blow out an eardrum, shatter a bunch of vertebrae, die cold and in excruciating pain, and then, like five minutes later, you're a squirrel in a top hat and tap shoes, fighting a pigeon with a spork over a used donut. I have seen things, Kevin, terrible, dark, disturbing things. You do not want to go there."

"Really, a spork?"

"Yeah, Kevin, the fucking detail you want to grasp on to is the spork. That was the point of the story. Not that you'll be a squirrel in tap shoes, fighting a pigeon over a donut? That's a custard donut, Kevin. Custard is running out of the donut onto the pavement. There are ants on your donut, Kevin."

"Whoa, ants?"

"Ants are still not the important part, Kevin, you douche waffle."

"Hey, I don't even like custard donuts."

"Jump, Kevin. Over you go."

"What?"

"Geronimo! Let loose a long trailing scream as you go—warn any boaters or windsurfers to look the fuck out. No sense dragging someone along with your dumb ass."

"Hey?"

"Take the leap, Kevin. Into the maelstrom of suffering that will open for you."

"At least it will be different."

"Yeah, different in that it will be worse. Since when did a two-hundred foot drop into icy waves full of sharks spell hope to you, huh? You think you're depressed now? You think you're hopeless now? Wait until you're reincarnated as a crazed, scurrying little creature, desperate, afraid of everything, wearing stupid outfits. I've seen them, Kevin. I'll show you. You take a look at them, see what you'll become, and if you still want to jump, I'll drive you back there and push you off. Deal?"

"You're lying."

"I am. I don't have a car. But I'll pay your cab fare and say good-bye to you over the phone as you go. Worst-case scenario, you get to see some really creepy little animal people and two hours from now you're in the same place you are now, and I'm giving you hot phone sex as you're plummeting into the shark cafeteria."

"Really?"

"Really. Your phone got a camera?"

"Yeah."

"Send me a selfie."

"Right now?"

"Yeah, how am going to know what you look like?"

"Okay. This shirt has a little coffee stain down the front."

"Got it. Now head for the city side of the bridge. I'll be there in ten."

"You don't have a car."

"I'm going to borrow my boss's. Head for the tollgates. I'll park the car in the visitor center and walk up."

"Can't you stay on the line until you get here."

"Would love to, Kevin, but I can't tie up the crisis line. Look, I'll call you from my cell in a second. They make us leave them in the locker room, so give me five minutes. Head for the tollbooths. I'll call you in a bit."

"How will I know you?"

"I'm Asian." She wasn't Asian, but there would be a metric fuckload of Asian girls on the bridge for him to think were her. "Ten minutes. Don't jump, okay?"

"Okay."

"Promise?"

"Promise. But my battery is low."

"You'd better not jump because your fucking battery ran out, Kevin. Have a little faith, for fuck's sake."

"I wish you'd quit swearing."

"Oh, right, I'm your fairy godmother. Now, allow me to grant your wish. See you in ten." She hit the disconnect button.

Lily sent Kevin's photo to the Ranger station on the bridge with a note: *Jumper, headed your way. Temporarily paused him. Detain and hold for psych eval. Another save for Darquewillow Elventhing!*

"Woooo-hooooo, bitches!" One for the big board! Lily rose from her seat and headed for the big whiteboard at the head of the bullpen. The other three counselors dove for their mute buttons. She snatched up the marker and wrote SAVES THIS MONTH, then wrote her name and drew in a big *5 1/2* next to it with an exclamation point.

"Five-point-five, losers, and it's only the seventeenth of the month. That's right, at least two more weeks to try to catch this train of effective fucking crisis intervention!"

"That's not a thing, Lily," said Sage, a freckled blond girl about Lily's age, wearing a huge fisherman's sweater and cargo pants, who had clearly given up on giving a shit about her hair before she'd even started grad school. That kind of neglect didn't show overnight. She was working on her master's thesis in crisis counseling or something.

"It's not a thing for *you*," said Lily. "Because you are a loooooooser. La-la-la-looooozzer." Although she knew she was too old for it, and it was far beneath her dignity to indulge in such things, she did a subtle booty dance of victory to mark the moment.

"You're so broken," said Sage. "How did you ever get a job here?"

"Death is my business, Sage. They came to me because they knew I would dominate! Five and a half—yay-ooooooh!"

One of the other counselors, a tall fortyish guy with a mop of blond hair, looked over his glasses. He had his finger on the mute mic button like he was holding the mouth of a poisonous snake closed. "Lily, any chance you could wrap it up? I have to get an address and find out what pills this girl swallowed before she passes out."

"Oh," said Lily. "Sure. Go ahead. You'll save her, Brian. Want me to mark it on the big board for you?"

"That's not a thing, Lily." He lifted his finger and said into the headset, "Yes, Darla, I'm here. Can you tell me the address where you're staying?"

Sage said, "The board is supposed to be for bulletins, BOLOs, events going on in the city, things we all need to know before we answer a call."

"You mean like Lily got FIVE AND A HALF!" Lily said, tapping the board next to her number. She thought as she moved: *Booty dance. Booty dance. Right up on Sage's desk with my great big booty—*

"Lily, please stop twerking my desk."

"Fine," said Lily. "I'm going on break. Try not to kill anyone while I'm gone."

"You're so sad," said Sage.

"No, *you're* sad," said Lily. She threw a booty bounce of dismissal toward Sage as she walked into the locker room.

She dug her mobile out of her locker and headed outside to smoke as she checked for messages. He'd cried on her voice mail, which had been satisfying at first, but then kind of pathetic. She wasn't going to be fooled into calling him back just because he'd succumbed to a moment of wuss. He was Death, after all! Or at least *Assistant* Death. How could you compete with that? They all had something special, Charlie Asher, even little Sophie, had been singled out by the universe as special, while she, Lily *Darquewillow Elventhing* Severo (the *Darquewillow Elventhing* was silent) was just a failed restaurateur and part-time suicide hotline counselor. But she did have that. She saved lives. Most of the time. Kind of.

She listened to the message of Minty Fresh weeping after her again, a message which she had no intention of erasing, ever. The next message was from him, too, and hoping there might be begging—she could use some begging—she listened, but as soon as she heard the words "motherfuckin' forces of darkness and whatnot," she cut off the message with a punch of the callback button.

FRIENDS OF DOROTHY

ike Sullivan found himself waking up every morning thinking of the ghost, Concepción, and again, every night before he went to sleep. He made a special effort to wash his coveralls, so they were sparkling white speckled with International Orange, which didn't come off in the wash, and he polished the scuffs off his hard hat with car wax. As he shaved in the morning, he practiced the expression on his face he would have when he told her the fate of her Russian count, and all day, every day, throughout the day, he tried to be prepared for her appearance. He had spent five days painting the structure under the roadway before she returned.

"Oh, Señor Sullivan, I am so happy to see you," said Concepción, swinging around one of the trusses under the bridge like a real girl might swing around a lamp post in the park on a joyful summer day in a musical comedy, her skirts flaring out around her.

"I'm happy to see you, too," he said. "Please call me Mike."

"Mike it is, then," she said with a shy smile and a fluttering of her eyelashes. If she'd had a fan, she would have flirted from behind it. "What have you found out of my Nikolai?"

All of Mike's preparation had not prepared him for this, for a ghost that was light of spirit. A sullen, grieving, heartbroken ghost, yes, but not this bright and laughing Conchita who skipped amid the heavy steel like a feather on the wind.

He checked his safety lines, then took off his hard hat and held it over his heart, just as he had practiced. Then he told her. Watching the light go out of her eyes made him feel as if he'd just kicked the angel of mercy in the mouth.

"A horse?" she said.

"Sorry."

"A horse? A horse! A goddamn horse! I wept for two centuries and he fell off a horse six weeks after he sailed away?"

"Really sorry," Mike said. "But he *was* riding across Siberia to St. Petersburg to get permission from the Czar to marry you when he fell."

"Nobody just falls off a horse. Who falls off a horse?"

"It said on the Internet that he snapped his neck when he hit the ground, so he didn't suffer."

"All this time, I thought I might have said something wrong, I worried he had fallen in love with another, that the Czar had imprisoned him for breaking the rules of trade, but no, for him it was over in an instant. He didn't have to go all the way to Siberia to fall off a horse. We had horses here. My father had men who could have pushed him off a fucking horse."

"Excuse me, Conchita," said Mike, "but that doesn't sound like the Spanish lady who—"

"What do you know about Spanish ladies? You, with your stupid bucket, you, spattered with your orange paint."

Mike swallowed hard and put his hard hat back on. "But you can rest now, right? You can be at peace."

"Peace!" Her dress and hair whipped around her as if in a hurricane wind, although it was a calm day on the bay. "Oh, there will be no peace. I am two hundred years grieving, it will take at least a hundred to get over my anger. Oh, yes, señor, there will be haunting. Such haunting as no one has ever seen. If anyone in those cars passing above is of Russian blood, I shall visit such horrors upon them, they will wish *they* had fallen off a horse. They will beg to fall off a horse."

"But he loved you," said Mike. He was grateful to whatever circuit breaker in his brain had stopped from telling her that she was beautiful when she was angry, for, although she was, she was also scaring the shit out of him, nearly as badly as the first time she'd appeared to him.

She stopped raging for a moment. "Do you think so?"

"It says so in all the books. His love for you is legendary. A few years ago they brought earth from his grave to mingle with yours in Benicia. Your name is inscribed on his tombstone in Russia, with the words '*May they forever be together.*' "

"Oh," she said. She bit a nail, kept a delicate finger against her lower lip, as if to keep it from trembling.

"I'm very sorry, Conchita," Mike said.

She smiled again, all for him. "I know. You are my gallant champion. You have done as I asked and I have given you no thanks."

Mike shook his head. He couldn't speak, couldn't think of anything to say, he was having trouble even swallowing—being forgiven for not being able to change history had touched him more than he would have ever guessed.

She reached out and caressed his cheek and he was sure that this time he could feel her touch.

"I must go now," she said. "But I will come to you again, if I may?"

Mike nodded.

"And I must ask you, my gallant champion, for another favor."

"Anything," he managed to say without his voice breaking.

"There is another one here on the bridge that would speak with you, but if you don't wish to hear him, I will understand, my champion."

"As long as I'm hooked in, I suppose it will be okay. No sudden surprises, okay?"

"I will send him now," she said. "I will see you soon. Thank you, my love."

"Wait, your what?" Mike said, but she had stepped into a beam as if stepping behind a curtain and was gone.

Before he could pick up his paint bucket to move on, a guy in a suit and a wide-brimmed fedora floated down from the roadway and settled in a seated position on the beam where Mike was standing.

"Nice-looking broad," said the guy in the hat.

Mike realized that at the appearance of the second ghost, even though he was braced for it, he peed just a tiny bit in his shorts. Just a bit. There's something about being suspended over a two-hundred-foot drop that snaps you to attention, and in a second he was back in control, dealing with a weird situation in the only way you could, weirdly.

"I thought you knew her," Mike said. "She brought you to me, right?"

"Well, yeah, but I've never *seen* her. Persons are less put together on this side of the bridge, you don't so much see each other as you get an impression of them as they go by, and the impression I get most of the time is they're loopy as a snake salad. Not this broad, though."

"So you two talked?"

"Sure, you could say *talked*. Ghosts mostly communicate by odor. Gotta tell you, you got a house that smells like farts, you got a haunted house. Next time you think, oh man, Grandma farted, think again, it might be your dead grandpa. Unless your grandma eats a lot of cabbage, then it's probably her. Cabbage can be a rough road for old people. But's there's good, too. Every time you smell peaches, a ghost just got his rocks off. I should have known that broad was a dish before I even saw her, she smelled like peach pie."

Mike wanted to punch him. The ghost looked as solid as any person, sitting there on the beam, his feet dangling, ships and wind surfers passing two-hundred feet below, and Mike wanted to punch him right in the mouth for saying Concepción smelled like peach pie—like ghost come. Instead he swung his paint mop, which is what they used most of the time—a rough, fist-sized mop on the end of a two foot stick, to spot paint the bridge —swung it backhand, hoping he could knock off the ghost's stupid ghost fedora. Instead the mop just whiffed right through the shade and flung paint off into space. The ghost didn't even notice.

Exasperated, but trying to hide it, Mike said, "Well, why are you here? Why did she send you to me. She said it's difficult for you to appear this way, so why?"

"Whoa, don't get sore, I'm getting there."

"Well, get there."

"Fine," said the ghost, thumbing the lapels of his jacket. "You don't have to hit *me* with a brick."

I was working in the Naval Investigations Service out of Chi-town when we first got word of a potential enemy propaganda operation called the Friends of Dorothy operating on the West Coast, probably originating in Frisco. I know, *What's Naval Investigations doing in Chicago, a thousand miles from the nearest ocean?* That's the slickness of our strategy, see: Who's gonna suspect navy cops in the middle of Cow Town on the Prairie, am I right? Of course I am.

Anyways, we get word that new troops shipping out to the Pacific out of San Fran are being approached on the down low by this Friends of Dorothy bunch, who are playing up on their prebattle jitters, trying to cause some desertions, maybe even recruit spies for Tojo.

So the colonel looks around the office, and as I am the most baby-faced of the bunch, he decides to send me out to Frisco under cover as a new recruit to see if I can get the skinny on this Dorothy and her friends, before we got another Axis Annie or Tokyo Rose on our hands, only worse, because this Dorothy isn't just taking a shot at our morale on the radio, she's likely running secret operations.

I tell the colonel that despite my youthful mug, I am an expert on the ways of devious dames and I will have this Dorothy in the brig before he can say *Hirohito is a bum*, maybe faster. So five days later I find myself on the dog-back streets of San Fran with about a million other sailors, soldiers, and marines waiting to ship out.

Well, San Fran is getting to be known as Liberty City, as this is the spot where many guys are going to see the good old U S of A for the last time ever, so in spite of restrictions and whatnot all along the Barbary Coast, every night the town is full of military guys out for one last party, looking for a drink or a dame or the occasional crap game. It's a tradition by this time that the night before you ship out, you go up to the Top of the Mark, the nightclub on the top floor of the Mark Hopkins Hotel on California Street, where a guy can have a snort whilst looking at the whole city from bridge to bridge, and if he's lucky, a good-smelling broad will take him for a twirl around the dance floor and tell him that everything is going to be okay, even though most guys are suspicious that it's not. And these are such dames as are doing this out of patriotism and the kindness of their heart, like the USO, so there's no hanky-panky or grab-assing.

Word has it that the Friends of Dorothy are recruiting at the Top of the Mark, so I don a set of navy whites and pea coat like a normal swabby, and stake out a spot by the doorman outside the hotel. As guys go by, I am whispering, "Friends of Dorothy," under my breath, like a guy selling dirty postcards or tickets to a sold-out Cubs game (which could happen when they make their run for the pennant). And before long, the cable car stops and off steps this corn-fed jarhead who is looking around and grinning at the buildings and the bay at the end of the street like he's never seen water before, and he's sort of wandering around on the sidewalk like he's afraid of the doorman or something, and I gives him my hush-hush *Friends of Dorothy* whisper.

So Private Hayseed sidles up to me and says back, "Friends of Dorothy?"

"You're damn skippy, marine," says I.

And just like that, the kid lights up like Christmas morning and starts pumping my hand like he's supplying water to douse the Chicago fire, or maybe the Frisco fire, as I hear that they also have a fire, but I cannot but think that it was not a real fire, as Frisco is clearly a toy town. Kid introduces himself as Eddie Boedeker, Jr., from Sheep Shit, Iowa or Nebraska or one of your more square-shaped, corn-oriented states, I don't remember. And he goes on how he is nervous and he has never done anything like this before, but he's about to go

off to war and might never come home, so he has to see— and it's
all I can do to calm the kid down and stand him up against the wall
beside me like he's just there to take in the night air and whatnot.
You see, I am dressed like a sailor, and he is a marine, and although
technically, swabbies and jarheads are in the same branch of the
service, it's a time-honored tradition that when they are in port they
fight like rats in a barrel, which is something I should have perhaps
thought of when I picked my spy duds.

So on the spot I compose a slogan of war unity so as to shore up
my cover. "*Fight together or lose alone, even with no-necked fucking
jarheads.*" I try it out on the doorman like I'm reading it off a poster
and he nods, so I figure we're good to go.

"C'mon, marine," I says to the Private Hayseed, "I'll buy you a
drink."

So we go up the elevator to the Top of the Mark, and I order
an old-fashioned because there's an orange slice in it and I'm wary
of scurvy, and I ask the kid what he'll have, and he says, "Oh, I ain't
much for drinking."

And I says, "Kid, you're about to ship out to get your guts blown
out on some godforsaken coral turd in the Pacific and you're not going
to have a drink before you go, what are you, some kind of moron?"

And the kid provides that, no, he's a Methodist, but his ma has a
record of the Moron Tabernacle Choir singing "Silent Night" that she
plays every Christmas and so I figure the answer is yes and I order the
kid an old-fashioned with an extra orange slice hoping it might help
cure stupid as well as scurvy. But I also figure that old Eddie here is
exactly the kind of dim bulb that Dorothy and her cohorts will try to
go for, so I press on, pouring a couple more old-fashioneds into him,
until the kid is as pink-faced as a sunburned baby and gets a little
weepy about God and country and going off to war, while I keep
trying to slide in questions about Dorothy, but the kid keeps saying
maybe later, and asks if maybe we can't go hear some jazz, as he has
never heard jazz except on the radio.

Well, the bartender provides as there is an excellent horn player over in the Fillmore, which is only a hop on the cable car, so I flip him four bits for the tip and I drag Eddie down to the street and pour him onto the cable car, which takes us up the hill and over to the Fillmore, which is where all the blacks live now, as it used to be a Jap neighborhood until they shipped them off to camps and the blacks moved in from the South to work in the shipyards bringing with them jazz and blues and no little bit of dancing.

And as we're getting off the car, I spots some floozies standing outside the club right below a War Department poster with a picture of a similar dame that says, *"She's a booby trap! They can cure VD, but not regret."*

And as we're walking up, I says, "Hey, toots, you pose for that poster?" And one of the rounder dames says, "I might have, sailor, but I ain't heard no regrets yet," which gives me a laugh, but makes Private Eddie just look down and smile into his top button. He whispers to me on the side, "I ain't never done anything like this before."

I figured as much, but I say to the kid, "That's what the Friends of Dorothy are for, kid," just taking a shot in the dark.

And he gets a goofy grin and says, "That's what the guy said."

And I say, "What guy?" but by that time we're through the door and the band is playing, the horn player going to town on the old standard "Chicago," to which I remove my sailor's hat, because it is, indeed, my kind of town. So we drink and listen to jazz and laugh at nothing much, 'cause the kid doesn't want to think about where he's going, and he doesn't want to think about where he came from, and I can't figure out how to get behind this Dorothy thing with the band playing. After a few snorts, the kid even lets a dame take him out on the dance floor, and because he more resembles a club-footed blind man killing roaches than a dancer, I head for the can to avoid associating with him, and on my way back, I accidently bump into a dogface, spilling his drink. And before I can apologize, when I am still on the part that despite his being a pissant, lamebrained, clumsy, ham-handed army son of a bitch, it is a total accident that I bump into him and spill his drink, he takes a swing at me. And since he grazes my chin no little, I am obliged to return his ministrations with a left to the fucking breadbasket and a right cross which sails safely across his bow. At which point, the entire Seventh Infantry comes out of the woodwork, and soon I am dodging a dozen green meanies, taking hits to the engine room, the galley, as well as the bridge, and my return fire is having little to no effect on the thirty-eleven or so guys what are wailing on me. I am sinking fast, about to go down for the count. Then two of the GIs go flying back like they are catching cannonballs, and then two more from the other side, and through what light I can see, Private Eddie Boedeker, Jr., wades into the GIs like the hammer of fucking God, taking out a GI with every punch, and those that are not punched are grabbed by the shirt and hurled with no little urgency over tables, chairs, and various downed citizens, and it occurs to me that I have perhaps judged the kid's dancing chops too harshly, for while he cannot put two dance steps together if you paint them on the floor, he appears to have a right-left combination that will stop a panzer.

Before long, guys from all branches of service are exchanging opinions and broken furniture and I hear the sinister chorus of MP whistles, at which point I grab the kid by the belt and drag him backward through the tables and the curtain behind the stage and out into the alley, where I collapse for a second to collect my thoughts and test a loose tooth, and the kid bends over, hands on his knees, gasping for breath, laughing and spitting a little blood.

"So, kid," I says. "You saved my bacon." And I offer him a bloody-knuckled handshake.

Kid takes my hand and says, "Friends of Dorothy," and pulls me into a big hug.

"Yeah, yeah, Friends of fucking Dorothy," I say, slapping him on the back. "Speaking of which," I say, pushing him off. "Let's take a walk—"

"I gotta get back to Fort Mason," the kid says. "It's nearly midnight. The cable cars stop at midnight and I gotta ship out in the morning."

"I know, kid, but Friends of Dorothy," I says. I'm aware all of a sudden that I have strayed somewhat from my mission, and that if the kid goes, I'm going to have to start all over again, although I suspect I have not exactly stumbled onto the mastermind of the diabolical Dorothy's organization. But still.

"Look," says the kid. "This has been swell. Really swell. I really appreciate you, you know, being a friend, but I gotta go. I ain't never done nothing like this, never met anyone like you. It's been swell."

"Well, you know—" I says, not knowing how to bail this out. That one tooth was definitely loose.

Suddenly the kid grabs me again, gives me a big hug, then turns and runs off toward the cable-car stop. He's about a half a block away when he turns and says, "I'm going to go see the Golden Gate Bridge in the morning. Oh-six-hundred. Ain't never seen a sunrise over the ocean. I'll meet you there. Say good-bye."

And I'm am tempted to point out several things, including that he will have to see the Golden Gate Bridge as he passes under it when he ships out, that we are on the West Coast and the sun doesn't rise over the ocean, and that there is no need to run, as I can hear the bell of the cable car and it is still blocks away, but these being finer points than I want to yell up an alley when there are MPs still on the prowl, I say, "I'll be there."

"Friends of Dorothy," the kid says with a wave.

"Friends of Dorothy," I say back at him. Which goes to show you, right there, the difference between sailors and marines: marines are fucking stupid. Running when you don't have to.

So next morning I'm on the bridge, crack of dawn, so hungover I feel like if I don't close my eyes I might bleed to death, but not having to worry about it, since my eyes are too swollen up to bleed, and I see the kid, all by himself, about halfway down the bridge, out in the fog, waving like a goddamn loony when he sees me. So I limp out to him, and when I get close he starts running at me, so I says, "No running! No goddamn running!"

But he keeps running, and now he's got his arms out like to give me a big hug, which I am in no mood for.

So I back away and say, "At ease, marine."

And he stops, bounces on his toes like a little goddamn girl.

"I couldn't wait to see you. I thought about you all night. I couldn't sleep," he says.

"Yeah, yeah, that's good," I say. "But about the Friends of Dorothy—"

"I'm sorry about that," the kid says. "Really sorry. I mean, I want to, but I never did anything like that before. I mean, in Kansas nobody's like that. I thought—I mean, if my folks—I thought I was the only one. Then this guy in boot camp told me about the Friends of Dorothy."

That's right. It was Kansas. Anyway, I says, "That's it, you got to tell me about Dorothy, everything you know, Eddie."

"But I don't know nothing. I just, I just have these feelings—"

Then the kid grabs me, right then, and gives me a great big wet one, right on the kisser. I was so surprised I just about shit myself. So I push him off of me, you know, big flat palm to the chin, and when I get done spitting, I say, "What the hell was that about?"

And the kid looks like I just shot his dog. "Friends of Dorothy," he says.

"Yeah, the Friends of fucking Dorothy, that's why I'm here, but what the fuck was that? You queer or something?"

And he goes, "Friends of Dorothy. Like the Scarecrow. Like the Tin Man. Like the Cowardly Lion. People ain't got anyone else like them. But Dorothy don't care. Like you. Like us."

"I ain't like you, kid. I got people. I got a wife and kid back in Chicago. I'd be out shooting the ass off of Tojo myself if I hadn't blown my knee out in football in high school. I'm not Dorothy's friend, I'm not your friend, kid."

"Friends of Dorothy," the kid says. "We find each other," he says.

"Queers? That's what this is about? A bunch of fairies? Marines? Sailors? Are you fucking kidding me?"

"Friends of Dorothy," the kid wails.

"Not anymore. Naval Investigative Service. I'm taking you in, kid. You're going in the brig, and if you ever wanna get out, you're going to tell me everything you know about the Friends of Dorothy. Everyone you ever talked to about them. I need names, places, dates."

"But I'm shipping out today. I ain't never done nothing like this."

"And you're not going to again," I says. "It's time of war, kid, and being queer is a court-martialable offense. You and your Friends of Dorothy are traitors. Hell, they might even shoot you. You might make it back to Kansas, but it's going to be in chains, to Leavenworth." Rough, I know, but I'm hungover and annoyed that I've been made a sap, and I'm just trying to scare the kid so he's easier to handle.

The kid starts shaking his head and backing away. "You can't tell my folks. You can't tell my dad. It would kill him."

"Everyone's going to know, kid. It's going to be in the papers, so you might as well come clean."

Then he turns and really starts to run.

"Where you think you're going, kid? I got the whole fleet I can send after you. A deserter. A queer traitor and deserter."

"Friends of Dorothy," he wails. His face is melting into a big glob of snot and tears.

"Yeah, Friends of fucking Dorothy, traitor. Let's go, Boedeker."

The he just starts wailing, crying it, "But Friends of Dorothy! Friends of Dorothy!" and then, again with the running, but this time for the rail, and before I can get close to him, he's over, headfirst. Hit the water like a gunshot. I bet they could hear it all the way to Fort Mason.

I look down and he's just all bent up, like a broken scarecrow, floating dead in the waves.

"That's the saddest story I've ever heard," said Mike Sullivan.

"Yeah, it was the war. Tough times."

"So, you, did you, I mean, did you jump, too?" asked Mike.

"Nah, I went back to Chicago. Heart attack in '58."

"Then why are you here?"

"Smoked a lot, ate a lot of bratwurst, we didn't know stuff in those days."

"No, why are you on the bridge?"

"No idea. Guess that's why the Spanish broad wanted me to tell you my story. You want I should fetch her?"

"Maybe that would be good," Mike said. The ghost's story had made him a little woozy. He couldn't figure out if it was nausea or anxiety, but neither were to be taken lightly when you were up on the bridge.

"So long, bridge painter," said the ghost. "And by the way, you can tell the dame that you have not been helpful in the least. I feel like I'm the only one did any talking here. No offense."

"You'll want to fuck off, now," said Mike, who despite being a nice guy, had his limits, which he was very close to reaching with this particular spirit.

"You don't have to tell me twice," said the ghost.

In an instant he had rolled into the beam he was sitting on and Concepción materialized on the beam next to Mike, so close she could have sat on one of his safety lines.

"Thank you," she said. "My brave champion."

"Why?" asked Mike. He felt better just seeing her, in fact his emotions had swung from morose and anxious to elated and nearly giddy as soon as she appeared.

"I think you can understand now that we need you," she said. "He is just one of many."

"You need me for what?"

"To join us, of course," she said.

COFFEE WITH LILY

When she arrived, he was already in the coffee shop, sitting in one of the conversation areas in a wingback chair, his long legs stretched out before him like a fun slide.

She said, "Just because the forces of darkness are rising and the end of the world is nigh, don't think I'm going to play Armageddon bone monkeys with you, M. This is just coffee."

She called him "M," because she refused to call him Minty, it being, in her mind, entirely too cheerful and perky and kind of stupid, and because he told her once that when he had worked security for a casino in Vegas he said they referred to him as M.F., which everyone thought stood for *motherfucker*. So "M" for short.

"A double espresso for me, then," he said with a smile.

She put her enormous spike-studded purse on the chair to the side of him. "How about two singles?"

He nodded. "That would be perfect, Darque."

She turned to conceal her own smile and headed off to the counter to get their coffee. She knew he'd conceded to having two single espressos because he knew that watching him drink from the teeny-tiny cups made her laugh, so she'd won coffee already. But he *had* called her Darque, which she loved, so maybe *he'd* won. Fucksox!

When she returned with their coffees she said, "Are you sure you want to talk about this stuff here?"

"You didn't want to come to my place."

But she *did* want to come to his place, be charmed into insane make-up sex where he enveloped her pale and luscious beauty like a great spider, rendering her helpless in his grasp, stinging her again and again (although not in the butt) until she screamed. But he was too old, too tall, too rich (she would not be a slave to his economic stability—even at the price of moving back into a crap apartment in the Sunset), and most of all, he was way too dark and cool.

She said, "Well, in public I thought there'd be less sobbing. It would be less embarrassing for you."

"Very considerate of you," he said. "You know that one voice mail, I was having a bad reaction to some cold medicine. So, you know, just ignore that one."

"Which one was that?" she said, eyes wide, which, with her dark and abundant eye makeup, made her look like a silent film star overplaying an insane person—Brigitte Helm, crazed anarchist/robot in Fritz Lang's *Metropolis* was what she was going for.

"You know which one," he said, then he took a sip from a tiny cup.

"Oh, you mean my new ring tone? Sure. Okay." She smiled coyly into her latte. This was what the personal ads would refer to as "light dominance and humiliation" and she decided this was something she was keeping in mind as one of her dating profile preferences.

"Charlie Asher is alive," Minty said.

"What?" She looked up so fast she spilled a little coffee in her lap. "Wait, what?"

"Audrey put his soul into one of those Squirrel People things. He's been living with her at the Buddhist Center since we buried his real body."

Lily had actually been there when he died from the Morrigan's poison . . . well, right outside the room. She had gone to Asher's funeral.

She'd been devastated. He'd been annoying, but she'd thought he'd always be there. She'd probably ended up with Minty Fresh because she had been so traumatized over Asher's death, at least that's what her friend Abby had told her. Now Asher was alive? Tears welled in her eyes and she wiped them back. She said, "Wait. What?"

"Asher needs a new body and I'm going to try to help him find one. I need to find someone who is going to die, but of an accident that won't ruin their body too much. Audrey has some *Tibetan Book of the Dead* gris-gris she going to do."

"Wait," said Lily. "What?"

"Rivera, the homicide cop that was following Asher, working the soul vessel cases? The one that shot the Morrigan while she was giving Charlie a hand job? He's a Death Merchant now."

"Rivera?" Was everybody special but her? For fuck's sake. Armani cop, Rivera? "Wait, how long . . ."

"I sent him the *Big Book of Death* myself. Asher told me that Rivera was able to see him while he was collecting a soul vessel, so even back then he was becoming. He opened a bookstore over on Polk."

"Rivera?" she said.

"A woman appeared in his shop out of nowhere, a banshee, shrieking, warning him that shit was going down—'an elegant death,' she said. Then she Tased him and disappeared."

"A banshee?" How did you get that job? She would be awesome at that. They give you a Taser?

"Rivera hasn't collected a soul for a year. Turns out, Charlie Asher was supposed to keep collecting soul vessels as well. He hasn't. His shop should have stayed open. We should have never opened that restaurant."

"Well I could have told you that," she said. Pizza and jazz, really a stupid combination. Would have been obvious to here if she hadn't been all woo-wooed over the enormous mint Death Merchant at the time.

Minty said, "We're not sure that the Death Merchants who were killed when all that went down were replaced. I'm trying to find out, now. There could be a thousand or more uncollected soul vessels. That's way, way worse than what caused the last un-fucking-raveling. No telling what kind of shit going to show up."

"Well little Sophie is the Big Death, right, the Luminatus, she can just smack them down like before, right?"

"She might not be. Asher says her hellhounds are gone."

He put down his first espresso and tossed back the second. Lily found no joy whatsoever in watching.

"Gone? Wait. What?"

"And the Emperor is running around, talkin' about he got to make a list of all the forgotten dead, which would be on par crazy per usual if all this other shit wasn't going down."

"But no one has seen the Morrigan, right?" Lily was the one who had first figured out who—what—the raven-women were, and she'd seen firsthand the entity that had led their attack, a winged bull-headed thing that had nearly destroyed Charlie Asher's secondhand shop looking for soul vessels. Charlie had seen the Morrigan rip the creature to shreds in the vast underground grotto that had formed under the financial district. Historically speaking, it had been a fucked-up day.

"Nah, Sophie took them out, we're hoping *that* was a forever thing."

"I'm going to need another coffee. You?"

He shook his head. She nearly lost her balance when she stood up—the maelstrom of new and disturbing information she was trying to process making her light-headed. He caught her arm and steadied her.

"You all right?"

She nodded. "I just need a minute with you not telling me stuff."

She stumbled over to the counter and ordered, stood there and waited even after the barista told her he would bring it to her. It had all gone to shit so fast—one minute she was the boss of the whole situation, the next she's stumbling around trying to grasp the idea that Charlie was alive and was trying to escape from the body of a squirrel person. (And what deeply creepy little fucks they were, even for her, for whom deeply creepy had long been a goal.) Had M dumped all this on her just because she'd been winning? Didn't matter. She needed to talk to Charlie Asher, she needed in on this grand and dark debacle that was about to happen. She picked up her coffee and returned to the Mint One.

"So?" she said as she sat. She sipped her coffee.

"So," Minty Fresh repeated, tenting his long fingers on his chest.

"What can I do?" she asked.

"Rivera is trying to catch up on his list, retrieving soul vessels. He's back on the force."

"When was he *not* a cop?"

"Retired. Temporarily. Back now. He needs someone to work in his shop. He asked for you."

"Wait. What?"

"Eventually we're going to have to figure out a way for Asher's shop to open again, too, if everything doesn't blow up. But first things first."

"You called me, had me come down here, dumped all this world-shaking shit on me because you want me to work in fucking retail?" Oh, it was so wrong. So, so, unfair. Bullshit, that's what it was. Bullshit!

"He needs someone," said Minty.

"Someone, but not me. Some anonymous, unspecial person with no talent, not me. I've saved five and a half lives this month already."

"A half?"

"Jumped but lived, so, you know, technically, I didn't stop the guy from jumping, but he failed, too, since he lived, so it's a tie, so half a save. Anyway, the point is, I have important things to do."

"I told him that."

"No, you didn't."

"I did. I told him you were special," he said.

"Wait," she said, then dug into her purse for her phone to buy time to think. What was he trying to pull now? She was not going to let him get away with that weak-ass charm thing he did. She looked at her phone to check the time, then stood up. "Look, I'll let you know. I've got to go. I have a date with the guy who paints the Golden Gate Bridge."

That sounded way less impressive than she had hoped it would.

"There's only one?"

"Yes," she said. She had no idea. There was now.

"Y'all have a good time, then," Minty said. "Good seeing you, Darque."

"Yeah, you too," she said, fussing with stuff in her purse as if she were searching for car keys, which she wasn't, since she didn't have a car, but it was a thing you could do when you couldn't think of what to do.

"Thanks for the coffee," he said. He watched as she walked away and thought, *She's too young, too short, and way to motherfuckin' spooky, and I miss her. But at least I won coffee.*

At the door of the coffee shop she turned and said, "You did not win." Then she walked out.

Motherfuckin' spooky, he thought.

Dawn, pink and chilly. The Emperor of San Francisco was trudging along the waterfront by the Aquatic Park when a guinea pig dressed in the pumpkin pants and satin doublet of an Elizabethan dandy ran by on disproportionately long, wading-bird legs, a small model tugboat thrown over its shoulder. It was followed by two equally patchwork creatures dressed in what appeared to be red shop rags, the type that are sold in rolls; one creature had the head of a calico cat, the other that of an armadillo, the latter chanting "go, go, go" as they passed.

"Well, you don't see that every day," said the Emperor. Lazarus, the golden retriever, ruffed in sympathy, but Bummer, the Boston terrier, was already after them, hell-bent for leather, emitting a staccato growl that sounded as if he had swallowed a very small and angry motorcycle and was trying to keep it down as he ran.

Not in my town, Bummer thought. *Not in my town.*

Lazarus looked to the Emperor as if to say, *We have to go after him, don't we?* He fell into a tolerant trot while the Emperor tucked his walking stick under his arm and hitched up the army-surplus map bag he had slung over his shoulder to hold the heavy journal containing his list of the dead, and strode along behind.

His bad knee had been bothering him more than usual lately, since

they'd started sleeping nearer the water, in and around Fort Mason, sometimes in a nook or cranny at the St. Francis Yacht Club, instead of in the
utility closet behind the pizzeria in North Beach whose benevolent owner
had cleared out the space and even provided a key for the Emperor and
his men. Something about being closer to the bridge helped the names of
the dead come to him, and on recent mornings he could scarcely work the
stiffness out of his hand before the names and numbers began flooding his
mind, and he would have to sit down wherever he was and record them.
At first he'd gone to the library, and to the police station, and even to City
Hall to get the names the dead had asked for, but these were names he
hadn't found there, and the dates went back much further than the year the
dead had originally asked him to record.

At the edge of the park, streetcar tracks, long unused, ran into a long
concrete trench where the street cars used to pass before entering the
tunnel under the great meadow above Fort Mason. Bummer chased the
hodgepodge creatures into the trench, knowing that there was a set of
steel doors closing off the tunnel at the end and soon he would tear ass
out of whatever these things were, or at least stand tough and give them a
stern barking at.

As the doors came into his view, Bummer smelled a foul, avian odor
that he'd encountered before, and he stopped so abruptly he nearly toppled
over. The doors covered only the lower portion of the tunnel; the arch
above, nearly four feet high, was open and dark. At the base of the doors
was a wide puddle that looked like tar or heavy oil.

The Emperor and Lazarus caught up to Bummer just as one of the
creatures, the calico-cat-headed one, bounced up and over the doors, into
the dark arch. As the second one, the guinea pig, crouched to leap over
the top of door as well, out of the puddle came a sleek feminine hand
with long talons that impaled the little dandy in the chest. Another hand
snaked out of the dark liquid, snatched the toy tugboat, and submerged,
then a third emerged, talons bared, and with the first one tore the guinea
pig to shreds; blood and silk splattered the door and the concrete walls of
the trench.

The third creature turned and ran back toward the Emperor and his men, who also turned and followed it out of the trench.

Above his own rasping breath the Emperor heard, "Oh, that's delicious, isn't that delicious?" in a breathy, female voice, that wafted from the dark tunnel.

They'd agreed to meet at an independent coffee place off Union Street in the Marina called The Toasted Grind. *Did nobody drink anymore?* Lily wondered. She loved coffee, but this was turning out to be a stressful day and a couple of stout Long Island iced teas would certainly take the edge off, especially if the bridge guy was buying. She'd only agreed to this because the bridge guy had called as she was getting ready to meet M, and she thought it would be something she could tell the Mint One that would make him jealous. Oh, well.

"Are you Mike?" Lily said, walking up to the guy who she figured was Mike. He was, as he'd described himself, "kind of normal-looking": midthirties, medium height, medium build, dark hair, greenish eyes, a lot like Charlie Asher, only with more muscle. He was wearing jeans and a clean, blue oxford-cloth shirt, but it was clear he had shoulders and arms—Charlie's arms had just been props he used to keep his sleeves from collapsing. Why was she even thinking about Asher?

He stood. "I am," he said. "Lily?"

"Sit," she said. She sat across from him. "You know this is not a date, right?"

"Of course. Thanks for meeting me. You know, on the phone, that first day, you said you knew things, and well, I wanted to pick your brain."

"In Fiji, they have a special pick just for eating human brains. They call it a brain fork."

"Not like that."

"I know," she said. She signaled to the server, a girl about her age with a short blond mop of mini-dreadlocks.

Lily ordered a black brewed coffee and Mike followed her lead until the server said, "You want anything in that?," directed at Lily.

"Like?"

"We just got our liquor license. We don't have the bar put together yet, but we can make you an Irish coffee."

"A shot of Irish whiskey would be great," Lily said.

"You?" the girl asked Mike.

Mike cringed a bit and looked at Lily when he answered. "I'm trying to stay away from depressants. I've just gone through a breakup and some stuff."

"Me, too," said Lily. "Put his shot in mine as well."

The server smiled. "I know. I'm dating an old guy, too. Don't you love how they act like every decision is life-altering?"

"I'm not an old guy," said Mike.

"It's not a date," said Lily.

"I'll be back with your coffee," said dread girl. "Anything else right now?"

"A Viagra and a pair of handcuffs," said Mike, deadpan.

"Nice," said dread girl, then to Lily, "If you don't want him, I'll take him." And off she went.

"You're sharper than you look," Lily said.

"Thanks. I think. You're younger than you sounded on the phone."

"My experience weighs on me far more than my years show." She sighed, a tragic sigh that she didn't get to use much anymore since she'd been forced by a brutal society to behave like a grown-up, and since she'd lost weight, most of her mopey Goth clothes didn't fit, so she was almost never dressed for tragic sighing. "I've seen too many things that can never be unseen, Mike."

"I guess I thought you were older because of how you dealt with that jumper."

Was he trying to say something? She didn't need anyone else judging her and she wished she had worn something low-cut so she could accuse him of looking at her boobs, which he totally was not, which was annoying. "I don't know what you mean," she said.

"You were so calm, unconcerned. I mean, that guy *died*."

"You think I'm unconcerned? That I don't care? Do you know why I'm cynical and snarky on the crisis line?"

He shook his head.

"Because it works. It's normal. They need normal, fast. They need out of the spiral they're in, so if they're suddenly offended by me, or horny for me, I don't care. What they're *not* focused on is their own pain, they're not alone, there's someone else on the planet with them who is annoying and possibly sexy, and it gets them to put the pills or the gun down, it gets them off the bridge in a safe way. That's my jam. It used to be being *dark and mysterious*, but you can't out-dark the people I was hanging out with, and if I get the least bit drunk or high, I tell everyone everything I know, so I'm a fucking loser at mysterious. Yeah, we lost that guy, but I saved five others this month. I'm good at what I do." *Five and half, bitches!* she thought.

"I know, that's why I called you," Mike said.

"Wait. What?"

"And because she told me to."

"Who told you to?"

Their coffees came before he could answer and he waited for Dread Girl to leave before he answered her.

"This is going to sound really strange," he said. "I can't quite believe I'm going to say it—"

"If you start talking about your ex, I will knock you out of that chair—"

"A ghost. The ghost of Concepción de Arguello, daughter of the governor of Alta California."

"Where is that? I don't even know where that is," Lily said. He was doing that big lie with a little detailed lie to give it the credibility thing.

"It's here," Mike said, gesturing to the street and around them. "*This* is Alta California."

"This is the Marina. This is where you go between the fraternity or sorority house and your first divorce. Look around, except for our waitress, who I guarantee doesn't live in this neighborhood, it's all people who are completely self-absorbed without a shred of self-awareness."

"Wow, that's harsh," Mike said.

"You haven't served them," Lily said. She smiled, not a lot of teeth but a sparkle of mischief in her eye, then sipped her hot liquor through the straw.

"Ghost," Mike said.

"So?" Lily said.

"This was Alta California in the early 1800s."

"You're not going to just forget you said that, then? I'm willing. I mean, to be honest, you've probably lost your shot with me, because I have a rule about not boning the mentally disturbed, but we can be acquaintances, and I promise not to cock-block you with the waitress—she seems into you. But don't you think that was disrespectful, her hitting on my date like that."

"I'm not your date."

"She doesn't know that."

"You told her that."

"Whose side are you on, anyway?"

"She said that you knew Death and could help with the Ghost Thief. That I should call you."

"The waitress?"

"The ghost."

"You're going to tell me, so tell me?" she said. She signaled for the waitress to bring her another, then, in her head, she conjured sad French accordion music playing, mimes and ballerinas entering the stage to act out Mike's story, guys rhythmically kicking Gérard Depardieu in the kidneys as a backbeat, because fuck him, why did he have to be in everything French?

So he told her, about Concepción, about the other ghosts, about how they had only spoken to him, about the Friends of Dorothy, about all of it, and as he told her, she believed him, because his wasn't even close to the most bizarre story she'd been part of, and then she realized . . .

"Oh my fucking god, the guy who paints the fucking bridge orange for a living is *special* and I get to go back to retail. Oh, fuck me. Fuck me roughly with a big spiky demon dick!"

"Huh?" said Mike, who hadn't expected that particular reaction. "People are looking."

"Fuck them!" Lily said. "They're not special. I know, because I'm not special and I recognize the symptoms. Although all you Marina people *think* you're fucking special, don't you? You entitled fucks!"

The waitress was making her way over to try to settle Lily down, but Mike signaled that he had this and she went the other way.

"Concepción evidently thinks you're special," Mike said. "She said you would be able to help save them from the Ghost Thief."

"I don't even know what that is," Lily said.

"Maybe you're supposed to find out," Mike said. "And right now I *need* you."

"What for? You're the magic ghost-talker guy."

"I need you to talk me out of jumping off the bridge."

PART TWO

With nothing will be pleased until he be eased
With being nothing.
— William Shakespeare, *Richard II,* Act V, Scene V

10

REMEMBRANCE OF THINGS PAST

She was so slight that her body made barely a rise in the sheets, like a wave on a calm pond from a phantom wind—her face might have been a skeletal mask laid upon the pillow for presentation, her long white hair brushed out to one side the way she liked it.

"You are trying to disappear," Baptiste sang from the doorway, "but *I* see you." He wheeled his mop bucket into her room.

"*Bonjour, Monsieur Baptiste,*" Helen said, her voice little more than a whisper.

"*Bonjour, Madame Helen,*" said Baptiste. "*Comment allez-vous?*"

"*Pas trés bien. Je suis fatiguée, monsieur.*"

"I won't be long, then you can rest. Can I bring you anything, *chère*?"

"No, thank you. Thank you for speaking French with me, no one does that anymore. I spent my semester abroad in Paris, you know?"

She told him this every day he worked, and every day he replied, "Ah, the City of Light. So many delights. What, I wonder, is your favorite?"

And here, her answer often changed. "I loved walking through the Jardin du Luxembourg in the autumn, when the wind was blowing a little, and chestnuts would drop out of the trees and sometimes hit one of the old men who sat on the benches reading. Plop, right on the head." She laughed, then coughed. "Now I'm the old one."

"Nonsense, *chère*." He was not so young himself, and by the end of his workday, gray stubble would show on his dark cheeks as if they had been dusted with ash.

"You want some oxygen?"

"*Non, merci,*" she said.

He was not authorized to put the cannula in her nose and turn on the oxygen, but he had done it before when she was in discomfort, and he did a lot of things he was not authorized to do. He rolled his bucket to the corner, dipped his mop in the water, then leaned on the ringer until it was nearly dry. When he wiped the mop out into the corner, the room filled with the smell of the lemon disinfectant, but above it he could still detect the acid smell of her organs shutting down. Helen had been in hospice for six months, longer than most of the patients. He had become attached to her and he was sad her time was coming to an end. Speaking French to her was a kindness he didn't get to grant to most of the patients, although he made an effort to try to do something actively kind for each one of them, every day, even if it was only asking after a grandchild, changing the channel on the television, or singing a soft song to them as they slept.

They all would pass, and he would grieve for each one, even if he was only the man who mopped the floors, gathered the laundry, emptied the bins. He would say hello to each one every day, if they were conscious or not, and say good-bye each evening as well, so if they died in the night, good-bye would not go unsaid. But Helen concerned him more than the others. Her name had not appeared in his date book and he did not see the object around her glowing red. From her symptoms, he could tell he had only days to retrieve her soul vessel, and he did not want to go to her house, as he sometimes did. He did not want to see the life she had left, which was grand and full and opulent; he knew because she had told him, and he did not want to see what she was leaving because it would make him more sad.

He mopped from the wall to her bedside, then ran the mop under her bed and up onto some very nice Italian shoes. On the other side of the bed stood a sharp, well-dressed Latin man who was looking around the room with some urgency—trying to look around Baptiste, not at him.

"Who are you?" Baptiste asked, and the man in the nice suit leapt back as if he'd encountered an electric fence at Helen's bedside.

"Santa Maria!" he said. Then he looked back quickly, as if something might be following. Finally, he looked at Baptiste. "You can see me?"

Baptiste smiled. "I can, but Madame Helen cannot."

"I'm blind," said Helen.

"What are you, some kind of ninny? Say hello to *Madame*," said Baptiste.

Charlie paced across the parlor of the Three Jewel Buddhist Center, the claws on his duck feet snagging occasionally on the Persian rug, at which Audrey tried not to cringe. She was not attached to material things, but it was a nice rug.

"I'm telling you, Audrey, they're squirrelly," Charlie said.

"Really? Squirrelly? Who would have thought?"

"No, I don't mean it that way. Well, yes that way, but what I'm saying is that the Squirrel People are going loopy, not exactly dirt-eating loonies, although there is a little of that. Okay, fine, they've turned into dirt-eating loonies. There, I've said it."

"So they won't help us find the Death Merchants or the missing soul vessels?"

"I went to ask them, but they . . ." Charlie considered for moment whether he wanted to say exactly what he had seen, and if he knew, in fact, what he had seen. "Look, they're my friends, but the Squirrel People are loopy."

"We prefer *People of the Squirrel*," said Bob, the beefeater-bobcat guy, who stepped out from behind a wastebasket in the butler's pantry and strode into the parlor using his spork as a walking stick. "Or just, *the People*."

"You shouldn't lurk, Bob, it's not polite," said Audrey.

"Your hair looks nice," said Bob.

Audrey had not put any product in her hair and had just brushed it up and over, so it fell softly to her left shoulder. It did look nice, Charlie thought, and he wanted to punch Bob for having said so before him.

"He's just trying to distract you," Charlie said.

"I heard you two talking," said Bob. "So we checked the places where we found the souls before, the Death Merchants."

"And?" Audrey said.

"When were you spying on us?" Charlie asked.

"They're all gone," Bob said, ignoring Charlie's question. "All of the Death Merchants that *we* took soul vessels from were killed by the Morrigan except Charlie and the tall Minty One. I don't know if there are others."

"When were you going to tell us?" Audrey asked.

"Now?" Bob ventured.

"So the Squirrel People are still going out in the city?" Charlie asked. "Using the sewers?"

"Mostly," Bob said.

"What about the Death Merchants' date books?" Audrey asked. "The soul vessels?"

Bob shrugged.

Charlie said, "So, if they're like me, their books kept getting names—"

"They aren't like you," Bob said. "Their souls moved on. You're a monstrosity with a human soul."

Audrey cringed but pushed on: "Have your people seen any new Death Merchants?" The Squirrel People could see the glow of soul objects, as could she, and she'd never really questioned why, but it had been a useful talent when she was misguidedly having them steal souls from the Death Merchants' shops.

"We haven't looked," said Bob. "I only had them look in the places we'd been before because I heard you two talking."

"No soul vessels lying around either?" Charlie asked.

"Nope," said the bobcat.

"If all those souls have gone uncollected—"

"Plus the ones in your and Rivera's books," Audrey said. She looked to Bob. "Could the People of the Squirrel help Charlie find the soul vessels in *his* book, at least?"

"We need new outfits," said Bob.

"Pardon?" Audrey said.

"You only made us one set of clothes each. They're wearing out." He presented the elbow of his red coat, revealing a hole there.

Audrey said, "I suppose I could patch—"

"I'd like leather armor," said Bob. "Like a samurai. Like a shogun."

"But strictly speaking, you don't even need clothes," Audrey said.

"Strictly speaking, no one does," said Bob.

"Your clothes take a lot of time to make, Bob. They're miniature theatrical costumes. The stitching is actually more difficult than regular clothes because they're smaller. I don't think I can—"

"Fine," said Bob. "*The People* do not need you." He walked back into the butler's pantry.

"She buys the groceries," Charlie called after him.

"We can find food."

"Clothes are merely adornments of ego, anyway," Audrey said.

Bob stopped, walked back, stood in the doorway, and dropped his spork. He undid the brass buttons of hs long red coat and pulled it open, revealing crisscrossed strands of muscle running over bone—some of the ham-colored fibers had crept up his neck and were starting to form the beginnings of cheeks on the bobcat skull that was his face. The high beefeater collar had hidden the progress.

"Adornment of ego?" Bob said.

"Oh, yeah," Charlie said. "Well have a look at this." He started to untie his robe and Audrey held her hand out to stop him.

"I'll make new clothes," she said.

"For all of us," Bob said.

"For all of you," Audrey said.

"And extras. So we can change."

"Fine," said Audrey. "I'll get started tonight."

"Good," said Charlie. "Because if we don't get this done, the dark could rise again, and you know what comes then . . ."

"About that," said Bob. He buttoned his jacket, picked up his spork, and turned to walk away. "You may want to get yourself a spork or something."

"What?" Charlie scampered into the butler's pantry after Bob, but he was gone. Charlie returned into the parlor. "There's a vent in there behind the wastebasket—drops right into the space under the house."

"You're not a monstrosity, Charlie," Audrey said.

"It's okay," he said, waving the thought away with a raptor's talon. "But I can't collect souls like this, and I don't trust the Squirrel People."

"I have an idea, but it might be a little, uh, humbling."

"We just got owned by a guy who carries a spork."

"Good point. Also, because you're officially still a Death Merchant, at least your date book is still active, I'm hoping that you'll still be invisible when you're collecting a soul vessel."

"Not invisible; people just don't see you. If you call their attention to you, they can."

"You didn't have to be naked for that to work, did you?"

"No."

"Good, because—"

"Yeah, I know," he said.

"You know about the cat carrier?"

"No, I was thinking of something else."

Y ou can see me?" Rivera asked the guy with the mop. After actually collecting several soul vessels from the names on his list, he was starting to gain some confidence as a Death Merchant. He'd even managed to enter the houses of two of his "clients" unnoticed, passing right by people who didn't realize he was there. All his years as a cop had conditioned him to take special care in entering a residence, so to ease his mind he had started to think of the names in his date book as warrants, which also expired if not served. The fresh names had worked, the older ones, not so much, but this name had only appeared in his book this very morning. Now he was busted while standing over this poor woman's hospice bed like some kind of ghoul. There was only one proper way to deal with this: badge the shit out of the mop guy.

"Inspector Alphonse Rivera," he said, flipping open his badge wallet to flash the seven-pointed gold star. "SFPD homicide."

"Uh-huh," said the mop guy, much less impressed than Rivera had hoped. "I am Jean-Pierre Baptiste. Are you lookin' for something, Inspector?" He was black, about sixty, and spoke with a musical Caribbean accent—from a French-speaking island, Rivera guessed.

"I'm working a case, and I'm looking for a book that I was told I might find here." All the soul vessels he had found had been books, which had been convenient, since he owned a bookstore, but then, it appeared that the universe preferred specialty retailing.

"This book you're looking for, you think it might be glowing red?"

Rivera felt an electric shiver run from his heels to the crown of his head, only a little less paralyzing than when the banshee had shocked him with the stun gun.

"I don't know what you mean," Rivera said, not even convincing himself. He'd interviewed witnesses who lied so badly that he was embarrassed for them and had to look away to keep from wincing. Usually, after a few minutes, they would realize they weren't pulling it off and would just cave in and tell the truth. Now he knew how they felt.

"Let us step out into the hallway," Baptiste said, "so *Madame* Helen can get some rest." To Helen he said, "*À bientôt, madame,* I will stop in before I go home."

"*Monsieur Baptiste,*" said Helen, gesturing for him to come closer.

"I am here, *madame,*" he whispered.

"Don't let that man alone in here with me. I think he's Mexican. I think he's after my Proust."

"I will keep it safe, *madame.* But I don't know where it is."

"I had Nurse Anne wrap it in a towel and put it in the bottom drawer. Don't look now, but check once you get rid of him."

"I will, *madame*." Baptiste looked to the little white dresser. There was one in each room, where patients' personal things were kept. "I will."

He left his mop bucket in the room and joined Rivera in the hall, then signaled for the policeman to follow him outside. He told the nurse at the desk that he was going on break and led Rivera outside to a spot by a covered bus stop. The hospice was in the outer Sunset, where San Francisco met the sea, and even though it was a sunny day, a cold wind swirled in the streets.

"You heard her?" Baptiste asked.

Rivera nodded.

"Don't think badly of Helen. She has also asked me to keep the *darkie nurses* out of her room. A long time ago, when she was a little girl, someone planted a small seed of fear in her, and now, when all of her fears are bubbling up, this is one she has yet to let go, but she has not lived her life this way."

"Then she doesn't know you're—"

"I speak French with her," said Baptiste with a shrug—*c'est la vie.* "Now, for you, Inspector, how did you know it was a book?"

"How did you know I was looking for something?"

"How many people that you meet are surprised when you can see them, Inspector?"

"I'm asking the questions here," said Rivera, feeling stupid for having said it. He remembered Charlie Asher having a similar reaction once when Rivera had spotted him up on a roof about to brain a Russian grandmother with a cinder block. Charlie had known then that Rivera was going to be a Death Merchant, long before the *Big Book* showed up in the mail.

"Oh, I understand. I work in a hospice. There is always a vessel close here, so much of the time I have to whistle or sing while I am working or people will run into me."

Rivera decided to drop the pretense. It wasn't as if he hadn't already gone against the *Great Big Book of Death*'s warning about contact with other Death Merchants before this.

"You are one of us and you work in a hospice? Seems kind of easy. Lazy."

"Me? You are a homicide detective and I am the lazy one?"

"I've never collected a vessel from one of my cases."

"Seems like a waste of coincidence. Maybe you are just not very good at finding things. The *Big Book* says it is very bad to miss a soul vessel. Very bad indeed."

"I could be better at it," said Rivera. "I didn't pick it up right away. I only started a little more than a year ago."

"Me, too," said Baptiste. "The book came in the mail a year ago and my wife opened it. I thought it was a joke until people started running into me at work and I began to see the soul vessels' red glow. I have never met another person who does this."

"There are a lot of us. I don't know how many, exactly."

"But you have met others?"

"Yes. A couple. Many in the city were killed a year ago. All of them shopkeepers. I think you and I must be their replacements."

"Killed? What do you mean they were killed?"

And because to keep the secret would have been unfair to the point of endangering him, Rivera told Baptiste about the darkness rising, about the Morrigan, about the Underworld somehow expanding itself into the sewer system of San Francisco, about the battle under the city, and of how Charlie Asher had sacrificed himself to put things back in order. Baptiste, already well adjusted to this soul-selling world, actually seemed pleased to have some dimension put on the responsibility that had been dropped on him from his mailbox.

"You said these Death Merchants were all shopkeepers? You and I are not shopkeepers."

"I have a bookshop on Russian Hill. That's how I knew that the soul vessel would be a book. Probably, anyway. If you don't have a shop, then how—"

"My wife sells them on the Internet."

"You sell souls on the Internet?"

"It's not always the Internet. Some Saturdays she will take them to the swap meet at the Cow Palace parking lot and sell them off a blanket.

People pay a lot of money for the silliest things. We may be able to buy a house soon."

"How do you know the right person gets the soul?"

"How do you know in your bookshop?"

Actually, Rivera didn't know. While he had several soul vessels in his shop, he had yet to sell one. But when he did, there was no way to verify the right person was getting it. According to the *Big Book,* each soul would find its right person. He shook his head and they both looked into the gutter. Rivera had a million questions for the orderly, and he guessed that Baptiste felt the same toward him, but there was a feeling of wrongness to it, like somehow they were cheating on a test.

Finally, Baptiste said, "How long? For Helen?"

"Three days," Rivera said. "But you know, the number isn't always how long they have to live, only how long we have to collect the soul vessel. So probably less. I'm sorry."

"Why do you suppose I did not get her name in my calendar?"

"I don't know," Rivera said.

"I should probably get the Proust book for you, then."

"I would let you collect it, but I'm afraid I may have already set things out of order by falling behind on my calendar."

"I understand," Baptiste said. "Wait here. I'll be right back."

Rivera waited, closed his eyes, and just felt the chill wind biting through his light, worsted wool suit. In a few minutes Baptiste came back out of the front door, moving quite a bit more quickly than he had gone in.

"It's gone," he said.

"Did you check all the drawers?"

"I checked and I asked the shift nurse, who said that Helen had her check on it this morning. It was there then, she said."

"Did Helen see anything?" Rivera asked.

Baptiste just looked at him.

"Sorry. Did she *hear* anything?"

"Rats. She complained of the sound of rats scurrying in the room. She rang for the nurse after we came out here."

"Rats?"

"Her hearing is very good."

They just looked at each other and there was a lull between gusts of wind when the leaves that were skittering around in the street slid to a stop. A woman's voice whispered, "Meeeeeeeeat." A woman's voice that seemed to be coming from under an Audi wagon parked on the curb across the street. They both looked and did a slow, synchronized deep knee bend until they could see under the car, where there appeared to be nothing but leaves and a candy wrapper.

"Did you hear that?" Baptiste asked.

"Did you?" asked Rivera.

"No," said Baptiste.

"Me either," said Rivera.

11

CROCODILE TEARS

ily let herself into the empty storefront that had once been Asher's Secondhand and later the location of Pizazz, the pizza and jazz place she and M had opened. The sight of the sign, leaning in the corner, and the idea that she'd let the Mint One talk her into that name made her want to start cutting herself again, something she'd indulged briefly when she was fifteen but had quickly stopped because it hurt. The space filled the entire ground floor of a four-story building at the corner of Mason and Vallejo streets, where the North Beach, Chinatown, and Russian Hill neighborhoods met like slices of an international pie.

All the booths and tables were gone, as well as most of the restaurant equipment. Only the oak bar and a great, brick, wood-burning pizza oven remained. There was still a storeroom with a staircase that led up to Charlie Asher's old apartment (now Jane and Cassie's), but now it contained only a walk-in refrigerator and a few bar stools and chairs instead of the collection of knickknacks that had filled it when it had been Charlie's store.

Lily dragged some stools out to the bar and sat down to wait in the diffused daylight from the papered-over windows. This would be weird, but she found she was excited at the idea of seeing Charlie again, even if he was a wretched little carrion creature now.

Soon there was the silhouette at the door of a woman who apparently had a crescent-moon-shaped head and Lily hurried to the door to let her in. Oh yeah, this was going to be weird.

Audrey, wearing yoga pants, a sweater, and sneakers, stood on the sidewalk holding a cat carrier shaped like a Quonset hut. It was made from heavy nylon embroidered in blue and orange swirls, heavy mesh halfway down on either end.

"Hi," Lily said, stepping out of the way so Audrey could come in. They'd met once before the debacle, when Lily had been the one with the postmodern hair. "Where's Asher?"

Audrey lifted the cat carrier.

"Well dump that little fucker out," Lily said. "Let's have a look at him." Charlie had described his new body on the phone but she wanted to see him for herself.

"Hi, Lily," came a voice from inside the luggage.

"Asher!" Lily bent down and tried to look into the cat carrier, but beyond something dark reflecting two points of light—eyes, she guessed— she could see nothing.

Audrey swung the cat carrier away from Lily. "He'd prefer you didn't see him this way."

"Oh, hell no," Lily said. "I agreed to meet you here where all my PTSD began, I get to look at the little monster."

Lily tried again to squint into the cat carrier. Audrey swung it around the other way.

Charlie said, "Audrey, if you keep swinging this thing around, I'm going to be sick."

"Please," Audrey said to Lily. "He's really sensitive about his looks."

Audrey put the cat carrier on the bar and sat down at one of the stools. Lily sat and squinted through the carrier's mesh, trying to see something. Still just points of light.

"Asher, is it really you?"

"It's me now."

"I feel like I'm talking to a tiny priest in a tiny confessional. But you can only hear my tiny sins." She affected her *bowed-head-of-deep-contrition* look, which was new to her, so she wasn't confident in it. "Bless me, Father, for I have sinned: I once drank the last of the milk and put the empty carton back in the fridge. I drew pubes on my Barbies and posed them in a threesome with a Ninja Turtle. I sometimes wish that dicks were mint flavored. I won't say what made me think of it. I never wished that you were dead, Asher, but when I worked here, I sometimes wished that you would fall down the stairs and land in a cake. I don't know how the cake gets there, it's just a fantasy."

"I don't think any of those things are sins," Charlie said.

"What do you know? You're not a priest."

"Although he *is* wearing a beautiful wizard's robe," said Audrey.

Lily gave Audrey what she considered her, withering, *silence, worm!* look.

"How about I run out and grab us some beverages?" Audrey said. "Give you two a chance to catch up."

"Skinny latte, please," Lily said, flashing her, *I am cute so all my prior bitchiness must be forgiven* smile. "Here, my treat." She took a bill from her purse and handed it to Audrey, who, having spent years as a monk begging for her daily meal, accepted it without protest.

"I'll get your usual, Charlie," Audrey said, and she was out the door.

As soon as the door closed Lily said, "Asher, you fucker!" She slapped the top of the cat carrier. It took the hit and sprang back.

"Ouch!" said Charlie. "Hey!"

"How could you do that to me? You fucker! You fucker!" Lily was crying now, as if she'd been saving it all for when Audrey was no longer in the room, which she had. "I thought you were dead! You let me think you were dead! You fucker!"

"Stop saying that," Charlie said. "I'm sorry."

She smacked the top of the cat carrier again.

"Ouch!"

"I would never do that to you, Asher, you fucker. Never! How could you do that? I thought we were friends, well, not friends, but something. You fucker!"

"I'm right here. Stop crying."

"I'm crying *because* you're right here, you fucker. I finished crying because you *weren't* here a long time ago."

"I thought it would be easier—I couldn't keep running the shop, being Sophie's daddy, being Charlie Asher like this. I thought it would be easier. I'm a freak."

"You've always been a freak, Asher. That's your best quality."

"That's not true, I was always nice to you, at least when you weren't being stubborn and moody."

"Which is like, never."

"Is that why you called the Buddhist Center and blackmailed me into meeting you? Because you're angry?"

"Yes, I'm angry, but that's not why. M told me you were in trouble, so I thought I might be able to help."

"I'm sorry it didn't work out between you and Minty Fresh."

Lily cringed at the sound of M's full name. "What could I do? You guys and the whole death-dealing thing . . . And he knows so much, and I don't know anything, and he was always giving me stuff and forgiving me when I was a bitch—acting like he respected my opinion."

"Maybe he does respect your opinion."

"That's what I'm saying. How do you win a relationship like that?"

"I don't think you're supposed to *win* a relationship, Lily."

"What do you know? You're hiding in a cat box."

"This isn't a cat box."

There was a commotion from the back room, a door opening at the second-floor landing, then footfalls on the stairs.

"Is voices. Hello," said Mrs. Korjev. The stout Russian grandmother came down the backroom stairs, followed by Sophie Asher. Sophie, her dark hair in pigtails with clips that resembled gummy bears, was dressed in layers of pastels that would have looked perfectly fine on taffy or ice cream. The soles of her pink sneakers lit up with every step.

Lily leaned over the bar so they could see her. "Hey."

"Lily!" Sophie scampered into the abandoned restaurant and jumped into Lily arms. "We miss you and your pizza."

"I miss you, too, kiddo."

"Lily, the goggies are lost. We're going to put up posters."

Sophie ran back to Mrs. Korjev, who handed her a letter-size printed sheet from a stack she was carrying. Sophie plopped the poster on the bar in front of Lily, then climbed onto the bar stool next to her. "See?" Sophie said. "There's a reward."

Mrs. Korjev pulled a staple gun from her shopping bag and held it. "Is reward for Mr. Chin at butcher shop, too, if he give Vladlena trouble about boning chicken again. Is lost-dog-poster staple on his front-head."

"Forehead," Sophie corrected the Cossack matron.

"If shoe fit," said Mrs. Korjev.

"So you're doing your shopping, too," Lily said. "Multitasking."

"Chinatown have best vegetables, even for white devils," Sophie said, with only a slight Cantonese accent, a remnant of Mrs. Ling's shopping tutelage. "Auntie Jane used to take me to Whole Foods on her day off, but she says she has to take too much vitamin X to keep from killing everyone there, so now we get our veggies in Chinatown."

"Let's see here." Lily pulled the poster over. At the top there was a picture, printed in black and white, of Sophie perhaps a year or two younger, with the hellhounds. Sophie was in the tub, her head above a sea of bubbles, crowned with shampoo horns. Alvin and Mohammed flanked the claw-foot tub like guardians at the entrance to a bubbly tomb, making them look completely unreal to scale, which is kind of how they looked in real life.

"We blacked out my eyes with this square for my privacy," said Sophie.

"Good idea," said Lily. "You didn't have any other pictures of them?"

"Nope," Sophie said.

The poster read:

LOST

2 Irish Hellhounds.

Very black, like bear.

Huge, like bear.

Answer to Alvin and Mohammed.

Like to eat everything. Like bear!

REWARD!

"Did you write the text, Mrs. Korjev?" Lily asked.

"I put in two bears and the Irish part," said Sophie. "Daddy said that no one would believe you if you called them hellhounds, but if you said *Irish* hellhounds everyone thought they'd heard of them."

A scratching noise came from the cat carrier on the bar and Sophie seemed to notice it for the first time. "Hey, what's that? Do you have a—"

Lily clamped her hand over Sophie's mouth. "No. I don't. There's nothing in there. Nothing. Do you understand?"

Lily's hand still on her mouth, Sophie nodded. Lily tentatively pulled her hand away.

"I wasn't going to say it," Sophie said.

"I know," said Lily. "I'm just taking the empty carrier to a friend. There's some food in there that shifted."

"Okay," said Sophie.

"We need to go, *lapochka*," said Mrs. Korjev. The Russian matron had come around the corner of the bar like a great, bosomy whirlwind when Lily grabbed Sophie and still held her staple gun at the ready. Lily was relatively sure that she had been only seconds from having her own forehead stapled.

"Okay, you two," Lily said. She carefully lifted Sophie off the bar stool and set her on the floor, then crouched in front of her. "I hope you find the goggies."

Sophie gave Lily a hug. "Come see us. Bring special-special pizza."

"I will," Lily said. "Bye, Sophie. Bye, Mrs. Korjev."

"Bye," Sophie said, leading Mrs. Korjev out the metal door that led into the alley. Mrs. Korjev looked back at Lily, siting down the mole on the side of her nose, letting Lily know that she had her eye on her.

As soon as the door closed behind them, a heartbreaking wail rose from the cat carrier.

"You okay, Asher?"

"I miss her so much. She's gotten so big."

"Sorry." Lily patted the top of the cat carrier.

"What's special-special pizza?"

"It's a flaming-dome pizza with mac and cheese inside. I created it for Sophie to celebrate her becoming a vegetarian."

"She's a vegetarian? She didn't even *like* vegetables last year."

"It's okay. She's only a vegetarian because it was a thing with the other girls. Jane convinced her you could still be a vegetarian if you only eat animals that eat vegetables, too."

"So anything but what?"

"I don't know, lion, bear, crocodile—"

"Jane is ruining my daughter. I have got to come home. I'm missing everything."

"But you *are* coming back, right?" said, Lily trying to cheer him up.

"Probably not. We'll never find the right body."

"No, that's the good news. That's why I'm blackmailing you—I mean, why I called. I think I have the body for you."

"Lily, I have to be there almost at the moment of death. You can't just grab a body out of the fridge."

"Are you implying that I keep bodies in my fridge?"

"It's just an expression."

"That's not an expression, Asher."

"Okay, sorry. No, I don't think you have a human body in your fridge."

"Douche." She pouted. She'd forgotten how much fun it was to pout in front of Asher. If only she could see the distress on his little face.

"I said I'm sorry," he said. "Go on."

"It's a guy I met on the crisis line. He's about your age, pretty nice-looking, if you like that type, doesn't seem to have any family, no wife or girlfriend, and he's got balls the size of toaster ovens."

"Trust me, Lily, enormous genitals are not as fun as they sound."

"It's just a figure of speech. He's a painter on the Golden Gate Bridge, so he's up on high steel, hundreds of feet above the water, every working day."

"And how do you know he's going to die? Did Minty find him in his date book?"

"No, M doesn't know anything about this, the guy told me, himself. He wanted me to talk him out of jumping off the bridge."

"That's horrible. Is he depressed?"

"No. He says he's not jumping to get *away* from anything, he's jumping to get *to* something."

"But don't you have a moral obligation to talk him out of jumping?"

"It's a gray area."

"How can that be a gray area? You work on a suicide hotline. You can't just say, 'Okay, have at it.' "

"I have before." She chewed a nail.

"Lily!"

"Shut up, they made a good case. Besides, nobody that I told to jump ever actually jumped."

"I don't know," Charlie said. "We'll have to ask Audrey. She's the one who knows the rituals and stuff."

"Do you want to see your daughter again or not?"

"Of course I do."

"Then shut the fuck up and let me kill this guy for you."

"Let's talk to Audrey."

"But if she says go, it's a go, right?"

"Sure, I suppose.

"Good. Where's the nun with our drinks?"

The nun with the drinks came through the door fifteen minutes later, a cardboard tray in one hand, a lost dog flyer wedged between the cups.

"Have you seen these?" Audrey said. The flyer was one of the ones Sophie had shown them. "They're all over North Beach."

"Sophie and Mrs. Korjev just came through," Charlie said.

"Are you okay?" Audrey said. She unzipped one end of the cat carrier and handed in the little paper espresso cup. "Two sugars."

"I'm okay," said Charlie. "But Lily wants us to kill a guy and take his body."

Audrey sat down on the bar stool next to Lily and sipped a frosty brown thing through a straw while she considered the proposition.

"Won't work," said the nun.

Lily nearly aspirated skinny latte. "Why not? M said that you needed someone who was healthy, male, and whose body would be fresh and not too broken up."

"It's why she blackmailed us into coming here," Charlie said.

"Stop saying that," Lily said. "I wouldn't have told Sophie about you and you know it. It was only a symbolic threat."

"We would have come without the threat."

Audrey said, "Does this man you're going to kill know what you're going to do?"

"I'm not going to actively kill him. He's going to kill himself. But no."

"For the ritual of Chöd to work the subject has to *willingly* give up his body to be occupied."

"Seriously? I not only have to talk a guy into jumping off a bridge, but I have to talk him into just giving me his body? He's not going to go for that."

"Maybe if you wear something low-cut," Charlie said.

"I will crush you and your little cat box, Asher."

"Let's calm down and work through this," said Audrey.

"Yeah, Lily," said Charlie. "Audrey is badass. Buddhist monks invented kung fu, you know."

"Not my sect," said Audrey. "We mostly chant and beg."

"I don't even know who you are anymore," Charlie said.

"Fine," said Lily. "Audrey, is there anything in your tradition about a Ghost Thief?"

"No, why?"

"Well, because evidently there's a whole choir of ghosts on the Golden Gate Bridge farting a message of doom if we don't find the Ghost Thief. I'm pretty sure that's going to be a condition of getting my guy to give up the goods."

"That's new," said Charlie.

12

PORTABLE DARKNESS AND THE BOOTY NUN

In a turnout on Interstate 80, about forty miles east of Reno, the hell-hounds had killed a Subaru and were rolling in its remains as two hor-rified kayakers looked on. Alvin had the last shreds of plastic from a red kayak hanging out of his jaws as he squirmed in the still-smoking bits of the engine, while Mohammed was biting at his reflection in the hatch-back window, trying to pop the final intact window like a soap bubble, which he did with great growling glee, before crunching down a mouthful of rubber gasket and safety glass.

Something popped and hissed under Alvin's back and in an instant the four-hundred-pound canine was on his feet barking at the stream of steam, each bark like a rifle report in the ears of the kayakers. The hound reared up in a prancing fashion, and came down repeatedly on the offend-ing steam thing with his front paws until it ceased and desisted. He cele-brated by settling down with the engine between his forelegs to chew off the remaining hoses and wires. Mohammed made to join him, but was distracted by a stream of green antifreeze which he stopped to lap up off the asphalt.

"Uh, I think—" said one of the kayakers, a fit man of twenty-five in an earth-toned array of tactical outdoor clothing, who had heard of dogs being poisoned by antifreeze.

"I don't think it will bother them," said the other, who had been driving when Alvin's jaws first latched on to the bumper, causing him to skid into this turnout and scaring him badly.

"Your insurance will cover this, right?" said the first.

"We should probably film it. Do you have your phone?"

"In the car."

"Damn."

They were both adrenaline junkies and had been on their way to run some level-five rapids on the Salmon River in Idaho, but now they were reconsidering, since the kayaks were the first things the hellhounds had eaten after bringing down the Subaru. They were both a little in shock and had already run a couple hundred yards into the desert before realizing the enormous hounds weren't in the least bit interested in them, then skulking back to watch the destruction of their car and possessions.

"You ever seen a dog like that before?" asked one.

"I don't think anyone has seen *anything* like that."

The hounds were long-legged, with the squared head of a mastiff and the pointed ears of a Great Dane; heavily muscled, with great barrel chests and rippling shoulders and haunches. They were so black that they appeared to absorb light—their slick coats neither shone nor rippled with their movement—sometimes they appeared simply to be violent swaths of starless night sky.

"I was doing seventy when they hit us," said the driver.

Interstate 80 was a main artery across the northern part of the U.S., but today the traffic was sparse and they were far enough off the road that someone would have to be looking for them to actually notice what was going on.

The driver was about to suggest that they hike up to the interstate to flag down some help, when a creamy yellow land yacht, a 1950 Buick Roadmaster fastback with a white top, a sun visor, and blacked-out windows, pulled off the highway and cruised by, just beyond the dead Subaru.

The great hounds stopped what they were doing and jumped to their feet, their ears peaked, their backs bristling. They growled in unison like choral bulldozers.

The passenger-side window whirred down and a black man wearing a yellow suit and homburg hat leaned over and addressed the kayakers as he rolled by.

"Y'all all right?"

They nodded, the driver gesturing to the opera of destruction playing out before them, as if to say, *"What the fuck?"*

"Them goggies ain't shit," said the yellow fellow. "I'll have them off you in a slim jiffy."

With that, great clouds of fire burst out the twin tailpipes of the Buick and it lowered its stance like a crouching leopard before bolting out of the turnout. The hellhounds dropped what they were chewing and took off after it, their front claws digging furrows in the asphalt as they came up to speed, their staccato barking trailing away like fading machine guns in a distant dogfight. In less than a minute, they were out of sight.

"I have my wallet," said the Subaru's owner, feeling he might have had enough adrenaline for a bit. "I say we catch a ride back to Reno. Get a room."

"Video poker," said the other. "And drinks," he said. "With umbrellas."

In a previous incarnation, he had been torn apart by jackals—black jackals—so overall, the fellow in yellow had developed a healthy distaste for the company of canines, which was why he was leading them away from San Francisco.

"You ladies doing all right back there?" he asked as he gunned the Roadmaster out of the turnout and back onto Highway 80. The big V-8 rumbled and the four chrome ports down each side of the hood blinked as if startled out of a nap, then opened to draw more air into the infernal engine. The tail of the Buick dipped and the grinning chrome mouth of the grille gulped desert air like a whale shark sucking down krill. Far below the crusty strata, long-dead dinosaurs wept for the liquid remains of their brethren consumed by the creamy, jaundiced leviathan.

"Was that them?" came a female voice from inside the trunk behind the bloodred leather backseat.

"That sounded like them," another female voice.

"Y'all can take a peek, you need to be sure," said the man in yellow. "Trunk ain't locked."

"You should go faster," said a third voice.

"They sound close," said the first. "Are they close?"

"They won't catch us," said the yellow fellow. "Them goggies ain't shit."

"I hate those things. They're so barky." said the second voice.

"So bitey," said another.

"Well, they loves y'all," said the yellow fellow. "That's why y'all are along."

"Can they bite through this metal? because I don't think I'm ready for the *above*?"

"No, not in the light. Not yet."

"Macha, remember that time they almost tore you apart?"

"I'ma slow up a bit, ladies, so they stay close."

A chorus of "No!" and "Oh, fuck no!" erupted from behind the seat.

Just yards behind, the hellhounds heard the voices, answered with enraged howls, and quickened their pace. The Buick jerked with impact, something hitting the rear, tearing metal, once, then again. The ladies in the dark screeched. The driver checked his side mirror and, finding it overflowing with angry dog face, slammed the accelerator to the floor, because while "them goggies might not be shit," he did not particularly want to be proven wrong by being reduced to yellow specks in great piles of hellhound poo dropped across the Nevada desert.

"I want to make Salt Lake before they know what happened," said the driver.

"What's at Salt Lake?" asked one of the trunk voices.

"They's a portal there that these motherfuckers don't know about."

"To the Underworld? We just got out of the Underworld."

The yellow fellow chuckled. "Relax, ladies. We gonna dump these goggies in Salt Lake, keep 'em out of my business in San Francisco. I'll have y'all back in some less portable darkness lickity-split, then y'all can freshen up."

"What about the child?" asked one of the voices.

"We cross that bridge when we get to it," said the yellow fellow.

"She's worse than the hounds."

"Nemain!"

"Well, she *is*."

"You know, it's not so bad in here," said Babd, changing the subject.

"Plenty of room. And it's not damp."

"And it's warm."

"You want," said the driver, "y'all can stay there when we get back to the city. I get you some curtains and cushions and whatnot."

He smiled to himself. Through many centuries and many incarnations, he had learned one universal truth: *bitches love them some cushions.*

They sped on, and after the two unfortunate bites, stayed just far enough ahead of Alvin and Mohammed so that from a distance, the hellhounds might appear to be particularly animated clouds of black smoke emitted from the tailpipes. They were creatures of fire and force, pursuing a yellow Buick with a creamy-white top through the desert. Like many supernatural creatures, they winked in and out of the visible spectrum as they moved, so when a highway patrolman outside of Elko, Nevada, looked up from his radar readout, first he blinked, then he was tempted to radio up the road to his colleague and say, "Hey, did you just see two pony-sized black dogs, doing seventy, pursuing a giant slice of lemon meringue pie?" Then he thought, *No, perhaps I'll keep that to myself.*

About that same time, five hundred miles west, in the Mission District of San Francisco, a Buddhist nun and little crocodile-wizard guy were working out the finer points of a murder.

"Is it really murder," said Audrey, "if he is going to jump anyway?"

"I'm pretty sure it is," said Charlie. "I think the Buddha said that one should never injure a human or, through inaction, allow a human to come to harm. If we know he's going to jump and we don't stop him, I think we're going against whatever sutra that is."

"First, that is not a sutra, that's Asimov's First Law of Robotics, from *I, Robot*, and second, we're not just allowing him to harm himself, we're trying to get him to do it on a schedule."

"I didn't know Isaac Asimov was a Buddhist," said Charlie. "Buddhist robots. Ha!"

"Asimov wasn't. But the robots thing is close. I mean, you"— she was about to say, *You are kind of a Buddhist robot,* but instead she said, "You know those terra-cotta warriors they found in China, buried since the second century B.C.? Those were kind of supposed to be Buddhist robots. The Emperor Qin Shi Huang was going to have a priest use the *p'howa of forceful projection* I used on the Squirrel People to put soldiers' souls in the terra-cotta soldiers, making himself an indestructible army. It might have worked if they'd filled them with meat."

"You said that Buddhism didn't come to China until the fifth century." Charlie had always had a difficult time understanding Buddhism.

"It was always there, they just didn't call it Buddhism. Buddha was just a guy who pointed out some fairly obvious things, so we call it Buddhism. Otherwise we'd just have to call it everything."

"Sometimes I think you're just making up Buddhism as you go along."

"Exactly." Audrey grinned. Charlie grinned back and Audrey shuddered. She would not miss all those teeth grinning at her. She had been under pressure when she'd put his body together, but given the opportunity to build her perfect man again, she would definitely go with fewer teeth.

"Maybe this Sullivan guy is in someone's calendar," Charlie said. "If Minty can find his name on one of the Death Merchants' calendars, then we'll know his death is inevitable. In a way, we'll be saving him, or his body, at least?"

"He still has to offer his body as a vessel for your soul. He must do it willingly or the Chöd ritual won't work. I'm not sure it will work, anyway, Charlie. I've never done it. I don't know if anyone has ever done it."

"Well, Lily's going to ask him. If he says yes, we're good to go."

"Would you believe Lily if she told you that she needed your permission to move a new soul into your body, and in order to do that, you had to jump off a bridge at a certain time?"

"I would. Lily is very trustworthy. She worked for me for six years and never stole anything. Except the *Great Big Book of Death*." Charlie scratched under his long, lower jaw, wishing he had a beard, even a chin, to stroke thoughtfully. "Okay, that caused problems, but otherwise . . . Yes, good point. But he told her a ghost talked him into this and she believed him, so he kind of owes her."

"Really?" She raised a questioning eyebrow.

"You're right, we should go talk to him."

"Charlie, you know I adore you, but I'm not sure that the finer essence of your being will shine through to a stranger, in a first meeting, and we *are* asking this guy to believe something that sounds, if not impossible, certainly preposterous."

"I know. That's the beauty of it. I'm like the preposterous poster child."

"I'll go see him."

"Fine. Maybe just brush your hair to the side so it's soft, nonintimidating," Charlie suggested.

"What's wrong with my hair?"

"Nothing. So you studied robots in the monastery? Who would have thought."

Because her discipline stressed living in the moment, and not obsessing on the past or the future, Audrey found herself more than somewhat off balance when Mike Sullivan answered his door.

"Hi, Audrey," he said, extending his hand. "I'm Mike." Dark, short hair; light eyes, green, maybe hazel, kind.

He was younger than she expected, even though Lily had told her that he was in his early to midthirties, and he was better-looking than she'd expected, even though Lily had also mentioned that he was not unpleasant to look upon. What surprised her most was that he was so healthy and alive, because in the past, everyone she had prepared for *bardo,* the transition between life and death, had been sick and dying, and most often old. Mike Sullivan did not look like a man who was dying.

She shook his hand and let him lead her into his second-story apartment, which took up the middle floor of a Victorian in the Richmond District, adjacent to Golden Gate Park. She felt prickly and self-conscious as she sat on the couch and watched him move around the apartment, playing host, getting them tea, relaxed, barefoot, in old jeans and a T-shirt. Despite her training to stay focused on the moment, she glimpsed into the future, and she realized that if everything went as it was supposed to, in a few days she'd be shagging this guy. She blushed; she could feel the heat rise in her cheeks, and she realized he must see it.

"You're not what I expected," Mike Sullivan said. "The director of a Buddhist center—although I don't know what I expected."

"That's okay," said Audrey; she touched her hair, which she'd spun into a bun behind her head, so that wasn't what he meant. "There aren't many women in my sect, even in the East. I'm privileged to have my position."

Mike sat down on the edge of a recliner across the coffee table from her and leaned forward. "From what Lily tells me, you're one of a kind."

Audrey felt herself blush again and suddenly, and for no reason she could think, thought of poor Lizzie from *Pride and Prejudice,* and then remembered how she also felt that Lizzie, nay, all of the Bennet women, in fact, all of the characters in *P&P* could have benefited from a good roundhouse kick to the head, and how, if she kept blushing, she should ask this guy to deliver one to her. (Despite what she had told Charlie, she did know a little kung fu, which she had learned in college, at San Francisco State, not in a monastery in Tibet. *Namaste.*)

"Mike, you should know, I've never done this before. I have transferred conciousnesses from people to, uh, other entities, many times, actually, but not anything like this. I don't even know if Chöd works. I mean, I've read scrolls written about people in the mountains who gave their bodies up for an enlightened being, but I've never seen it."

"I figured," said Mike. He smiled.

"So if you're going to do this, you should go into it prepared for your life to simply end, as all our lives will end. Part of you will endure either way, but you shouldn't do this just to offer up your body."

"I know," said Mike. "I know all that. I've always known that. I'm not doing this for your friend."

"You need to be sure."

"I'm sure."

"And you understand that if it works, someone else will be walking around in your body. If someone you know sees him on the street, they'll think it's you. Your friends, your family."

"I don't have any family, and no close friends."

Audrey paused. She wasn't sure how to react to that. Well, she wanted to ask why not, but that seemed a bit cruel, considering why she was here.

"Audrey, I'll be honest, I have never really connected with anyone. I mean, I've had girlfriends, even serious ones, but they've always left, and I've always let them. I'm not sad, or heartbroken, I just go to work the next day and try to do my job. Another girl comes along, and then we're off to the races until the race ends again. Same with friends. I get along with people, I like listening to them, I play in a softball league with some cool guys, but if they all went away tomorrow I'd be fine. My folks are dead, my brother and I have been out of touch for years, all the rest of my extended family is all over the country and we don't see one another. Not bad blood, just blood. I guess I only realized after these people, these ghosts, came to me on the bridge, but I've been like a ghost for a long time. It sounds like this friend of yours can put better use to this body than I ever have. He's welcome to it."

Audrey was breathless. He was so calm about it, so sure. This was the place you tried to get people to in *bardo,* to accept their death as part of their life, as a door through which all must pass, will pass, and have passed. He was standing calmly in the doorway, unafraid. It was the sexiest thing she'd ever encountered, and if it weren't for Charlie, she would have wrestled him to the couch and screwed his brains out right then. No. From desire comes suffering. And besides, she could jump him after he was dead. Her Buddhist practice had suffered somewhat, she realized, since coming back to the States.

"Mike, have you thought about something less violent? Carbon monoxide? Pills?" Was she actually planning a murder with the victim?

"No, it has to be the bridge. That's where I'm going. I mean, that's why I'm going. Concepción, did Lily tell you about her?"

"Yes, but I don't know about any Ghost Thief. I've never even heard the term before."

Mike nodded, looked into his teacup, which he held loosely by the edge between his knees. "I figured. But they need me."

"For what?"

"Don't know." He shrugged, smiled. "If your Charlie said he needed you, would you ask him what for?"

Oh yes, she was going to do him until he begged her to stop. He'd be lucky if he could walk straight when she was done with him.

She cleared her throat, fidgeted. "I guess not," she said demurely.

She really did need to get laid more than once every twelve years. This must be what it's like for locusts. Long periods of dormancy followed by crazy tantric bug-fucks. Maybe not.

She cleared her throat again, hoping it would clear her restless mind as well. "Well, we'll have to be there, when you . . . when you . . ."

"Jump?" he offered.

"Really, do you have to jump? Maybe you can crawl up in a cubbyhole with a bottle of sleeping pills? You don't have to jump, do you?"

"I think I do. Believe me, that part sort of gives me the willies. I mean, if you're up on the bridge five days a week for ten years, there's not five minutes that pass that it doesn't occur to you that you are just one mistake from plummeting to your death."

"That's it!" she said.

"That's what?"

"That's why you're who you are. That's why you can do this, why we'll be able to do this. Probably. You've lived every day of your life preparing for your death."

"Not really preparing."

"But you're not afraid when you're up there, right?"

"No. Well, I was a little bugged out when the ghosts first showed up."

"But you're aware, always."

"You kind of have to be."

"We can do this, Mike." She put her tea down and reached out for his hands. He put his tea down and took her hands across the table.

"I'm sure we can do this; we just have to coordinate everything."

"One thing . . ."

"Yes?"

"Can you pull me out of my body *before* I hit the water? I kind of don't want to be there."

"I think that's going to be on you—the timing of *your* part of the ritual."

"Great. I'm in. Now what?"

"Well, there's your life to close up. Charlie's going to have to sort of take over for you, at least for a while. Because even though you jump off the bridge, and you die, to everyone else it will appear that you *survived.*"

"So, what? You want me to close my credit cards, stuff like that? Get my affairs in order?"

"I guess just do things to make it easier for Charlie to move from your life to his."

"And now his soul is trapped in some kind of jar? A vessel? Lily wasn't clear."

"Sure, let's say vessel. Some kind of vessel."

"Poor guy. And he has a little girl. You know, I wouldn't believe any of this if the ghosts hadn't appeared to me. I mean, Concepción was the one who told me to call Lily. A ghost! Who would have believed that?"

"I know," said Audrey. "I've trained for this kind of thing for most of my adult life and it wigs me out a little."

"I love her," said Mike. "I've never been in love, but I love her."

"Yes," said Audrey, patting his hand.

"The ghost."

"Right, I know," said Audrey. "Let's make lists. Lists will help. Let's start with ten things to keep you from getting too broken when you fall hundreds of feet into the bay."

So, I guess we're going to kill this guy, she thought. Then she said, "How does Thursday look for you?"

13

THE SHADOW OF A THOUSAND BIRDS

Minty Fresh had felt dread rising like acid in his throat since Rivera first showed up in his shop with the story of the banshee, but never had it been more immediate than when he walked into the pawnshop in the Fillmore to find Ray Macy standing behind a glass case full of watches and jewelry. Ray had worked with Lily at Charlie Asher's secondhand store. Lily had described the fortyish, balding ex-cop as her nemesis, her natural enemy, and a fucktard of astounding density. Minty tried to dismiss Ray as just more of the saturated humanity that lived under the wide spray of Lily's contempt sprinkler, except that the ex-cop had become openly hostile when Lily and Minty Fresh closed Charlie's store to open their pizza and jazz joint. Shortly afterward, Ray moved out of Charlie's building and Fresh thought he'd seen the last of him. But no, here he was, guarding the gate, so to speak, to the only living Death Merchant Fresh knew besides Charlie and Rivera. It was cool. He was cool.

"Mr. Fresh," said Ray. He was a beta male, so open confrontation wasn't really his game. Passive aggression being the beta weapon of choice.

"Ray," said Minty Fresh. "Good to see you landed on your feet."

Ray turned behind the counter a bit so Minty Fresh could see he was wearing a revolver on his hip, the gesture made overly obvious by Ray's inability to turn his head. A bullet to the neck had ended his career as a cop and doctors had fused his vertebrae. Ray Macy looked at life head-on, whether he wanted to or not.

"Did you just turn so I could see you had a gun?" asked Minty Fresh, amused.

"No," said Ray, turning back quickly.

Ray must have been a horrible, horrible cop, Minty thought. He said, "I need to talk to Carrie Lang. This is her shop, I'm told."

"She's not available," said Ray.

"I'm right here," a woman called from the back room. "I'll be right out."

"She must have just come in," Ray explained.

A blond woman in her midthirties came out of the back room.

"Whoa," she said, when she spotted the big man. She stopped and backed up a step. "You're a tall drink of water."

"Honey," said Ray, "this is Minty Fresh. Remember, I told you about him. *Him and Lily.*"

Minty considered the "honey" and gave Carrie Lang a second look: she was short, but weren't they all? She wore an awful lot of silver Indian jewelry layered over denim and chambray, but she had a sweet smile, a nice shape, and there was a spark of intelligence in her eyes that really should have put Ray out of the running for her attention. *It's a lonely business,* Fresh thought.

"Ms. Lang." Minty offered his hand over the counter. "A pleasure." As he took her hand he looked at Ray and nodded approval, giving the non-cop props for achieving out of his league.

"Mr. Fresh," said Carrie Lang. "I've been by your store in the Castro. I always mean to stop in. What can I do for you?"

"I wonder if there's someplace we can speak in private."

"We're pretty busy," said Ray through gritted teeth.

"It's about that special part of your business," Minty said. "I, too, deal with very special secondhand items."

Carrie Lang's perky smile wilted. "Mr. Fresh, I don't discuss the details of my business."

"Under normal circumstances, neither do I, as the *Big Book* instructs, but these are really special circumstances."

Ray turned to Carrie. *"Big Book?"* She patted his arm.

"I have an office in the back," said Carrie. She turned and walked back through the doorway through which she'd come. "Watch your head."

"Always do."

Ray Macy audibly growled as Minty Fresh stepped behind the counter and ducked to go through the door.

Ray blurted, "You know Lily did me once in the back room at Asher's."

Minty Fresh stood to his full height and looked back over his shoulder at Ray. Carrie Lang popped back through the door, walked under Minty's armpit, and glared at Ray.

"That is not news to me, Ray," said Minty. But he'd bet it was news to Carrie Lang. "Miss Severo and I have parted ways. She is far too young."

Carrie Lang held up her index finger to Ray, marking a place in the conversation where they would return at a later time—for fucking sure. Ray understood completely, and had he been able to nod, he would have, but instead he assumed the expression of someone who had just accidentally plunged an ice pick into his junk and is trying to hide the effect. Carrie exited under the big man's armpit. "My office," she said, leading him across the stockroom.

Her office was utilitarian, small, with all metal desk, chairs, and filing cabinets. Minty Fresh sat in a guest chair across from her. His knees touched her desk and the chair was backed flush against the door.

Lang sat, sighed. "Mr. Fresh, you know the last time we started talking—"

"That's why I'm here, Ms. Lang. All those secondhand dealers who were killed a year ago, ten of them, I think. They were all like us."

She nodded. So she knew? What she didn't know was that she'd been saved by the Squirrel People, who had knocked her out, duct-taped her up, and thrown her in a dumpster until the danger passed. They'd come in the dark and she'd never even seen them. Fresh knew.

"I don't think they've been replaced. We—myself and a couple of other Death Merchants—think that the soul vessels they should have collected are still out there somewhere."

She shrugged. "The *Big Book* says that stuff just gets taken care of. We don't need to worry about what other—what did you call them, Death Merchants—are doing with their soul vessel?"

"I know, but apparently, they're not taken care of. Look, have you noticed an increase in the number of names, or any strange circumstances? More important, have you seen any weird shit when you're out and about?"

"You mean like giant ravens or voices coming out of the sewers."

Minty Fresh tried to push back in his chair, but there wasn't room to do it and he bumped his head on the steel door. "Yes."

"No. I did before, last year. But it's been quiet since. The soul vessels are about the same. I bring them in, they go out."

"Good. That's good. And Ray, he doesn't know?"

"I think he suspects I'm a serial killer, but he's clueless about the other thing."

"You know Charlie Asher was one of us?"

"Yes. That's how I met Ray. I went to Asher's shop after the Latino cop told me what had happened and picked up the soul vessels that had been taken from me. The cop said it was over."

"Rivera didn't know. He was just being a cop. He's one of *us*, now."

"So maybe the others have been replaced, too."

"No way to tell. We only knew about you because Charlie Asher went in your store once and saw the soul vessels. We don't know what rules are still in effect. That's what we're trying to find out. I won't contact you again unless it's an emergency, just in case our contact is bringing up the forces of darkness like before. You can always reach me at my store if anything strange happens." He threw a business card on her desk. "My mobile's there. Anytime. Even if it's just to fuck with Ray."

She laughed. Her eyes had been getting wider and her expression more frightened as he had spoken, but now she smiled. She picked up his card. "Okay."

"Just one more favor, then I'm in the wind."

"Sure."

"I need to look at your book. Your calendar."

"We allowed to do that?"

"Who knows?"

"Okay." She opened her desk drawer and pulled out a leather date book, and slid it across the desk to him. "There's only one uncollected. Just appeared today."

"I'm looking for a specific name. Mike Sullivan. Sound familiar? Within the last six weeks or so?" They'd figured out long ago that Death Merchants had the forty-nine days of *bardo,* the transition from life to death, to collect the soul vessel; sometimes they got it before the subject died, sometimes after.

"Nope," she said.

He opened the book to the current date and she saw another entry on the page. "Two, I guess," she said. "That last one wasn't there this morning."

Minty saw the newest name on her calendar and the number of days she had to retrieve the soul vessel: *one.*

"Oh, shit," he said. "Shit. Shit. Shit."

"What? What? What?" She stood and leaned over, trying to get a better look at the new entry.

"I know this guy. He's a cop."

Sundown. Rivera was sneaking into a house when his phone buzzed in his jacket pocket and he checked it: *Minty Fresh.* He hit mute and soldiered on, walking into a bedroom where a portly man in pajamas was holding a pillow over the face of a thin person propped up in a hospital bed.

"Just a little bit more," said the man. He looked to the clock on the nightstand as if timing himself.

After being restrained for twenty-five years by warrants, or at least *knock and announce*, Rivera was still getting used to sneaking into a house under the cloak of kinda-sorta invisibility. He kept reminding himself that he was not here as a cop. But then the guy looked over at him.

"Holy—!" The fat guy leapt back, threw the pillow in the air, and grabbed his chest. The woman's head in the hospital bed lolled to the side. She was dead.

"You can see me?" said Rivera.

"Well, yeah."

"I'm afraid I've got some bad news, then."

"Worse than you walked in on me smothering my mother?"

"I'm afraid so."

"Who are you?"

Rivera badged him. "Inspector Alphonse Rivera, SFPD Homicide."

The guy was backed against a dresser, trying to catch his breath, still holding his chest. He looked quickly to the dead woman, then back to Rivera. "Well, this is awkward."

"You think?" said Rivera.

"It's not what you think. She asked for it."

"Okay," said Rivera. He noticed a crystal perfume bottle on the dresser behind the fat guy, glowing a dull red.

"No, she really asked for it. She's been sick. She's my mother." He looked at the dead woman again. "*Was* my mother. I have a videotape of her asking me to do this. We even discussed show tunes I could sing to cover the noise of her struggles."

"Uh-huh," said Rivera. "Decided to skip the singing, then?"

"Forgot. How did you get here so fast? You guys are a lot better at this than cops on TV. It usually takes like forty minutes to find the killer on TV."

"Yeah, that's not real," said Rivera.

"So, do I need a lawyer? Are you going to take me in?"

"That depends," said Rivera. He looked at the names in his case notebook that he'd copied out of his calendar. "Is that Wanda DeFazio?"

"Yes. Yes, it is," said the fat guy, breathless once again.

Rivera nodded, referred back to the notebook again. "You wouldn't be Donald DeFazio, would you?"

"Donny," said Donny.

Rivera nodded again. He'd wondered what was going on when he had the two names appear on his calendar with the same surname. He figured it might be a car accident, husband and wife thing. He'd wanted to call Minty Fresh to ask him about it, but then, no . . .

"Donny, give me that perfume bottle behind you on the dresser."

Donny DeFazio did what he was told, handed the crystal bottle to Rivera, who slipped it in his jacket pocket.

"You live here, Donny?"

"I have been. I had to move in six months ago to take care of my mother."

Rivera nodded. Noncommittal cop nod. "So your possessions, they all here in the house?"

"Yes, why? Are you going to seize my stuff when you take me in? Freeze my accounts?"

Rivera shook his head at his notebook, flipped it shut, put it into his inside jacket pocket. "Nah, you're good to go, Donny. I'm going to have a look around, though. Which is your room?"

"Down the hall." Donny moved away from the dresser. "Wait, don't I need to get a lawyer? Don't you want to see the video? She was in pain. She asked me to do it?"

"I know. You feel bad about it?"

"Well, of course. I feel horrible about it. It's the hardest thing I ever had to do." He started gasping again.

"Well then, I'm sorry for your loss." He pointed. "Just down the hall this way?"

Donny nodded, then grabbed his chest again, and either from relief or stress, stiffened, twitched, and slid down the front of the dresser to a splay-legged sitting position on the floor. He twitched for a few seconds, then slumped forward.

"And there we go," said Rivera. He looked around, just in case Donny's soul vessel might be sitting out like his mother's, but nothing else was glowing. He backed out of the room and headed down the hall.

His phone buzzed again. There was also a text that had come in during the DeFazio deaths. *Pick the fuck up*, it said.

Rivera hit talk. "You said we weren't supposed to talk unless it was an emergency."

"Where's your partner?" asked Minty Fresh.

"He's watching my store while I'm out on a collection. I didn't hear from you on the Lily girl, so he's filling in until I find someone."

"Where are you, not near him?"

"No. In Noe Valley. Looking for a vessel. I found another Death Merchant, and there's more—"

"Yeah, we'll get to that. Y'all might want to sit down, Inspector."

Nick Cavuto was reading a Raymond Chandler short story called "Red Wind" behind the counter when the banshee stepped out of the stacks.

"*AIEEEEEEEEEEEEEEEEEE!*"

Cavuto dropped the paperback as he slid off the stool into a crouch, drew a ridiculously large revolver from his shoulder holster, and leveled it at the banshee. One motion.

"I will drop you, raggedy," he said.

"I come to save your life, you great dolt, and you cast aspersions on me frock?"

Cavuto kept the gun trained on her and looked around it. "Save my life, huh?"

"You need to get out of here before dark, lad. There's a nasty bit of business heading your way. They're not strong enough to move in the daylight yet, but they'll be here soon."

"Raven women coming to take my soul?" Cavuto lowered the gun to his side. "Stay there."

"They can't kill a man for his soul, don't know why, just the way of things, otherwise you'd all be rotting in the fields. But they will kill you for the sport." She moved toward him, gestured that she was moving wide of the counter, toward the front door. "Let's go, love, have a ride in your lovely carriage. I'll hang me head out the window when I scream." She smiled, black lips and bluish teeth—batted her sooty eyelashes.

Cavuto glanced over his shoulder and out the window. The streetlights were on and the little stripe of sky he could see was dying pink.

"There'll be no screaming."

"Aye, lad, let's go, then." She made a motion as if shooing errant chickens toward the door, the long tatters of her sleeves making trails like smoke.

There was a rumble from behind the shop and they both looked to the single window at the back of the store, high and narrow, four steel bars across it. As they watched, the window, lit yellow from the light in the alley, went black.

"Back door locked, then?" asked the banshee.

Cavuto nodded, not looking away from the window.

"Spendid. We're off, then. Come along. Go swiftly and stay long, I always say."

The rear window cracked and the shadow of a thousand birds oozed in between the cracks and down the back wall, spreading, form and light exchanging as it moved, like oily lace woven into the shapes of flying things. The shadow slid down onto the hardwood floor, splashed in waves over the shelves as it approached them. At one narrow, central shelf where Rivera displayed recently acquired books—soul vessels—the shadow coalesced, covered the whole shelf like a shroud.

The banshee could see the five souls, glowing dull red, and one by one, as the shadow enveloped them, they started to fade.

"Mad dash, love. Mad dash," she said.

"You go," said Cavuto. He trained the .44 Magnum on a spot at the middle of a dark shelf, fifteen feet away.

As the last soul vessel went dark, the shadow throbbed, gained dimension, split into three distinct masses that then undulated, changed, formed into three female figures, human to a degree, shimmering with fine, blue-black feathers; talons sprouted from the tips of their fingers, long and hooked like marlin spikes, the silver color of stars.

"Gun," said one, her voice like gravel swishing in a pan. "I hate guns."

"Well, lad, you've shat the bed now," said the banshee.

14

PERCHANCE TO DREAM

It was a Wednesday night in San Francisco, and despite the fog having laid a soft blanket over the city and the foghorn singing its sad and low lullaby, no one slept well.

RIVERA

Inspector Alphonse Rivera was electrified by the shock and grief of finding Nick Cavuto dead in his bookstore. There were four units and an ambulance on the scene by the time Rivera got there. The EMTs were working on the big man on the floor—compressions on his chest, squeezing the bag to breathe for him, slamming syringes of adrenaline, and hitting him with defibrillator paddles. As soon as they got a heartbeat they would move him, they said.

There was blood, but not a tremendous amount, on Cavuto's cutaway shirt.

Rivera could still smell the gunpowder in the air, as well as the more smoky aroma of burning peat. Cavuto's big stainless-steel revolver lay on the floor by him.

"How long?" he asked the first officer he saw with a notebook who wasn't interviewing someone. Nguyen on his nameplate. Rivera going into autopilot, not allowing what was happening a few feet behind him to become part of his reality.

"They've been working about ten minutes—since I've been on scene."

"Gunshot wound?"

"Probably not," the cop said. He cringed. "EMT said it looks more like a stab wound. Thin blade. Ice pick maybe."

"Witnesses?"

"People all over on the street, drinkers, diners, people walking their dogs, you know this neighborhood. No one saw shit yet, still looking. 'Shots fired' call came from the nail place next door." The officer looked at his notes. "Seven-oh-two. First unit on scene a minute later. Found him like this."

Rivera checked his watch: 7:15.

Rivera looked around. The shelf where he had displayed the soul vessels was sprayed with a fine, oily fuzz, like black down, and even as Rivera watched, it was evaporating into vapor. He'd seen it before, a year ago, on the bricks in the alley where he'd pumped nine 9-mm rounds into one of the Morrigan to rescue Charlie Asher.

"We're moving him!" barked one of the EMTs.

"He's back?" Rivera asked.

The EMT whipped his head. "No, I'm calling an audible. We can get him to St. Francis in five. He needs a surgeon. Wound may have hit the heart."

The other EMTs had already lifted Cavuto onto a gurney. Uniform cops were clearing the way to the ambulance.

"We'll work on him until we can't," said the EMT over his shoulder as he went out the door.

"Tell them to check for venom," Rivera said.

The EMT raised his eyebrows.

"Just do it."

The EMT nodded and was out the door.

"People next door said they heard six shots, quick," said Officer Nguyen. "Very, very loud."

Rivera walked to the display shelf. The books, the five soul vessel books, were still there, lying on the floor, but they no longer glowed. Two rounds had hit the books on the top shelf, tearing cantaloupe-sized holes through the books, leaving shredded paper in the cavity like it had been nested by hamsters. He looked to the back of the store. Two more portals of shredded paper where the rounds had hit the books on the back wall.

Nguyen moved to his side as the last of the black feathers vaporized.

"What the fuck is that stuff? It was all over the place when I got here."

"No idea," said Rivera. Then, still on emotional autopilot, crime-scene robot on the scene, he said, "All the shots were Cavuto's." He pointed to the four impact points with his pen. He saw Nguyen's eyes go wide at the craters in the books before him.

"He used SWAT loads," Rivera explained. Cavuto loaded the .44 with very-high-speed, prefrangilized bullets—a copper jacket filled with lead beads encased in resin, half the weight of a normal .44 round, thus the high speed, but when they hit they expanded explosively, doing enormous damage to flesh, or in this case, paper. Used by law enforcement because they didn't ricochet, and would not go through walls or car doors to hurt innocents. Essentially, they blew up on the first thing they hit, and Cavuto had hit what he was aiming at, thus the spray of hellish down.

Nyguen ran his own pen around the edge of one of the craters in the books, careful not to actually touch it. "So these rounds went through someone before they hit here?"

"Some*thing*," Rivera said. "If it had been some*one*, there'd be a pile of ground meat here to identify and clean up."

"Fuck," said Nguyen.

"Yeah," said Rivera. "I'm headed to St. Francis. Tell the watch commander, would you?"

Rivera did not hurry because he knew there was no reason to hurry. They wouldn't be bringing Nick Cavuto back to the land of the living. They continued to work on the big cop for forty-five minutes after Rivera arrived at the hospital without getting so much as a blip of a heartbeat. They pronounced him dead a little after 8 P.M.

A captain from Personal Crimes debriefed Rivera at the hospital, after which two commanders took turns telling him to go home and stay away from the case, which he finally did when they threated to suspend him if he didn't.

At home, he texted Minty Fresh about Cavuto's death, then ate something, but he didn't remember what, turned on the TV and sat in front of it, but he couldn't have said what was on, then went to bed and lay there, staring at the ceiling, his Glock .40 cal in his hand, until 6 A.M., when he finally fell into a fitful, jerky sleep, with dreams full of the sound of frantic birds scratching at windows.

MINTY FRESH

Minty Fresh lay awake mentally arranging jazz albums by artist and recording date, cross-referencing who played what on which record, listening in his mind's ear to the signature riff of each artist as he came to mind. It was a rich, complex, demanding exercise, but it kept him from thinking about the dead cop, the dark rising, and the task he would have to perform tomorrow. It kept him from reaching that place that he hit so, so often in his life, the mind-bending, sob-inducing limit where he said to himself, *I just cannot endure any more motherfucking death. No more!*

Order. Put everything in order. Serve order. That was the *why* and *what* of it. Order.

In his head, he flipped albums, looked at liner notes, grainy photographs taken in smoky clubs, listened to notes played by men long dead, and he put them in order. 'Round Midnight, he drifted off.

MIKE SULLIVAN

Mike couldn't remember being this excited to go to sleep since Christmas Eve when he was a kid: the excitement, the anticipation, the replaying, over and over, of how it would be, knowing that no matter how you imagined it, you'd be surprised. This was just like that, but instead of waking up to find that Santa had brought him a new bike, or a fire truck with an extending ladder (he loved that fire truck), he was going to get up in the morning and throw himself off a bridge and die.

He knew he should feel sad about it, in fact, he even felt a little guilty for not feeling sad, but he didn't feel sad. He'd miss his apartment, and some of his friends, but not that much, really. Not compared to what it might be like. And there was the Christmas-morning part: he was going to die, but he was not going to end. There was something else out there, more exciting and unknown than even a bike under the Christmas tree, and somehow there was an inevitability to all of it. He didn't feel like this was a choice he was making, but more like a choice that had been made long ago and he was just fulfilling it—like riding on a train, waiting for your station, you don't decide at each station to stay or go, you get to your station and you get off. He was coming to his station.

He ran the Sanskrit chant through his head, which wasn't hard. It was only a few words, Audrey had written them out phonetically for him, and since he'd first learned them and repeated them, they had rung in his head constantly. With the chant sounding in the background, he checked and rechecked the arrangements he'd made for Charlie Asher to take over his life, going so far as to label certain shirts that he thought looked good on him, certain background details he shared with the guys at work, listing each of their social network profiles so if Charlie ever ran into them, he might recognize them from their pictures.

He liked that someone was getting his stuff, even his body, as if he was giving someone who was really hungry half of his sandwich, after deciding he might have to throw it away. It was all so exciting. Charlie had called him, and in his strange, scratchy little voice, thanked him for what he was going to lose. Ha! Lose? "You're welcome, but no, not lose," he'd said. "A gift," he said, and, "Thank *you*."

Concepción! Concepción! Concepción! Concepción! My Conchita! My love! He had never felt like this and it was glorious. He ached for her, his soul sang electric with the thought of her, and tomorrow he would be with her.

He didn't remember falling asleep and he didn't care that he did, because in the morning he would get up, go to the bridge, then jump off and die.

LILY

Lily lived in the Sunset District, where San Francisco was open to the sea, so even when the rest of the city was warm and sunny, the fog rolled in over Ocean Beach and the Great Highway to settle between the rows of postwar tract homes. Lily liked the fog, and didn't even mind the cold wind. She reckoned that Ocean Beach, the dunes there, and the Sunset were the closest San Francisco was going to come to the foreboding, wind-swept moors of England, where she had aspired to suffer romance and heartache when she was a kid. The foghorn, however, rather than a lone-some lament that conjured images of Heathcliff's dark figure, waiting with clenched jaw on the moor for her to bring light and warmth into his life, sounded like a distressed moose tied up in her neighbor's garage, having his nut sack singed with jumper cables at a precise interval calculated to keep her from falling asleep. Which, in turn, made her think of what complete douche bags people could be when all you wanted to do was borrow a defibrillator. Then she was awake and angry.

"Look, I just need it for a few hours," she told the ambulance guy.

"They have to stay with the ambulance, miss," the stupid guy had said. "We can't lend them out."

"Look, *nurse*, I'm trying to save lives over here. I swear, I'll have it back to you in like three, four hours max."

"Still can't do it. Even if we could, these aren't the consumer models like they hang on the wall at the airport. We're trained to use these."

"*Quoi?*" she had said, in perfect fucking French. They just hung defibrillators on the wall at the airport? Those things cost like five thousand dollars. (Which she hadn't known when she said she'd take care of getting one.) And they just hang them there for anyone to use? She needed to travel more.

A quick search on her phone revealed that they hung them on the wall at City Hall, as well as at the airport, and she was only a few blocks from there. But she hadn't really been sure she wanted to try to get on the bus or the BART while making off with a stolen defibrillator, so she had called her friend Abby, who had a car.

"Abs, we're getting the band back together," Lily'd said.

"I have to work at four," Abby said.

"It's an emergency. Like an hour, max. Can you pick me up at the corner of Polk and Pine?"

"Okay, but I'm going to be dressed for work."

Twenty minutes later, Abby showed up in her beater Prius and Lily jumped in. "What are you wearing?" was the first thing Lily said.

"For work," Abby said. She was wearing a khaki skirt, black tights, a crisp white blouse and flats. If not for her hair, which was still short and dyed a deep maroon, Lily wouldn't have recognized her.

"Retail?" Lily asked.

Abby nodded. "I'm a failure. What are *you* wearing?"

Lily was in black jeans, ankle boots, and a red SF Fire Department T-shirt, which she had thought might help her with the ambulance guys. "Me, too," she said.

The two failed Goth girls shared a high-five and hugged it out for their shame, then Lily said, "Head up Van Ness and pull in in front of City Hall."

"I can't park there. There's a bus stop."

"You're not parking. It's an emergency."

Lily outlined the plan on the way: "I need to steal a defibrillator."

"Okay, I'll drive," said Abby.

"No, you have to come in with me."

"Why? They aren't heavy. Are they heavy?"

"No, but I haven't done this before."

Abby pulled the Prius up onto the sidewalk in front of City Hall and they both jumped out.

"My friend is having a heart attack. My friend is having a heart attack,"

Lily chanted as she led Abby up the steps, and continued chanting it as they ran up the hall.

"My friend is having a heart attack, make way."

When people looked, Abby said, "Hey, fuck off, I'm having a heart attack."

Finally they spotted a bright red plastic box inside a larger, clear plastic box near a fire extinguisher.

"You want this, too?" Abby said, her hand on the fire extinguisher handle.

"No, just this."

Lily pulled open the plastic box and pulled out the defibrillator, which was about the size of a small laptop computer. There was a readout and a single yellow button. Then the box started talking.

"Place pads on patient's chest," said the box.

Unfortunately, Lily and Abby had attracted enough attention on their way to the defibrillator that a group of about a dozen people had gathered around them to either help the skinny girl or watch her twitch.

"Place pads on patient's chest," said the box.

Lily popped open a little door on the defibrillator and two vinyl pads about the size of coasters, stuck together, fell out, trailing wires behind them.

"What do we do?" Abby said.

"Place pads on patient's chest," said the box.

Lily held the box between her legs, separated the two pads, then tore open Abby's blouse and slammed the pads on her boobs.

"You bitch!" said Abby. She grabbed the front of Lily's shirt and made to tear it open, but instead just stretched it out and spun Lily halfway around.

"Heart rhythm normal. Do not shock," said the box.

"What's going on here?" came a voice from down the hall.

It was a heavyset, coplike guy, in that he had a gun and a uniform, but he didn't look like he ever had to do any difficult cop stuff.

Abby took off running the way they had come. Lily grabbed the defibrillator just as it was about to be yanked out of her hand and followed.

"Heart attack! Heart attack!" Abby yelled ahead. "Out of the way, I'm having a fucking heart attack."

"She is," said Lily, holding up the defibrillator as she ran. "Slow down, Abs, you're pulling out the wires."

Abby jumped into the Prius. Lily bundled the defibrillator into her friend's lap, then jumped in the Prius's back door behind her. "Go! Go! Go!"

And with all the roaring fury of a golf cart escaping the back nine, they sped into the traffic on Van Ness and were immediately stuck behind a bus, which, it turned out, didn't matter, because no one was chasing them.

"Do not shock. Heart rhythm normal," the box said.

"You got electro-stickum on my best bra," Abby said. "I have to change before work, now."

"They look good on you, though—like a sexy torture robot."

"Yeah?" Abby was trying to look at her chest while driving. "See if there's extras in the little box."

So that had happened, and Lily had called M and told his voice mail, "No problem on the defibrillator, I'll have it for you," but then doubt started rising as evening came on, and by midnight she really, really wanted to be asleep, not thinking about killing a guy, but the stupid foghorn. *What, ships didn't have radar and stuff, they still had to use nineteenth-century technology to keep from crashing into rocks?*

She went to her bedroom window, threw up the sash, and stuck her head out as the foghorn sounded.

"Really?" she shouted.

Again the horn.

"Seriously!"

"How 'bout you be quiet," said Mr. Lee, the old Chinese guy who lived in the apartment below her and was hanging out the window smoking.

"Sorry," she said, and slunk back to bed.

AUDREY AND CHARLIE

Since meeting with Mike, Audrey had spent three days fasting, chanting, and meditating, preparing herself to perform the ritual of Chöd, trying to achieve the mental state necessary, without, of course, thinking about achieving the mental state necessary, which is sort of the tricky part of Buddhism.

Late Wednesday night found her sitting in the lotus position on a wide, padded stool at the end of the bed while Charlie paced frantically around her, nervous about his big moment. She had not slept and would not sleep, having achieved the state of waking trance that she would need to maintain through the ritual, but Charlie's toenails, *snickt, snickt, snickting* on the carpet threatened to pull her out of her trance.

Calmly, evenly, quietly, she said, "Charlie. Please."

"I can't sleep. I've tried. All the things that could go wrong. What if it doesn't work and Sophie never has her daddy? You could have done all of this for nothing. Mike might back out, and who could blame him. I'm sure there's a way I could screw this up. And you know if there's a way to, I will. And not only that—"

"Please," she said, not a note of alarm or anger, every breath with purpose.

"I just can't sleep, there's the—" and he was off again. *Snickt, snickt, snickt.*

Audrey, her face a model of the beautiful and compassionate Buddha, stood on the cushioned stool, ever so slowly—Venus rising from the sea on the half shell—and let her silk saffron robe slip off her until she stood there naked.

"Hey," Charlie said. "Wow. What, are you—"

Charlie, all of his vital energies and most of his fluids having been inspired to swiftly migrate to his enormous dong, was spun around as the member unfurled from his waist until it achieved its full appreciation, then he plopped over on his side unconscious on the rug, where he remained, snoring, until dawn.

Audrey slowly lowered herself back into the lotus position and continued her meditation through the night.

THE MORRIGAN

They had once been death goddesses of the Celts, the three, and had reigned over the battlefields of the North for a thousand years, plucking souls from the dead and dying, and driving warriors on with fury and terror, switching from their raven and crow forms to the silky, razor-clawed harpy-women as whim and wind suited them. Now they were patchwork shadows, licking their wounds in a closed train tunnel under Fort Mason Great Meadow, unable even to hold three-dimensional form, distinguishable from the oil stains left by the tractors and other heavy equipment stored in the tunnel only in that they were moving.

"Did guns get worse?" asked Nemain, the venomous one, trying to hold on her left arm, which was attached by only a thread of pitch. "I was shot when I was above before, and I don't remember it being this bad." She tried to will herself to hold form, but melted back a flat shadow. She looked to the man in yellow, who sat in the seat of the skip-loader, leaning on one elbow.

"And it wasn't the same one who shot you before?" asked the Yellow Fellow.

"Different. Bigger. Bigger gun. But I stung him in the heart before he shot my arm."

"We're going to need more souls to heal," said Macha, who had reverted to the shadow of her bird form, a hooded crow. The cold, fog-diffused moonlight in the tunnel shone through ragged holes in her wings and breasts. "The five that were in the bookstore were barely enough for us to take form. Now . . ."

"I want to take the head of the banshee," said Babd, the third of the sisters, who leaned on the wheel of a skip-loader for balance, her left leg gone from the shin down. She had wielded the terrifying screech that drove warriors to suicidal frenzy on the battlefield, so the more gentle screamer, the banshee, had always been especially annoying to her. "But I can't do it with only one leg. We need souls."

"Ladies, ladies, relax. I will bring you what you need," he said. And he would. He hadn't anticipated the setback of a heavily armed policeman who had been forewarned by a banshee when he sent them into the soul-seller's store. They hadn't been strong enough for that, and now they weren't even strong enough to go above and hold a useful form, or, if necessary, face the Luminatus and her hellhounds. He wasn't exactly sure he wanted them to be. They *had* torn his predecessor, Orcus, to pieces. It was a dilemma he needed to ponder. He would bring them what they needed to heal, but *only* what they needed.

"For now y'all can lick your wounds in the trunk of the Buick. I'll be back in a butterfly wink."

He limped off down the tunnel alongside the heavy equipment, limped not because he was injured, but as a matter of style.

When he was gone, Babd said, "How long is that? Is that more than a week?"

"He's being colorful," said Nemain. "He's very colorful."

"If I want any color out of him, I'll open one of his veins," said Macha.

"Ooo, I like that," said Babd. "I'm going to say that to the banshee."

"Not the same," said Macha, shaking her shadowy head.

"Yeah," said Nemain. "No blood."

"Butterflies," said Babd. "Yuck." She shuddered so that even in her shadow form her feathers bristled with revulsion.

15

THURSDAY AT THE BRIDGE

Thursday was similar to any other workday for Mike Sullivan, in that he got up, got dressed, and drove to the bridge. But this Thursday was a little different in that he wouldn't be driving back. He was awakened by the knock on his door, and when he opened it, a thin woman with severe blond hair dropped a gear bag at his feet.

"What are you, about a forty, forty long?" she said instead of hello.

"Huh?" said Mike.

"Jacket size."

"Yeah, a forty."

"Yeah; me, too," she said. "Thirty-eight actually, but I like shoulder pads. I have to have the waist taken in a little, too."

"Okay," said Mike.

"I'm Jane. I'm going to be your new sister."

Mike shook her hand. "You wanna come in?"

"No, gotta go. I'm on the catch team. There's motocross leathers in there. Not really leather, though, some kind of bulletproof fabric. They were my brother's. Should fit you. If they're snug, that's good, they'll hold your bones in place."

Mike was suddenly wide-awake. It was the *"hold your bones in place"* line that did the trick.

"There's plates over the spine, elbows, forearms, knees. All should fit under your coveralls without showing. I also threw in a kayaker's helmet—"

"No," said Mike.

"Look, I'm just trying to keep you from getting too mashed up."

"I'm not wearing a helmet."

"You wear a hard hat on the bridge, don't you?"

"Yeah, but."

"Fine, wear that."

"I will."

"Okay, there's also a five-pound paper bag of sand in the satchel. You want to throw that in right before you jump. I mean, *right* before you jump. You're basically going to jump into the hole that the bag makes in the surface of the water."

"How do I get a five-pound bag out onto the bridge unnoticed?"

"Do you ever bring your lunch?"

"Well yeah, but—"

"You aren't going to need your lunch today. Take the sand instead. If everything goes right, you'll just knock yourself out and drown."

"You're kind of being mean to me, considering . . ." He realized then that she hadn't looked him in the eye once since she'd shown up. Now she did.

"I'm just trying to get through this, okay, Mike? I can't get my head around what you're doing for us, and it's easier if I think of you as some random insane guy."

"Sure, I get that."

"Sorry. I'm sometimes overly stern with the mentally ill. I'll work on that."

"Uh, thanks?"

She held her arms out stiffly, offering a hug above the gear bag at their feet. Mike leaned over and shared an awkward, only-collar-bones-touching-back-patting hug with her.

"Okay. Good talk," Jane said, pushing away. "You have the number."

"Yes," Mike said.

"So, unless something different happens with the weather, I'll see you at nine?"

"Nine," Mike said.

"Thanks," she said. "Really." Then she quickstepped away down the hallway like she was trying to get through a haunted graveyard as fast as possible without actually running.

They had rented a twenty-four-foot Boston Whaler from the marina by the ballpark. Rivera was to have been their pilot, but they'd agreed to call him off when they got news of Cavuto's murder. Jane stood at the center console, steering. Minty Fresh stood to her side, holding the stainless rail on the console, towering over her. On the deck behind Jane, Audrey sat in the lotus position, apparently in some kind of trance, although she could move and react when they needed her to. Her head bobbed as the boat bounced over a light chop in the bay. Charlie, in his wizard robe and a dog's life jacket that had come with the boat, was at the stern, wedged between the bait box and a large waterproof suitcase that Minty Fresh had brought on board.

"So, a green wet suit?" said Jane. "Bold choice."

"I wanted it in a sea foam," said the Mint One, who was already wearing his fins. "But the guy who was making it could only get neoprene in forest green."

"Very froggy," said Charlie, shouting to be heard over the big twin Mercury outboards.

"You need to consider your glass house," said Minty.

"But hey, webbed feet," Charlie said, wiggling his duck feet before him. "Nice, right?"

Jane glanced back. "I can't even look at you like that. It's just like Mom used to say, you're a freak of nature."

"Mom said that?" Charlie thought he was pouting, but since he had no lower lip to protrude, it looked more like his jaw was flapping in the breeze.

"Well, she did one time—she was repeating what I had just said when she asked me to drive you to school one day. Still."

"Not for much longer," said Minty Fresh, letting them both off the hook of family history.

"Shhhh," shushed Jane. "We're harshing Audrey's chi or something."

Jane throttled down the outboards a little as they rounded Alcatraz and the current coming in the Golden Gate kicked the waves up.

"Where'd you learn to drive a boat?" Minty Fresh asked.

"Our dad used to take us fishing," shouted Charlie. "Jane always got to drive the boat."

"Shhhh," shushed Audrey, who evidently was not as deep in trance as they thought.

"Sorry," said Charlie.

"Uh-oh," said Jane as she steered toward the north tower of the bridge. "That's not good."

A finger of fog was streaming in through the Golden Gate; from their position, it appeared to be above the water, but below the deck of the bridge.

Minty Fresh lifted his sunglasses to get a better look. "You can see to steer, right?"

"So far," said Jane. "But I don't know if we'll be able to see the bottom of the bridge from under it. It might be a whiteout by the time we get there." She checked her watch.

Five minutes later, when they were a half mile out, the fingerling of fog had taken on the aspect of a snowy knife blade, inserting itself between the bridge towers and the water just below the roadway.

"We won't be able to see the bottom of the bridge," said Jane, digging in her rain-jacket pocket for her phone. "I'm calling it off."

Lily was supposed to be at work at nine, and she had actually been headed that way, but after dropping off the defibrillator at Charlie's store for his sister, and learning that the big gay cop, Cavuto, had been killed, she started to shake, and as her bus approached her stop near the Crisis Center offices she realized she just couldn't do it. She got off the bus and flagged down a taxi.

"Take me to the Golden Gate Bridge," she said.

"You want me to take you to the visitor center, or to the bridge. Because if I take you to the bridge, I'm going to have to go to Marin to turn around and pay the toll to come back and it's going to cost you."

"Sure, the visitor center," she said, not really thinking it through.

She got out of the cab at the visitor center and paid, then started running up the trail for the bridge. She hadn't even gotten to the tollbooths before she was out of breath and had to slow to a walk. She checked the time on her phone: 8:55. Five minutes. She started to jog in the wobbly, ankle-breaking way that drunk girls do, although she wasn't drunk, just really out of shape.

He was going to jump off from the steel structure under the road, about two hundred feet south of the north tower. She looked up. She wasn't even to the south tower. She'd never make it. And if she did, what was she going to do? You couldn't even get to where he was going to be from the walkway; at least *she* didn't know how to get there.

But there was fog coming in under the bridge, like a plank or something. He wouldn't jump in the fog. That was one of the plans, she was sure of it.

She scrolled up his number and pressed dial. This was her thing, this was what she did. This was what made her special. She would get the bridge painter off the bridge.

"Hi, Lily," Mike said.

"Mike, you can't do this. Not today."

"I have to, Lily. But I wouldn't be here if not for you."

She made an exasperated growling noise.

"Are you okay?" Mike asked. "You sound like you're choking. Are you crying."

"No, I'm running." She was crying. "I'm right above you on the walkway." She *was*, kind of, above him, and she *was* on the walkway, she just wasn't *right* above him on the walkway, by about a quarter of a mile.

"That's very sweet of you," Mike said. "But really, I'll be fine. I don't know, I feel like I'm done here."

"You're totally not done. You paint the bridge I'm looking at it. I can see a spot you missed right here. There's rust."

"This is what's supposed to be, Lily. She needs me. *They* need me."

She held the phone to her chest until the urge to scream that he was a fucking lunatic passed, then, very calmly she said, "Just come up, Mike. This is a bad idea. There's fog. You can go back down if your mind is set on it, but for now, please just come up here. Hang out with me for a little bit. I'm waiting."

"Are you using the 'promise of sex' thing on me, Lily?"

"No, that's not what this is. That's a different thing completely. This is—"

"Well, that would be lovely, and under other circumstances, I'd jump at the opportunity."

"Really?" *He did not just say that. Did he really say that?*

"I mean, I'm flattered, but Concepción is waiting for me, and she has my heart."

"Mike, did you just call that ghost your boo?"

"Good-bye, Lily. Thank you. I have to go, I have another call."

Her phone beeped as he disconnected. She stopped walking and just looked at it.

"Are you fucking kidding me?" she screeched.

A father who was walking his two elementary school kids across the bridge took their heads and steered them away from the foulmouthed girl with too much eye makeup. He glared over his shoulder at her.

"Oh, lick my love-luge, Dockers, I'm trying to save a fucking life here."

She couldn't see the screen of her phone through the blur of her tears. She wiped her eyes on her sleeve, and looked again: nine o'clock.

Hi, Jane," Mike said into the phone. He stood on a beam under the roadway, facing the city, one arm wrapped around a crossbeam. He'd already slipped out of his safety harness, leaving the lines attached to the bridge. At his feet, the bag of sand. The chant Audrey had taught him was repeating in his mind, over, and over, and over, as constant as the ocean.

"Mike, it's not a go," said Jane. "We can't even see you."

Mike looked down on the strip of fog that was streaming not more than twenty feet below him. Incredibly dense, but wispy and soft-looking on top. Looking out, the bay was clear all the way to Berkeley, the fog only coming in from the ocean side, the strip of vapor like the fog bank testing the temperature of the bay before coming through the Gate. He'd seen it before, he'd seen it all.

"It's clear all around you, though, right?" Mike said.

"Yes, but not above us. It's not safe."

Concepción materialized before him, about ten feet away, smiling, her arms out.

Mike laughed. "Good-bye, Jane. Take care of my body." *Eyes forward, knees a little bent, hands in a fist,* he thought. He crouched, put his phone on the beam, then stood and faced Concepción, holding the bag of sand before him.

"Come to me," she said. "Come to me, my sweet Nikolasha."

The Sanskrit chant circling in his head, Mike dropped the bag of sand and stepped out into space.

The man in yellow could just hear them saying—after the Morrigan killed the cop and took the soul vessels from the bookstore, completely wasting them—he could just hear them saying, *"They're creatures of darkness, it's not like they're just going to waltz right in in broad daylight and take the souls."*

Everybody likes a surprise, he thought.

So, just a little after nine in the morning, when a pasty guy in big glasses flipped the "Open" sign on the front door at Fresh Music, the man in yellow waltzed right in, in broad daylight, to take the souls.

It was a nice store, stained glass in the front windows true to the Edwardian architecture of the building, poster-sized black-and-white photos of jazz, soul, and rock greats. Iconic album covers in frames over the racks of used vinyl: *Bitches Brew, Lush Life, Sticky Fingers, Abbey Road, Born to Run.* The yellow fellow strolled by the racks, flipping an album here, there, looking for that beautiful red glow that the ladies loved so.

The store was laid out in a barbell shape; he paced the whole front, then paused at the counter before going to the back. The guy behind the counter was about thirty, wearing a too-small plaid cotton short-sleeve, the bottom buttons unbuttoned, the shirt flaring over too-tight, too-short, gold polyester dress slacks, his hair a tangled mushroom shape, his beard more the function of not shaving than grooming—*that shit was growing down his neck.* The yellow fellow looked over the counter at the guy's shoes: like something out of a Dorthea Lange Depression work-camp photo, toes all bent up and nasty.

"Can I help you," said Neck Beard, a little indignant, the yellow fellow in his personal space.

"What's your name?"

"Evan," said Evan.

"Evan, this everything?" Yellow stirred the air with a long finger to include the whole store. "This your whole inventory?"

"There are a few things in the back room, mostly duplicates, some estate stuff I'm supposed to unpack and file. Nothing good."

"Uh-huh," said Yellow, noticing the locked glass case on the wall behind the counter was conspicuously half empty. "What you got in there?"

Evan looked over his shoulder dismissively, shrugged. "Some rare pressings, first editions. Usually these three shelves on the right are what the owner calls his 'special collection': just crap, mixed-up genres, vinyl, 78s, 45s, like a Fleetwood Mac CD, a beat-up wax Edison cylinder, worthless—not anything anybody'd want, no need to lock them up."

"But he do? He lock them up, keep watch on them like they solid gold, right?"

"Yeah," said Evan, just weary of it all. "I don't understand it, unless he's keeping them ironically, because they *are* worthless, so he's kind of making a statement by pretending they have value."

"So where, *ironically*, do you think he put them?"

Shrug. "Who cares?"

Yellow's hand shot out and struck Evan's throat like a viper, catching his windpipe between his thumb and fingers, pinching it. Evan made a cat-yakking-up-a-hairball noise, but could not move.

"Son, I'ma tell you something ain't nobody else in the world can tell you: you got no soul. And I'ma tell your future, too: you ain't never gonna get a soul, you keep makin' people's shit small."

Evan's eyes started to roll back in his head and the big man shook him like dust mop until he came back to the room. "You ain't shit, Evan, and you ain't never gonna be shit until you show some passion for something. Y'all got to *love* something. Y'all got to *hate* something. Y'all got to *want* something. Pissing on other people's passion 'cause you trying to be cool just make you a coward—a little bitch." Shake. Rattle. Roll.

"You don't love nothin', Evan. You're no use to me. You're no use to anyone. In fact, I'ma choke you out. Say good-bye to the world, Evan."

"Wait!" Evan gasped.

"Wait, what? Ain't no thing. I'ma choke you out *ironically*, Evan, so you be too cool for school. Cool as a motherfuckin' corpse, Evan." He let a little air through.

"I love something! I do love something."

"You do?"

"My cat, Cisco."

"Cisco? After the outlaw?"

"After the networking company."

"Yeah, I'm sho-nuff gonna choke this motherfucker out!" Yellow said to the ceiling, just an amen short of preaching.

"There won't be anyone to take care of him. The people in my building will take him to the shelter and they'll put him down."

Yellow loosened his grip. "Evan, did you just say something that wasn't about you?"

Evan nodded as best he could.

"Where is the shit was in that case?"

"With Fresh. It was gone this morning when I got here."

"Tell you what, Evan, I'ma give you a gift—a gift of passion. You got a passion for finding the shit was in that case."

Yellow let him go. Evan fell back against the glass case, gasping. The man in yellow reached in his vest, pulled out a business card, and threw it on the counter. "That shit turn up, you call that number."

Evan nodded.

"And that's all you know about this encounter, Evan. You got a passion for finding that shit and calling that number. You didn't see nobody, you didn't hear nobody, you don't even know how you got that card."

Evan nodded.

"And shave your motherfucking neck." Yellow pulled a silk handkerchief from his breast pocket and wiped his choking hand as he left the shop. "That shit is nasty."

The bell over the door rang and Evan looked up, surprised that no one was there. No one had been in all morning. Just as well, he could feel a sore throat coming on.

It's done," Audrey said. She opened her eyes and looked around.

"What's done?" said Jane, she looked up from her phone just in time to see a dark shape plummeting out of the fog bank above them. Two things hit the water with explosive impact only about fifteen feet from the boat— *Pow! Pow!*—a water spout shot up and dispersed over and around them.

"Holy fuck!" Jane said, staring at the water.

"Audrey, can you hand me that," Minty Fresh said, pointing to the big, gray suitcase at the stern. His diving mask was on his head. He hit a button on his watch.

"Holy fuck!" Jane said.

Audrey stood, grabbed the handle, and swung it over to the big man, who stepped past the console and set it in the bow.

"What's in there?" Audrey asked.

"Soul vessels," said the Mint One. "After Cavuto, I wanted them with me."

"Holy fuck!" Jane said, still staring at the settling spot where Mike had hit the water.

"Jane!" said Minty Fresh. She shook off the amazement and looked at him. "We need to get into the water."

Jane shook her head. "Too much current, someone has to drive the boat." She wore a wet suit under a yellow Gore-tex rain jacket, which she had refused to take off because she wasn't happy about her butt.

Minty looked to Audrey, who shook her head.

"Fine, fold down that swim platform, Audrey," said Minty. He moved to the rear of the console—his fins now in the space where Audrey had been sitting—sat on the gunwale, then pulled down his mask, put his snorkel in, and flipped over backward into the water. He took one breath on the surface and dove, his fins standing straight up out of the water like the flukes of a sounding whale. Sirens began to sound on the bridge.

"There's enough foam in those motorcycle leathers to bring him to the surface," Jane said. "Isn't there?"

Audrey shrugged . . . *who knows?*

Jane maneuvered the boat to keep it near the point of impact. Without a word, Audrey reached over the stern of the boat and folded down an aluminum and teak swimming platform that formed a little dock at water level next to the big Mercury outboards. Jane pulled a backpack with the defibrillator in it out from under the console and handed it back to Audrey.

They watched the water fizz where Mike had gone in, looking for any sign of movement. A shadow rose in the deep green water and heads broke the surface. A geyser of seawater sprayed into the air as Minty Fresh cleared his snorkel. He looked around, located the boat, then hooked Mike under the chin in the crook of his arm, and started kicking for the boat.

"Backboard," said Audrey. She was still in her nun robes, yellow and maroon silk, now beginning to whip in the cold wind.

There was an orange plastic backboard lashed to the rail on the console. Jane slipped the knot and handed one end of the board back to Audrey, who caught it by one of the many handles. The two of them lowered it over the side and waited. Minty Fresh swam Mike's limp body up to the backboard, then pushed him onto it as Jane and Audrey held it steady. The big man cinched a nylon strap around Mike's chest, then another around his feet, then kicked back to the swim platform, which he launched himself up and around into a sitting position. He allowed himself one breath, pulled his fins off and threw them into the boat, then was on his feet, reaching over the side to grab the backboard.

"Just pull his head up, we'll slide him up out of the water," said Audrey.

They did, sliding the board up, then turning it so it would fit in the open part of the boat behind the console. Audrey and Minty Fresh immediately fell to their knees over Mike.

"Jane," called the Mint One, tossing his head to point. The boat, in neutral, had drifted and was dangerously close to the south tower pier, which loomed above them.

"Holy fuck!" Jane said. She dove for the console, threw the throttle forward and powered away from the massive concrete monolith.

"Easy," said Minty.

Audrey flipped the strap off the backboard, unzipped the front of Mike's coveralls, then his leathers. Mercifully, he wasn't wearing anything under the leathers. The defibrillator started making a high-pitched whine as the capacitor charged.

"Place pads on patient's chest," said the defibrillator. "Charging."

Minty Fresh handed Audrey the pads, which she separated and stuck on Mike's chest.

"Please stand clear. Do not touch patient."

Audrey pulled back her hands, the defibrillator fired, Mike's body convulsed, relaxed, then he started coughing.

"What? What?" said Jane.

"He's back," Minty said. Audrey fell forward across the body and let loose a soul-shaking sob.

Audrey felt a hand on her head, pushed back, looked at the guy on the backboard.

"Charlie?"

"Hey, baby," he said. She lost herself again, sobbing into his chest.

"Ouch, ouch, ouch," said Charlie. "I can't move my other arm."

"Your shoulder is dislocated," said Minty Fresh. "Just try to lie still." He nodded toward Audrey. "She says the ritual will heal a lot of the damage. Don't ask me how. We'll hand you over to the Coast Guard rescue boat like we planned. They'll take you to the hospital."

"Coast Guard closing," Jane said. She turned at the console and looked down on Charlie. "Hey, little brother, welcome back. You're all growed up."

"Hey, Jane." He grinned at her, then looked up, trying to see past his feet. "What about him?"

In the stern of the boat was Charlie's former crocodile-guy body, his wizard robe saturated with seawater, his little duck feet twitching as if he was being electrocuted.

16

A BRAND-NEW DAY

harlie was actually grateful that they made him stay in the hospital over the weekend while doctors evaluated his injuries, mostly, it seemed, because they wouldn't believe he wasn't hurt worse than he was. It gave him a chance to get used to being someone else.

"Mr. Sullivan," said a Dr. Banerjee, scrolling through the chart on a tablet computer, "We analyzed the full-body CAT scan, which we often do in the case of fall this severe, and it appears that you have no broken bones."

"That's great, isn't it?" said Charlie, spraying a little spit. He was still getting used to how Mike's mouth worked compared to the crocodile guy. It was like driving a different car for the first time after not driving for a long time, but human-sized stuff was coming back to him quickly.

"It is. It's amazing, really, considering. You're very, very lucky."

"I think if I was very lucky, I'd have remembered to check the buckle on my safety harness."

"So this was an accident?"

"Absolutely," Charlie said. He'd already talked to a psychiatrist, a social worker, and two people from the Bridge Authority, as well as a couple of guys from the painting crew whom he'd pretended to know.

"We don't see any organ damage from impact, and beyond the bruis-ing, which is fading, and your dislocated shoulder, which should be fine after a week or so in a sling, it's only your mental condition that concerns me. There's no physical evidence of damage to your brain, although you did sustain a concussion, but the memory loss concerns us."

"It's just certain things," said Charlie. "Like I can name every street in the north end of the city, in both directions, but I couldn't tell you the address of my apartment if you gave me two numbers and a letter to start."

The doctor nodded, ticked something on the tablet, scrolled back. "I've also looked at your medical history, and it seems pretty clear going back, ten years. Hernia operation, that's it."

"That's it," said Charlie.

"So you haven't had a major accident in the last year or two? Motor-cycle?"

"No, not that I remember. I think I'd remember a motorcycle acci-dent. Or, knowing how to ride a motorcycle. Do I know how to ride a motorcycle?"

"I don't know, I just wondered. We had to cut motocross pants off of you. The CAT scan showed evidence of a pretty major accident within the last two years. Both hips broken, five cracked vertebrae, cracked ribs, all healed nicely, but recently."

Charlie shook his head. They'd had him in a neck brace at first, but after the CAT scan they'd taken it off. "I think I'd remember something like that."

He caught movement, looked up to see Audrey peeking in the door. "Is it okay?" she said to the doctor.

"Well, hello, sir or madame," said Charlie. "Please come in."

"I'll leave you two," said the doctor, bowing out.

"That's not funny," said Audrey.

"What? You changed your hair."

"I've given up the swoop."

"Who does he think you are?"

"Your girlfriend."

"My girlfriend or Mike's girlfriend?"

"Obviously Mike's girlfriend."

"And yet you were living with *me*. Floozy!"

She leaned over, grabbed his hand, laughing, and started to kiss him, then stopped herself and stepped back. "Weird," she said.

"It's okay," he said. "It's me. I feel like me. Kind of."

"Might take a little while," she said.

What it took was two more days, when she picked him up at the hospital. When he got in the passenger seat of her Honda, as he was reaching for his seat belt, she threw her arms around him and kissed him, hard and long, lots of tongue, not coming up until both of them were breathing hard, then she pushed him away and reached for her own seat belt.

"There," she said.

"Wow," he said.

"We're going to be fine," she said.

"Weird, though, huh?"

"Absolutely." She put the car in gear and drove them across town the to Buddhist Center.

There was an empty apartment in his building—well, Jane's building, now—and Jane was having it cleaned and painted for him to move into, but they still had to figure out how they were going to tell Sophie before they went there.

"It's a lot for a little kid to take," said Charlie, when they got home. He sat at the oak table in the kitchen drinking coffee. "I don't want to traumatize her."

Audrey fussed with the coffeemaker at the counter. "Charlie, she's seen the Squirrel People, she's Death —the *Big* Death. She holds dominion over the Underworld. You're not going to shock her."

"I know. That's got to be really hard. And we don't even know if she still is Death."

"I think you should just go over there and have Auntie Jane explain. Sophie will know it's you. You sound like you already. You move like you. You just, you know, just don't look like you."

"Speaking of which, how's he doing?"

Charlie's former body, the wizard-crocodile guy, sat on the floor in front of the dishwasher, rocking from side to side with the rhythm of the motor. Audrey had brought him home from the boat in a sack and had been caring for him while Charlie was in the hospital.

"He's good. He's doing really good. I mean, he's, well, you'll see. Charlie, come meet a new friend!"

"Really?" Charlie said.

The croc guy made a delighted growly noise as he climbed to his feet and scampered across the kitchen, his head and torso sort of wiggling back and forth as he moved, his lower jaw flapping, leaving a drop of drool on every downstroke, his long dong skittering on the tile between his feet as he moved. He stopped in front of Charlie and made an excited and juicy growling sound.

"Charlie, this is big Charlie," Audrey said, presenting big Charlie with a bow.

Big Charlie looked at her. "You named him Charlie?"

"What was I supposed to do? He was Charlie for a year. I've talked to him for countless hours as Charlie, so when I see him, I think *Charlie*. You're not the only one going through a transition here. Anyway, I've decided on another name for him."

"Which is?"

"Wiggly Charlie."

The croc guy jumped up and down, clicked his talons as if clapping, excited drooly breaths.

"See, he likes it."

"He *is* pretty wiggly."

As if on cue, Wiggly Charlie resumed jumping, his torso, head, and jaw wiggling as if connected by loose springs.

Charlie felt bad for the little guy, then he felt bad for Audrey. "Was I this goofy when I first, you know, when I first moved into that body?"

"No, you were much more coordinated. There was kind of more *there*. Less drooly."

"Really? I mean, look at him." Charlie looked at Wiggly Charlie, then at Audrey. "All that time, you weren't—you weren't creeped out by me?"

She sat down in the chair across from him, moved his coffee cup, took his hand. "To be honest, I was always captivated by your enormous unit."

"Really?"

She nodded, eyes down, humble and sincere.

"Are you fucking with me?"

She nodded, eyes down, humble and sincere.

She laughed. Wiggly Charlie made his breathy, excited noise.

"Come here," Charlie said, bending down. "We need to fix you."

Charlie untied Wiggly Charlie's wizard robe, then wound his dong around his waist and cinched his robe shut under it, so now instead of a creepy little patchwork creature dragging around a completely dispropor-tionately sized sex organ, he just looked like he needed to spend a little more time at a creepy little patchwork creature gym to work off his roll.

"There you go," Charlie said, sitting up to admire his work. "Better?"

Wiggly Charlie frisked and drooled, clicked his talons together in applause.

"Are you hungry?" Charlie asked. "Do you want something to eat?"

More jumping, frisking, and drooling. Audrey sat back in her chair with Charlie's coffee in hand and watched this very strange bonding.

"Let's get you something to eat," Charlie said. He got up and led Wig-gly Charlie over to the big stainless-steel refrigerator.

"I'm making him some shoes," said Audrey. "The toenails on the tile and carpet drive me nuts."

"Why didn't you say something?"

"Because my annoyance at toenail noise seemed kind of trivial com-pared to the fact that I'd trapped you in that," she said. Then to Wiggly Charlie, "No offense."

Charlie scanned the shelves. "Do you want a cheese stick?" He held up an individually wrapped mozzarella cheese stick.

Wiggly Charlie jumped, reached up. Charlie gave him the cheese stick. He immediately clamped down on it, working it with noisy, wet smacks of his jaws, the cheese stick sort of becoming very distressed, but more of it hanging out either side of his mouth than in it.

Charlie crouched down. "Look at me. Look at me."

Wiggly Charlie stopped chomping and looked at him.

"Do your tongue like this? See, like this."

Wiggly Charlie did his tongue the way Charlie was doing it, rolling it. Charlie remembered having to learn to eat with teeth that were made only to tear, not to chew. In the hospital, he'd had to consciously get used to having molars again, not to swallow chunks of food.

"Good," said Charlie. "Now do this with your tongue while you're chewing."

Wiggly Charlie did, and the cheese stick slowly disappeared into his mouth.

"Good! Next time we'll take the wrapper off." Charlie said. "You want another cheese stick?" He grabbed another cheese stick from the shelf.

"Want a cheez," said Wiggly Charlie, very wet, very scratchy, but very distinct.

Charlie looked at Audrey. "He talks." His voice broke.

She nodded, smiling into the coffee cup.

"Want a cheez," said Wiggly Charlie.

Charlie, who was alive in another man's body, who had lost the mother of his child and the love of his life, who had found and sold human souls, been present at hundreds of deaths, who had died and been resurrected, twice, closed the refrigerator and slid down the door as he unwrapped the mozzarella, then began to weep. Wiggly Charlie, whatever the hell he was, was alive, and Charlie wept for the joy of it—that spark of life.

"I know, we can call him W.C. for short," said Audrey, acting as if she didn't notice that the man she loved, evidently, was sitting on the floor, sobbing—giving him that measure of pretend privacy.

"A cheez," said Wiggly Charlie, bouncing on his ducky feet.

Charlie gave him the mozzarella stick, then looked up at Audrey, tears in his eyes. "Let's go see my daughter."

"I'll get my keys," Audrey said.

"Need a cheez," said Wiggly Charlie.

It took them ten minutes to get to North Beach from the Buddhist Center in the Mission District and twenty minutes to find parking.

"I'll get you a permit and you'll be able to park in the alley where I used to park my van," said Charlie.

"That will be great when I visit," said Audrey.

"Wait, what? Wait."

They were at the front entrance, next to the storefront. Charlie had buzzed and they were waiting, since Charlie no longer had a key.

"I can't live here, Charlie. I have to be at the Three Jewels Center. It's my job."

"You can go there for meetings and classes," he said. "I thought you'd live here with Sophie and me."

"I have to be there for the Squirrel People."

Charlie threw his arms around her and pulled her close. "No. I'm never letting you out of my sight."

Audrey patted his back for him to let her loose, but he pulled her tighter to him.

"Are you guys going to do it?" came Jane's voice over the speaker.

Charlie let Audrey loose and looked around. There was a domed security camera in the doorway that hadn't been there when he had lived here. He looked directly into it. "No, can you buzz us in?"

"I guess *technically* it's not necrophilia," Jane said.

"Please," he said.

The door buzzed and they went in and up the stairs. Jane stood in the doorway of what had once been Charlie's apartment, wearing Cal Berkeley sweatpants and a Stanford sweatshirt. "Come on in."

"Is Sophie here?" Charlie whispered.

"School," said Jane.

"Cassie?"

"The yoga center is mad at her for borrowing their backboard without asking, so they're making her stay extra to scrub out all the old chakras."

"Yeah, that's not a thing," said Audrey.

"Whatever," said Jane. "She's going to run by school and walk Sophie home, so we've got an hour or so to kill."

"Why aren't you at work?"

"I'm in banking. We have ATMs that do almost everything."

"Aren't you in real estate loans?"

"I am, but I'm pretty high up, so I don't really do anything. Sign papers and go to meetings. I have an assistant who does the work. They don't even miss me. I'm golfing with important clients right now, I think."

"You golf?"

"Nope. You want to go through your old suits? I've had a lot of them tailored for me, but there's some I didn't get to yet. They should fit you—you look about the same size as former Charlie. You're going to need something for the cop's funeral and this Mike guy doesn't seem like a suit guy."

"He owned one," said Audrey. "It's pretty ratty."

"Wait," said Charlie. "How do you know what clothes he owns?"

"Because I went to his apartment to get the clothes you're wearing now."

Charlie suddenly became aware of the clothes he had on, felt the front of the oxford-cloth shirt, looked at the jeans, the shoes, some sort of sporty black leather walking shoe. "I'm wearing dead man's clothes?"

Jane looked at Audrey with a "What are you gonna do?" shrug. She headed into the master bedroom, waving for them to follow.

"You seem very—I guess, very okay with this," Charlie said.

Jane spun on him at the closet door. "I know! How are you doing? Are you feeling comfortable? Is it weird?" She looked over Charlie's shoulder. "Is it weird for you? Have you guys—"

"She just brought me home from the hospital this morning," Charlie said.

"So?"

"He's our Charlie," said Audrey.

Jane punched him in the arm. "Freak."

She went to the closet and picked a subtle, dark gray plaid wool suit, handed it to him, then took Audrey out into the great room to wait for him to emerge. The suit felt very familiar, yet not. Watching Mike's expression change in the mirror when he moved was strange, like he was remotely working a robot, but he was getting used it. He wasn't comparing it to old, human Charlie, so much, as little, crocodile Charlie, so the differences, for the most part, were positive. He straightened the lapels and presented himself to the judges, who were seated on the couch.

"Turn around," Jane said.

"Very nice," Audrey said.

"A little snug in the shoulders and arms." Jane rose, pulled at the shoulders, brushed at some imaginary lint. "That's how guys are wearing their suits now, though. I think you're good to go. Do you have shoes?" Jane looked at Audrey, who nodded. "Sweet. You guys want something to drink?" She headed to the kitchen.

"I like my tea like I like my men," Audrey said.

Jane looked at her quizzically.

"Weak and green," Charlie said. "You know, that line was a lot funnier the first time I heard it, when I actually hadn't spent a year being weak and green."

"Oh, yeah," said Audrey. "Sorry. Jane, do have you any wine?"

Jane scoffed. "I have red, I have white, I have pink, I have green." She looked at Charlie. "Get over it, Chuck, you're not green anymore."

"Red, please."

Before Charlie could ask for anything to drink, there was the ratcheting sound of a key in the lock and the door opened, flying back on its hinges. In marched Sophie, pink backpack dragging behind her, followed by Cassie, carrying two bags of groceries. Sophie slung her backpack up on the breakfast bar and jumped up onto the stool.

"I need a snack up in this bitch or I'm going to *plotz*," said the darling little brunette with the heartbreak blue eyes.

Jane looked past Sophie to Charlie and cringed, then to Cassie, who was trying to land two bags of groceries on a counter with only one bag's worth of space. "Cassandra, what kind of filth are you teaching this child?"

Cassie finally let one bag of groceries slide into the sink and looked over. "Oh." She combed her red curls with her fingers. "Hi." Then she recognized Audrey, having only really seen her once, and her eyes went wide. "Oh, hi!" She looked at Charlie, really more checking him out than looking at him, as if she might be sizing him up to figure out a fair price for him. "So . . ."

Sophie looked over her shoulder quickly, then to Cassie, and whispered, "Who is that guy wearing Auntie Jane's suit?" Her whisper skills were still developing and were decidedly wetter than required.

"Family meeting," said Jane. "In the kitchen. Family meeting." She crouched down so she was behind the breakfast-bar pass-through. "Family meeting." Her hand shot up and grabbed a handful of Cassie's sweater, pulling her down.

Sophie spun on her stool, her eye on Audrey. "Hey, I remember you. You're that *shiksa* that came here with Daddy." She squinted at Charlie suspiciously.

"Yes," said Audrey. "It's nice to see you again."

"Family meeting!" said Jane and Cassie as they stood, each taking one of Sophie's arms and dragging the child over the breakfast bar into the kitchen and out of sight in the depths below.

Furious whispers, some of them damp, Jane peeked up, ducked, more whispers.

Audrey patted Charlie's arm. He'd stood when Sophie had come in and looked on the verge of either crying or being sick to his stomach.

Frantic whispers, a pause, then a little kid voice: "Are you fucking with me?!"

"Jane!" Charlie barked.

Jane stood, "You taught her that one." Back down.

Cassie stood, nodded confirmation, ducked.

Charlie looked at Audrey for help. "It *is* kind of your catchphrase," she said.

Jane popped up, then Cassie. Sophie came around the breakfast bar as if the great room had been mined, stepping carefully but keeping her eyes on Charlie.

Charlie crouched down. "Hey, Soph," he said.

She approached him, looked him in the eye, looked *into* his eyes, looked around, like she might spot the driver in there. He had felt less foreign even when he was the croc guy. "It's me, honey," he said. "It's Daddy."

Sophie looked to Audrey, who nodded. "It your daddy, Sophie. He just got a new body because the old one was broken."

Charlie put his arms out. She stood there, three feet away, just looking at him. He let his arms fall to his knees.

"Go ahead, honey, ask me anything. Ask me something that only Daddy would know."

"That won't work."

"Why not?"

"You could be tricking me. I'm a kid, we're easy to trick. It's a proven fact."

"Just try."

She rolled her eyes, thinking. "What word are we never allowed to say? I mean, *you* can say it for the question, but *I* can never say it."

"You mean the K-word?"

She didn't move. "You could have just guessed that."

"It's okay, honey. I know this is strange."

More eye rolling, foot shuffling, then her eyes lit up when the question occurred to her. "When we went to Tony's to get pizza, how did we eat it?"

"Like bear."

"Daddy!" She jumped into his arms.

There were hugs and kisses and no few tears, which appeared to be contagious and went on for a few minutes until Jane started making gagging noises. "God, I hate this movie!" She blew her nose on a paper towel.

Sophie pushed back from Charlie's embrace. "Daddy, the goggies!"

"I know, honey, Auntie Jane told me. It's one of the reasons I had to come back."

"Are you going to find them? We have to find them."

"We'll find them," Charlie said.

"Let's go get ice cream, and look for them," said Sophie. "Can we go get ice cream?" Sophie looked to the kitchen, to Jane, who froze like a pistol had been pointed at her. Sophie looked back at Charlie. "Who is the boss of me now?"

"Family meeting," Charlie said.

Sophie ran back to the kitchen. Cassie and Jane ducked down.

"Out here, please," Charlie said.

They all came out of the kitchen, heads down, and shuffled out into the great room. Charlie sat in one of the leather club chairs, Cassie and Jane sat with Audrey on the couch. Sophie crawled into the chair with Charlie and he looked up, helpless.

"Do not start crying, Chuck!" said Jane. "Do not!"

Audrey looked down, veiled her eyes with her hand.

"You either, booty nun." Jane elbowed Audrey.

"Are you a nun?" asked Sophie.

"Different kind," said Jane.

"Flying?"

"Yes," said Jane.

"Sweet," said Sophie.

"Sophie has nun issues," Jane explained to Audrey.

"Flying?" asked Charlie.

"It's a show on TV Land," Cassie said.

"Right," Charlie said. "So, can I take my daughter out for ice cream?"

"That would be great," Jane said, "except everybody in the neighborhood knows Sophie, and knows that Cassie and I are raising her. All of a sudden she shows up with a strange man—"

"Wearing Auntie Jane's suit," added Sophie.

"It's *my* suit," Charlie said.

Jane said, "Maybe we can say we brought you in so she would have a male influence on her, like Big Brothers of America or something."

Cassie said, "Or, we could say that we are thinking of having a kid of our own and we're auditioning you as a sperm donor. See how you are with kids first."

"That seems kind of dubious," Charlie said. "Not that easy to explain casually on the street."

"Yeah, you're right," said Cassie. "I've got it, you're Uncle Mike from Seattle. Rachel's estranged brother. And you're staying with us because you can't hold a job due to your drug problem and some run-ins with the law."

"Yeah, so we've let you work as our manny, until you get on your feet," Jane said.

"Except that money keeps disappearing from our purses," Cassie said.

"And local dogs have started to go missing," Jane said.

"So we made Sophie show us where you touched her on a My Little Pony," said Cassie.

"On my horn," said Sophie.

"She's an *alicorn*," Jane explained.

"A unicorn, a Pegasus, *and* a princess at the same time," Sophie clarified.

"Of course," said Charlie, thinking they were enjoying this family meeting way, way too much. To Jane he said, "You have broken my daughter."

"Everybody thought you were fine," said Jane, completely ignoring him.

"But then," said Cassie, "I went to your apartment to borrow a cup of sugar, and you weren't there, but the door was open, so I went in— "

"And discovered the secret room full of your mummified victims," said Jane.

"We have one of those at the Buddhist Center," Audrey said cheerfully. "Under the porch."

"Audrey, please stop helping," Charlie said.

"What? It's nice to be included."

Cassie hugged Audrey and kissed her on the cheek, which Charlie found both disturbing and slightly arousing at the same time.

"So, if anyone asks, that's the story," said Jane.

"It'll be great!" said Cassie.

"Sure, good." Charlie stood and held his hand out to his daughter. "Come on, Soph, let's go get ice cream."

They walked a few blocks through North Beach, down Grant Avenue past Café Trieste, where Francis Ford Coppola supposedly wrote the script for *The Godfather;* past Savoy Tivoli, the bright yellow-and-maroon-painted bar and café with booths open to the street, where Kerouac, Ginsberg, and Ferlinghetti dined; past North Beach Pizza, two galleries, two leather boutiques, and a lingerie store, then up Union Street, headed toward Coit Tower, to a gelato place that had been there as long as Charlie could remember, and whose seating consisted of one teak garden bench outside and one against the wall inside across from the counter. They ordered scoops in sugar cones and took their cones to the bench outside.

"Your Nana used to love this place," Charlie said.

"Jewish Nana or dead Nana?"

"Dead Nana."

"Your mom, right?"

"Yes."

"Does it hurt when you think about your dead mother?" A serious question coming from a small child with a corona of bubble-gum gelato around her mouth.

"A little, maybe, but a good hurt. I wish I would have paid better attention when I was little."

"Yeah; me, too," said Sophie, who had never known her mother as anything but pictures and stories. She sighed, licked her gelato, painting a dot of pink on her nose. "We're not going to be able to tell Jewish Nana about you being back, huh?"

"No, probably not."

"She'd *plotz*, huh?"

"I don't know what that means, punkin."

"You couldn't find a Jewish body?"

"Been spending a lot of time with Jewish Nana, then?"

"It feels like it."

"Oh, I know, honey."

She patted his arm in solidarity.

"After this, we need to find the goggies, Daddy."

17

COME LAY MY BODY DOWN

For the next two days Charlie tried to get used to the idea of living his life as someone else. He walked around the neighborhood, running errands and adjusting to being outdoors again, among people and traffic and sunshine. He went to the courthouse and applied to change Mike Sullivan's name to Charles Michael Sullivan, so he'd have a quick explanation for why everyone in his life would be calling him Charlie. He accepted sympathy about his accident from the people at Mike's bank, and made sure everyone he encountered knew that he was suffering from mild amnesia and asked them to be understanding if he seemed a bit sketchy on the basic details of his life. Mercifully, most of the people who he encountered seemed to think Mike Sullivan was a pretty decent guy, although no one seemed to know him very well, which worked out great for Charlie.

"This amnesia thing is great," he said to Audrey as she sat bent over a sewing machine, making one of dozens of costumes for the Squirrel People. "You just say, 'I'm so sorry, I don't remember your name, I fell off the Golden Gate Bridge and hit my head and I'm having a few memory issues.' Everyone's so nice about it."

"They're probably envious they can't use the same excuse," said

Audrey. "This is ridiculous!" She snapped the needle up out of the fabric and snipped the thread. "I can't make all the Squirrel People ornate costumes. This list Bob gave me is impossible. I made their original costumes from fabric scraps I'd collected over months. This would be a full-time job, even if all I was doing was collecting material, let alone making a unique costume for each of them."

"Maybe I can help," said Charlie.

"That's sweet of you to offer, but you have plenty to do already. I'm just going to get a couple of bolts of cotton in different colors and make them basic outfits from it, with drawstring trousers, like hospital scrubs. They can cinch them up to fit."

"Sounds good," said Charlie. "You can use Wiggly Charlie for the pattern."

Charlie had gotten used to Wiggly Charlie following him around the big house that comprised the Buddhist Center, the little monster imitating his movements. When Charlie went to the bathroom, W.C. followed him and peed in a plastic mixing bowl that Charlie had used for the same purpose when he had been a little monster. When Charlie sat down to practice Mike Sullivan's signature, W.C. sat on his mixed nut can, using a stack of books as a little desk, and practiced his penmanship as well, which consisted mostly of tearing stationery and licking the pen, then putting inky tongue prints on the paper. Charlie hung some of the more interesting ones on the fridge.

Wiggly Charlie was learning skills, but didn't seem to be getting any more vocabulary, picking up only the odd word here and there and working them into some syntax around the phrase "need a cheez." He also alternated between making an excited, happy noise and a disappointed sigh sound, which he only seemed to make when a cheez was not forthcoming or when Charlie left the house and did not take him. Charlie felt for the little guy, having been imprisoned in that improbable body himself, but W.C. seemed strangely untroubled.

"Maybe life is just easier if you're a little goofy," Charlie said to Audrey. He gestured as he said it, a bit of a game-show-spokes-model-presenting-a-dishwasher flourish. W.C. made exactly the same gesture, perhaps half a second behind Charlie. Audrey shuddered a little at the sight of it.

"I'm not sure how he's even, uh, alive," said Audrey. "Not that I understand the mechanics of any of the Squirrel People, but the engine is their consciousness, their soul. W.C.'s soul—you—left the building and found a new place to live."

"I don't know," Charlie said, rubbing his brow. W.C. mirrored the gesture. "There's *something* in there."

Audrey nodded, a little creeped out by the synchronized mime. "I think maybe when you left that body, there was a shadow or an echo of you left in there."

"Nah, I'd feel part of me missing, wouldn't I?"

She shrugged. "Just don't get too attached to him, Charlie. We don't know how long he will last. He might be like the ladies I used the *p'howa of undying* on."

"Boobies," said Wiggly Charlie, who hopped and made his excited noise.

"See," said Charlie. "He's his own man."

"Really? What were you thinking about just then?"

"I'm going to go grab something to eat," Charlie said. "Can I bring you anything?"

"Need a cheez," said W.C.

Meanwhile Charlie got used to the peculiarities of Mike Sullivan's body. Mike had been meticulous and incredibly considerate to write down all of his bank account numbers, his passwords, even the context of the contacts in his phone, but he didn't explain what the dark spot on his left calf was: it could have been where he'd been poked with a pencil as a child, or it could be a deadly melanoma, but in Charlie Asher's beta-male imagination, it was probably the latter. Despite a dubious medical history, there were qualities of Mike Sullivan's body that were new to Charlie, and delighted him, among them a much more solid hairline than Charlie Asher had been blessed with, and, of course, arms . . .

"Look, I've got guns." He flexed his biceps for Audrey. "I've never had guns before. Do you think they're good for anything, or are they, you know, like breasts, just for looking at and touching." He presented an arm for her to squeeze.

"Breasts are for breast-feeding babies, you doof."

"Sure, there's that, too, I guess."

"I'm pretty sure you'll need them to paint the bridge. That's probably how Mike got them."

Charlie sat down, a little stunned.

"I can't paint the bridge. I can't. I have to collect souls, I have to reopen the shop. I have my own stuff to do."

"But that's Mike Sullivan's job."

"I'll claim that the fall damaged me, so I can't do it."

"But it's obvious you're good as new," Audrey said.

"I'll say I'm mentally unable to do it. The amnesia excuse has worked great so far."

"So you'll tell them you can't remember what color to paint?" She tried very hard not to laugh, but failed.

"You, young lady, are not too old to be spanked," said Charlie, using his stern dad voice, tickling her and trying to pull her over his knee as she squirmed and giggled.

Which was only one of the many, many cues that had sent them into a raucous session of sweet monkey love. In fact, once they had breached the wall of tentative awkwardness his first day home, if it hadn't been for Audrey's duties at the Buddhist Center, and Charlie's need to establish his new life as Charles Michael Sullivan, they might never have gotten out of bed except to slide naked down the stairs to the refrigerator. But when the last attendee for the last meditation session left in the early evening, the crazy new-love sex fest began, and went on until they collapsed into exhaustion or laughter or exhausted laughter.

"Wow," Charlie said, late that first night, lying next to her, catching his breath; a sheen of sweat on both of them, golden under the candlelight.

"Yeah," said Audrey. She ran a fingernail between his abdominal muscles. "Yeah."

"Is this better?" he said, rolling on his side to face her, look in her eyes. "Better than the first time, when we were together?"

"Charlie, this is wonderful, but we only had one night. It was wonderful then and it's wonderful now. I knew I loved you then. I love you now."

"Me, too," he said. He touched her jaw, smiled. "But is this body, you know, am I better now?"

"It doesn't really matter what I say, I'm not going to stop you from being jealous of yourself, am I?"

"I'm sorry. I guess, yeah. I just feel so lucky to be here, with you, to not be, you know, like before."

"I loved you then, too," she said. "But this is nicer. It's okay to say that, right?"

"I guess. But some part of me will always just be a little reptilian monster following his penis around."

"I know that's how I always think of you," she said.

Again, the tickling, and they were off again.

On their second night together they learned just how close Charlie was to W.C. They were making love, slow and sweet and without the slightest worry of getting anywhere, just being there, when there came a scratching at the door. For a second their eyes went wide, then the scratching began again, then stopped, and having been brought back to the world outside themselves, they finished, and Audrey got up and padded naked over to the bedroom door.

"Oh no!" she said, when she opened the door.

Charlie looked over to see Wiggly Charlie lying on the floor, as if he'd been leaning against the door and had rolled in when she opened it. He just lay there, a motionless lump.

"Is he . . ." Charlie sat up. "Is he dead?"

Audrey knelt, reached out, and gently touched W.C. on his wizard robe. He lolled to the side.

"Oh no. That's not right," Charlie said.

Then Audrey lit up, looked back at Charlie over her shoulder with a smile. "No, look, it's okay. He just has an erection."

She picked up Wiggly Charlie by his enormous erect willy and turned to show Charlie. The little unconscious monster jostled limply like a puppet on a stick. "He'll be fine." She bounced W.C. on the end of his stick.

"Wow, you were right about the echo. It's like we have some kind of psychic connection."

"Right, this used to happen to you, remember?" Audrey said, swinging W.C. by his dong to make her point. "As soon as it goes down he'll be back."

"Which is never going to happen if you keep yanking him around by it."

"Oh. Good point. Sorry." She carried Wiggly Charlie back to the doorway and carefully set him outside in the hall—rolled him on his side and patted his little shoulder. "You rest, little guy."

She palmed the door closed, then turned, leaned on the door, and looked at Charlie. "I'm glad he's okay."

Charlie lay back on the bed, looked at the ceiling. She joined him and found a spot between his chest and shoulder that seemed to have been built to lay her head upon.

"He was eating some out-of-date cat food this morning," she said. "I hope you don't have any ill effects from it."

They lay quietly for a moment, considering the situation, pretending they didn't hear Charlie's stomach growl. There was the noise of something stirring in the hall and she smiled and kissed his chest. "See?" she said. "He's fine."

"Before, when I was—you know—when I had Wiggly Charlie's body, did you ever pick me up like that? I mean, it seemed like a pretty automatic response for you . . ."

She nuzzled into his chest. "You mean, pick you up and swing you around by your huge unit? Spray furniture polish on your wizard robe and dust under the bed with you? Like that?"

"Uh, yeah."

"Of course not."

"Was that why my clothes always smelled like lemon?"

"Don't be silly. You couldn't smell things in that body. Hey, what should I wear to the funeral tomorrow? I don't think my monk robes are appropriate, but it's been so long since I've worn a dress."

"Wait a minute. I used to wake up under the bed wondering how I got there."

"Shh, shh, shh, quiet time. Rest. Rest. Sleep." She gently stroked his penis like she was petting a kitten.

There was a thump in the hallway like someone had dropped a bag of dicks.

Which Little Pony is appropriate for a funeral?" Jane asked, flipping through Sophie's closet.

"I don't think any," said Charlie. "It's a wake, Jane."

"Smurf? Little Mermaid? This big red dog, I forget his name?"

"Doesn't she just have a normal little dress?"

"Why are you taking her to a funeral anyway? She's just a little kid. Despite her being the big D, she doesn't really get death. After you, uh, died, it was pretty awful trying to explain."

"What did you tell her?"

"I told her that when you die, fluffy monkeys take you shoe shopping with a black card."

"That's horrible."

"And very hetero," said Cassie from the other room.

"No, it's not. I see what you're saying, Chuck, but Sophie didn't even know Cavuto."

"We're not going for Cavuto. We're going for Inspector Rivera. He saved my life. Sophie wouldn't even have a daddy if it weren't for him, so we're going. Funerals are for the living."

"Fine. What's Audrey wearing?"

"A black dress."

"Well, I can't go now, that's what I was going to wear."

"No, you weren't. I saw my charcoal Armani hanging on the doorknob in your room."

"Okay, I wasn't, but Cassie was, so she can't go, so I can't go."

"Gray dress," Cassie called from the other room.

"Not helping," Jane shouted. To her brother, under her breath, she said, "Can you believe we marched for the right to marry, for *that*?"

"You didn't march," Cassie called.

"How did you hear that?" Jane said. "Do you have this room bugged?"

"Jane, please, can we find something?" Charlie said. "Audrey's waiting downstairs."

Before Jane could dig back into the closet, Sophie marched into the room, past them, pushed her toy box over to the closet, climbed on it, pulled out a blue dress, jumped down, went over to the bed, where she laid out the dress, then crossed her arms and looked at them.

Charlie and Jane slunk out of the room to give the child the privacy she seemed to require.

"It's *my* Armani," Jane said. "You were dead."

"You swiped it when I still lived here. What tie are you wearing?"

"No tie. Cream satin camisole."

"Nice." He put his arm around her, side hug, then hip-bumped her into the couch.

Cavuto's wake was held in the grand ballroom at the Elks Lodge, which took up the third floor of a large building just off Union Square. The enormous room was paneled in dark mahogany, with tall cathedral windows that looked out over the square. There were perhaps five hundred people in the room when Charlie and his family arrived: Audrey on his arm, Jane and Cassie following, each taking one of Sophie's hands between them. Most in attendance were San Francisco cops, all in dress uniform, but there were also police and firemen from a dozen different departments, and more polished buttons than a royal wedding procession.

Charlie immediately spotted Minty Fresh across the room, towering above the crowd, and near him, Lily, in a black lace and brocade Victorian dress with a plunging neckline and bustle, and a black-feathered hat with a veil. Charlie escorted Audrey in their direction, and as they cleared the crowd, saw Fresh was talking to Inspector Alphonse Rivera.

There were introductions all around, condolences, and when Rivera shook Charlie's hand he grasped it with both hands and held it for a second. "Charlie, you have no idea how happy I am to know you're here," Rivera said, looking directly into the eyes of a stranger he'd never even seen before.

But Charlie *did* know, and he believed him, because in the face of a death, overwhelming, irresistible death, what moves you is life, and Charlie being here, even in the body of this stranger, was the thing that would touch this strong, collected cop the most. "Wouldn't be here at all if not for you, Inspector," he said.

Rivera still held his hand. "I'm sorry I wasn't there to help pull you out of the bay. I—"

"You needed to be somewhere else," Charlie said. He could see Rivera was still a little stunned, as could happen to you, mercifully, after the death of someone close. The grief or remorse might come over him later, like a rogue wave, but right now he was functioning, doing his duty, carrying on. There'd be no sloppy songs with his fellow officers for this one, no raucous, funny stories, of which he'd have had hundreds. He was part of the fraternity, but he stood out from every other cop in the room, in the city, in the world, because he knew who, *what*, had killed Nick Cavuto. "I'm going to get them, Charlie."

"Absolutely," Charlie said.

Minty Fresh leaned down, said, "We're going to meet tomorrow. Everyone. We just need to pick a time and place."

"The Buddhist Center," Audrey said. "Noon?"

Minty Fresh looked to each of them for a nod.

Charlie looked around for Jane, Cassie, and Sophie, and saw they were already in a reception line that ran four deep halfway around the great room and was moving, slowly, by a thin, middle-aged, balding fellow in an immaculately tailored suit.

"Brian," Rivera said. "Brian Cavuto. Nick Cavuto's husband."

"I didn't even know he was married," Charlie said.

"Neither did I," said Rivera.

"We should pay our respects," Minty Fresh said, directing Audrey and Lily to go before them to the line with a slight bow.

As Lily went by, Charlie whispered, "Nice bustle."

"I liked you better when you were in the cat box," she said.

Brian took Rivera's hand and held it in both of his the way Rivera had held Charlie's only moments before, gripping and shaking his hand with the rhythm of his words as he spoke. He had that lean, stringy strength of a marathon runner. Cavuto used to say guys like that wanted to be the last one everyone ate if they went down in a plane crash in the mountains.

"Inspector Rivera, I'm so glad you came."

"I'm sorry for your loss," Rivera said, because that's what you say. "Nick meant a lot to me."

"You were his best friend," Brian said. "Nick talked about you constantly."

Rivera couldn't keep up any pretense. This guy had been Nick's husband. He'd know bullshit even if he didn't call bullshit.

"Evidently I didn't even know him at all."

"You knew him," Brian said, patting Rivera's hand. "He was a huge lunch whore." Brian smiled and released Rivera's hand.

"Okay, maybe I did know him."

"That was one of his favorite things. He would tell me at least twice a week, while we were eating dinner, like I'd never heard it before." Brian then did an uncannily accurate impression of Nick Cavuto: " 'Fucking Rivera says I'm huge lunch whore.' That's what he always called you, 'fucking Rivera.' "

"Well," said Rivera, pinching the bridge of his nose for a second, waiting for the power of speech to return. After a quarter of a minute or so, in which Brian waited patiently, not touching Rivera's arm, which might have caused the detective to break up in front of four hundred cops, not offering comfort, just waiting, politely looking at his shoes, until Rivera said, "he *was* a huge lunch whore."

Brian laughed.

Rivera laughed and said, "You've done this before."

"Inspector, I'm gay, I'm fifty, and I've lived in the Castro for thirty-two years. I buried half a generation of friends and lovers before the cocktail. Yes, I've done this before. Not like this, though."

"You can call me Alphonse," Rivera said.

"I'll call you 'Inspector.' Nick liked that. He was proud of being an inspector, a detective, *a working cop.*"

"He wouldn't even take the tests to move up," Rivera said.

"He was where he wanted to be, and for that we can both take comfort."

"I'm going to get them."

"I know," Brian said.

Rivera nodded and moved on. He walked by his partner's open casket but could only bring himself to look at Cavuto's tie, and smile, because someone, probably Brian, had put just the slightest smear of mustard there.

Across the room, Sophie waited with Auntie Cassie for her daddy and Audrey to get through the line, and for Auntie Jane to return from the bar. Among all the cops, the mayor, city councilmen, firemen, EMTs, nurses, prosecutors, jailors, and friends, was the occasional junkie, or hooker, or ex-gangster, most of them standing off to themselves, or trying to, not feeling as if they fit in, but feeling like they needed to be there, because as much as Nick Cavuto had been a rough, profane, bull of a cop, he had also been a kind, fair man, and in the course of his long career had touched a lot of people's lives. Standing out from those, though, were three man-nuns from the order of the Sisters of Perpetual Indulgence, a group who did their service and performance for the community with good humor and, of course, in drag.

The three were all in Kabuki-style whiteface makeup with three different styles of habits. The one closest to Sophie wore a wimple with wings.

"Are you a nun?" Sophie asked.

"Why yes, darling, we all are," said the sister.

"The nuns at my school are mean."

"I'm a different kind of nun."

"Flying?"

"No, but thanks for asking." The sister primped his wings.

"A booty nun?"

"I don't know what that is, honey, but I like where you're going with it. No, we're more like—like fairies."

"Fairies?" She grinned in a kid-rictus and pointed to a vacant spot in her lower gum. "You bitches still owe me some money for this."

"Oh my. We'll see about that. Sister has to go do good deeds now, honey." The nun led her sisters a few feet to the right, where they turned their attention to others in need of mercy.

"Who was that?" asked Cassie.

"Just a fairy."

"Honey, we don't use that term, it's not nice."

"Like Magical Negro?"

"Auntie Jane really has ruined you. Come, let's go blame her."

Lily finished in the reception line first and headed for Cassie and Sophie. As she passed the Sisters, one of them looked at her corset-elevated cleavage and tsked-tsked her as she passed.

"Really, doll, the devil's pillows at a funeral?"

"Only dress I had that was clean," Lily said. Which was not entirely true, but even she knew it was ill-advised to throw down with drag nuns at a funeral, and she felt very mature for the lie.

"Well, they're stunning," said a second nun. "If you got it, flaunt it, I guess—"

"God loves hussies, too," said the third. "Bless you, child."

The funeral was held at St. Mary's Cathedral of San Francisco, which has the distinction of being the only church in the world designed after a washing-machine agitator. There was a wide courtyard that led out onto Geary Boulevard, the main east-west surface artery of San Francisco, and today it was filled a block wide and a half a block deep with policemen from a score of departments all over the state, in dress blues, standing in ranks, saluting their fallen brother in arms.

The cathedral was full, not just the main sanctuary, with its soaring concrete ceiling broken with strips of stained glass, but all the pews that reached back into grotto-like overhangs. The doors on all sides of the main nave were propped open and hundreds of people stood in the outer lobbies, which had highly polished floors and glass walls that looked out on the courtyards and the streets.

If the outside of St. Mary's resembled a washing machine, the interior was a minimalist starship, with the round dais and altar at the head of the nave, and a pipe organ built into a platform that rose and cantilevered over the mourners on the side, like the control center of the great vessel.

Rivera and the other pallbearers stood to the side of the casket, along with an honor guard with rifles and a corps of eight with bagpipes and drums. He stood at ease, hands in white gloves folded in front, as first the bishop, then two priests, then the mayor, the chief of police, the district attorney, a senator, two congressmen, and the lieutenant governor spoke of Nick Cavuto's courage, dedication, and service to the city for twenty-six years. The entire time, Rivera tried not to smile, not because he wasn't grief-stricken or nearly shaking with a desire for revenge, not because he didn't feel the profound space that his friend had left vacant, but because he could hear Cavuto cracking wise through the entire ceremony, calling bullshit on everything the politicians and clerics said: *"You know why those guys with the bagpipes have daggers on their belts, right? So they can stab themselves in the fucking legs to take their minds off the music."*

He could hear him like his friend was standing next to him:*"You know why they play bagpipes at a funeral? It's to rush the soul to heaven because he's the only one who can leave early. Tell me if my ears start to bleed, this is a new shirt."*

Thousands were watching, and Rivera knew that he, the fallen's partner, dare not smile, and he knew that Cavuto would be laughing at him, razzing him, daring him to laugh.

And when they had all spoken, the great organ had played, the final prayer given, the bagpipes started to play, to signal them to move the casket, but instead the crowd parted and a solitary figure came up the aisle, female, thin, dressed head to toe in beaded lace, a veiled pillar of femininity and grace, moving as if floating above the floor. And no one moved. The pipes whined to silence. She turned, faced the mourners, and began to sing.

Without a microphone or amplifier, her voice filled the cathedral, the lobbies, the courtyards and the streets. She sang the notes of heartbreak and loss, of grief unassuaged and glory unrewarded. She sang to the heartstrings of all who could hear—tears streamed and eyes clouded until the sunlight through the stained glass looked like stars. She sang "Danny Boy" and "The Minstrel Boy," in a Celtic dialect, because even though Cavuto had been Italian, all cops are Irish in death. She sang a dirge in an ancient language that no one recognized except that the notes resonated with that part in each of them that could feel the passing of a soul—a part they had never touched before. And when she finished, she was gone. No one saw her leave, but somehow, everyone was left with a bittersweet sadness, satisfied that they had said good-bye. Their vision was cleared of tears.

As he helped lift Cavuto's casket, to take it out to the hearse under the salute of five thousand cops, Rivera smelled the faint odor of burning peat and at last allowed himself to smile.

18

STRATEGY

They met at the Three Jewel Buddhist Center the day after the funeral: Charlie, Audrey, Minty Fresh, Lily, Rivera. Minty Fresh had called Carrie Lang, the pawnbroker, and Jean-Pierre Baptiste, the Death Merchant from the hospice. Charlie had found the Emperor and his men in the utility closet behind the pizza place in North Beach, and strangely enough, had no problem convincing the old man that he was, indeed, Charlie Asher in a different body, and saw to it that he and the men made it to the meeting. The Emperor entered carrying the map bag containing the heavy journal Rivera had given him.

Audrey was accustomed to leading meetings at the Buddhist Center, and they usually held them in what had been the parlor in the grand old house, with attendees sitting on the floor, but for this one she decided that they should all sit on chairs. She and Charlie set them up in a circle. Introductions were made all around, with as little biography as possible, because they could have filled the entire day with the reasons each of them was there.

"Well," said Minty Fresh. "I think Audrey ought to start, because it seems like once again we are dealing with metaphysical shit that she's spent a lot more time thinking about than the rest of us."

"Oh, that's just a load of moo-poo and you know it, Mr. Fresh. You all are much more experienced than I am."

"Uh-huh," said Fresh. "You did a ritual that moved Charlie's consciousness out of a monster you made from deli meat into that dude over there, who you more or less talked into jumping off the Golden Gate Bridge so you could do it. Anyone else feel like they got more experience with spooky-ass supernatural shit than that? Show of hands."

No one raised his hand. Carrie Lang and Baptiste, who knew nothing of the Squirrel People, looked dumbfounded, even for people whose work involved collecting human souls. Wiggly Charlie had been locked in the butler's pantry with the last two mozzarella sticks and a tennis ball he'd taken a liking to, largely to avoid a lengthy and somewhat irrelevant explanation of how he came to be, but also to keep Bummer from eating him. The stalwart Boston terrier had growled and scratched at the pantry door until the Emperor was forced to exile him and Lazarus to the porch.

"I'll start," said Lily, and when Minty Fresh started to object that he had just made a perfect explanation of why Audrey should run things, Lily glared him into silence.

"Proceed," said the big man.

Lily said, "Seems to me, we need to figure out what is happening, why it's happening, and what we need to do about it, agreed?"

Everyone nodded except Baptiste, who said, "I don't even know why I am here. I do my part and everything works out as it should, just like it says in the *Big Book*."

"Speaking of which," said Carrie Lang, who was wearing a casual business suit instead of her usual denim and Indian jewelry ensemble. "I'm guessing that there's a reason that we're totally ignoring the instructions in the *Big Book* not to have contact with each other.

She looked at Minty Fresh.

"We think that the rules have been changing," said the Mint One.

"Right," said Lily, taking back the floor. "Did each of you bring your copy of the *Great Big Book of Death*?"

Rivera, Carrie Lang, and Baptiste all nodded. Minty Fresh said, "Rivera has mine now."

"Good," Lily said. "Do they all say 'revised edition' on the cover?"

Everyone nodded.

"And none of you has ever been out of possession of the book since you received it?"

No all around.

"Yet it's changed, right? M, you knew the text backward and forward, and it changed?"

"Yes."

"All of them did," Lily said. "Spontaneously." She looked at Audrey. "What's up with that?"

"No idea," said Audrey. "All this was going on when I met Minty Fresh and Charlie in their shops, when I was looking for soul vessels. I thought they were somehow trapping the souls. I didn't know they passed on to the next person through the object."

Lily looked at Minty Fresh. "See, she doesn't know anything about it." To the group she said, "We know that the book set down rules to keep the Underworlders or whatever from rising, which everyone broke, causing the shit storm last time, bringing up the Morrigan and that thing with the wings, that Asher saw them tear apart."

Rivera said, "If we try to figure out *why* it's happening, we won't get anywhere. We need to figure out *what* is happening. And I can tell you, I haven't seen the Morrigan, but I've heard them."

Baptiste nodded.

"And they killed Cavuto," Rivera went on. "There's no doubt in my mind. I've seen that feathery goo that passes for their flesh, and we've all seen what their venom does." He nodded to Charlie.

"That hand job in the alley was completely against my will," Charlie said.

"He means killing you," said Minty Fresh.

"Exactly," said Lily. "How did the *Big Book* change? It assumes that you've already broken the rules." She snatched Rivera's copy off his lap and paged through it. She read, *"So you fucked up—* It says, *A new order will be established. In the meantime, try not to get killed or let your world be overwhelmed by darkness forever."*

"That's really not that helpful," said Charlie. "I think we need pushpins and red string. You're supposed to put all the stuff you know on a bulletin board with pushpins, then connect them with red string. It's a must for figuring things out." He looked at Rivera, who was a cop and would know about such things.

Lily looked at the others. "Clearly Asher is still an idiot, so at least we have that on our side."

"Hey!"

"A new order," Lily said. "That's you." She pointed to Baptiste. "He's selling souls on the Internet, at swap meets, that's new. Rivera is new, too. He didn't collect any souls for a year, and Asher's calendar was active as well, yet bad stuff only just started happening. Before the big battle, that kind of screwup would have brought up a world of trouble. It's new."

"Plus the banshee," Rivera said. "She warned me of a new, elegant Death. Something more insidious than what came before."

"I thought she was one of them," said Minty Fresh.

"That was her at Cavuto's funeral yesterday, singing," Rivera said. "That wasn't enemy action. You felt it."

Everyone who had been there, which was everyone but Carrie Lang, had felt it.

"Comfort and consolation," said the Emperor. "I felt it."

"And I think she was there the night Cavuto was killed, but not to hurt him. To warn him. It's what she does. She's a good guy."

"What about the other thing she warned of, the 'elegant Death'?"

"He's here," said Minty Fresh.

Everybody looked to the big man, the same look: *You're telling us this now?*

"I wasn't sure. I saw a car in my neighborhood, early the day we pulled Charlie from the bay. A 1950 Buick Roadmaster fastback. Can't be a dozen of them in that condition left in the world. It's why I brought the soul vessels with us on the boat, besides what happened to Cavuto. In fact, y'all need to carry all the soul vessels you have, old and new, with you at all times to keep them safe."

"Can't they just kill people and take their souls, like the cop?" asked Carrie Lang. She looked quickly to Rivera. "Sorry, I mean the policeman. Your partner."

"That's just it," said Minty Fresh. "They didn't get his soul. He came up in your calendar just before they attacked him. I saw it when I was at your shop." He looked to Rivera. "Show them."

Rivera reached into a leather briefcase beside his chair and pulled out a very large, short-barreled, stainless-steel revolver. He held it up so everyone could see. "Brian, Cavuto's husband, asked me to come by their house yesterday after the services. He said Nick wanted me to have it."

"I thought they'd gotten it," said Carrie Lang. "That I wouldn't be able to retrieve it at all."

"What? What?" Lily said.

To everyone in the room except her and the Emperor, the revolver was glowing a dull red. Charlie leaned over and whispered to Lily. "It was Nick Cavuto's soul vessel."

"Oh!" Lily said. "You said he shot the Morrigan with a revolver. Shouldn't it be in evidence or something."

"This is a different one," said Rivera. He handed the big revolver to Carrie Lang, who tucked it into her oversized purse.

"He had two of those?" Lily looked to Minty Fresh, who shrugged. He had two enormous Desert Eagle .50-caliber automatics he'd carried during the last debacle. "Okay, so it's not a penis-size thing," Lily said.

"Some evil shit out there, Darque," Minty said. A smile.

"Wait," Charlie said. "Back up. How do you know that this Buick is this 'elegant Death' the banshee warned about?"

"Teeth marks," said Minty Fresh.

"Huh?" said Charlie, and a chorus of various "huhs" and "whats" sounded around the room.

"You have any idea how much steel they put in the bumper of a 1950 Buick?" Minty asked. "In the bodywork?"

"A lot?" ventured Charlie, not seeing where this was going.

"A shitload. That car is as heavy as any two modern cars, and in the back of it, through the bumper and up onto the rear of the body, were two bite marks. Clear as day." He held his hands apart as if he were holding an imaginary volley ball. "About this big. Through the metal. Through the mother-fucking bumper. Y'all ever seen a creature could do something like that?"

There was a pause. Thinking.

"The goggies," said Charlie.

"Hellhounds," Lily said at the same time.

"That's right, motherfuckin' hellhounds. Whatever was driving that Buick got hellhounds on his tail."

Charlie said, "And they disappeared, about the time—"

"That the Morrigan showed up," said Rivera.

Lily said, "And the hellhounds showed up in the first place to protect Sophie from the Morrigan."

"Where *is* Sophie?" asked Minty Fresh. "She's kicked their ass before, she can—"

"She's seven," said Charlie.

"She's the Luminatus," said Lily. "She's the *Big Death*."

"Maybe," said Charlie. "Maybe not. Does anyone have pushpins in their car? I just think I could get a better handle on all of this if we had pushpins and some red string."

"*Maybe not?*" said Minty Fresh. "Did you say *maybe not?*"

Charlie rubbed his forehead as if he was thinking, when he was actually just stalling for time. Mike Sullivan had less forehead and more hair than Charlie was used to, so he found that the forehead rubbing wasn't really working.

"*Maybe not?*" Minty Fresh repeated. "Sophie is *maybe* motherfucking *not* the Luminatus—the only thing that kept the whole damn city from being destroyed last time? Maybe not?"

"We think she might not have her powers anymore," Charlie said.

"You think *maybe* you ought to find out?" asked Minty Fresh.

"Probably," said Charlie.

"A few months ago, Bummer lost the hellhound powers she bestowed upon him," said the Emperor, being helpful. "It was a relief, really. He had such a penchant for biting the tires off of Volvos. I don't know why. He still enjoys barking at them."

"Excuse me?" said Jean-Pierre Baptiste. "Could someone tell me what all of you are talking about, please?"

"*Us*," said Carrie Lang. "Tell *us*."

And so they did, running through the whole history of what had happened before, glossing over the bits about Audrey and the Squirrel People as if that was just a minor thing that had passed, not mentioning that they had been the ones who had saved Carrie Lang from the Morrigan by duct taping her up and hiding her in a dumpster, as she was still a bit traumatized by the event, focusing more on how Sophie had basically vaporized the Morrigan with a wave of her hand.

When they were finished, Carrie Lang said, "Whoa. A little kid?"

"She's in the advanced reading group," said Charlie.

Carrie Lang said, "So now you think there could be a thousand souls unretrieved?"

"Maybe more," said Rivera. "I've gone back to the early names on my calendar. I haven't found one soul vessel from those."

"Plus all those on my calendar," said Charlie. "While I was— uh— unable to retrieve them."

"The *Big Book* revised edition still says that it would be really bad if they ended up with the powers of darkness," Lily said, tapping the page in Rivera's copy of the *Big Book*. "There's no way to know how many souls have been missed."

"I have a list," said the Emperor, and they all turned to him. He pulled the journal from his map bag and held it up. "Here."

Lily handed the *Big Book* back to Rivera and crossed the circle to get the Emperor's journal. They all watched as she leafed through it, hundreds of pages of names in two, single-spaced columns per page, printed in the meticulous hand lettering of an engineer. "You have nice handwriting," she said. She flipped back and forth. "You have dates next to them. These aren't just for the last year."

"I was given the dates along with the names."

"Some of these go back to the 1700s."

"Yes," said the Emperor.

"Who gave you the names, Your Grace?" Charlie asked.

"I got many from the library. And public records. Inspector Rivera was very helpful with that. But some were given to me by the dead themselves. While I slept. The older ones. When I awoke, I would know all the names and the dates next to them."

Lily closed the journal with a finger in it to hold her place. "So, basically, I'm the only one here who doesn't have a superpower. Even the crazy homeless guy has a special power, but not me?"

"That's not true, Lily," Charlie said. "The Emperor may be fabricating all of this."

"A distinct possibility," said the Emperor.

Lily looked around the circle. "I need each of your date books. Cough 'em up." She collected the date books from the five Death Merchants then slung her messenger bag over her shoulder. "Audrey, I need a place to work and I need your Wi-Fi password."

"What are you doing, Darque?" Minty Fresh asked.

"I'm going to check the names in all of your date books against the Emperor's list. Then I'm going to check as many of the names with the old dates with what I can find on the Web. If they match, we have a list of the unaccounted for."

"There's a table in the kitchen where you can spread out," said Audrey, standing. "And an outlet where you can plug in your laptop."

As Lily followed Audrey out of the parlor she grumbled, "I feel like the accountant for the Justice League. If someone finds a magical cat or an enchanted stapler or something, I'm calling dibs, you got it?" She looked around the circle as everybody nodded. "Good, give me half an hour."

While Audrey was out of the room, Minty said to Charlie, "So when do you have to go back to painting the bridge?"

"I don't. They offered me a disability settlement. Post-traumatic stress. I can take the settlement or they'll train me for a job that's not on the bridge. The gardens or the tourist center."

"Take the settlement, and the time off," said Fresh. "Get your shop up and running again. You saved the city, gave your life, really. *THE MAN* can help you out for a while."

"I know," said Charlie, fidgeting in his chair. "But whenever I used to hear that expression I always thought I was *THE MAN*."

"No, you're *A* man," said Audrey, returning to the room. "Kind of . . ."

Minty Fresh laughed and high-fived Audrey. "I always liked you," he said.

There came a scratching at the door to the butler's pantry, just behind where Charlie was sitting. He tapped the door lightly with his palm. "Settle," he whispered, in a way that made no one at all look away from him. "New puppy," he explained.

The scratching became more frantic. He reached back and opened the door just a crack.

"Need a cheez," came a little voice at about shin level.

"Play with your ball. We're out of cheese."

"Need a cheez," said the voice again.

Charlie closed the door, grinned at everyone, embarrassed, as the scratching resumed. "Maybe if you show him your boobs," he said to Audrey.

Now, Charlie pretty much had everyone's attention.

"No," Audrey said, crossing her arms.

"Excuse me," Charlie said. He got up, moved his chair, then got down on his knees and opened the door again.

"Need a cheez," said the voice.

Charlie opened the door a couple of inches, reached in, grabbed something, and threw it. "Go play." They could all hear the distinct sound of a tennis ball bouncing off surfaces and something scurrying after it, then nothing.

"There," Charlie said, getting back in his seat. "He'll be fine."

"I have a basset hound," said Carrie Lang. "Showing him my boobs doesn't really have much of an effect on him."

"Hmm," Audrey said. "Go figure." She moved to the center of the floor. "Okay, here's what I've been thinking, about this new order." She paused a moment, seeing if they would let her out of further explanations about her dog-training methods. Everyone appeared to be letting it go and she felt loving kindness toward all of them.

"The universe seeks balance, order. For every action there is an equal and opposite reaction, right?" Audrey was suddenly grateful that Lily was out of the room. She was feeling somewhat vulnerable to sarcasm as she waded into this concept. Everyone waited.

"So, for every dark, there is a light, the wheels turn, the planets spin, the machine seeks and finds order. But the universe also oscillates, pulses, expands and contracts—and, I've lost all of you, haven't I?"

"Pretty much," said Charlie. Now that it was out there, everyone agreed.

"Okay, let me come at it this way, *The Book of Living and Dying*, what you call *The Tibetan Book of the Dead*, talks about hundreds of demons and monsters that one will encounter on the journey from life to death and beyond. It describes them in detail, but warns not to be afraid, because they are all illusions, manifestations of human consciousness."

"Like the Morrigan . . ."

"But, they aren't an illusion," said Charlie. "They are very real and deadly."

"They *become* real," Audrey said. "The *Big Book* warns not to let souls fall into the hands of those from the Underworld, but at one time, they weren't in the Underworld, were they? Human souls empower them. They were part of someone's living religion. So was that bullheaded thing, so was, or is, this elegant Death entity in the Buick, so are you guys, you Death Merchants. The *Big Book* is revised because things change, the rules change, and I don't think this whole system of moving souls from one life to the next has always been that way. Every supernatural entity is a projection of human consciousness, going back for, well, who knows how long? And any change is going to be countered, always has been."

She looked around the room. "Nobody?"

"We need to figure out what to do," said Rivera.

"I don't think you can solve a problem if you don't know what it is, Inspector," said Audrey. "I think that the order the universe found, for a time, anyway, was this ridiculously complex system of souls transferring through objects. Maybe there was a wobble a thousand years ago, and this is the universe trying to correct that, but now there's another wobble. Maybe when Sophie was born, somehow as the Luminatus, there had to be a balance, so that horned death thing rose, and the hellhounds came to protect Sophie, and the Morrigan appeared to balance that. The whole conflict changed things, and for the last year it's been seeking a new order. Subtle, like Mr. Baptiste being able to sell souls over the Internet instead of having a shop."

Charlie said, "But if Sophie was on the light side, and has lost her powers, and this new Death has come, with the Morrigan, doesn't that mean that everything is out of balance again?"

"Yes," said Audrey. "It means we're in a wobble. And there's way too much on the dark side of the wobble. Something has to balance it out."

"Some good guys?" said Charlie.

"Not necessarily," said Audrey. "There's order and disorder, we may not perceive whatever is balancing the dark as good. I'm just saying there has to be something to balance the dark, and if it's not Sophie, there's something else, some other being or force—"

"So," Charlie said, "you're saying that every god, throughout history, every supernatural being ever, is a manifestation of the power of the human soul?"

Audrey shrugged.

"The Ghost Thief," Lily said from the doorway. Everyone looked up at her. "Mike Sullivan said that the ghost on the bridge told him we had to find the Ghost Thief."

"Which is what?" said Rivera, starting to show some impatience now.

Lily held up the Emperor's journal. "This is not a list of everyone who has died in the Bay Area, but it *is* a list of a lot of people who have died, most I confirmed. And so are all of your calendars. But none of the names on the Emperor's list are in any of your calendars, except those in Charlie and Rivera's calendars, and only Charlie's from the last year."

"Which means?"

"It means that if your soul object was retrieved, your name isn't on the Emperor's list. And after all those Death Merchants were murdered, the list got a lot longer fast. It means that there are a shit ton of unretrieved souls—souls out of order—floating around or taken by another entity. If what Audrey says actually applies, if they gain their power from human souls, there's something very big and very scary that's been taking these souls. I think that's what Mike's ghost girl was calling the Ghost Thief."

"You know this for a fact," said Charlie.

"No, Asher, I don't know *anything* for a fact, I'm just putting it together from what we know and what Audrey is saying. I'm saying there's a big hole in the system right now and I'm calling that hole the Ghost Thief. Could be good, could be bad."

"So, there," said Rivera. "What do we do?"

Lily looked to Audrey, "All yours."

Audrey said, "I think you need to carry on, collecting soul vessels, getting them to new people, keep as many as you can out of the hands of the Underworlders. The cycle of living and dying is the order the universe is seeking." She paused, scanned faces, got nothing. "I think."

"Maybe it's better to do it Mr. Baptiste's way," said Minty Fresh. "Not have them in our shops. Put them somewhere out of the way, a vault or something. Sell them remotely over the Internet."

"My wife and I can sell them," said Baptiste. "We would just need a photo of each vessel."

"We could move them all to a vault somewhere," said Minty Fresh. "Only go there to get the ones you will ship."

Rivera said, "That might keep the soul vessels out of their hands, but it does ignore the more immediate problem, which is when they come for the souls, they kill us. Does no one else find that a problem?"

"Yeah," said Minty Fresh. "That's why I'm suggesting we hide the objects, then we hide. Stay out of our shops. Just go out to retrieve the new vessels. What do *you* want to do about it?"

"Go after them," said Rivera. "Sure, we try to figure out who this Ghost Thief is, and I'll use what resources I can to help, but the Morrigan require a little more direct action. We know they can be hurt by weapons, and they only get stronger as they accumulate human souls, so the sooner we go after them, the better chance we have of stopping them."

He looked at Charlie. "You need to figure out if your little girl still has her powers, because if she doesn't, her history with them is probably all that's protecting her, and without her hellhounds, that's about it. So even if we can't kill them, we can at least weaken them, slow them down."

Minty Fresh rubbed his shaved head, as if polishing an idea in there, then looked at Charlie. "How did you find them last time?"

"Bummer found them," Charlie said. "I sort of wandered around in the sewers with the Squirrel People until we ran into Bummer. He led us to them."

"They're definitely going to be out of the light," Lily said.

"We heard one, the Inspector and I, in a sewer in the Sunset," said Baptiste.

"That's my neighborhood," said Lily. "I'm officially *pro*-fuck-up-the-sewer-harpies'-shit. Now you just have to find them."

The Emperor held up a hand. "I know where they are."

"Okay, well, that was easy," said Lily. "You don't know where the thousands of souls listed in your book are, do you?"

The old man shook his head dolefully. "I'm sorry."

Baptiste thought it was perhaps the strangest meeting he had ever attended, and even when it was over, and they were all leaving, he looked to Minty Fresh and said, "Mr. Fresh, can you tell me please, what happened just now?"

"You know in a horror movie, when the scientist comes in and explains that there's a zombie virus or there are vampires in the city?"

"Yes."

"That's what this was, but instead of a scientist, we had a crazy old man who thinks he's the Emperor of San Francisco."

"Oh, I see," said Baptiste, who really didn't see.

He stood on the porch of the big Victorian, gathering his thoughts, searching in his messenger bag for his car keys as the others made their way to the street.

"Pssst!"

A noise at his feet, no, below his feet. It was coming from beside the stairs.

"*Monsieur Baptiste!*" An urgent, small whisper.

Baptiste went to the rail and looked over. Below, on the walk, stood a creature about fourteen inches tall with a rotund little body, small hands that looked like those of a raccoon, and the head of a calico cat, wearing what looked like miniature pink hospital scrubs and doll shoes.

"*Monsieur Baptiste, comment allez-vous?*" it said in perfect French.

"Not so good," said Baptiste.

PART THREE

Cry woe, destruction, ruin and decay:
The worst is death, and death will have his day.
—William Shakespeare, *Richard II*
Act III: Scene II

19

WIGGLY CHARLIE'S ADVENTURE

Wiggly Charlie lived in a big house with his friends Audrey and Big Charlie. He liked mozzarella cheese sticks, chasing his tennis ball, and putting his purple wizard hat on his willy and pretending they were friends.

One day, he was playing with his ball in the butler's pantry (which was a small room where rich people used to keep their prisoners until they needed them to bring them a beverage). When Big Charlie reached in the door, took the ball, and threw it for Wiggly Charlie, it bounced into a vent behind the wastebasket and disappeared.

Wiggly Charlie didn't even take time to be sad or think how throwing his ball down a vent was kind of a dick move, but instead jumped right into the vent after it. He slid down and down and plopped out on his bottom in the dirt. All around him were little lights in many colors. He stood up and turned all around, looking up at all the pretty colors. He saw that there was a little doorway, just his size, and on the other side he could see his ball.

He went through the doorway and found himself in a passageway made of green glass, so he could still see the colored lights attached to the floor joists of the big house, as well as others that were strung through the glass hallway. He threw his ball and chased it down the hallway, catching it in his mouth just as it was about to roll down some stairs. Then he saw something wonderful.

In front of him was a big round room, like a hole, only nicer, and all around it were little people just like him. He dripped drool on his toes as he looked around in wonder at all the little people, all with different heads and feet, different hands and different clothes, all just about his size. They gathered around a stage in the center of the round room as one of them talked at the others.

"Bring the head for Theeb," said the little person on the stage. He was wearing a red uniform, had a face that looked like a cat skull, and a very nice black-and-red hat. When he talked, he waved around a spoon that was a fork, or a fork that was a spoon—whatever it was, Wiggly Charlie thought it was very clever.

The little people parted and two of them carried a tray with the head of an animal Wiggley Charlie didn't recognize down an aisle. (It was the head of an opossum, but the *o* was silent, as often happens with the decapitated.) The red suit guy took the head and put it on a table on the stage.

"Bring the body for Theeb."

"Bring the body for Theeb," everyone chanted, and two more little people brought a big piece of meat on a tray and fitted it on the table with the head.

"Bring the legs for Theeb!"

And the legs were brought.

"Bring the voice!"

As each pair of little people brought their pieces, they took tools out of little pouches and sewed the pieces on the body. When the arms were attached, a person with a lizard face wearing a pretty pink dress brought some clothes, and the new body on the stage was dressed. Wiggly Charlie had seen Audrey making clothes just like the ones they fitted onto the body. *These must be Audrey's secret friends,* thought Wiggly Charlie.

"Bring the soul, so Theeb the Wise may give it life," said the special fork-spoon guy.

"Bring the soul. Bring the soul. Bring the soul."

There were many, many little people in the round room now. More than a hundred, but Wiggly Charlie didn't count very well, so he just thought there were many, many. Each of them had a red light in his or her chest, glowing even through their clothes. Now they opened two doors in the side of the round room, and behind it were many different kinds of objects: shoes, trophies, boxes, tools, bowls, rings, clocks, radios—there were many, many things, and each of them glowed a dull red, just like the little lights each of the little people had in his chest.

"*Bonjour*," said a voice right next to Wiggly Charlie, and he was so surprised that he dropped his ball. It bounced down the steps and into the crowd of little people. He looked to where the voice had come from and he saw the very pretty face of a calico cat.

"*Soyez la bienvenue*," she said. She had a pink ribbon around her neck and wore a pink outfit like the ones Audrey made. In the center of her chest a red light glowed very brightly and Wiggly Charlie jumped and clicked his talons because he liked it so much.

"Shhhhh," said the cat person. She held a finger to her mouth, which Wiggle Charlie knew meant he should be quiet because Audrey and Big Charlie did it all the time. She pointed to the middle of the big room, then patted a spot next to her on the stairs for him to sit next to her. He did, and watched.

"*Je m'appelle Helen*," said the cat person.

Wiggly Charlie didn't know what kind of nonsense she was talking about, but she was nice, so he sat down and watched the show going on in the middle of the big round room. "Ball," he said, pointing to the spot in the crowd where he thought his ball might have rolled.

A radio was brought on the stage and set beside the body they had stitched together. The fellow in red raised his fork-spoon and said:

"Now Theeb the Wise will bring life to one of the People."

The crowd chanted, "Theeb the Wise. Theeb the Wise. Theeb the

Wise." Not everyone could say the words, and some just growled in rhythm or stamped their feet. "Theeb the Wise! Theeb the Wise! Theeb the Wise!"

Fork-Spoon Guy took papers from his red coat and spread them out on the stage, then started to chant in a different language. Wiggly Charlie had seen pages like that in Audrey's book room, and he knew that you were not supposed to lick or chew or drool on them, but what he didn't know was that these were very special pages that had been given to Audrey by the high lama of her monastery in Tibet, and she should have probably not left them lying around like she did with most of her things because she was still not good with having things.

Anyway, the Fork-Spoon Guy chanted and chanted, and before long, the light in the radio moved through the air and settled in the chest of the body they had stitched together, and everyone said "ooooo" and "ahhh," unless they couldn't talk then mostly they just hissed or clicked, but when the light had moved the body twitched. It twitched again.

The Spoon-Fork Guy stopped chanting, stood over the body, and said, "He's alive!"

"Alive!" everyone chanted, and Wiggly Charlie bounced up and down and made his most excited sound and clicked his talons because everything was so wonderful and everyone was just his size.

"Alive!" everyone said. And the body sat up. The new little person looked around.

Wiggly Charley jumped to his feet, and as he chanted with the others he bounced down the stairs, clicking his talons. "Alive! Alive! Alive!"

The Spoon-Fork Guy lowered his spoon-fork and everybody stopped chanting.

"Alive! Alive! Alive!" Wiggly Charlie chanted on. And everyone turned and looked to him, even the new person, so Wiggly Charlie chanted much quieter and stopped on the stairs, halfway down.

"Not one of us," said the Spoon-Fork Guy, pointing his fork-spoon at Wiggly Charlie.

"Not one of us! Not one of us! Not one of us!" they all chanted, and pointed.

"Not one of us! Not one of us! Not one of us!" chanted Wiggly Charlie, glad that he wasn't chanting by himself anymore.

The Fork-Spoon Guy came off the stage and the crowd opened up for him as he passed through and came up the stairs until he was standing right in front of Wiggly Charlie.

"Theeb the Wise demands silence!" shouted the Fork-Spoon Guy.

"Not one of us. Not one of us. Not one of us," chanted Wiggly Charlie, the rest of the crowd leaving him hanging. Finally he trailed off and looked around, hoping someone else had been chanting, but they hadn't.

"I am Theeb the Wise," said the Fork-Spoon Guy. He pointed to his red coat with the shiny gold buttons.

"Steve," said Wiggly Charlie.

"No. Theeb," said Theeb. "I did not know who I was, but now I have remembered. I am the leader of the People. I am Theeb."

"Steve," said Wiggly Charlie.

"Steve! Steve! Steve!" chanted the crowd.

"No!" shouted Theeb. "She put our souls in these vessels, and they gave us false names. I was called Bob, then, but our real names have come back to us. We remember!"

"Steve! Steve! Steve!" chanted the crowd.

"No, you dumbfucks!" shouted Theeb, although he didn't look as sure of himself as when he had started.

"You are not one of us. You are not one of the People. You are incomplete." He pointed to the little light in his own chest, then at the enormous pile of things that were red. "You are missing something!"

"Need a cheez," said Wiggly Charlie.

"Need a cheez! Need a cheez! Need a cheez!" chanted the People.

Theeb bellowed, "She gave us hideous form, and no memory, but *now* we *have* memory."

"Need a cheez! Need a cheez! Need a cheez!"

"Shut up!" shouted Theeb, and the crowd did.

"She gave us no voices, but the new People have voices!"

"Need a cheez! Need a cheez! Need a cheez!"

"She gave us no lips. But we have grown lips!" said Theeb.

"Lips! Lips! Lips!" the People chanted.

"Lips," said Wiggly Charlie, handing Theeb his enormous dong, which Theeb the Wise wisely let drop to the ground.

"Sure, you have *that*, because you are her favorite, but you have no soul."

"Lips," said Wiggly Charlie.

"We were people, and she trapped us in these hideous creatures, but we have her books, and using them we have become more. There will be more of us. Thousands of us! And the People shall all have voices! All shall have lips! So sayeth Theeb the Wise!"

"Steve the Wise! Steve the Wise! Steve the Wise!" everyone, including Wiggly Charlie, chanted.

Theeb the Wise was not pleased, for he was pretty sure his name as a human had been Theeb, not Steve, but then, Steve really did make quite a bit more sense, didn't it? Now he was angry.

"Guards!" called Theeb, possibly Steve, previously Bob.

Four of the People, all wearing the new colored cotton outfits that Audrey had sewn, came out from behind all the soul vessels. Each carried a different weapon, a knife, a hatchet, a sickle, and a screwdriver, although not a spork, for the *Spork of Power* was reserved only for Theeb the Wise. Each also wore a little belt, more crudely fashioned than their clothes, and tucked in it were canisters of pepper spray.

"Seize him!" said Theeb.

"Seize him! Seize him! Seize him!" chanted the People.

"You don't have to chant that!" shouted Theeb, and they pretty much fell silent but for a few stragglers, who were still working the "lips" chant and were behind.

The guards took Wiggly Charlie by the arms and he let them, asking each of them if they might have a mozzarella stick handy, using the traditional "need a cheez" phrase.

"You, her soulless minion, have been sent to us as a sign, Charlie Asher. We will take Audrey's soul, and put it in your soulless body, so she, too, will know what it is to be trapped in a hideous little creature!" Theeb waved his spork maniacally and laughed.

Wiggly Charlie struggled, and two more guards came and grabbed his feet. Audrey gave him cheezes and had boobies and other parts that made him sleepy. He didn't want them to hurt her.

"Take him away," said Theeb. "Tie him up, and prepare to seize the heretic maker, Audrey!"

"Tie him up! Tie him up! Tie him up!" chanted the people, although to be honest, most of them weren't sure what was going on. The guards dragged Wiggly Charlie out of the big round room.

"*Mon Dieu!*" said the cat person called Helen, who was still at the top of the stairs. She hurried off the other way to the passageway that led out under the porch.

20
TESTING, TESTING

On his first day back living in his old building, Charlie picked Sophie up at school and walked her to get ice cream. On their way home, cones in hand, they encountered a rat that was dying in the gutter, probably from poison. Charlie thought, *"A dead rat, well, that would be disgusting and cliché, but an* almost *dead rat, that sir, is an opportunity!"*

Charlie looked around. He didn't see anyone else out walking on this particular stretch of street, at least none close enough to tell what he was doing. He didn't notice the yellow Buick Roadmaster parked on the next block, someone sitting behind the wheel.

"Sophie, honey, you know the word that you're never supposed to say, and that thing you're never supposed to ever do?"

"Yep." She nodded, plowing a nose-shaped furrow into her orange sherbet.

"Okay, I need you to do that. With this rat."

"You said never, ever."

"I know, honey, but this creature is suffering, so this would help it."

"Audrey said that life is suffering."

"You can't listen to her, she's a crazy woman. No, I need you to try it. Just point at the rat and say the word."

"Okay," Sophie said. "Hold this." She handed Charlie her cone and crouched down.

She pointed to the rat, looked over her shoulder at Charlie, just to make sure, and he nodded.

"Kitty," she said.

Lily was sitting at her call station, headset on, tablet before her, watching a French film about a man who goes insane when he shaves off his mustache, when her line rang. She could see on the terminal that it was one of the hard lines from the Golden Gate Bridge. She paused her movie, took a deep breath, and connected.

"Crisis hotline. This is Lily. What's your name?"

"Hi Lily, this is Mike Sullivan."

"Hi, Mike. How are you doing today."

"Lily, this is *Mike Sullivan*. The Mike Sullivan who jumped . . ."

Lily stopped breathing for a second. No one who had actually jumped had called back before. She wasn't sure she was trained for this. Sure, she would have ignored the training, but it would be nice to have it to fall back on.

"So, Mike, it says here you're on the bridge, on one of the hard lines."

"Yes. I'm just sort of connected. I don't know how."

"So, you're not, like, standing there talking into the speaker box or anything?"

"No, nothing like that. I'm just sort of here. Not physically, but it feels like I'm talking to you."

"You're calling from the other side?" Lily said.

"What? Marin? No, right *on* the bridge."

"It *is* you!" His doofuscocity had transcended even death.

"I'm here, Lily. On the bridge, like Concepción promised, like I thought it would be—well, not like I thought it would be, but I'm here. So it worked? Did Charlie get my body?"

"Yes, but that was a while ago. Do you not have the same perception of time?"

"It did seem to take a long time to figure out how to get through to you. I tried asking people on the bridge, even risked going to one of my old coworkers. Nothing. I don't have whatever it is that Concepción and the others had to appear to me."

"Maybe it was you," said Lily. "Not them."

"Really?"

"You're talking to *me* from beyond the grave, although not literally. A lot of people have been on that bridge over the last seventy-five years, yet you're the one she picked."

"Oh, yeah. How's your friend doing with my body?"

"He seems pretty comfortable. He's boning a nun with it."

"Oh no!"

"No, it's okay. She's into it. You met her."

"Oh, Audrey?"

"Yes. So, what's it like being dead?" Lily was suddenly aware of the other counselors in the room looking at her, which normally didn't bother her. Sage was writing down the time on a Post-it, no doubt so she could find the call on the recordings when she reported Lily. "Just a second, Mike." She'd forgotten for a moment that all the calls were being recorded.

She pressed the mute key and turned to Sage. "This guy thinks he's a ghost," she said. "I just need to indulge his delusions long enough to figure out how to get him down. You want to take over? I can put him on hold, probably."

"No. Go ahead," said Sage. "Sorry."

"I'm back, Mike. You okay? One of my co-counselors was noting the time for the recording."

"Recording? That's not good, is it?"

"I just need to get you safely off that bridge, Mike," she said, louder than was necessary.

"Well, I just called to tell you that I was okay, better than okay. I'm, well, I'm not just the me you've met, I'm a lot of people. And there are others here. Thousands."

"Mike, as a trained crisis counselor, I'm not qualified or authorized to give you a diagnosis, but if someone less grounded than you were to say that—that he was *'a lot of people,'* then I would have to recommend he seek counseling."

"Isn't that what I'm doing?"

"Not really a mystery that you didn't have any friends in life, Mike."

"Oh, the recording. Right. I need to know if you guys found the Ghost Thief yet. Concepción says we need to hurry."

"Not yet, Mike. We're trying to figure that one out."

"Oh, okay. Thanks. Keep trying. I guess I won't jump today, Lily. You've changed my outlook. I'm going to go seek some counseling right now." He was possibly the worst liar she'd ever heard.

"Wait, Mike—"

He disconnected. Lily looked over her shoulder to see if Sage was still listening, but the frizzy-haired traitor in cargo pants was already on her way to the director's office.

Well, she's totally useless," Charlie said as he entered the apartment.

Sophie ran by him into the apartment—wailing like a tiny fire engine—through the great room where Jane and Cassie were sitting, and into her room. She slammed the door.

Jane sat up, wineglass in hand. "I'm suddenly feeling a lot better about my parenting skills."

Sophie opened her door and poked her head out. "I liked you better when you were dead!" she shouted at Charlie. She slammed the door again.

"So, good first day back?" asked Cassie.

Charlie plopped down on the couch next to his sister. "She can't even kill a rat that's already circling the drain. In fact, I think he perked up a little. She kept pointing and saying, *'Kitty! Kitty! Kitty!'* but nothing happened. A couple walking down the other side of the street gave me smiling pity nods because they thought she was slow."

"You're not supposed to say slow," said Cassie. "It's unkind. Although, Jane always says it."

"That's because she takes like an hour to vacuum the living room, not the developmentally kind of slow."

"Unkind," said Cassie.

Charlie scooted away from Jane on the couch. "You make a seven-year-old vacuum the living room? That's horrible. You're like a wicked stepmother."

"First, I pay that child a living wage; second, the reason it takes her so long is because she gets to do whatever she wants during the process; and third, she wants to be a princess, so a wicked stepmother is like a pre-rec."

"Well she's not going to be a princess. She's not even the Luminatus anymore."

"You told her she isn't the Luminatus?"

"Well, of course. I need to keep her safe."

"Jane wouldn't even tell her that she wasn't a vegan," said Cassie.

"It's not a diet thing," said Jane. "She really wants to fit in."

"But she's not a vegan, right?" Charlie said. "Lily said you told her she could eat animals that only eat vegetables."

"Yeah, that's when she was a vegetarian. Now that she's a vegan she only eats orange food: mac and cheese, carrots, sweet and sour pork."

"Sweet and sour pork is *not* vegan."

"The kid had two dogs the size of cows at her command. If she wants sweet and sour pork to be vegan, then it is."

"So you just let her do whatever she wants—run around here like a crazed barbarian."

"She likes to think of herself as a warrior princess," said Cassie.

"Are you guys fighting?" Charlie asked.

"It's how we show affection," said Cassie.

"Honestly, I'm kind of sad she's not the Luminatus," said Jane, slouching on the couch. "I feel bad for her. Plus, it really got me through discussions in line at Whole Foods. When the other mothers were going on about how awesome their kids were, I'd think: *Oh, your little Riley is an all-star in youth soccer, can play Bach on the cello, speaks Mandarin, and has a brown belt in ballet? Well, Sophie is the Luminatus. DEATH! The grim reaper. The big D. She rules the Underworld and can vaporize demons with a wave of a hand. She's guarded by indestructible hellhounds that can eat steel and burp fire, so your little Riley can lick dog drool off my Sophie's spiky red Louboutins, bitch!* Now I'll never be able to say that."

"Sophie has spiky red Louboutins?" Charlie said. "I don't think those are good for a kid's posture."

"No, I was embellishing. Really not the point of the speech, Chuck. It was that Sophie had a *thing,* but it had to be a secret. They're all so *gifted.*" Jane said 'gifted' with a tone normally reserved for reference to skin-boring parasites. "You know one mother has her kid in Ninjitsu. Ninja lessons! Kid is seven, why does she need invisible assassin skills?"

"Well, as important as your self-esteem in the line at Whole Foods is, I'm more concerned that if she doesn't have her powers, with the hell-hounds gone, we don't have any way to protect her from—you know."

Cassie and Jane both knew how Cavuto had been killed. They played darting-eye tennis between them until Cassie lost and so had to say something positive.

"Maybe she's just having a hiatus or something. She had them when she needed them, right? Well, maybe her powers will return. Like when she hits puberty. Maybe one day when she's in sixth or seventh grade she'll get her period, the skies will darken, and the Apocalypse will be on."

"That's how it happened for me," said Jane.

"It did not," said Charlie. "I don't remember that."

"You were at camp."

"Well, even if that's the case, we need to get her to sixth or seventh grade. Look, I need you guys to take her somewhere out of the city until this is all sorted out."

"I can't. I have work," said Jane.

"You're sitting around drinking wine at three in the afternoon on a Monday."

"If you give me a day," said Cassie, "I'll get my classes covered. How far do you think we should go and how long do you need us to stay away?"

"Thanks, Cass," Charlie said. "I think maybe a day's drive will do it. Whatever is going on, it's clearly centered in the city. The others are talking about going after the Morrigan. I'll ask them to wait until you're safely out of town."

"Done," said Cassie. "It's sad that your best sister is not related to you by blood."

"I was going to do it," said Jane. "I just wanted to make a bigger deal out of it."

"Why is all this centered in San Francisco?" Cassie asked. "Seems like it should be a worldwide thing, right? Did you guys figure that out in your meeting?"

"I suppose that's something we should have talked about," said Charlie.

When Mike Sullivan first stepped into space, into Concepción's arms, he was surprised not only that it didn't hurt, but just how completely joyful he felt.

"My beautiful Nikolai," Concepción said.

"You said that before," Mike said. "But I'm not—" Then he felt it, the thread of time, going back from the bridge, through a dozen lives in a dozen times, men, women, births, deaths, strung out like lights, the brightest the Russian, the count, Nikolai Rezanov, made radiant because of the light of Concepcíon de Argüello, his love. He kissed her, as he perceived that he could kiss her, because the boundaries of their bodies no longer existed, and they were, for a moment, completely and absolutely one. But she pulled away, and again he could see her, and she him.

"Not yet," she said.

"No? But you waited so long."

"I had to wait, but I was happy to wait, I could do nothing but wait, and I can wait a little more? Then—"

"So, you had to find me before you could rest?"

"Rest? Oh, no, my love. We will be together, at last, but it will not be to rest. Look at them, feel them, all of these ghosts?"

Mike looked, then reached out, aware of every strand and rivet of the bridge and the ghosts that flowed over and through them, over and through one another, oblivious, the bridge their only anchor to any world.

"There is much to do," said Concepcíon.

"I can feel that," said Mike, feeling the tug of the thread of his past lives like fish on a long line.

"And they and many more than them are trapped if we do not find the Ghost Thief."

"Did you look under the couch?" Mike said. "In my many lives, I remember that lost things are often—"

"You fell off a fucking horse?" said Concepcíon, the spell between them broken for now. "You couldn't have told someone to send word. A note?"

The Morrigan were gathered at a sewer junction under Mission Street, staying pressed against the walls, flat as shadows, to avoid the light filtering down from a grate above. Babd was manifesting a slight, blue-black, feathered pattern on her body, while her sisters were merely flat masses of darkness. Babd had managed to snag one of the little creatures who carried human souls—souls that they could consume as they once consumed the souls of dead warriors on the battlefield in the days when they had ruled as goddesses. She ate it in front of her sisters as it squealed, and they watched jealously as the feathers appeared on her with the power in the soul. When she had consumed all but a few gooey drops of the red soul, she threw them each one of the creature's legs, which they sucked out of the air like groupers snapping down fry.

Babd speared the piece of meat the creature had been carrying, bit into it, then spit it out in revulsion. "Just meat," she said. "Ham, I think."

"I thought we liked ham," said Nemain, looking enviously at her sister's talons, which had manifested with the power of the soul she'd just consumed.

"These things holding the souls, aren't they made of ham?" asked Macha. She very much wanted to pick up the little creature's head, which lay in a stream of water in the pipe, but didn't have the corporeal substance to pick up and hold anything. It would make a lovely pendant, at least until she could get a human head to replace it, which was her preference.

"No, it's just meat," said Babd. "But they are gathering it for something. Maybe they have a nest."

"A nest?" said Macha, a dreamy tone to her voice. "A nest, built with bones of men. Lamps of skulls all around—"

"And cushions," said Nemain, joining in the reverie. "To lie on."

"To push a dying warrior down on and fuck him to death," said Babd.

"—lick his soul from your claws as his light goes out," said Macha, shuddering at the pleasure of the thought.

"Oooo, a nest," said Nemain. "We should go back to the tunnel near the Fort, for when Yama brings us the souls."

"No, we should wait for more of these things," said Babd, pointing to the skull. "Follow them to their nest."

"With the souls we get from Yama we can go above," said Macha. "Above! Find the soul sellers. Grow stronger. Hold dominion. Build a nest."

"With cushions," added Nemain.

"I don't trust Yama," said Babd, emboldened by her easy soul score. "The last time—the banshee."

"And the gun," said Macha.

"And the way he walks in the light," said Nemain. "How does he do that?"

"Shhhh," shushed Babd. There were voices in the pipes. Not filtering down from above, but *in* the pipes with them. Small voices. She bridged herself over the top of the pipe, disappearing into the darkness there as best she could, fighting the form she had gained. Her sisters moved away from the grate above and became part of the darkness once again.

The procession of creatures moved by them, perhaps ten of them, each with the little light showing through his clothes, each carrying some bit of meat or animal part, except the last, who carried what looked like a porcelain candy dish that also glowed with the light of a human soul.

The Morrigan followed them for blocks, flowing along the sides of the pipes, watching as the little creatures climbed a makeshift ladder and hopped, one by one, through an open storm grate. Babd moved to look out but the daylight singed her and she pulled back.

"Wait," she said.

When darkness fell an hour later they gathered at the storm grate and looked out.

"I remember this place," said Nemain.

"That tall green one kept running over us here," said Macha. "Cars suck."

Babd rose up, spotted a very large Victorian house across the street, a sign in front that she could not read.

"What is it?" asked Nemain.

"The nest," said Babd.

The director messaged Lily to see him in his office when her shift was finished. She set an alarm on her phone that would go off five minutes into her appearance and would sound like a phone call. The door was open and she could hear Mr. Leonidas and Sage talking. She listened long enough to determine they weren't talking about her, then knocked.

"Come in," Leonidas said. He was dark and a little doughy, with eyebrows that Lily found it hard to look away from because they really looked like they might have ideas of their own. Because of her fascination with his eyebrows, Leonidas thought that Lily paid rapt attention to everything he said and consequently showed her favor over the other counselors. Leonidas had a background in psychology and public health, so being a snarky bitch around him was deeply unsatisfying because he would always try to find the root of her discontent, the hurt behind her hostility; getting a rise out of him was like trying to give a handjob to a parking meter: you were going to end up frustrated and exhausted long before a cop came along to haul you away. In spite of herself, she kind of liked Leonidas. Having Sage in the room, the enemy, was presenting a dilemma.

"Mr. Leonidas," Lily said. "What can I do for you? I can wait until you're done with Sage if you'd like."

"No, please have a seat. Sage brought something to my attention and I thought it fair that she be here to see how it was handled."

"Oh, right," said Lily. "For her thesis. Sure." She sat down, looked over the array of a dozen or so family pictures propped across Leonidis's desk. "How's the fam? Have any more kids?"

"No, still just the six, same as when you asked me two weeks ago."

"Well, I know how busy you are," Lily said. "What's up?"

"Lily, Sage heard some disturbing dialogue in the call center today, and I thought we would all listen to the recording together so we could understand what happened."

"I don't see what she has—"

Leonidis held up his hand to stop her right there. "Let's just listen."

He hit a key on his PC keyboard and Lily heard her own voice coming out of the speakers. Sage sat back and nodded, as if she'd just wrapped the big case on *Law & Order.*

"Crisis Center, this is Lily, what's your name?"

And there was silence. Nothing.

"Hi, Mike," Lily's voice said on the recording. "How are you doing today?"

And there was another gap. And Lily's voice continued, her entire half of the conversation, and only her half, and as the recording ran, Sage started to squirm in her chair and Lily fought, *fought very hard,* not to grin, and was really thankful when the alarm on her phone went off so she could make a big deal out of ignoring the imaginary call.

They listened to the entire conversation, Lily's side only. When it ended, Leonidas looked at Sage and said, "That's it. That's the entire call."

"But she always does—" Sage stopped. "I've heard her before, she's so profane."

"I think we can see what was going on here," Leonidas said. He raised his eyebrows at Sage in what he probably thought was an open, understanding manner, but Lily thought they looked like two bristly caterpillars crouching, ready to pounce. He turned to Lily and she pushed back a little from his desk—the eyebrows, they were sizing her up. "Lily, while I don't approve of high jinks in the call center, I understand the point you were making with this little performance."

"Uh, thanks, Mr. Leonidas," Lily said. *Point them at Sage. Point them at Sage.*

"And, Sage, while you may not immediately see the efficacy of Lily's method, she does get results, she connects with the clients, and ultimately, that saves lives. Perhaps less focus on her process and more on yours and we'll be able to connect with more people. Help more people. Don't you agree?"

Sage nodded, looking into the abyss of one of the buttons on her cargo pants.

It was a Leonidas ass-chewing—as close as he ever got to one. Lily resisted doing a booty dance of triumph against Sage's stupid sweater because that would be immature, so she did it mentally and said. "Friends?" She stood and held out her arms to force Sage into hugging it out. And as she held Sage a little too long, feeling the slight woman get tenser and tenser as the embrace continued, even as she puffed Sage's frizzy-ass hair out of her mouth, exhibiting her victory—nay—her domination, Lily also warmed with the satisfaction of her own specialness.

She was the only one who could hear him—the only one who could talk to the ghost of the bridge.

21

KILLING VILLARREAL

Mike Sullivan hung from one of the vertical suspension cables by one hand. "Look, I'm as light as a feather. There's hardly even a breeze and I'm standing straight out."

"You are lighter than a feather, my love. Let go and you will not fall, and the bridge will not let you blow away."

"Yeah, I think I'm going to wait on the letting-go part."

"You are beyond fear. And you are bound to the bridge just as you were drawn to it."

"Just the same, you died of what, diphtheria? What if right after you died I was to offer you a big steaming cup of diphtheria, how would you feel?"

"They can put it in a cup now? It was invisible in my day."

"A Cleveland steamer was a ship, in your day, my sweet Conchita."

She reclined on the oceanside railing—the walkway on that side of the bridge was closed most of the time, the foot and bicycle traffic confined to the bay side. Not that it would have mattered. People would have walked right through her and have only felt a chill, which was normal for the Golden Gate.

She said, "There is someone who needs to speak to you, my love."

"Another one? I don't understand. Why do they want to talk to me?" There had been scores of them, each telling a different story; a woman who was trapped overnight in a stationery cabinet with a janitor after the earthquake of 1989 and didn't share the Pepsi she had in her purse, a man who hallucinated he was being pursued by a giant squirrel in John Muir Woods. The only thing the stories had in common was some unresolved element, some lesson unlearned, something sad.

"I don't know why, my love, any more than I know why I had to wait two hundred years for you, and that you have been on your way here for two hundred years, but I trust there is a reason. I have faith."

"Faith? But all those years as a nun, didn't you—I mean, did it prepare you for this?"

"For this? No. True devotion is done not for a reward, but for the devotion itself. All my works, all my prayers, were for forgiveness of my selfishness, my weakness, because I could never love God as much as I loved you. What my time as a nun prepared me for was the damnation of being without you for these centuries, which I deserved. For this, you, here, with me, this joy, for this I was not prepared."

Mike settled on the walkway beside her and took her in his arms; she embraced him, and in an instant they were a single entity—the only thing the third ghost could see of them was a white gardenia that Concepción wore in her hair, glowing.

"This is where I'm supposed to talk to the guy, right?" said the third ghost.

Mike and Concepción divided like a luminous amoeba and each stood on the walkway.

"My love, I am going to drift," she said. "Good day, sir."

The third ghost, who wore a baseball uniform, tipped his cap. "She asks someone what a Cleveland steamer is, might be your last—uh, whatever that was you two were doing for a while."

"You heard that?" asked Mike.

"Yep. You want to have a smoke or something?"

"I'm good. How long have you been there?"

"Awhile. You don't get many conversations here, as you probably know. Most people are kind of flighty."

"Good description."

"Besides, I wanted to see what happened if things got hot. Never seen that before either."

"How long you been on the bridge?"

"Ah, not long, ten, maybe fifteen years. Hard to say exactly. Time, right?"

"Do you know why you're here? I mean, any of us, but let's just say you?"

"Cursed, I guess," said the ballplayer. "Cursed long before I took the last out."

"Yeah?" said Mike. "Tell me."

"You a baseball fan?"

"I watched a game now and then."

"So you heard of Skipper Nelson, Giant's shortstop, right?"

"Nope," Mike said. "Sorry."

"So I'll start where it started," said Skipper.

I used to think I was cursed because of the bird, but now that I've thought about it, it was probably because I planned the murder of Villarreal. I first ran across Villarreal in the minors, before the bird, so it was probably him. Probably.

I was drafted as a shortstop right out of high school by the Giants and sent to their double-A team in Richmond, Virginia, the Flying Squirrels, which is where I got my nickname—the squirrel—when I finally got sent up to the majors, because of the way I could track down a grounder and turn double plays—"like a squirrel after a nut," the announcer says, and it sticks. It coulda been worse, though. I could of gone to the Grand Chute, Crotch Crickets, and then had to deal with that nickname for my whole career. A year after me, Villarreal was drafted out the Dominican

League to the Chattanooga Lookouts, which were the double-A club for the Dodgers, a catcher, switch hitter, batted .325 in the Dominican, arm like a cannon. He was an early draft pick, so you knew he wouldn't be in double-A ball for long, but a butterball, five nine, two-fifty—you could time his forty-yard dash with a sundial, so the Dodgers wanted to see if they could take some weight off of him and give him a little more speed on the bases.

First time I meet him he's catching for a one-pitch lefty name Markley, one of those guys you see a lot in the minors—scary heat, pushing a hundred miles an hour, but no movement, a laser beam— you know if it's going to be over, it's going to be right at your knees in the middle of the plate, then, after about eight pitches, he's going to be spraying deadly leather all over the goddamn place, so if you can avoid getting a burning, baseball-sized hole through your body somewhere, you draw a walk. One out, guy before me whiffs so bad, I can feel the wind off his bat in the on-deck circle. But I'm not worried, I can see heat. It's a gift. Then, as I'm walking up, before I even get in the batter's box, Villarreal starts talking . . .

"How you doing? Nice to meet you? Are you married? Got any kids? How's your mother? How was the bus trip? You guys staying at the Travelodge? How's the rooms? You got a mini-fridge?" And he just keeps talking, mostly questions, for the next fifteen fucking years, but I don't know that. Right then, I know, absolutely know, I can hit Markley before he goes all Wild Thing on me, I just have to watch one go by to measure, but I'm listening to Villarreal the whole time, and I whiff. And so it begins . . .

Fortunately, that first one was an exhibition game, so we don't play Chattanooga again, before I get brought to the bigs the next year when the Giants' starting shortstop is trying to turn a double play and gets a knee bent back by a sliding base runner. Already I have a reputation as being nimble on the turn, and no matter what the odds of it happening twice in a season, a ball club loses a starter to a certain kind of injury, they want to avoid it happening again, so

I get the nod instead of the shortstop at Fresno, who has a better batting average then me, but can be flat-footed at times.

Villarreal gets called up by the Dodgers the same season, backup catcher, because their starter has taken a lot of shots to the head and is kind of goofy. In those days, before the concussion rules, if a guy could count to ten and tell his left from his right, he was good to play, and to be honest, I know a couple of ballplayers couldn't pass that test without getting hit in the head, but they have Villarreal ready, and he's been batting over .300 in the minors with a lot of home runs, so he was coming up soon anyway, despite still being shaped like a pregnant mailbox.

So, I finally get my first at-bat in the bigs against the Dodgers. It's bottom of the ninth, and we're tied two to two. The utility infielder playing short ahead of me, Manny Ignacio, a lefty, strikes out three times, and they got a left-handed closer pitching, so the skipper needs a righty at the plate. We're playing in Candlestick Park, which, as you know, sits out on a peninsula in San Francisco Bay, and usually has a prevailing seventy-five mile an hour wind, but what I'm not used to, is about the ninth inning of every game, the seagulls start coming in, getting ready to swoop down on the uneaten fries and hot-dog buns, and they do it like they're psychic or they can read the scoreboard or something.

So it's two outs, we got a guy on second with some speed, and I come up and who is catching, but Chava Villarreal. Chava is short for Salvador, which makes about as much sense as a guy named Villarreal that can't pronounce the letter V even if you put him in a Volvo and drive him to Visalia for Valentine's Day. And he's off; "Hey, man, nice to see you again. How you doin'? You get married? You got any kids? How's your mother? You like San Francisco? You been to the Mission?" And he goes on, and on, and on, until between him and the seagulls diving on the outfield beyond the pitcher, I think it's going to be a miracle if I even see the ball, let alone hit it.

And, "You like Caribbean food? I take you for the best plantains in the city when you come to Los Angeles."

And the pitcher throws me a hanging curve that moves like a balloon, time slows down, Villarreal is a mosquito buzzing in another city, and I let go on that son of a bitch—whole body swing, toes to hips to fingertips, and it has that clack-stick sound of a homer, I can feel it and the crowd can hear it and they're on their feet—it's going to be a line-drive homer, not high, just a rocket off the field, except before it gets off the infield there's an explosion of feathers, a literal explosion—I'm not even out of the batter's box and this circular snowstorm of feathers appears right over the second baseman's head, and this bird drops, crushed and limp, and the ball drops, plop, and the second baseman shakes his head like he's got water in his ears, because he was following the ball to go out like the rest of us, but now it's sitting at his feet and he picks it up and throws me out at first. We go on to win, but my first big league at-bat, I kill a bird, and not a seagull or a pigeon, oh no. My line drive killed a friggin' goony bird. An albatross. Like a five-foot wingspan. I basically knocked a turkey out of the sky with my first hit in the bigs, and the last thing I hear before the ball hits the first baseman's mitt is Villarreal. "Oh, man! Oh, shit! I can't believe it. Oh, man!"

So that's it, right? I'm cursed. But it turns out, I'm not *that* cursed, and I bat .260 that season and we get to the National League playoffs and by next year I'm starting shortstop, but here's the thing, Villarreal is starting catcher for the Dodgers, and we have to play those sons-a-bitches nineteen times during the season. And three or four times every game, for nineteen games, when I come up, that fat fuck is, "So how you doing? You feeling good? I heard you got married. You have any kids? How's your mom?" And between that and the albatross I get to be almost worthless on offense against the Dodgers, batting a flat buck-fifty against them when I'm batting in the high two hundreds, low three hundreds against everyone else.

My third season with the Giants, we're neck and neck with the

Dodgers for the division and the guy I jumped over at Fresno is batting .375 and fielding just as well, so I figure I'm maybe two, three bad games from losing my starting position, so when I come up in the second game against the Dodgers, I say, even before I get in the box, "Villarreal, just shut the fuck up. Just shut your fucking mouth while I'm in the box, you hear me?"

Evidently, though, he didn't hear me, because through three balls, four foul balls, and a swing and a miss, Villarreal jabbered, "I'm sorry, man, I didn't know it bothered you. You want me to shut up, I'll shut up. I'm a pro, man. A batter needs it quiet, I'm quiet. I was just wondering, you know, how your mom was."

Two Dodger games later, right after the ump calls a third strike which was a gift to the pitcher, because it's like a foot off the plate, I turn around and say, "You cocksucker, you don't shut the fuck up I'm going to knock your fucking head off."

And the ump says, "You're out of here." And makes to throw me out of the game. "You can't use language like that," he says, which is more explanation than he has to give.

And I say, "I wasn't calling you a cocksucker, I was calling this cocksucker a cocksucker. You ought to throw him out of the game. He's got to drive you nuts, right? He never, never shuts the fuck up."

It was a Sunday day game, and there was a lot of kids at the park, and it was televised nationally, and they muted me, but it turns out that people read lips a lot better than you'd think, so the cocksucker—and this time I mean the ump—suspended me for two games, and that cocksucker Villarreal hit a game-winning homer against us that day. So I think you can see where I'm going with this. That's right, it might not have been the albatross. And every baseball fan in the country thinks I have a black box over my mouth because they can't even play the highlights without I'm calling every granny watching the six o'clock news a cocksucker.

Every game, it's all I can do to not hit Villarreal in the throat every at-bat. And then we're coming into the fall, and I get my chance. I'm on second when Joe Rollo smacks one into the gap in center, sending it to the wall. I'm hell on wheels going for home, and their center fielder has a good arm, but the third-base coach sends me, and I look up and see Villarreal is blocking the plate, and the ball is going to get there before I do. So I got one choice, and one choice only. That's to cream him and knock the ball loose. I've got four seasons of frustration going down that baseline with me, and not only is this a run, it's my chance. I'm going to take his fucking head off. I'm going to explode him like that ball exploded the albatross. I'm going to leave broken bits of can't-shut-the-fuck-up Dominican cocksucker scattered over the infield. So when I'm a good five feet from him I make my move. I go like I'm going for Olympic gold in the pole vault, which led to what was to be known as the Superman Slide.

Yes, he was a fat fuck, and he ran like he had tubs of lead tied to his cleats, but he was quick, so as I leave my feet, Villarreal has the good instinct to duck, and I sail, vertical, over him, not even grazing him, past the ump (on the replay you can see him saying "what the fuck?" even through his mask) and I land a good three feet on the far side of home plate, having never touched it. Villarreal spins and tags me out while I'm still wondering what happened.

When you kill a goddamn albatross with your first big league at-bat, you think, yeah, that's going to be the highlight they play when I do something good. They're going to go, "Oh, nice turnaround by Nelson, but let's take a look at that time he killed the rare seabird." But no. You show the world that you have the athletic prowess to not be able to run into a fat Dominican when there's a fucking line painted up to him, that piece of film is going to Cooperstown, and ne'er a day shall pass from now to the end of time when your name is mentioned that with it is not shown your dumb ass flying through the air to land with your dick in the dirt to be tagged out as gentle as Jesus picking a baby to be born.

Doesn't get any worse, right? Can't, right? Nineteen times

a season. Regular season. Twenty-five times if you count spring
training games. I got to the point where a week before we played
the Dodgers I'd start losing my shit. Making dumb mistakes in the
field. I get some beta-blockers from my doc to slow my heart down
when we're playing L.A. so I can hit, but I can't field for shit on them
either. So they bring up a kid from the minors who takes my place
as the starter. I become the utility guy, playing when someone is
hurt or bats from the wrong side. Pinch hitting, unless it's against
the Dodgers, because believe me, I'm not the only one who notices
I'm cursed. As bad as it can get, right? If I'm a pitcher and I let a guy
get into my head this bad, I'm selling Chevys in Petaluma, because
fuck-knows I can't go into broadcasting and have the Superman clip
play every goddamn day, and the front office isn't going to hire the
dead bird/cocksucker guy to coach or scout, right? So I still have a
job, year-to-year contract, minimum money, which isn't bad, except
now I have a kid and wife who wants to hang with the wives whose
husbands are making major coin, and she spends and dresses like
them, too. Could be worse, though, right?

Then the Giants' starting catcher decides to shoot his coke
dealer in the off-season in a Miami disco, at the same time that
Villarreal's contract is up at the Dodgers, so that babbling fucking
ball of chorizo becomes our starter. So it's every day, every goddamn
day I go into the clubhouse. "How you doin, Skipper? How's your
wife? Your kid getting big, huh? How's your mom?" Guy has been in
the States ten years now and he's still only got about forty words of
English, which he rearranges a hundred times a day to get up my ass.

"She's dead, Chava. Just like she was this morning! Just like she
will be in twenty fucking minutes when you ask me again, Chava.
She's dead!"

She wasn't dead. My mother is still alive and lives in Jupiter,
Florida, with seven miniature poodles, but that's not the point. The
guy was annoying.

He says, "Oh, I'm sorry, man. Anything I can do? Man, that must be so hard. I lose my mother, I don't know what to do. My heart goes out to you, man. How's your wife holding up?"

So that's when I decided to kill the cocksucker. But not right away, because now that he's not playing for the Dodgers anymore, my batting average is going up and I don't want to jinx it. So instead, I compromise and decide to get him kicked out of the game and ruin his life in the interim.

This is a time in baseball when steroids have become a pretty big deal. On our team, you got Barry Bonds, who is hitting home runs like a mortar barrage, and whose head has grown to a size where when they make his promotional bobble-head, they just do the whole thing to scale, while across the bay in Oakland, Mark McGwire now has forearms like Popeye and will only speak in dialects of horse, and they're keeping José Canseco chained to a post under the ballpark and throwing him raw meat until right before game time, so the league is starting to get sensitive about it. Personally, I stay away from the juice, as I already have what my wife calls "anger issues" and steroids are suppose to be bad for that, but the league is starting to spot-check players, so I figure this might be my chance to get rid of Villarreal without jinxing my hitting.

By this time, my wife was breeding Yorkshire terriers, so naturally I'm nearly able to claim her vet as a dependent on my taxes, so in exchange for a stack of prime tickets behind home plate, the vet hooks me up with some animal steroids in powder form, which are supposed to be tasteless except for a slight hint of dog balls, which I figure Villarreal will never notice because he constantly eats jerk chicken and Caribbean pulled pork, which, for all I can tell, are spiced with garlic, fire, and dog balls anyway. So I start slipping a spoonful of powdered dog balls in Villarreal's Gatorade in the clubhouse, and after a week or so, when I figure it has built up in his system enough to be detected in a piss test, but before he starts barking and humping an ump's leg, I have my wife call the anonymous tip line to rat him out.

Now, it's a hard sell with the league to convince them a guy is on performance-enhancing drugs when he's so slow that when he hits a double, fans can go take a leak and still get back to their seats to see him slide, but my wife, it turns out, is a terrific liar, so I'm thinking that Villarreal is going to be peeing in the hundred-game suspension cup any day, but the day before the spot test, the son of a bitch whiffs on a backdoor slider, winding himself into a knot and snapping the hamate bone in his right hand, which gets him put on the disabled list for three weeks while he has the bone removed. (Turns out the hamate bone is one of those things like the appendix, the tonsils, and algebra, that you don't really need but is left over from a time when we used to live in trees and didn't have calculators.)

But with Villarreal out of the clubhouse for a month, my batting average jumps up twenty-five, my blood pressure drops twenty points, and I'm starting to make some good plays on defense. At this point, when my guard is down, my wife decides that we need to buy a house in Marin with a bigger yard for her dogs, and I'm in such a good mood, I give in, and before you know it, I'm commuting to the ballpark across the Golden Gate Bridge every day.

A week before he can actually start playing, Villarreal comes back from Arizona, where he was doing rehab on his hand, and he's in the clubhouse, all day, every day, "How you doing? You getting some good at bats, man. How's your wife? She like the new house?"—six thousand times a day, and my batting and fielding go to shit again and I'm afraid I'm going to get sent down to the minors unless Villarreal shuts the fuck up. But how?

So my wife is on me about the new house, how there are all these plants in the backyard that aren't safe for her precious puppies and maybe even the kid and she wants them out of there. Foxglove, she calls them. Really tall flowers. I look at the Yorkies, which are about a foot tall at best, and the foxglove, the poison part are the flowers, which are about four feet off the ground, and I tell her I'll get to it next time we have a day off.

"Digitalis," she says. "It's in the flowers. If one of them eats one of those flowers, their little heart will explode and we won't even know what it was from."

"What?" I say. I say, "What?"

"Digitalis. They make heart medication from it. If you have a weak heart—"

Before she finishes her sentence I decide it's time to do some yard work because, goddammit, those little dogs give her a lot of joy and you can't have one of their little hearts explode from eating those horrible flowers. So I cut those sons-a-bitches down, pile them up until I have a whole bale of them, then put them in the garage workshop where the puppies can't get to them, and so they can dry and I can get rid of them responsibly.

So next day off at home the team has, I strip all the dried flowers off the stems and crunch them up in a coffee grinder, until I have about a baby-food jar full of fine powder, I mean really fine, like you pinch it between your fingers and it just sticks in that shape. Of course I don't taste it, but it doesn't have very much odor at all, and I can't wait to get to the clubhouse next game day and get ready for the team meal. I mean I am excited. I cram as much of the powder into the jar as I can, and I'm off to the ballpark. But as I'm driving down the hill out of Sausalito and onto the bridge, I'm almost too excited. I mean, I'm sort of out of breath, and I'm sweating like crazy. Then my vision gets kind of blurry, like vibrating blurry, and I lose sight of the road for a second, I drifted out of my lane a little, I guess.

It turns out that there was a semi-truck coming the other way that stopped me from really hurting anyone else, although don't let them fool you, no matter what they say about how safe Mercedes are, they cannot withstand a head-on with an eighteen-wheeler at fifty miles per hour. Guy driving the truck was fine.

Yeah, it turns out that digitalis can be absorbed through the skin, so I probably should have worn gloves when I was preparing my powder. Who knew?

Villarreal batted .335 that year and you can bet your ass he didn't shut up the entire time. I'm just glad I wasn't there for my funeral, because I know he probably talked until half the people there wanted to join me in the casket just for some peace and quiet.

"So, like I said, I'm cursed. You think it was the bird or the murder plot?"

"I don't know," said Mike.

"Do you believe in karma? Because if karma is a thing, I'm thinking it's the murder plot."

"That sounds reasonable," said Mike. "But why are you telling *me* about it?"

"You don't know?"

"That's why I asked."

"Well, because I'm stuck. I'm not moving on. This isn't how it's supposed to be. Mind you, I don't know how it's supposed to be, but this isn't it—stuck on a bridge forever with a bunch of other loopy spirits. I thought you were the one that was supposed to move things along."

"And telling me about an annoying catcher is supposed to help that how?"

"It's supposed to make you realize it, I suppose," said the ballplayer. "It's like stealing second base. The manager can tell you to go, the first-base coach can signal you to go, the batter can know you're going to go, but you have to watch the pitcher, watch the catcher, watch the first baseman, you have to see all the signs, then *you* know it's right to steal. I'm just one of the signs, but you have to make the move to steal."

"That's the least helpful sports analogy I've ever heard."

"Well, you're not the one who needs help, are you?"

22
FRESH

ird played "Summertime" on the speakers. Minty Fresh stepped
out of the back room of his store when he heard the bell over
the door jingle and saw a man in a yellow suit and homburg hat
coming down the aisle. Minty caught himself against the counter. The
man in yellow pulled up, almost losing his balance, but for sure losing his
cool with the misstep. The man in yellow had no more expected to see
Minty Fresh than Minty expected to see him. He turned his surprise into a
fingertip-to-the-brim-of-his-hat salute.

"Minty," he said.

"Lemon," said Minty Fresh, all of sudden feeling his shit tightening
down.

"I didn't expect to find y'all here."

"I expect not," said Minty.

"I had some business with Evan."

"Yeah, he don't work here anymore."

Lemon looked to the back of the store, where a fortyish African American man in a nice suit was browsing the jazz vinyl.

"I don't suppose y'all got them souls vessels here, do you?"

"No, cuz, I do not. Those motherfuckers are not here."

The man in the suit—he wore caduceus pin on his lapel, a doctor—came to the counter with a first pressing of Mile Davis's *Birth of the Cool*. He set it on the counter, and as the Mint One rang it up on his old-style mechanical register, the doctor looked from Minty, to Lemon, to Minty, then back to Lemon. From the seven-foot, shaved-head man wearing a mint-green shirt and chocolate dress slacks in light wool, to the linebacker-sized gent dressed head to toe in yellow, even down to his yellow python-skin shoes.

"Are you two for real?" he asked.

"Pardon?" said Lemon.

"You two. You look like you walked out of a seventies blaxploitation film. You know, when you reinforce the stereotype like that, you make it harder on all the younger brothers coming up, right? Difficult enough for a young man to make his way without every old white lady in town terrified she just spotted Superfly down on Market Street. Forget about a black *woman* trying to be taken seriously."

He laid down his cash and took his change and the record. "I have a hard enough time getting my son not to talk like a thug as it is, and having you two dinosaurs riding in on the *Soul Train* from the Cretaceous is not helpful. You are grown-ass men. Act like it. Do you feel me?"

Lemon and Minty both nodded slowly, remembering doing that same contrite, synchronized nod when they were boys. The doctor shot his lapels, tucked his record under his arm, and strode out of the store.

Lemon glared at the door, then turned back to Minty. "Harsh."

"Seventies? Motherfucker, I had these shoes made *last* year," said Minty, his voice two indignant octaves higher, looking down at his Italian patent-leather loafers in mint green, as smooth and shiny as pillow mints.

"Excuse me for perpetuating your stereotype," said Lemon, "but we got some archetypical shit to do up in here and we need to dress the part."

"You don't never be lyin'," said Minty, using the phrase for the first time in twenty-five years. "You don't never be lyin'."

"But he *do* have a point," said Lemon.

"Yeah, you *do* be a bit ostentatious," said Minty.

"Me?" said Lemon, pointing to himself, touching his diamond tie tack in the process as if pushing an irony button. "Me? You ever look at yourself, niggah? Nine-feet-tall motherfucker weigh thirty-two pounds—shit, you be ostentatious standing in the weeds wearin' camouflage."

"Style can't be denied, Lemon. That's the difference between you and me: you a slave to fashion and I'm a sultan of style."

Lemon laughed, started to talk, then laughed some more, pointing at Minty to hold the moment until he got his breath. When he did, he shrugged grandly, raised his arms as if appealing to the holy spirit, and said, "Since when was this fashionable?"

"'Bout the time that piece of trash Buick was new," said Minty, grinning.

"Know what? Fuck that niggah, he don't know us when we didn't have but a single pair of raggedy-ass trousers each, am I right?"

"You know you are?" Minty in the groove now of how they talked to each other.

"How your mama?"

"Still dead."

"So sad, that woman a saint, what she put up with. I learned some shit over the years. Counseling. Your daddy was emotionally unavailable, you know that?"

"That's right."

"And *my* daddy treated women like they was throwaway things—you know that fucked up my shit."

"You a broke-dick dog, Lemon Fresh."

"You know I ain't at all what I used to be."

"I was picking up on that. New hat, right?"

Lemon laughed again, wheezing a little bit. "You funny. Hey, you still got that book I sent you?"

"No, I passed it on, like you do."

"You did all right, though."

Minty looked around the shop, at his handmade Italian shoes, back at Lemon. "I coulda used some coaching."

"You know how it is, we was young and stupid."

"We?"

"But we ain't now."

"No, we ain't."

"In fact, I'm not even who I am no more, you know, 'cept for my good looks and charm and whatnot."

"That right?"

"My shit is informed by a thousand-year-old super-enlightened being from the Underworld up in here." Lemon thumped his lapel with an open hand.

"Super-enlightened, huh?" Minty looking baffled.

"What you sayin'?"

"Super-enlightened and he still let you drive that ugly-ass, dog-bit old Buick."

"You saw that, did you? I was gonna get that shit pounded out."

"Look like something happen when you was running. You always was afraid of dogs. Walk a quarter mile not to go by that white dog Miss McCutcheon had fenced up in her yard. Was you running from them doggies, Lemon?"

"That white dog come over that fence once, you wasn't there. I spent best of an afternoon top a Oldsmobile before Miss McCutcheon come get him. I hated that dog."

"You *was* running." Minty smiled. "S'alls I need to know."

"You think you smart. I know you, Minty Fresh. I watch yo mama whip yo ass for having pee pants when you was five. But you don't know me. This ain't gonna be like it was before. I ain't like Orcus."

"Who?" Minty tsking like, *What you wasting my time with now?*

"Orcus. Big, black motherfucker with wings, tore shit out of this town. Kill him a bunch of y'all motherfuckers. You know who I mean."

"Oh." Minty searched his memory. "Oh, yeah, what ever happened to him?" He knew what happened to Orcus. He'd been torn apart by the Morrigan.

"Not the point," said Lemon. "I ain't like him, all bustin' shit up, biting people's heads off and shit. I'm moving in smooth, in the daylight." He held out his arms, just letting sunlight through the front windows get all over him. "Shit about to get real up in here, Minty."

"It feel like it is."

"But nobody don't get between me and what I want got a worry in the world."

"That's good to know."

"Not even that pale white girl of yours."

"Mmmp," Minty said. A percussive sound, like disappointment hitting home. He shook his head slowly, looking at the counter, just wishing, regretting, truly unhappy that Lemon had gone there, and when he looked up, when his head snapped up, his eyes were like golden fire. "You ain't bad, Lemon."

Lemon's eyes went wide for a second, then he tightened down, tried to show some swagger. "You don't know *me*. You ain't just talkin' to *me* anymore, cuz."

"You ain't shit, Lemon."

"You don't know what I am now, Minty. I been fifty years in a cave, I have outwaited mountains, I have slain multitudes, I have brought dark death down on whole cities. Do not fuck with me."

"Uh-huh." said Minty, unimpressed. "Of all of us, all of us that collect souls, pass them on, do the business of Death, *you* all of sudden chosen by this badass lord of darkness to lead his conquest over light? You, Lemon Fresh? You? Why you? What make *you* special? Your blood? Is it your golden eyes?"

Minty leaned on the counter, leaned forward, eyes wide, so Lemon could get his point. "Is that it, motherfucker? *You* the only one in the whole world picked to start a new order, the only upstart from the Underworld to rise in *my* motherfucking city? You? Bitch-ass Lemon motherfucking-broke-ass-Buick Fresh? Niggah, please."

"You need to chillax, cuz." Lemon was suddenly interested in the rack of CDs near him. "You got any Xanax, or gin or something back there you can self-medicate with, 'cause that anger is not healthy. Our peoples got high blood pressure. They a vein standing out on your head, right here."

He took off his hat and pointed to a spot on his own head. "Right here, like throbbin' and shit. You probably havin' a stroke."

Minty said: "You touch any of my people, what happened to Orcus will look like a spa day compared to what happen to you. Now get the fuck out my store."

Lemon looked up from the CDs. "Don't push me, niggah. I will end you right here."

Minty now held his arms out to his sides, angry Jesus style, *suffer all the bitch-ass motherfuckers need an ass-whoopin' unto me, for I shall rain wrath down upon them*—that look.

Lemon took a step toward the counter, then saw something there in Minty's stare that stopped him. He checked his watch, which was thin and gold and looked feminine on a man his size. "You lucky I got appointments and shit." He turned on his heel and strolled away, limping a little from his burden of unshakable chill. The bell over the door jingled and he was gone.

"You a lying motherfucker," Minty said. He went to the back room, found a bottle of cognac he kept in the desk, uncorked it, then paused, corked it, put it away. He didn't need to steady his nerves. He went back out front. Flipped and cued the album on the turntable, then sat on the high-backed stool he kept behind the counter, stretched his legs out, threw his head back, closed his eyes, and let Bird's notes wash over him.

He didn't know what he would have done if Lemon had come at him, if whatever Lemon was now, or what deity was wearing Lemon had come at him—he didn't have a plan, didn't have a clue, but he was steady, cool as a sea breeze, unafraid, because there *was* something, even if he didn't know exactly what it was. Even as he'd asked Lemon, *What make you special?* he had felt it. *You ain't the only one, Lemon.*

Lily said, "Has it ever occurred to you that this Death Merchant thing is just a shitty job?"

"A dirty job," Charlie said. "The *Big Book* says it's a dirty job. But, yeah.

I used to think that we were like Death's middle management, but we're not. We're Death's grunts."

They were sitting at the bar in Charlie's empty shop, there to plan what they were going to do with it. "Whatever you are, it's ridiculous. There's no vacation time, no retirement, and if you fuck up, the universe as we know it will collapse. Plus, the system is insanely complex, and you know what chaos theory says about that."

"Sure," said Charlie. "But go ahead and say so I'll know that you know, though."

"Chaos theory, more or less, says that in any complex dynamic system, it's impossible to predict behavior because even the tiniest variable can have a huge effect down the line, throw everything into chaos."

"Right," Charlie said. "But Audrey doesn't think that chaos is necessarily bad. It sounds kind of bad to me."

"That's because you're thinking of chaos as disorder, but they're not the same thing. And she's a Buddhist, and they're all about just making sure you're paying attention or something. Remember what she said about the universe seeking order, balance, and the wobbles when it can't find it? Well, chaos is the condition between order and disorder, the transition between one system and another. So that's what's going on."

"Well good," Charlie said. "I should check on Sophie. I left her playing upstairs."

"You have no idea what I'm talking about, do you?"

"Yes, it's just that when I try to apply it . . . No. How do you know this stuff? Isn't chaos theory math or something? I thought you went to culinary school."

"That's where I learned it. First day, right after you learn to wash your hands and sharpen a knife. You have to know chaos theory to make basic biscuits."

"Really? For biscuits? I never gave my mom credit . . . Really?"

"No, not really, Asher. Did your brain stay tiny and reptilian when Audrey changed you into a real boy? I'm trying to tell you I don't think we should reopen your store. I don't think you're going to need it, because there's a new system happening. I'm trying to tell you I don't want to work in retail, for you or for Rivera. I have a thing now. I'm beyond working in retail."

"The crisis line, I understand."

"No, not the crisis line—yes, the crisis line, but there's something else. Look, I've always had an empty place in my life that I've alternatively tried to fill with food and penises, but now I have something. Mike, the guy who used to be you, that guy you look like, he's calling me. He's calling me from the bridge—from beyond the grave. Just me, only me."

"Wow," Charlie said. "Like, now? Since—I mean—after he's dead?"

"Yesterday," Lily said. "From one of the hardwired lines on the Golden Gate."

"Wow," Charlie said.

"Yeah," Lily said.

"How's he doing?"

"Kind of hard to say. He sounds happy, but a little freaked out that he'll be accused of boning a nun."

"Hey, that's consensual. And she's not really a nun anymore." He hung his head. "I miss her."

"And it's been how long since you've seen her?"

"Yesterday."

"Oh, for fuck's sake, Asher. One day? M and I broke up months ago, and still when I think about him as I'm going to sleep, my heart sounds like someone falling down the stairs. One day?"

"But I just got her back, sort of."

"One day? Mike told me the ghost on the bridge has been waiting for her lover for two hundred years. And there's thousands of others, waiting. Who knows how long. Blow me, *one day*, Asher."

"Wait, thousands?"

"What? Yeah. He said there are thousands of ghosts on the bridge."

Charlie swiveled on his stool, looked at her head-on—up until then they'd been more or less talking at a Cinzano poster that had been left up from the pizza and jazz days. "Lily, when you looked at the Emperor's ledger the other night, was Mike Sullivan's name in it?"

"Yeah, he was one of the last. But I thought that was just because his soul wasn't retrieved by one of you guys, like all the others."

"Can you call him?"

"Of course I can't call him. He calls through magic or something, there's no number. But I'm the only who can hear him. That's what I'm saying, Asher. I have to stay at the Crisis Center. That's my special thing."

"I've got to go call Audrey. I left my phone upstairs."

"You massive wuss. Are you missing the fact that I am the only person who can speak to the dead, Asher?"

"Right, just you and the Emperor," Charlie said. "Be right back." He ran through the back room and up the stairs.

"It's a big fucking deal!" she shouted after him, then settled into her well-practiced pout. *Fuckstick*, she thought. "Fuckstick!" she called after him, knowing he wouldn't hear it, but saying it because it needed to be said.

"Lily!" called a voice from the stairwell.

Sophie ran, stumbled, hopped, tumbled, down the stairs the way she did, then climbed up on the bar stool next to Lily.

"I needs me my gin and juice," she said.

"No gin," said Lily.

"Just juice, then," Sophie said.

Lily slid her Starbucks over to the kid, who took a sip, made a face, then slid it back.

"Where's Daddy—I mean Mike?"

"You just missed him."

More noise on the stairs, deliberate, heavy steps, lots of them, a tired horse descending.

Sophie leaned over and whispered wetly, "I'm not 'sposed to call my dad *Daddy* in front of anyone because it would be weird."

"Well, we wouldn't want it to be weird," Lily said.

Mrs. Korjev came out of the back room, eclipsing Mrs. Ling, who was right behind her, but identifiable by the squeak of the little cart she always rolled her groceries in, despite having to fold and unfold it to get it up and down stairs, and up curbs, and on and off buses, or trains, about a thousand times every trip.

Lily greeted each of the grandmothers and they returned her greetings with the same distaste and distrust they had paid her since she was sixteen and had first come to work for Charlie Asher.

"Lily," each of them had said in turn, slowly, as a greeting, just short of spitting in three languages after.

"We take Sophie to buy vegetable," said Mrs. Korjev.

"Maybe snack," said Mrs. Ling, defiantly, for no apparent reason.

"Both of you?" Lily asked.

Mrs. Ling stormed forward in teeny-tiny steps, stopping twice to uncatch her cart from the edge of the bar, but stormed right up in Lily's face, well, in Lily's general bosom area, but she was looking at her face. "You think we not know how to take care Sophie? We take care Sophie since baby. We know what good for her. Not Mike."

"What is manny?" said Mrs. Korjev. "Is not real. Is imaginary. He is drug fiend. I see on *Oprah*."

"Dlug fiend!" said Mrs. Ling. Then she said something in Cantonese, most of which Lily didn't get except for "white devil," which she'd learned a long time ago because it was how Mrs. Ling referred to anyone who wasn't Chinese.

"Maybe you ladies should wait for Mike to come back. He shouldn't be long."

"We go," said Mrs. Ling. "We go, four block to market on Stockton Street, four block home. Two hour, tops. You tell. We go."

The two matrons herded Sophie through the back room and out the steel door into the ally, and Lily let them because, really, it was only four blocks, and it was the middle of the afternoon, so there was no danger from the Morrigan, and because she was a little afraid of both of them. "Bye, Lily," Sophie called as the door closed behind them.

Lily's phone buzzed. It was M. She contemplated sending it to voice mail for a half a second, then remembered that he hadn't yet found out about her specialness.

"Speak," she said.

"Lily, where are you?"

"I'm at the restaur— at Asher's."

"You okay?"

"I'm mysterious."

"Good. Look, Asher said he's sending his daughter out of town with his sister. I want you to see if you can go with them."

"No. I have a job. I can't—"

"Dammit, Lily. Would you—" She could hear the exhale, his effort to calm his voice. "I need to know you're safe."

"Chill, M. I'm fine. It's broad daylight."

"Doesn't matter. It's not the Morrigan. We're talkin' 'bout a whole different level of badass. This motherfucker can go anywhere, any time of day. You hear me, girl? You need to get gone, right now, and stay gone until this shit is over or everything is over. I need that from you."

She slid off the bar stool, ran around the bar, into the back room, and opened the steel door into the alley. No one was out there.

"Uh, M, I'm going to have to call you back."

CHAPTER 23
STRANGE ATTRACTORS

Audrey was missing her Charlies. Big Charlie, because he was her companion, her lover, her best friend, and Wiggly Charlie because in the absence of Big Charlie, he was good for a laugh, better company than a dog, and a little more self-maintaining. Sort of like a talkative cat who wasn't a jerk, but could still be entertained by a piece of string.

Charlie had been in his new apartment in his old building for only a day and a half, and she was already trying to think of ways to alter their living arrangement so they could be together, yet both attend to their responsibilities. Her first instinct was to have Charlie and Sophie move into the Buddhist Center. After all, she carried Sophie's mother's soul; the kid would get over the fact that she wasn't Jewish soon enough. But Charlie didn't think it would be fair to Jane and Cassie, who had really thrown themselves into raising Sophie as their own, plus the fact that Charlie, who inhabited Mike Sullivan's body, did not look like the Charlie the world knew as Sophie's father and who the world thought to be dead. The simplest solution, although not the easiest for Audrey, would be for her to leave her position at the Buddhist Center and move into Charlie's building with him and Sophie, which would make her, what? Was her clinging to her title as the venerable Amitabha Audrey Walker Rinpoche, of the Three Jewels Buddhist Center, a regression in consciousness? Was she clinging to a *self* that had no meaning. Was she, in fact, a hypocrite for not letting go of ego, of desire, of attachment, as she prescribed in her teaching?

The bright side was that it might all be moot if the imbalance that seemed to be wobbling through the greater Bay Area destroyed the world of light as they knew it, and they would all be cast together into a dark pandemonium of destruction and disorder. So she had that going for her. She decided that she would call Charlie to celebrate their liberation into doom, but as she was scrolling through her contacts looking for Mike Sullivan's phone number, one of the center's landlines rang. She pocketed her cell and picked up a handset in the kitchen. MIKE SULLIVAN showed on the screen.

"Hi, Charlie. I was just going to call you. You really need to change the name on your phone."

"Audrey, the bridge, I think they're on the bridge."

"You may have to be more specific, sweetie."

"Lily talked to Mike Sullivan, the dead one. His soul, or his ghost, whatever, is on the Golden Gate Bridge. He says there are thousands of other ghosts there."

Audrey wasn't sure how to react, wasn't sure that she should really question Lily talking on a ghost phone, considering everyone's history. "So if that's true—"

"That could be where all the missing souls went. Lily said Mike Sullivan's name was on the Emperor's list. What if all those souls, going back hundreds of years, are on the bridge?"

"I suppose it makes as much sense as someone's soul trapped in an ashtray or a ceramic frog, and we've seen that."

"Or a CD," Charlie said. His wife, Rachel's, soul had moved into a CD when she died shortly after Sophie was born, then moved out of it into Audrey. He'd seen it happen.

"What do we do?" Audrey asked.

"I don't know, that's why I called you."

There was a skittering noise in the next room, then the sound of something falling over, maybe a wastebasket. Wiggly Charlie, she thought. "Wait a second, Charlie. I heard something. Wiggly Charlie has been missing, it might be him. Hang on, while I check."

"Sure."

As she came out of the kitchen into the dining room she saw one of the Squirrel People on the other side of the room and something grabbed her ankle. As she tried to steady herself, something caught her other ankle and she fell forward, losing the handset as she went.

"Audrey?" Charlie's voice over the phone.

"No, I'm okay," she said. "Tripped. Just a second—"

Audrey twisted her head and saw one of the Squirrel People with a duck's face and especially nimble paws pick up the handset and click it off. Then they were on her, all over her, the sound of duct tape ripping, tension around her ankles, tiny claws raking her, pulling her hands behind her back.

Mrs. Korjev led them up Stockton Street and into Chinatown, clearing the way through the crush of shoppers like a blocking-back, Sophie right behind her, and Mrs. Ling bringing up the rear, the wheels on her cart squeaking like distressed mice. At Jackson Street, Mrs. Korjev moved toward a luscious display of pears at the corner market, whose trays of fruit and vegetables ran along the sidewalk and around the corner for another quarter block on either side. Mrs. Ling went in low, did a quick hand-sweep that threw a competing grandmother off balance, and snagged the perfect pear before her opponent could do anything about it. Doing tai chi every morning in Washington Square Park to Motown songs with a hundred other oldsters might seem a waste of time at first glance, but when those slow, repetitive moves were cranked up to marketing intensity, only the grandma with the strongest kung fu would emerge with the perfect pear. *Eat dragon dung, loser.* Mrs. Ling dropped the pear into her cart and moved on to some bok choy of superior crispness.

Meanwhile Mrs. Korjev was quarrying carrots from a display, holding up one after another for Sophie's consideration.

"No," said Sophie.

"This one?"

"No, not big enough."

The market owner stood at his scale, watching the systematic destruction of his carefully arranged carrot display with muted alarm, one eye twitching slightly.

"You want broccoli?" asked Mrs. Korjev.

"Is there orange broccoli?" Sophie asked.

"Green broccoli is good for you, make you strong, like bear."

"But it's not vegan."

"We put on Cheez Whiz, make vegan for you."

"Okay, broccoli," said Sophie.

Sophie moved behind Mrs. Korjev, skipped around the corner, and yipped like a trod-upon Chihuahua.

"Hey, Shy Dookie."

Instead of finding a new crowd of shoppers, Sophie stepped into a cleared space, a bubble of quiet, and in it stood the man in yellow.

"That's not my name," said Sophie.

"That's my name for you," said Lemon.

"Eat shit and die!" Sophie shouted.

Mrs. Korjev came around the corner like a mother bear, spotted Lemon, put her hand on Sophie's shoulder.

"Sophie, is not nice to say. What you say to gentleman?"

"Pleeeeeease," Sophie said, grinning at Lemon, unafraid.

"Know something, Shy Dookie, you ain't the Big D no more. You ain't shit."

"You better be careful," Sophie said.

Perplexed, Mrs. Korjev started to pull Sophie away. "You are nasty man," she said to Lemon. "She is little girl, she not know better. *You—you* should know better."

"Yeah?" said Lemon. He held out his hand to Mrs. Korjev, fingers spread, then closed it in front of her, like a starfish closing over a mollusk. Mrs. Korjev gasped, and collapsed on the spot. Sophie screamed, leaned on the fallen matron's shoulder, and screamed some more. The crowd closed around them, their cell phones beeping for 911.

Sophie looked up to see the man in yellow strolling away. She made the same hand-closing gesture at him that he had just made to Mrs. Korjev. He looked back and said, "You got nothin', Shy Dookie." Despite the commotion and her own screaming, Sophie heard him as if his lips were pressed against her ear.

Rivera loaded shotgun shells into a riot gun, one by one, at the counter of his store. The shades were pulled down, the sign turned to CLOSED. He hadn't opened the store, or even cleaned up since Cavuto had been killed here. There were still books shredded by gunfire and a bloodstain on the floor.

He had collected two soul vessels on his calendar, easy finds, and they were tucked safely into the trunk of the brown, unmarked Ford parked out front. The plan was to pick up Baptiste and his soul vessels, then ride shotgun, literally, as they went to Minty Fresh's store, then Carrie Lang's place, and picked up their inventory. They'd take them all to a vault storage facility that people used for storing fine art and furs in the Hayes Valley, near City Hall. Ultimately, Baptiste would photograph each item, and his wife would post them to sell on the Internet. They would retrieve them for shipping as they sold—those details were not really worked out—the key was to get all the soul vessels they controlled out of reach of the Morrigan and this mysterious man in the yellow Buick. Once the souls were secured, and Charlie Asher got his daughter out of town, they'd move on the Morrigan.

Rivera pushed the last shell into the shotgun, then slipped on a knife-resistant vest that he had borrowed from the county jail, feeling a little silly. He had two bullet-resistant vests of his own, but they weren't going up against assailants with guns. His Beretta 9-mm was in a shoulder holster, and the smaller Glock on his ankle. As he put on a sport coat, one he'd had tailored especially for hiding tactical gear, his phone buzzed. *Baptiste.*

"Are you ready?" Rivera said by way of greeting.

"Hello," said Baptiste. "Yes, I am ready, Inspector, I have all of the soul vessels, even the one stolen from the hospice the day you were there."

"You found it? How?"

"Well, that is why I am calling. It—well—it is speaking French and walking around."

Rivera, armed and armored for battle, his plan arranged to the minute, and steeled by anger and the desire to avenge his friend, felt unprepared for this conversation.

"I don't think I follow," said Rivera. "It's, what, one of those talking dolls?"

"In a manner of speaking. I think she is what Audrey referred to at the meeting as a Squirrel Person. I can see her soul glowing in her chest, and it is Helen, she remembers me, but, well, she is knee-high and has the head of a cat. And hands"—whispering in the background—"the hands of a raccoon."

"And you think it's your Helen?"

"That's what she says."

"Well, you can't sell her on the Internet."

"No, that would be wrong. We are friends."

"How did you find her?"

"She came to me, when we were leaving the meeting at the Buddhist Center. She forced her way into my car."

"How did she force anything if she's not even knee-high?"

"She is very insistent."

"Audrey will know what to do. We'll take Helen back to the Buddhist Center after we leave Carrie Lang's pawnshop."

"She doesn't want to go there. She says they are all mad. She says we must help the cheese monster."

"The cheese monster?"

"Yes, that is what she says. I think. Her French is—she is working on her French. *The monster who wants cheese*, she says."

"Did you call Audrey?"

"No, I called you."

"Well, find a way to get Helen to the car. Put her in a box or something. Even with another stop, we should be able to get the souls in storage before dark. I'll call Audrey."

"Very well, but she heard what you said and she says she will not get into a box."

"Do your best," said Rivera. "I'll be there in twenty minutes." He disconnected then called the Buddhist Center. Voice mail. He couldn't really have a uniform unit run by the Buddhist Center to check on her. He was pretty sure there wasn't even a radio code for "cheese monster in distress." If they ran out of daylight, then the Helen creature could just stay with Baptiste. Or Minty Fresh. Or Charlie Asher. Just not him. He was not going to go into mortal combat tomorrow worrying about a cat-headed lady talking in French about a cheese monster.

You gave us life, but you gave us no voices!" He waved his spork menacingly, only inches from her face.

Audrey lay on the floor in the parlor, her feet and hands duct-taped, surrounded by Squirrel People, many of whom she didn't recognize except for the miniature hospital scrubs they wore. There were more than she had made, many more. Over a hundred.

"What's the matter with you, Bob? If you needed supplies, all you had to do was ask."

"Ha!" said Bob. "Don't call me Bob. That is my slave name. I now remember my name from before, when I was a man. I am Theeb the Wise!"

"Theeb! Theeb! Theeb!" the People chanted.

"Hey, you guys can talk," Audrey said. She felt she really should have been more frightened, but being menaced with a spork by a fourteen-inch-tall megalomaniac in a beefeater's uniform seemed too absurd to be frightening. Especially when she had collected and sewn his parts together herself. "What did you do?"

"We have collected our bodies from markets across the city, parts from Chinatown, from animals who died in the road, from trash bins. We have taken these unwanted parts, and we have made new People. We have stolen the souls from the Death Merchants and with the *Book of the Dead* we have given them voices."

"I didn't know how to do that when I made them," said Audrey. She really felt quite bad about it. She'd learned as she'd gone along. Bob and Wiggly Charlie had really been the finest examples of her craft, although there had been some mistakes along the way.

"You have trapped us in these horrible meat creatures, with no voices, with no genitals, except for him." Two Squirrel People, mostly lizard, pulled Wiggly Charlie through the crowd. His little arms were taped at his sides, his feet bound together, and his enormous willy dragged across the rug.

"Need a cheez," said Wiggly Charlie.

"Hi, W.C.," Audrey said. "I'm so sorry."

"What did you do to him?" asked Bob. "He seems, well, he's kind of goofy."

"Head injury," said Audrey.

"Really, but his soul is gone."

"He fell really hard. I really should make a helmet for him. I know, I'll make helmets for you all."

"No. You have done enough."

"It's no bother, really," Audrey said. "Helmets for everyone!"

"Helmets for everyone! Helmets for everyone! Helmets for everyone!" the little People chanted.

"Good crowd," Audrey said to Bob under her breath.

"There will be no helmets!" said Bob.

Various moans and murmurs of disappointment sounded around the room.

"That's on you, buddy," said Audrey. "Don't blame me if you take a tumble and end up like him."

"Need a cheez," said Wiggly Charlie.

"No! You have made us miserable meat creatures and now *you* shall be a miserable meat creature. Seize her! Take her to the hall of souls."

A score of Squirrel People lifted Audrey, which was very uncomfortable, but she didn't struggle because most of them had sharp claws and she'd already learned that the more she struggled, the more scratched up she got. They carried her through the parlor, into the butler's pantry, where one of them kicked the wastebasket out of the way while the rest shoved her head into an uncovered vent. Which was all that fit. Just her head. Her shoulders caught on the side.

"She won't fit," said a little voice.

"We can't take her in through outside, she won't fit though the hall of glass either," said another voice.

"New plan!" said Theeb.

"New plan! New plan! New plan!" the People chanted.

The Morrigan waited, peering out of the storm sewer at the Buddhist Center until darkness fell, then they flowed across the street like miscast shadows, their edges fringed with the ragged pattern of swarming birds. Babd saw a window cracked open just an inch on the second floor and so flowed up the wall and through the crack. Macha and Nemain flowed around either side of the downstairs walls, looking for an opening, then, finding none, slipped under the back porch, down the passageway made of auto glass, then up through the vent and into the butler's pantry, not even remotely aware that they were passing just a few yards from the Squirrel People's cache of soul vessels.

In the parlor, Theeb the Wise stood between Audrey and Wiggly Charlie, who lay trussed up on the floor, and finished reading the *p'howa of forceful projection* to move Audrey's soul into W.C.'s body. With a great flourish Theeb finished the reading, enunciating the Sanskrit perfectly with his newly grown lips, then loomed over Wiggly Charlie. "Now you know the suffering that is our lot."

"Need a cheez," said W.C.

"He still doesn't have a soul," said the duck-faced guy. "No glow."

"It didn't work," said Theeb. He hopped to a spot in front of Audrey's face. "What happened?"

"The *p'howa of forceful projection* moves the soul out of a *soul vessel*, into a new body, like yours. It won't work from a living human to, uh, you guys."

"Then from a dead human," said Theeb.

Audrey said, "That won't work either—"

"Guards!" Theeb called.

Four Squirrel People carrying weapons, came forward through the crowd.

"Theeb the Wise demands you stab her!" said Theeb, and in doing so, he stepped away from Audrey and next to Wiggly Charlie to give his guards stabbing room.

"No!" shouted Wiggly Charlie, and bit down on Theeb's leg, engaging a majority of his seventy-eight needle-sharp teeth. Theeb squealed and tried to pull away, but instead ended up sawing his leg against W.C.'s teeth.

The People all moved away from the calamity in the middle of the parlor, those with voices crying out in distress. A lizard-headed musketeer started to scamper up the big open staircase, only to be met by Babd, who was oozing down the staircase, claws first. She caught the musketeer, tore him in half, and bit into the red light of his soul, her head and talons taking on dimension as she fed.

Macha and Nemain slid out of the butler's pantry, Macha across the ceiling, Nemain across the floor.

"Run!" Audrey screamed. "All of you, run!"

Nemain impaled two of the People on her claws and they screeched piteously as she bit into one's torso, and the other squirmed on her talon, the light of its soul dimming in an instant. Macha dropped from the ceiling like an inky blanket and fell upon a half dozen of the People, gathering them in a death embrace, crushing them. Bones cracked, splintered, four souls went dark. Macha stood full form in the middle of the parlor, holding one of the People in each hand, gore dripping down her face and chest.

The People scattered, running for every exit, through the dining room, crowding the vent in the butler's pantry, some scrambling up the stairs, a few skittering through the foyer and trying to get to the front doorknob. Theeb struggled to free himself from Wiggly Charlie's jaws. Nemain stepped by Wiggly Charlie, and Theeb stuck her in the ankle with his spork.

"Fuck! Ouch!" She kicked Theeb, who was ripped out of W.C.'s mouth and went flying into the butler's pantry. Wiggly Charlie went spinning across the floor the other way. One of the guards, an iguana-headed fellow in green scrubs brandishing a screwdriver, charged her, and Nemain impaled him in the chest on a single claw and lifted him to her eye level. She turned him in the air, as if she was examining a particularly fascinating hors d'oeuvre. She looked down at Audrey. "Did you make these? They're delicious." Nemain closed her eyes, and tilted her head back in ecstasy as the light pumped out of the guard's soul —absorbed through her claw as if she was filling a syringe.

Across the room, Macha slung the lifeless body of a squirrel ballerina against the wall, then reached for Wiggly Charlie, saw there was no soul light in him, and tossed him aside. She dropped to all fours and crawled up to Audrey until their faces were nearly touching. Audrey squirmed to move away, wiggled a few feet back before encountering a chair leg, her breath coming in little yips, as if each breath had to resist turning into a scream.

Macha said: "I don't know whether to take your head, or just open your veins and watch your life drain out on the floor."

"Oh, you have to take her head," said Nemain, now standing over them both.

"I vote head," said Babd, moving up behind Nemain, blood dripping from her talons.

"There you have it," said Macha. She scissored her claws in front of Audrey's face.

"Hurry," said Nemain. "All the souls are getting away."

Macha snarled, reared back. Audrey screamed, tried to tuck her face into her knees.

"That will be enough, ladies," came a voice from the foyer. They stopped. Lemon filled the parlor doorway. "Go catch you some critters, ladies. I'ma have me a chat with the venerable Rinpoche Audrey."

24

BATTLE

It was 7 P.M. and Charlie Asher had been at St. Francis Hospital for two hours, with no word of how Mrs. Korjev was doing, if the soul vessels had been safely moved, or what was going on with Audrey. He had called everyone, and no one had picked up. He suspected either they didn't remember he was using Mike Sullivan's phone, or someone was fucking with him. Strangely enough, despite having jettisoned the body that carried his original, beta-male DNA, he still had the personality of a beta, and its built-in, double-edged imagination, which, in addition to helping him anticipate and avoid danger, engendered a suspicion that someone, usually someone unknown and cleverly wicked, was fucking with him. Possibly, and even probably in this case, the mobile phone people.

Fortunately the hospital cafeteria had macaroni and cheese, so he was able to feed Sophie (their other vegan selection being *Wood and Leaves with Suffering*). Now she was in the waiting room, sleeping next to Lily in one of the vinyl padded chairs designed so you wouldn't sleep in them. She'd refused to go home with only Lily, but if he could reach Jane and Cassie, maybe he could get her out of here without waking her. Finally, a text buzzed into his phone from Jane. *We're on our way.*

He walked over and slumped in the chair next to Lily.

"Something like this happens," he said, "you realize you don't really even know the people you know. She's lived in my building for ten years. She's helped me with Sophie since she was a baby. There are things I should have told her. There were things I wanted to ask her."

Lily nodded, knowingly. "Like why she never had that thing taken off her lip?"

"No. Important things. Things so she'd know that she was important to me, to my family. Now . . ."

"You couldn't have known."

"I did know," said Charlie. "And so did you. Which is why you should have stopped them from going out."

"This is my fault?"

"No, but I'd prefer it if it were."

"Fine. It's on me."

"You should never pass up an opportunity to be kind. You should never not thank someone. You should never *not* say something nice when you think it."

"I don't."

"Okay, then."

"You done?"

"I suppose so." He slumped down farther in the chair. "You hear from Minty?"

"Not yet. But . . ." She nodded through the double-glass door, which Minty Fresh was approaching. "Tell him I was badass."

"You were afraid to confront two old ladies."

"Okay, tell him I was helpful."

She had been helpful, in a way, in that she had broken into Mrs. Korjev's apartment and found her matron's address book so Charlie could call her sons, one who lived in Seattle, the other in Los Angeles.

Minty Fresh wore a black leather car coat with his usual ensemble of shades of green, but Rivera was wearing an ill-fitting tweed sport coat.

Charlie stood to meet them.

"The old lady okay?" said Minty Fresh.

"We don't know. It was her heart," said Charlie.

"But she's hanging on?"

"So far. They won't really talk to us—me—since I barely know her, officially. Maybe when Jane gets here."

"Oh, right. You know that Chinese lady from your building is out on the front stoop. What's she doing out there?"

"Pacing. They won't let her bring her cart in and she won't leave it."

"Well, leave it in your car."

"We came in a cab. Followed the ambulance."

Minty Fresh shrugged.

Rivera said, "I can have a uniform unit take her home."

"She won't go," said Charlie.

Minty looked to Lily.

"Why are *you* still here?"

Lily tilted her head toward the sleeping Sophie, saying, more or less, *because of the kid,* "I'm not going to leave town, M. Even if Jane and Cassie go. I have work tomorrow. I'm going to be on those lines if Mike calls in from the bridge."

Minty Fresh tapped out three beats with his size sixteens, a habit he'd acquired from arguing with Lily over the last year. "Well, at least go to your mother's place. Stay there tonight. There's no way Lemon will know to look for you there, even if he's been watching you."

"Whoa, whoa, whoa," said Charlie. *"Lemon?* This man in yellow that Sophie has been talking about is called *Lemon?"*

Minty Fresh glanced around the waiting room, as if there might be some obvious explanation written on one of the pieces of innocuous motel art. "Well, yeah, that's sort of a shorthand I made up, you know." To Lily, he said, "Anyway, will you at least stay at your mother's house and take a cab to work? Please."

Looking at Rivera, Charlie said, "Would you guys run by the Buddhist Center and check on Audrey. I was on the phone when all this happened. We got disconnected and I haven't been able to get hold of her."

"We will," said Rivera.

Charlie held out a key. "This is for the front door."

Minty Fresh took it and turned on a heel. "We'll call you in ten minutes."

"Thanks," Charlie said, and watched them go. He sat on the other side of Sophie and stroked her hair as she slept.

"He loves you, you know," he said to Lily.

"Not going to discuss this with you."

"Okay."

They passed the next few minutes by not talking and not looking at people who were trying not to look at them, except for those who looked at Sophie, sleeping, and smiled. Charlie leafed through some magazines to distract himself, only to find that he was made more anxious by wondering what kind of sociopathic fuck-weasel would do all the puzzles in *Highlights* in pen. *These monsters walk among us*, he thought.

His phone buzzed. "She's fine," said Rivera.

"How is she fine? Why didn't she call?"

"She said she dropped her phone and it broke and she didn't have your new number written down anywhere. She left a message on your sister's landline. She's in the car with us. You want to talk to her?"

"Yes! Well, yes!"

"Hi, Charlie," Audrey said. "Sorry. There was a little bit of a meltdown with the Squirrel People. Anyway, the inspector and Mr. Fresh are going to take me to your place, if that's okay."

"Sure." He looked at Lily, mouthed, *She's okay.* "Of course that's okay, but I'll be here awhile. Mrs. Korjev's son is flying up from Los Angeles. We still haven't heard on her condition other than she's still critical."

"I hope she'll be okay. I have W.C. with me. He's—well—the Squirrel People were mean to him."

"Okay. I think there's some mozzarella sticks in the fridge. I'll be home as soon as I can. I was really hoping we could spend tonight together, since, you know, we may not get any more after tomorrow."

"How could you say that? Don't say that? You guys—" There was a muffled rustling on the line that sounded like she was holding the phone against her chest as she spoke to whoever was in the car.

A doctor came through the double doors in scrubs, head down, looking very serious. He headed right for Charlie, who dropped his phone in his lap.

Jane and Cassie parked in the emergency-only lane at the hospital. Jane stayed with the car while Cassie snuck into the waiting room to retrieve the sleeping Sophie, who hung in her arms like a snoring rag doll. Cassie emerged from the double doors just as Audrey was climbing out of Rivera's unmarked police car, with a cat carrier containing Wiggly Charlie. Jane jumped out and herded Mrs. Ling down from the landing into the backseat of the car. Mrs. Ling's cart stubbornly refused to fold up, so Jane chucked Wiggly Charlie's cat carrier into the cart and fitted it into the backseat between Audrey and Mrs. Ling.

The same sort of stealth fire drill happened when they were bringing Sophie back to the apartment. Jane let Audrey into Charlie's new apartment and Cassie carried the sleeping Sophie into their apartment, leaving Mrs. Ling to fend for herself. When the elevator cleared, Mrs. Ling looked into her cart to see the cat carrier. She wheeled it to her apartment on the third floor, then unzipped the cat carrier just far enough to peek inside, and smiled for the first time since her friend had fallen down.

She had cooked a creature almost exactly like this one before, when one of the early Squirrel People who fancied himself an assassin broke into the building, only to find himself in Mrs. Ling's soup pot. Duck in Pants, she had called the dish. This one would make a nice soup that she could take to Mrs. Korjev at the hospital. She went to the kitchen and filled her blackened soup pot with water and turned on the flame.

"Need a cheez," said Wiggly Charlie from his carrier.

Rivera slammed two five-hour energy drinks as an act of faith. Not the faith of his father, which he now looked upon as quaint ritual, but faith in his own anger, because if he looked at the situation rationally, five hours was probably about four and a half hours longer than his current life expectancy. He was exhausted, having driven all over town through most of the night doing what he had come to think of as the "To-Do List of the Dead," but now dawn was breaking and he and Minty Fresh were pulling into the concrete channel where the old train tracks cut into the knoll at Fort Mason.

"Back in," said Minty Fresh.

Rivera flipped a Y-turn and backed the brown Ford into the channel until they were about twenty-five yards from the big steel doors that led into the tunnel, then stopped, popped the trunk, and got out. Minty Fresh unfolded out of his side of the car and met Rivera at the back; Minty in green leather trousers and black trainers, Rivera in his oversized sport coat, jeans, and black nylon tactical boots.

Rivera pulled two folding "Men Working" barricades out of the trunk and handed one to Minty Fresh. They set them up in front of the car and turned on the flashers.

"I told dispatch that animal control was going to be using some charges to chase rats and ground squirrels out of the tunnel, so if they get any calls for people hearing gunfire, they have an explanation."

"They believed that?"

"They love having an answer."

They walked back to the trunk.

"You got bolt cutters?" asked Minty Fresh, shooting a glance over his shoulder toward the steel doors.

"Yeah, but I think we can probably climb over. They're what, eight feet tall? I'm not that old."

"I ain't worried about getting in, but if shit go sideways, I sure don't want to have to get over those motherfuckers in a hurry getting out."

Rivera ticked off a point well-made in the air, pulled the bolt cutters from the trunk, and leaned them against the bumper. He handed Minty Fresh a light flak vest. "Blade-resistant," he said. "Prison guards wear them. Should fit, just may not cover you all the way down."

Minty Fresh shrugged off his leather coat and the double shoulder holsters with the massive Desert Eagle pistols. He put on the vest.

"Turn," Rivera said. "Lift your arms." The Mint One did as instructed and Rivera cinched the vest up tight on him. Minty put on his shoulder holsters, buckled them down, then his coat. Rivera held up a riot helmet. "I guessed at the size."

Minty Fresh looked at the helmet like it was a foul dead thing. "Yeah, I ain't wearing that."

"It's Kevlar. Lights and goggles. You said one of them flings venom from her claws."

Minty Fresh pulled a pair of wraparound sunglasses from the breast pocket of his coat, flicked them open, and put them on.

"Going to be dark in there."

"I have excellent night vision."

"Suit yourself," said Rivera. He put on his own helmet and pulled down the goggles.

Rivera handed Minty some orange foam earplugs. "You're going to want these."

"I'll be all right."

Rivera grinned, looking—in all the tactical gear—like a victorious soldier in the tooth-whitening wars. He reached into the trunk and pulled back the flap on a nylon satchel, revealing a row of grenades clipped into elastic straps. "Flash bangs. Trust me, you're going to want earplugs."

Minty smiled. "We going to throw grenades in the park and 911 going to tell people we're animal control?"

"Aren't we?"

Minty held out his palm and Rivera dropped the earplugs. Rivera handed him a riot shotgun with a pistol grip, a laser sight on the top, and a flashlight slung under the barrel. "You ever use one of these?"

"I have."

"Semiautomatic, just click off the safety and pull the trigger. I have double-ought buckshot in them. They'll tear the hell out of whatever they hit, but they're not Magnum loads, so they'll kick less, and if you have to shoot quickly you'll still be able to aim. You have nine shots with one in the chamber, five each extra on the elastic on the stock, four on the forestock." He pulled a box of shells from the trunk. "You want some extras for your jacket pocket?"

Minty Fresh laughed. "No, Inspector, I think eighteen shots and our handguns are either going to do the trick or we gonna get done."

Rivera nodded and shrugged off his sport coat, revealing the Beretta slung in a shoulder holster under his left arm, two extra clips under his right. He was checking for the tenth time that each was loaded when he heard gravel crunching and a silver-blue Honda pulled up in front of his Ford. He checked his watch.

"I thought you told him seven, it's barely six-fifteen."

"I did," said Fresh.

Charlie Asher climbed out of Audrey's Honda and stood by the door. "You guys are ready already?" He wore a leather jacket and was carrying a black cane with a silver handle, but otherwise he looked like Mike Sullivan out to buy a paper.

"How's the old lady?" asked Rivera.

"She's stable. Heart attack. Her son is there."

"But alive," said Rivera. He looked at Minty Fresh.

"That's good," said Minty, meaning more than it was good that she was alive, it was good that Lemon had attacked her and she'd managed to survive it. It meant Lemon was vulnerable.

"Where's the Emperor?" Charlie asked.

"Jail," said Rivera.

"Really?"

"Just until this is over. Actually I had them lock him in a cage at the animal shelter so his men could stay with him. They owed me a favor."

Charlie joined them at the back of the Ford. "My motocross leathers got all cut up when I—when Mike jumped off the bridge, so I only have this jacket. Should be okay, right?"

"Yeah, you ain't going to need them," said Minty Fresh.

"Go home to your daughter, Charlie," Rivera said.

"What are you talking about? This is *my* battle. I'm not a afraid of them. I've done this before."

"We know," said Rivera. "That's not even the issue. You have to go back to Audrey and your daughter and your sister because you have them to go back to."

"We don't," said Minty Fresh.

"I have guns now. Look at these bad boys," Charlie said, flexing his biceps. "I didn't have these before."

"Have you ever been to the animal shelter, Charlie?" Rivera said. "I could show you around."

"Go home, Charlie," said Minty Fresh. "I didn't go to all that trouble to bring you back to life so you could get killed again. If something happen to me, you look out for Lily, you hear?"

"You know I will." Charlie slumped, knowing he was defeated. They had decided this long before now. If he hadn't shown up early, it would all be over by now. And they had a point. He had charged into battle against the Morrigan once before, and Sophie had lost her daddy for a year. He couldn't do that to her again.

"Well, at least take this with you." Charlie held out the cane. "It's my sword cane."

"We look like we need more weapons?"

"It was my soul vessel—where my soul went before Audrey put it into that little body. It might be good luck or something."

"Didn't you have this with you when you got killed?" the Mint One asked.

"Kind of."

Minty took the cane from him and tucked it into his belt. "Thank you."

"Give a brother a pound?" Charlie held out his fist to receive a pound. The Mint One left him hanging.

"Don't do that," said Minty.

"Sorry." Charlie turned to Rivera, started to go in for a hug, which Rivera intercepted and turned into a handshake. "Something happens, you can have my suits," he said.

"Nothing's going to happen," said Charlie.

Rivera smiled. "If you're going to stay out here, tell anyone who comes up that we're animal control and they should move along because of the chemicals."

"What chemicals?"

"The dangerous imaginary ones," he said. Rivera looked to Minty Fresh. "You ready?"

Rivera started for the doors, Minty Fresh followed, the bolt cutters in one hand, the shotgun in the other.

Minty Fresh said, "Are you absolutely sure you want to do this? Seems like maybe it would make more sense to call in a SWAT team or Special Forces."

"That won't work, isn't Special Forces where everyone gets a hug?" Charlie called.

"That's the Special Olympics," Rivera said over his shoulder. To Minty he said, "How are you going to explain this, the Morrigan?"

"Just so we're clear, then," said the Mint One, "we're only doing this because we want to avoid an awkward explanation to other police, right?"

Rivera paused. "No. We're doing this because they murdered my partner and I don't think they're going to come along quietly if I try to arrest them. They're going to come for us, eventually, and if we wait, it will be on their terms. Now is better."

"You don't never be lyin'," said Minty Fresh. He stopped at the doors and leaned the shotgun against the concrete wall. "Do you smell something burning?

"Oh, hell," said Rivera. He cringed and braced himself.

"*AIIIIIIIIEEEEEEEEEEEEEEEEEE!*" called the banshee.

Minty Fresh dropped the bolt cutters, snatched up his shotgun, and brought the sight down on the sooty wraith.

"Don't shoot her, don't shoot her, don't shoot her." Rivera stepped away from the banshee and pushed down the barrel of Minty Fresh's shotgun.

"What do you think you're doing, ya ninny?" said the banshee. "Ya can't go in there."

"We have to," said Rivera.

"I tried to warn your great fat friend, and ya know how that turned out. And the harpies are even stronger now than they were then."

"I know. Thank you," said Rivera. "But we have to do this."

"Fine. I'll nae sing at your funeral, you bloody loony." The stun gun crackled in the air and she was gone.

"She thinks it's a box of lightning," Rivera explained. "She thinks it adds drama to her entrances and exits."

"Right, 'cause what the bitch need is more drama."

Because the Morrigan were goddesses of war, they were attracted to the sound of war drums. So when they first rose in the modern world, a pocket of the Underworld opened under the rumbling boom they followed. As it turned out, they had entered the world under a bowling alley, and it was there that they absorbed the dialect of English that they now spoke.

"This sucks," said Babd. "I don't know why we have to stay down here now." She was reclining in the bucket of a skip-loader, methodically licking the last remnants of some Squirrel Person from her claws.

They were all strong, and lithe, and they shimmered in the dim light of the tunnel like swaths of starry night. Macha leaned against the tunnel wall and preened her breast with her claws, retracted to the length of a cat's claws.

"We can go into the light," said Nemain, who was crouched over a wolf spider, dripping venom from her talon as the creature tried to escape, then blocking its path with another sizzling drop as it bolted the other way. "What does Yama know?"

They had flown in their raven forms to the tunnel while it was still dark. Bloated with the power of new souls, moving again as shadows was beyond them, at least for a while.

"We could find the rest of the soul stealers," said Babd. "Take their souls. Kill them."

"Yama says if we go into the light we'll attract the attention of humans," said Nemain.

"I thought that was the point," said Macha. "Have our names on their breath as they die. Have them cower when a raven passes over them."

"Why can't we just kill everybody?" said Babt, pouting.

An inhuman shriek sounded from the far end of the tunnel.

Nemain impaled the spider she'd been torturing with her talon and stood. "Did you hear that?"

Babd climbed out of the skip-loader basket, looked down the tunnel around the column of heavy machinery. "There's too much light. Someone's moving down there."

"Snacks," said Macha, grinning in anticipation, her fangs showing against her lower lips.

Something clattered against the wall on Macha's left and fell at her feet, it looked like a green soup can. Another object rattled and bounced down the other side of the tractor and settled a few feet from Babd.

The flash bangs exploded. Deafening concussion. Blinding light. Babd was thrown back into the bucket of the skip-loader. Macha staggered, spun, bouncing off the wall, her arms up by her ears as she willed them not to turn into wings to flee—not in the tunnel.

Babd shrieked, her most ferocious battle cry, the call that had made warriors soil themselves and cower in terror on the battlefield as their enemies harvested their heads. She was answered with a flash and a shot and her left arm was shredded. Another shot, her foot blown out from under her.

"You fuckers!" Her scream resonated in the metal of the machines.

On the opposite side of the tunnel Macha fell into a crouch, having deduced where the attack was coming from. A light and a red dot panned up the side of the tunnel, settled on her as she dove and the projectiles took her full in the side, rolling her over in the air to land against the bucket of the skip-loader.

Nemain fell between the unused train tracks. Light and lasers and explosive fire were blazing down either side of the tractor in front of her.

She watched as parts of her sisters were shaken and shredded with impact. Flares smelling of sulfur came bouncing down the tunnel and projected shadows of her sisters' torment across the ceiling. She scuttled forward under the tractor, rolled onto her back, pulled herself up onto the driveshaft, and hung there, perhaps a foot off the ground, as the conflagration raged on either side of her. Fear was foreign to her—in a thousand years on and over the battlefields of the North she'd never had to defend herself. It was war, someone was going to die and she was Death; it had always been win-win.

The roar of gunfire paused. Human footfalls, the hiss of the burning flares, a mechanical clicking noise. Light beams bouncing in the sulfur smoke.

"Anything?" A man's voice.

"Something on my side headed away—further down the tunnel."

"One here, too. The tunnel is walled up at the other end, heavy wooden slats, into Fort Mason parking lot. Reloading." *Click. Click. Click.*

Then she saw them, human legs moving up the tunnel, one man on either side of her, the one on her right closer. *Take down one and then make a dash after Macha and Babd.*

The one on the right, then, in the green leather. She unsheathed her claws on that side to their full length. Venom dripped and softly sizzled on a steel rail below . . .

Minty Fresh was trying to keep the light on the shotgun pointed down the tunnel as he pushed fresh shells into the tubular magazine, which made his grip on the gun precarious at best. When the Morrigan's claws struck his calf, he lost his grip on the shotgun and fumbled it away, the light bouncing around the tunnel like an epileptic Tinker Bell.

He pulled away from the pain and his feet were yanked out from under him. He landed hard on his side, his breath knocked out, and he felt himself being yanked under the tractor. With one hand he caught a piece of metal that protruded from the front wheel of the tractor, a steering bar, perhaps, while he swung a fist at his attacker, hitting nothing.

Rivera shouting. White pain in his leg. Frantic digging in his coat with his free hand for one of the Desert Eagles. He touched one, was yanked, lost orientation, reached again. His free hand whipped around, settled on something round—at first he thought another piece of the tractor—but it was Charlie Asher's sword cane. He pulled it free from the scabbard and swung in the direction of his attacker as hard as he could.

A screech, not Rivera. The grip on his calf gone, he fell slack on the train tracks. A shotgun firing, a figure, illuminated by the highway flares, rolling out from under the tractor, awkwardly scrambling to her feet. Another shotgun blast and she was spun around, fell, and scuttled off into the dark screeching.

"You okay?" asked Rivera, his face appearing by a wheel on the opposite side of the tractor.

"Yeah. The fuck?" Now, on the ground by his leg, he saw the severed claw of the Morrigan twitching, evaporating into a feathery vapor spewing from the severed wrist until, in a few seconds, it was gone. "She got my leg."

Rivera ran around the front of the tractor, crouched beside the Mint One. He pulled a flashlight out of his vest, played it over Minty Fresh, set it on the ground pointing at his leg. The blood looked like tar. Rivera took off his belt and wrapped it around Minty's leg just above the knee, tightened it down, putting his foot on it for the tension. "Hold this. Tight." He handed the free end of the belt to Minty Fresh.

"Go get them," Fresh said.

Rivera shook his head, dug his phone out of his jacket pocket, checked the signal. "Fuck. I'm going to have to go back out to get a signal and call help."

Rivera helped Minty Fresh sit up against the tractor wheel, then took the end of his belt from the big man and tied it off. He picked up his own shotgun and handed it to Minty. "Two still in it, the extras still on the stock."

"Yeah, reloading might have been my mistake," said Minty.

"I'll be back."

Rivera picked up his flashlight and stood. As soon as the light played back toward the entrance he saw the new, fitter Charlie Asher coming out of the darkness. "A really scary-looking woman in black rags told me you guys might need help," Charlie said.

"Grab an arm," Rivera said. "We need to get him out of here." He looked down to see that Minty Fresh was unconscious.

25

THE DEATH CARD

harlie hadn't told Audrey he was going to attack the Morrigan—he hadn't told her *anyone* was going to attack the Morrigan. The last she had heard about it, the attack was theoretical, Inspector Rivera blowing off steam, she'd thought.

Charlie had taken a taxi home from the hospital after Mrs. Korjev's son had arrived from Los Angeles, and let himself into the new apartment, which still smelled of paint and cleaning products. He crawled into bed with Audrey and kissed her awake enough to tell her that Mrs. Korjev was stable, and for her to tell him that Sophie was sleeping in her own bed in the other apartment, but she hadn't told him anything else.

They made love and she flinched once when he brushed against her ankle, which was raw from where she'd been duct-taped by the Squirrel People, but she'd passed the movement off as passion and she fell asleep in his arms, feeling safe for the first time in days. She had awakened when he rose at dawn, went right back to sleep when he kissed her on the temple and crept out of the apartment, leaving a note on the breakfast bar that said, *Had to go out. Will call you in a couple of hours. Tell Sophie I love her. Love, Charlie.* Not, *Going to engage the powers of darkness, because that worked out so well the last time.* Not, *I'm a complete moron with no common sense and no consideration for the people who love me.* No, just, *Had to go out.* So when he called her around seven and said he was headed to San Francisco General Hospital because that's where the ambulance was taking Minty Fresh and he would pick her up outside in five minutes, well, she'd been a bit surprised, and a little angry.

When he pulled up out front in her Honda and she crawled in, she really wanted to shout at him—hug him first, then maybe hit him a bunch of times, which caused her years of training to kick in, and instead she took a long, slow breath and let it out over a count of ten. One did not become the caretaker for the forgotten chapters of the *Book of Living and Dying* by indulging in random freak-outs every time one encountered difficulty. So she only hit him once.

"Ouch! What's that for?"

"Why didn't you tell me what you were doing?"

"I didn't want you to worry."

She let that sit for a while. Were her reasons for not telling him about the massacre at the Buddhist Center any more pure? Wasn't she just trying to keep him from being distressed? She had done so much wrong, with good intentions, but wrong nonetheless. She had done the right thing, not the easy thing, by not telling him. Probably. Maybe.

The man in yellow wasn't like the other creatures. He might be dark, he might be *of* darkness, but wasn't darkness necessary? Light, dark, male, female, yin, yang: balance. He'd convinced her as much after saving her from the Morrigan.

He'd righted an unbroken chair and pulled it over to where she lay bound on the floor, the remnants of shredded Squirrel People littered the room.

"Do you mind if I sit?" he asked. The absurdity of him asking her approval when she was trussed up on the carpet almost made her laugh.

"Please," she said.

He tipped his hat as if spilling silky sax notes off the brim, then took five shuffling steps to get around from the back of the chair to the front, shaking a leg on every other step. He sat, leaned forward.

"How you doin'?" he said. He had a gold crown on an upper right bicuspid and he showed it to her with a smile.

"I'm tied up on the floor and I've almost been murdered twice in five minutes."

"Well, the night is young," he said, a little too much cheer in his voice.

She took a deep breath, let it out while reciting a Sanskrit chant in her mind. Right now, in this instant, she was fine.

He laughed, "I'm just fuckin' with you. Ain't nobody gonna hurt you, Red. You mind I call you Red? That whole 'venerable Rinpoche' jazz a bit of a mouthful."

Strictly speaking, her hair wasn't red, but auburn, but she nodded approval anyway. "And you are . . . Death?"

"That really more a title than a name. You probably wanna gonna call me Yama."

"Yama?" She thought she'd been as surprised as she could be tonight. Apparently not. "Protector of Buddhism?"

"That's right, but we not using titles, right? Now, Red, I cut you loose, you not gonna freak out and go all kung fu and shit on me, are you?"

"I'll make tea," she said.

He laughed, pulled a straight razor from his jacket pocket, and leaned over. "Hold still, now." He cut the tape on her wrists, then handed her the razor so she could do her ankles herself. The handle of the razor was ivory or bone, yellowed with age. She cut the tape then folded the razor and handed it back to him. Careful not to step in anyone, she braced herself and ripped the remaining tape off her ankles and wrists. He cringed at the sound, in sympathy with her pain.

"You got somewhere else we can chat? Disorder in here harshing my mellow."

She led him through the dining room into the kitchen.

"Your minions made that mess. Those were human souls?" She wasn't afraid of him. She had come face-to-face with Death three times tonight already, including him, and she was unafraid.

"Well, that is true," he said, pulling out a chair at the oak table. "But they weren't the ones put them human souls in those little monsters, now, were they? They freed those souls to their natural course. They methods can be rough, but they do get the job done. Truth told, they ain't my minions, but I do admire a strong, black woman."

"They *slaughtered* them," Audrey said.

"Slaughtered who, Red? The ladies can't take a soul from a human. Mighta been a time, back in the day, but not now. Them things you made weren't people, they was prisons. The ladies just busted them out."

She was more shaken by that than by all the violence of the night. She *had* been wrong. Her intentions might have been pure, but her actions had not been. Had the Morrigan really freed the souls of the Squirrel People? She had seen them grow more solid, stronger, with each soul they devoured. She put on the kettle and went about the homey ritual of making tea. The fire on, she turned her back to the counter to face him.

"You're right. Why didn't you let them kill me?"

Lemon looked around, as if someone might be listening. "They no need for that. That's not why I'm here."

"They killed Inspector Cavuto."

"Not my intention. You know how things get out of hand? They got out of hand that night. They was a long time down, they get a little drunk with being up here."

"So they're not here to bring up the darkness to cover the world and reign for a thousand years, like they said before."

"Before? You mean when they with Orcus? That dumb motherfucker? Fuck no, that ain't what I'm doing here. You tell soldiers what they need to hear to go to war. Bitches need a mission, not a goal. It's *my* war."

"War on who?"

He shrugged. "Not for me to say. I'm just fillin' a need, puttin' things in order. Ain't no sides. Death don't discriminate. I don't judge. I don't deny anyone. I don't shun anybody. I accept everyone. Death be not proud,

Red." He shot his lapels, grinned. "Death be chic, baby, but not proud. I am loving-kindness. You think you know what life worth more than me? I speed these souls on to become one with all things. Y'all fucked things up. Y'all and all these motherfuckers selling souls in this city. You know that, Red. What you think call me up after a thousand years? This ain't your first barbecue; you think this through, you'll see I ain't the one knocking things out of order, I'm the one putting them back. Y'all just need to stay out of my way."

"Okay," she said. There was a truth to what he said. A logic. The universe sought balance and the universe oscillated, and when it oscillated, between the beats of the heart of the universe, there rose the agent of change: chaos. Chaos sat at her table. "What kind of tea would you like?"

"You got any decaf? Caffeine make me jumpy."

"Decaf green or decaf cinnamon spice?"

"Cinnamon spice sound nice."

"So, you're the Ghost Thief?"

"Thought we wasn't using titles."

"Why did you move the souls to the bridge, then?"

"The bridge? Yeah, the bridge. Well, you know, seems like a good place for safekeeping."

She had believed him then, believed that he was putting things in order, but now, after finding out about Mrs. Korjev's heart attack, which Sophie insisted had been brought on by the man in yellow, after Minty Fresh had fallen under the Morrigan, well . . . Yama hadn't really explained why he couldn't control the Morrigan. He hadn't explained why establishing his new order involved so much destruction, and for some reason, she hadn't questioned him. She'd felt strangely calm after talking to him, drinking tea at the kitchen table, at peace. But now, not so much.

Charlie parked in one of the hospital garages and they spent twenty minutes asking people where they might find a Mr. Fresh before Charlie's phone buzzed with a text from Rivera directing them to intensive care.

Rivera had shed his tactical gear but was still wearing the ill-fitting sport coat.

"I tried to talk the doctor into giving him some antivenom but he wanted to know the species of snake."

"Did you tell him 'big'?" Charlie said.

"Yeah, he wanted more than 'big.' He probably passed out from blood loss or shock rather than the venom. The wound wasn't as deep as we thought, but it nicked an artery. Lucky we got a tourniquet on him right away. He should be sewed up by now."

"Did someone call Lily?" Audrey asked.

"Would you? Her number's in my contacts." Charlie handed her his phone and Audrey stepped outside of the waiting room.

As soon as Audrey was out of earshot, Rivera said, "I went back in."

"What? Alone?" Charlie trying to whisper, but it was coming out louder than if he were talking in a normal voice. The few people sitting in the lobby looked up.

"They were gone. I went all the way to the other side of the tunnel. It's closed off."

"Do you think they are just gone, like before?" Charlie said. "Like when Sophie did whatever she did? Atomized them, I guess?"

"I don't think so. Certainly the one that clawed Fresh wasn't hurt very badly. We hit the other ones hard, though. I saw what happened. But they were really strong, a lot more than the one I shot in the alley when—you know."

"I was mesmerized by her or something," said Charlie, still embarrassed about the time he had let the Morrigan give a handjob in an alley off Broadway and Rivera had delivered nine rounds of lifesaving .9-mm cockblock. "And sad. I was weak and *sad*."

"Doesn't matter, Charlie. What I'm saying is they got out of that tunnel somehow, and there's no way out except the entrance we came in, not even a maintenance passageway like in the BART tunnels. And they didn't get by me."

"Did you check for drainage grates? You know they were sliding in and out of the storm sewers, they don't need much space when they're—"

"There's a Buick in the tunnel," Rivera said. "A big, old, yellow Buick. All the way at the Fort Mason end, which is boarded up with four-inch-thick beams. So either this man in yellow moved twenty pieces of heavy equipment out of the tunnel, parked his car, then moved twenty pieces back in, or he has another way of getting in and out of that tunnel. A way I can't see."

Audrey came back through the glass double doors and joined them.

"Her mom is bringing her over now."

"Oh, good, she's not alone," Charlie said. "Lily's mom is nice. Kind of surprisingly."

"You're dead to her," Audrey said.

"Why, what did I do to her?"

"No, I mean you need to remember that Charlie Asher is dead to her. She's not going to recognize you in this body."

"Oh, yeah. Right."

A nurse came in from the ward side of the waiting room and everyone looked up. She headed right for Rivera. "Inspector, he's awake and asking for you." She looked apologetically at Audrey and Charlie. "I can only let the inspector in, or family. I'm sorry."

"We're family," Charlie said.

The nurse looked at him, then at Audrey, and seemed as if she was trying to think of exactly how to answer without seeming horrible and racist, when Rivera said, "They are part of this investigation. I didn't want to tell the doctor, but this was an assault. Mr. Sullivan is a herpetologist and Ms. Rinpoche is a sketch artist."

The nurse appeared almost relieved, but did look for Audrey's sketch pad. Audrey held up Charlie's smartphone. "All digital now."

"We gave him something for the pain," said the nurse.

As the nurse led them into Minty's room, which was behind a glass wall facing the nurses' desk, Audrey whispered, "My last name isn't Rinpoche, that's a title."

"You're not a sketch artist either, are you?" Rivera whispered back. "I couldn't remember your last name."

Minty Fresh's injured leg was bandaged and held in traction so his knee was at a right angle. His hospital bed was propped up about thirty degrees and his other leg jutted a foot and a half out into space. He smiled when they came in. His face was starting to go gray.

"This is some bullshit," said the Mint One. "I'ma die and my foot is cold."

Audrey tried to adjust his blanket, but with the one leg propped up she couldn't make it work without uncovering him to the waist. She whipped off her sweater and wrapped it around his foot. "Until I can get the nurse to bring you another blanket."

"Thanks," said the big man.

"How you doing?" said Charlie.

"How was you doing when this happened to you?" Minty looked to Audrey. "Don't you put me in one of those creepy puppet things like you did him, just let me go, you hear?"

"Oh, I'm so sorry," Audrey said. She hugged his jutting foot. "I didn't know. I would have warned you. I watched them get strong, so strong, with each of the Squirrel People they killed. It was so horrible. I didn't know you were going to go after them. I didn't know."

"What are you talking about?"

So she told them about the attack on the Buddhist Center, about how the Morrigan had grown, taken form as they slaughtered the Squirrel People. She told them about Yama releasing her, saving her from the Morrigan, and what he had said about trying to establish the new order.

"He just let you go?" Charlie said.

"Who the fuck Yama?" said Minty.

"The man in yellow," said Audrey. "He's a Buddhist personification of Death. The legend was that he was a monk who was told if he meditated for fifty years, he would achieve enlightenment, so he went into a cave in the mountains, and he meditated for forty-nine years, three hundred and sixty-four days, and on the last day, some thieves came into the cave, leading a bull they had stolen, and they decapitated it, and when he asked to be spared, they decapitated him, too. He was reincarnated as Yama, a powerful demon-god, and he put the head of the bull on his own body and then killed the thieves and became the prime ruler over Death, the protector of Buddhism. He's one of the demons we're told to ignore when we are training to lead people through *bardo,* from life to death."

"Yama, huh?" Minty Fresh said.

"Yes, I'm so sorry, I should have told you all."

"That's okay. How 'bout you let go my leg."

Audrey had been hugging his calf and foot through the entire Yama story, now she was embarrassed as well as sorry.

"But you didn't ignore him, right?" said Charlie.

"Honestly, I didn't really remember him until now. Does that make sense?"

"It's all right, Audrey," Minty said. "He has some kind of gris-gris he put on people. Kid that works for me was all woo-woo with it, too, asking me about where my soul vessels went. I knew something was up with him. Motherfucker been sneaky since we was little."

"Pardon?" said Charlie.

"Yama my cousin."

"Wait," said Audrey. "What?"

"He might be Yama now, but when I knew him, his name was Lemon, and he was my cousin."

"Lemon Fresh?" asked Charlie. "So that isn't a nickname you made up?"

Rivera turned aside and tried to hide his smile.

"Don't you laugh," said Minty. "Lemon was not an uncommon name in Louisiana in those days. And I'm dying here."

"He said he's just trying to establish a new order," Audrey said, even more distressed now. "And that's what *we* thought was happening. That's part of the cycle, part of the wheel of life and death . . . Right?"

"Audrey," Minty Fresh said, his eyelids fluttering a bit now. "I don't want to rush y'all, but I probably got a limited time to live, so if you could just tell us—"

"I think I told him the lost souls are on the bridge," Audrey said.

Minty Fresh looked from Charlie to Rivera back to Audrey. "Was anyone going to tell me?"

"I was going to," said Charlie, "but I only found out yesterday afternoon and things have moved kind of fast since then. Were you going to tell us that the new menace to reality as we know it is your cousin?"

"Don't sass me, Charlie, I'm dying."

"You can't keep playing the death card."

"I don't want to keep playing the death card. But the death card been played. Just let me go with a little dignity." He closed his eyes, took a gasping breath.

"You mean instead of lying like a rug," said Charlie.

One of Minty Fresh's eyes popped open, his dignified death having been postponed by being called on his shit. "You know, Asher, just because you have biceps now doesn't mean you can talk to me like that."

"Your cousin?"

"He sent me the book, all right? He made me into a Death Merchant twenty some years ago, then he disappeared. Only reason I knew he was in town is he still driving that raggedy old Buick Roadmaster. I would spit but my mouth is dry."

There was a squeeze bottle of water on the nightstand, Audrey held it for Minty Fresh to have a drink.

"Where my shades? Let me die with a touch of cool."

Rivera took Minty Fresh's sunglasses from his jacket pocket, helped fit them on the big man, then they all stood there for a minute, waiting.

"Anybody got any 'Trane on they phone?" asked Minty. "Some Miles?"

Sad shaking of heads.

"Figures," said Minty Fresh. He lay back as if he was hearing the notes. They all listened to his breathing and watched the cardiac monitor's jagged line.

The nurse came through the glass door and everyone stood a little straighter and tried to look a little more official, as if she couldn't have seen them through the glass before she came in.

"Mr. Fresh?"

"What? What? What?" Minty Fresh said, lifting his head up. "It so dark. Why it so dark? Here I go. Here I come, Lemon, you bitch-ass motherfucker—"

"You have your sunglasses on," said the nurse.

"Oh, yeah. Sorry."

"Mr. Fresh, there's a young woman out here who says she's your priest."

"Big titties? Dress like a vampire?"

"Well, I guess," said the nurse, giving Rivera a nervous look. "She's kind of dressed more like a Catholic schoolgirl."

"Yeah, that my priest. Send her in."

"So, some good pain meds?" Rivera said.

"Fine as frog fur," said the Mint One. He offered Rivera a pound with his non-IV hand and Rivera returned it.

Charlie Asher frowned. Having never gotten a pound from the big man, he felt slighted.

"Let's give them some privacy," said Audrey. They passed Lily on the way out of the room, each giving her a pat on the shoulder.

In the lobby, among the other distressed and waiting, stood a slim woman in her forties with dark hair, wearing a sharp knit suit with military-style gold trim. Charlie recognized her as Lily's mother, but unless you saw them both side by side without eye makeup (which was a condition in which Charlie had never seen Lily) and saw that they had the same wide, blue eyes, you'd have never guessed they were related. Charlie elbowed Rivera and whispered, "Lily's mom, Mrs. Severo."

Rivera showed one second of an "are you kidding me" look then gathered his composure and introduced himself to her.

"Inspector Rivera?" she said, shaking his hand. "I'm afraid to ask how you know my daughter."

"I met her at Charlie Asher's shop when she worked there."

"Charlie Asher was a good man."

"He was," said Rivera.

"He was good for Lily. She was a wild child, but I think her job at Charlie's store kept her grounded, at least some of the time. I work so much, it's just been Lily and me—I'm not even sure she's over Charlie's passing; now this."

Rivera could tell she was feeling responsible for her daughter's pain and he wanted to tell her just how much this was not her fault. He wanted to put his arm around her and be a decent human being, but he wasn't finding it easy, because this—the attack on Minty—was murder, and he had a protocol for dealing with the loved ones of the victim. It didn't seem right.

"Mr. Fresh is a good guy."

"I don't know him. Never met him, of course. I worried he was older than her, but she really seems to care for him. I don't want her to be alone. It sucks to be alone."

"I know," he said. "I was going to offer to be here for Lily if you needed to get to work, but I'm guessing you'll be staying. Can I get you a cup of coffee?"

"That would be nice, Inspector."

"Alphonse," he said.

She nodded. "I'm Elizabeth. Liz."

"Liz," he repeated, smiled. "Liz, I've know Lily since she was sixteen," Rivera said. "You had your work cut you for you. She was a spooky kid."

"Oh, you have no idea," she said.

"Maybe I do. What do you take in your coffee?"

He was about to head back out the glass doors into the hallway when he saw a familiar doctor walk up to the nurses' desk, confer with the attending nurse, then look around until he caught Rivera's eye. Rivera intercepted him at the desk. Dr. *Hathaway*, Rivera reminded himself.

"How are you doing Inspector?" asked the doctor.

"That depends," said Rivera.

"I don't think there's anything we can do for him. We were going to move him to a quiet room where everyone could be with him, but honestly, I don't think there's time. His organs are shutting down and I'm surprised he's even conscious, so if you need to ask him anything, I'd do it right now."

"Actually, he's a friend."

"I'm sorry. Before—"

"It's okay, Doctor."

"Code blue, Doctor," called the nurse. She ran around the desk and into the room where Minty lay.

Without a word the doctor turned and followed her in. Lily came stumbling out of the glass doors, makeup-blackened tears running down her face.

26

THE UNDERWORLD

Under the San Francisco Bay, in a maintenance storage room just off a BART service tunnel, the Morrigan pooled among the heavy track-repair and debris-clearing tools. Every few minutes a train would go through the tunnel and they would dig what was left of their claws into the concrete to keep from being sucked out into the greater train tunnel.

"Close the door," said Babd, "and that won't keep happening." It was almost completely dark in the room and their eyes looked like silver disks floating in ink.

"I can't close the door," said Nemain. "It's big and rusty and I can't pull it loose. I only have one hand."

"We should go back through the sewers to that house with all the little soul puppets," said Macha. "Get our strength back."

"We could get the ones that escaped under the house where we couldn't fit."

"Well, we could fit now," said Babd. She, like her sisters, had barely any dimension now; even her shadow form showed holes and tears from buckshot.

Nemain, who was the most solid of the three, had lost a hand, and as much as she stared at it and cursed at it, it wouldn't grow back, even in a shadow form. "We should go someplace where there are no guns."

"Or cars," said Babd.

"Or Yama."

"Why is it," said Macha, "that every time we become strong enough to do something about Yama, someone shoots us up?"

"I feel used," said Babd. "Do you feel used? I don't know why we need him."

"I say we go eat the soul puppets, then flay Yama right away," said Nemain.

"Take his head," said Macha, who was always keen on taking heads, it being her specialty.

"I'm in," said Babd. "Let's go."

"Ladies," came a deep voice out of the dark, which was strange, because they could all see in the dark, and they couldn't see where the voice was coming from.

"Ladies," said Lemon. Now he stood there, a palm out, an open flame burning on his palm, illuminating the room. "What are you doing in this shit hole?"

"They came into the other place with guns. Blowed us up," said Macha.

"Look at us," said Nemain.

"Don't look at us," said Babd.

"We need to go get the rest of the soul puppets, the ones that taste like ham."

"No, we not going back there, ladies. But I know a place where you can scoop souls out the air like eatin' cotton candy. Thousands of them. Y'all ain't seen nothin' like it. Why, I bet once you done there, you be able to rip souls right out of a human like the old days. Ain't no gun or car can hurt you, then."

"Where?" asked Macha.

"Why, when y'all are done, you'll probably be able to bring the Underworld up anywhere y'all want. Maybe everywhere."

"Where? Where? Where?" asked Nemain.

"What's cotton candy?" asked Babd, who was the dimmest in a triad of very dark creatures.

"Well, I'll show y'all," said Lemon. "But we going to have wait until it's dark out. They's a lot of open ground to cover to get there."

"Open a door into that place," said Macha.

"I'll get y'all close, but you can't just wade in and scoop them all up. You nibble round the edges, maybe, and before anyone know what happen, they's one soul in particular you gotta shred. You don't get that one, you lose the rest."

"Take us there," said Nemain.

In the days when the Underworld was in flux with the light, and gods rose and fell like mushrooms in a damp forest, there came into being two brothers, Osiris and Set. Osiris, with his queen, Isis, rose to reign over the kingdom of light, and Set ruled over the dark, the Underworld, with his queen Nephthys, who was fine. Set was jealous of his brother's land and worshippers, and plotted against him, while Osiris, radiant and self-assured, yearned for a taste of the dark world in Nephthys, and so he did tap that ass. From that union came a son, the dark, dog-headed god, Anubis. (As well as his jackal-headed brother Upuaut, who would be put in a basket and set adrift in the sea, to make his way unguided in a new land, but his is another story.*)*

When Set learned of his wife's affair, he murdered Osiris, and to assure that Osiris would never be reincarnated, Set cut the body into pieces and hid the pieces among the darkest, most distant corners of the Underworld. Isis was overcome with grief and searched in vain for her beloved. But the dutiful dog-headed god, Anubis, Osiris's son in the Underworld, found the pieces of his father's body and returned them to Isis. Anubis mummified his father's body and Isis raised his spirit to rule over the people of the sun. For his service, Anubis was given the realm of the

---

* *Coyote Blue.*

dead in the Underworld, and it was his lot to see that order was kept and justice done to the passing souls of man.

Set was left to seethe with jealousy and wait for chaos to come about, and with it, his opportunity to rise again to power over the kingdoms of light and darkness.

In the waiting area, Lily sobbed in her mother's arms while Rivera, Charlie, and Audrey stood by feeling helpless. Audrey squeezed Charlie's hand until it hurt, but he was actually grateful for the pain, because it took his mind off of everything else. Rivera stood aside, observing, until Lily's mom looked over her daughter's shoulder at him. He recognized that same helplessness in her eyes that he'd seen in the families of so many murder victims—and he touched her back, lightly, and for only a second, to let her know he was there, another human being: backup.

The medical crash team had pulled curtains across the glass in Minty Fresh's room, but after twenty-two minutes the curtain whooshed aside and the doctor came through, paused a second at the desk, then turned to come through the double doors into the waiting room, the look on his face broadcasting what he was going to say: "There was nothing we could do."

Before the doctor reached them, Charlie felt himself go light-headed; his vision tunneled down, went black, and he collapsed. The doctor helped Audrey catch him and lower him into a chair.

Asher, what the fuck you doing here?" said Minty Fresh.

Charlie looked around, saw literally nothing but the big man, standing perhaps ten feet away from him, wearing only a bedsheet.

"Where's here?" asked Charlie.

The Mint One adjusted his sheet, which was too small for a man his size to wear as a toga, opting instead for a sarong/towel wraparound effect. He looked around. They might have been standing on a sheet of black glass under a starless night sky, except he could see Charlie and Charlie could see him, so technically, it wasn't dark. When he rubbed his eyes and looked again he could see that they were inside a large stone chamber, lit with bronze oil lamps that jutted from the wall and threw long shadows up to a high, pointed ceiling. Across one wall and plane of the ceiling stretched the elongated shadow of a dog's head with long pointed ears. Minty searched but couldn't see the dog that was casting the shadow, yet there it was, a shadow thirty feet tall, and still reaching only halfway to the apex of the ceiling.

"I'm going to guess the Underworld," said Minty Fresh.

"You've been here before?"

"I had it described to me once," said Minty Fresh. "And you look like your old self."

Charlie was his non-Mike Sullivan self, dressed in one of his Savile Row houndstooth suits.

"Oakland?" asked Charlie.

"Not Oakland," came a voice that echoed through the chamber.

A circle of torches appeared; in its center, a tall, dog-headed man in an Egyptian kilt stood by a stone table on which stood a gold balance scale. In front of the table was a stone pit, perhaps five meters across; something down there was growling and snarling.

"You know who I am?" said the dog man.

"I do," said Minty Fresh. "Anubis. A man I knew came here once, met you, told me about you."

"He was my brother's avatar on earth, you are mine."

Anubis crouched, leaned forward, opened his eyes wide; the irises glowed deep gold.

"The eyes," said Charlie. "Of course."

Minty Fresh looked at Charlie. "Of course? This all makes sense to you?"

"Sure," Charlie said. He inched forward until he could see into the pit. Thirty feet below, a creature the size of a hippo circled the floor, with the body of a lion and the jaws of a crocodile. The floor of the pit was littered with bleached human bones; Charlie could make out skulls here and there in the orange light of the oil lamps. He backed away from the edge until he stood next to Minty again. "Maybe not."

"You will go back," said Anubis. "You will be my avatar on earth and you will put things in order again. Do you understand?"

"I'm not good at taking orders," said Minty Fresh.

The dog-headed god seemed disturbed at the answer. "You're not afraid, then?"

"Of what? I'm dead already, aren't I?"

"You are," said Anubis.

"Then no, I'm not afraid."

"Good. And you?" Anubis nodded to Charlie.

"I'm fine," said Charlie. "Dogs love me."

Minty Fresh's gaze fell on Charlie like it had fallen off a table. "Really?"

"Sorry." Charlie looked at his shoes.

"The weapons of men will not help you. Your enemies are of the realm of the dead. You cannot kill them. You shall have my gifts to meet your adversary," said Anubis. "Defeat him, restore balance, order. You are mine and I am you. Now return."

"That is totally not helpful," said Charlie.

"Why are you even here?" said Minty Fresh.

"He must keep them from desecrating your body until you return to it. Away with you," said the dog-headed god.

The torches faded, the blackness returned, and once again they were standing as if they were in empty space at the end of the universe, nothing but the two of them and the faint barking of hounds.

And then Charlie was in the waiting room, Audrey standing over him. "Are you okay?"

"Fine," he said. "I'm fine. Fainted or something. How long was I out?"

Audrey looked at Rivera, then shrugged. "About eight seconds, I'd guess."

"Hmmm. Seemed longer." Charlie looked at the doctor. "No autopsy."

The doctor seemed surprised. This was not the reaction he was accustomed to getting from people who had just received the news of the passing of a loved one.

"In cases of a crime," said the doctor, "it's the law . . ."

"No autopsy," Charlie said to Rivera. "No embalming, no autopsy. It's important."

Rivera said, "Doctor, if we could hold off on the autopsy, I'd appreciate it."

The doctor nodded. "It will be up to the coroner after I sign off," said the doctor.

"I'll take care of it," said Rivera.

"I'm very sorry," said the doctor. He turned and went back through the doors.

Once the doctor was gone, Charlie went to Lily. "Hey," he whispered in her ear. Lily's mother looked up. Lily nodded to her that it was okay to let this stranger close.

"Kid, come here," Charlie said. He put his arm around Lily's shoulder and walked her away from her mother, away from the others.

"He told me to go to work," Lily said. "Those were his last words, 'Go to work, Darque.' "

"Yeah, that's the thing," Charlie whispered. "You probably need to go to work."

"Fuck you, Asher. I'm grief-stricken. And I'm not even being overly dramatic."

He didn't want to tell her that with the black eye makeup smeared down her cheeks like a sad clown, she was overly dramatic without saying a word, but in her hour of grief, he let it go. "Yeah, I know, and I know that's a first, but you need to have your mom take you to work, because you need to stay busy, and keep your mind off of this. And when I tell you this next thing, you can't overreact. Promise me."

Lily looked at him with the familiar "could you be any more annoying?" look that she reserved for him, and he knew he could plunge on.

"Promise?"

"Okay, fine, I promise. What?"

"He's not dead."

She stared. Just stared. Stunned.

"He's coming back," Charlie said. "Don't scream."

She didn't move. She stopped breathing, then started again, in short, halting gasps.

"I don't know when, but soon. I just saw him in the Underworld. There's a god called Anubis—"

"Asher, if you are fucking with me—"

"I'm not! Really, I'm not."

Now she was catching her breath. She leaned in. "He told me once that an Indian guy in Montana told him he was, like, the chosen of Anubis. That's why he had—has golden eyes."

"Yeah, apparently that's true."

She put her fingers to her lips as if she were holding in a laugh and bounced on her toes in a circle like an overjoyed little girl.

"You're going to need to stop that."

"Right," she said, stopping that. "Sorry."

"Now you're going to have to figure out what to tell your mom that I just told you that made you do that."

"No problem. I'll tell her that you said the last thing he said to you was that he only regretted never telling me that I was right about everything."

"He would never say that."

"She never met him."

"Fine. Now look sadder and get your mom to take you to work. You're our only contact with the ghosts on the bridge. You need to be on the crisis line. And we need her out of here so I can tell the others. I'll call your cell when I know more."

"Okay, I'm going to hug you now, Asher."

"Okay."

"It's not a real hug, it's theater. I'm faking it."

"Right. Me, too," said Charlie.

Lily and her mother had only been gone seconds when Charlie's phone buzzed: *Jane.* He answered.

"He took Sophie," Cassie said. "He just came in the door and took her. We couldn't do anything. We tried."

An electric chill surged through his body. "Who?"

"The black guy in yellow—the one she talked about hurting Mrs. Korjev."

"Where's Jane?"

"She's right here. He did something to her. She ran at him and he just put out his hand and she dropped. She's coming to, woozy, but she seems okay."

"You called the police?"

"Yes, they're on their way. I'm still on the other phone with 911."

Charlie heard her talking to someone, describing the man in yellow.

"Was he driving? On foot?"

"I don't know, Charlie. I couldn't move. He just looked at me and I couldn't move. Sophie kept yelling for him to put her down. Called him Dookie Face. She wasn't screaming, afraid screaming. She was yelling, angry yelling. I'm so sorry. We should have been gone by now."

"Tell the police everything," Charlie said. "I'll be there as soon as I can. Ten minutes, maybe."

Rivera and Audrey stood behind him, waiting for instructions, having read the situation from his end of the conversation. "We have to go," he said to Rivera. "Audrey, can you stay with Minty Fresh's body? Don't leave him for even a second. You have to be there when he comes back." He held out her car keys.

"What?" Audrey asked, taking the car keys by reflex.

"He's coming back, I don't know when, but stay with him. Tell them whatever you have to. I would do it, but I have to go."

"Go," she said, "Go, go, go." She kissed him and pushed him toward the door. She pushed Rivera after Charlie. "Call me when you know any-thing."

"You, too," said Rivera. "And if they give you any trouble—"

"Go. I've got this. Go."

Rivera ran after Charlie.

Crisis Center, this is Lily. What's your name?" Her screen showed the call was coming from one of the hardwired lines on the bridge. Her heart leapt.

"Lily, it's Mike."

"Holy fuck, do you have any idea what's going on?"

And once again, everyone in the call center turned to look at her.

"I mean, hello, Mike, how can I help? This call may be recorded," she said, letting him know why she was being formal, "but only my side, so you should feel safe to say whatever you'd like."

"Okay," said Mike. "I thought you should know. There's someone here, at the bridge, and all the ghosts are riled up. It's like a storm here. Not that you could see, but here in my world."

"I was going to tell you that I think we found that thief you were looking for." Lily was trying to figure out how her side of the conversation might sound on the recording. Incoherent was fine. She could claim she was responding to someone who was suffering from delusions. "So, it looks like the suspect is a large African American man who is dressed all in yellow. I see. And his name is Lemon Fresh, maybe, possibly Yama?"

"I don't know about that last part, but he's here, and he has a little girl with him. He's why everyone is riled up."

"On the bridge?"

"No, not on the bridge, he's right under the bridge. In Fort Point."

"Fort Point," Lily repeated. "I see. Shall I send someone to you?"

"If you think they can help," said Mike.

"Well, they'll certainly try. Can you hold on a minute while I contact those people to help you?"

"Sure," said Mike. "Lily, I can't find Concepción, either. It's like she's lost in this storm."

"Let me see what I can do, Mike."

Lily pushed the hold button, looked around the center. Mercifully, Sage wasn't working tonight, but a couple of the other counselors were glancing her way every few seconds. Leonidas was standing in the doorway of his office, his finger to the earpiece of a wireless headset. The fucker was listening in on her *live*. Fine, he'd only hear her side and think her terminal was out of order. Pretending to scroll through contact numbers on her screen, she pulled her phone out of her purse and texted Charlie Asher: HE'S AT FORT POINT. UNDER THE BRIDGE.

She looked over her shoulder. Leonidas was frowning. He would have expected to hear her call to emergency services, even if he couldn't hear Mike's end of the conversation. She clicked off the hold button.

"Hi Mike, I'm back. Sorry about that, something seems to be wrong with my terminal. I texted the bridge authority and they are on their way to you. I'll stay on the line with you until they reach you."

"I know you're covering, Lily. You need to know, I think I'm starting to get the point of all the stories the ghosts have been telling me, but I need to find Concepción. She just evaporated, right in front of me."

"I'm sure she'll be back any minute, Mike. I just had a similar experience and I know how distressing that can be, but just stay calm and—"

The line clicked. The screen showed disconnected. She had the ability to call back each of the hard lines on the bridge and she hit the button.

"Hello?" A male voice, but different. She could hear wind, traffic, not the ghostly static that she heard when Mike called.

"Mike?"

"No, this is Jeremy. Who is this?"

"This is the Crisis Center for the bridge."

"Well, you guys should have blankets up here or something. It's really cold. I thought it was supposed to be warm in California."

"Well, you're standing over the mouth of a bay, at night, in the winter, you fucktard, of course it's cold." She disconnected. When she looked back, Leonidas was heading for her desk.

Her phone buzzed with a return message from Asher: HE HAS SOPHIE.

Fuck! The little girl Mike mentioned.

She stood up, turned to Leonidas, did a traffic-cop signal for him to stop right where he was. "Get the fuck back in your office. This is my thing, and I need to be here. It's not my fault that this terminal isn't working right, but you didn't hear the other side of the conversation. If that guy calls back and I'm not here, someone is going to die, so get back in your office and chew my ass or fire me at the end of shift, but right now I need to be here."

Leonidas, paused, seemed to be thinking, then said, "End of shift." He turned and headed back to his office.

Lily texted Charlie: MIKE SAW SOPHIE WITH LEMON AT FORT POINT.

27

FORT POINT

Audrey dug her wallet out of her purse as she approached the nurses' desk. For the first time since she'd returned from Asia, she wished she was wearing her monk robes. She had three or four cards with her name and title ready, as well as her driver's license, which proved she was the person on the other cards. This was a first for her, but desperate times . . .

"Hello, I'm the venerable Amitabha Audrey Walker Rinpoche, head of the Three Jewels Buddhist Center." *Click, click, click* went the cards on the desk. "I am Mr. Fresh's spiritual guide. Our faith requires that I be present with the body at all times to help usher his spirit through *bardo*, from life to death. I need to be with Mr. Fresh."

The nurse looked skeptically over her reading glasses. Luckily, she wasn't the nurse to whom Rivera had presented Audrey as a sketch artist, but she'd been at the desk for a while. She'd seen them all come and go, their strange displays of sorrow and joy, but she was used to dealing with people who were often at the most stressful point in their lives, and they didn't always react rationally when things got rough.

"He said the girl in the slutty schoolgirl outfit was his priest."

Audrey knew she had some wiggle room here, because what most Americans knew about Buddhism came from a forty-year-old television show, the star of which had accidently hanged himself while having a wank in a hotel wardrobe, so it was unlikely she'd be caught stretching the truth on doctrine.

"She is, but hers is a different discipline. To those who practice our faith, outward appearance is an illusion, a distraction from the true nature of our dharma." *Wait, let that sink in. No one knows what dharma is. Wait. Wait. This will work.*

"He did have her down as his next of kin."

"All people of our faith are considered family." *No, that sounded culty.* She wanted to sound nice, not culty.

"And you need to be with the body how long?"

"Until the soul has passed. Usually less than a day."

"Could you step in here, please?" The nurse went to the part of the desk that was behind the glass partition and waited for Audrey to pick up her IDs and come through the doors.

"Look, Ms. Walker, we are going to have to send Mr. Fresh's body down to the morgue in a few minutes. Whether they let you stay with him will be up to them. You can stay with him until they come to get him, and I can vouch for you with the orderly who takes him down, but once you get down there, you're going to have to tell them why you're there and see if they let you stay with him."

"What if I told them I was with the police? You saw we were with Inspector Rivera."

The nurse's glasses slipped down again. "You're a Buddhist priest *and* a policeman?"

"Undercover. And, technically, I'm a nun."

"I would watch that show," said the nurse. "I wouldn't believe it, but I would watch it."

"Pardon?"

"Go stay with Mr. Fresh. But *stay* with him. No wandering around doing detective work while you're tending to his soul." The nurse wondered why people never figured out that once you got your way, you could stop lying. It almost made her want to back up and revoke the permission she'd just given.

"Thank you," said Audrey. "Blessings."

Thirty minutes later Audrey was standing in a hallway by the gurney on which Minty Fresh's body lay when his eyes popped open.

"Hi," she said.

She hit send on her phone, sending the message she'd typed in: HE'S ALIVE.

His eyes went wide and darted around, as if he were trying to remember how to speak.

"You were dead a little under an hour," she said. "Think of it like a nap, really. Charlie told me you'd be back." Audrey watched as the confusion seemed to settle in Minty's eyes. This process was all new to her, too, but she had been present when the Squirrel People came to life after they received a human soul; they were always disoriented and seemed to have to remind themselves of the confines of reality, because for them, reality had just been put in a jar and shaken vigorously. For some it would settle; for others, it never seemed to.

"You're probably cold. They cut your pants off of you, and I don't know what happened to your shirt. I brought you these." She held up a pair of green scrubs she'd plucked from a bin as the orderly had rolled Minty Fresh's body though the basement hallway. "I have your coat and your shoes, too. Shelf under the gurney. There's blood on one shoe. Sorry."

Minty's eyes stopped darting. It seemed as if whatever part of him had been searching for reality had finally found it.

"They cut off my motherfucking custom-made leather pants?"

"Look at you, all alive and stuff," she said. She thought she should have said something more profound, something from the heart sutra, "Form does not differ from the void, and void does not differ from form," perhaps, but instead she said, "Who needs pants? You're alive."

"Spoken like someone who is alive *and* has pants."

She threw him the scrubs. "I'll turn my back and watch the hall."

The big man sat up, turned sideways on the gurney, and began to worm his way into the scrubs.

"You presided at the death of a lot of people when you were a nun, right?"

"I guided one hundred and fifty-three souls through *bardo*."

"So how was my death?"

"Pretty good. A solid seven. Well above average."

"Did everyone cry?"

"Well, most of the crying was done when they were still trying to save you. Lily was a mess. I wasn't in the room when you actually died, but it wasn't long before Charlie told us you were coming back, so everyone cheered up. I think Lily said 'yippee' as she was leaving."

"Why isn't Charlie here? He told you, I'm guessing, where we went?"

"Yes, but your cousin Lemon took Sophie."

"Shit."

"The ghost on the bridge told Lily that Lemon has Sophie at Fort Point, under the bridge."

"Dressed," he said. The scrubs were extra large but not extra tall, so they fit him in the hips and shoulders. The pants, however hit him just below the knee and the shirt in the middle of his waist. He looked like a cross between a well-kept castaway and a very large Moroccan houseboy.

"Anyone hurt?"

"No. He just came to their apartment and took her. Jane and Cassie couldn't do anything to stop him."

"And the old Russian lady, she okay?"

"She'll recover, they're saying."

"And you, my cousin mess with you when he had you? Hurt you?"

"No. In fact, he stopped the Morrigan from hurting me."

"Why didn't he?"

"I don't know what you mean."

"I mean, why didn't he hurt you? Why didn't the old lady die? Why would he take Sophie? She's just a little girl, now, right? If he's such a badass, how is it you're all alive?"

"Maybe he just wants a new order, like he said."

"Don't care what he wants," said Minty Fresh. "I want to know what he can do. How'd he get in Asher's building through all that security?"

"They didn't say. Everything's always locked there."

"Then Lemon got a way of getting around that ain't a '49 Buick. You got a car?"

"In the parking garage."

"Lead on," said the Mint One. He hopped as he pulled on his black trainers, then grabbed his leather car coat from under the gurney. "We're going to Fort Point."

Audrey sent a text to Charlie as they walked: ON OUR WAY TO FORT PT.

Fort Point?" said Rivera. "Charlie, I don't know if I can get us in there. It's a national park. Since 9/11 it's been under Homeland Security. There are guards there with M4 rifles; even the park rangers are armed. After what we pulled at the Fort Mason tunnel, there's no way the department is going to back me up if they call in to verify me." They were in Rivera's Ford, just passing Fort Mason and the Marina Safeway on their way to Fort Point.

Charlie said, "It's okay, they'll let me in."

"Why would they let you in?"

Charlie pulled Mike Sullivan's bridge authority ID and held it up. "Because I'm an employee. They need me to find another job in the park that gets me off the bridge, so even if they call in, someone will vouch. Everyone knows Mike Sullivan's story. I'll say I wanted to check it out when there were no tourists."

"They'll never let us in with our weapons," said Rivera.

"Anubis said weapons won't do us any good. They won't touch him."

"Well, I'm not sure what good we can do here, then."

"We *have* to be here. He has my daughter. She's just a little kid."

"Actually, she's probably not."

"What's that mean, 'she's probably not'?"

"Why would this thing—this deity, go back and kidnap a little kid? What use is a random little kid to him? We would have taken a break if he hadn't taken her."

"I never thought about that. You think he still thinks she's the Luminatus?"

"He knows more about this stuff than I do, and *he* took her."

"She *is* in the advanced reading group."

"Well, there you go," said Rivera.

Charlie's phone buzzed. Message from Audrey. HE'S ALIVE.

Rivera pulled into the tourist parking area, which was still a good half mile from the fort. The remainder of the road had heavy vehicle barriers that rose out of the concrete to limit traffic to pedestrians and bicycles; however, currently, the barriers were down. Rivera killed the lights and drove to the parking lot adjacent to the fort. He stopped the car at the far edge of the parking lot and turned off the engine. There were a few vehicles near the fort, but they looked official, light trucks and SUVs with national park insignias.

Fort Point was a Civil War–era fortress with four-foot-thick brick and concrete walls, and gun ports designed for a battery of cannons to defend the entire entrance to the San Francisco Bay. Even though the fort had lost its strategic value by the 1930s, the Golden Gate Bridge had been designed specifically so the fort would be preserved as an example of military architecture. The entrance from the city side of the bridge was a great, structural steel arch that went directly over the top of the fort, rather than the more practical straight pylons that could have been built if the fort had been removed.

As they climbed out of the car, Charlie's phone buzzed again. Audrey's message: ON OUR WAY TO FORT PT.

Charlie said, "They're on their way. Maybe twenty minutes out."

"We should wait," said Rivera as he popped the trunk. "This Yama probably doesn't know we know he's here. We shouldn't blow our surprise when Fresh is the only one who has any way to fight him." Rivera put his Beretta and holster in the trunk. "I'm keeping the Glock on my ankle. If the guards notice it, I'll say I forgot I had it on."

"I have my sword cane," said Charlie. "As far as they know, I just fell off the bridge. They're not going to take away my walking stick."

"If it makes you feel better," said Rivera.

The wind covered the sound of the car trunk closing, but also whipped their trouser cuffs around their legs. Strangely enough, Rivera's hair stayed perfect.

"It's freezing out here," Charlie said.

"We should wait in the car," Rivera said.

They climbed back in the Ford. Charlie texted Audrey that they would wait for them in the parking lot. He hoped that she wasn't texting while driving, because that would be dangerous. No, she was smart, she'd hand her phone to the newly resurrected Egyptian demigod of death rather than do anything careless.

The light shining down from the bridge plus a three-quarter moon gave them light to see the entire southern side of the fort. No one was visible. Not even at the main gate.

"Where are the guards?" Rivera asked. "The park rangers?"

"You know I never actually worked on the bridge, right? Mike Sullivan did. I didn't even know there *were* guards here until you told me."

"When Fresh gets here, you and Audrey need to stay here."

"No."

"Charlie, where are the guards? You don't know that they haven't been shredded by the Morrigan and are lying in pieces inside."

"No," said Charlie.

"Fresh and I will get Sophie."

"My daughter is in there, Inspector. Plus, do you think I've done battle with sewer harpies, been poisoned and died, been resurrected and lived as a meat puppet, then had someone throw himself off the Golden Gate Bridge to give me his body so I could sit in the fucking car?"

Rivera considered it, ticked off Charlie's points in his head, considered his lack of concern for his own safety, then said, "Okay."

"Okay," said Charlie.

They sat in silence until Rivera spotted headlights in his mirror and watched them go out even as the car continued on. "Good girl, Audrey," he said.

When Minty Fresh climbed out of the Honda, Charlie ran to him and threw his arms around the big man's waist. Minty held his arms out to his sides and looked from Audrey to Rivera with the humiliated but resolved look of a dog enduring a bath until Charlie finally let go and stepped back.

"Sorry," Charlie said.

"It's okay," said the Mint One.

Audrey bailed Charlie out by performing the same, yet somewhat more appropriate run and hug move on him.

"So, how was dying?" Rivera asked Minty. Rivera raised an eyebrow at the Mint One's outfit.

"Not as relaxing as you'd think," said Minty.

"Charlie says you have some Yama-stopping mojo."

"Yeah, about that; Anubis was less than clear what particular talent I would have, other than I would be his avatar in this world. Right now I'm thinking pants would have been a good start."

"Audrey?" Rivera said, looking to the nun. "Any hints?"

"I'm Buddhist. We believe all gods are illusions and constructions of ego. As far as I know, even you guys might be illusions."

"That's helpful," Rivera said.

"*Namaste*," Audrey replied. "If that's even your real name."

"What?"

"Sorry, Buddhist humor. Carry on."

Rivera glanced over his shoulder at the fort. "Okay, here's what we know. We can't see any guards or park rangers, but if they're there, and they should be, they'll be armed with M4 automatic rifles. There was nothing on the radio about gunfire here, so we have to assume that if Yama is in there, as the ghost says, then they either haven't seen him, or they haven't seen him as a threat, which means he doesn't have the

Morrigan with him, because I can't really see them as coming off as non-threatening."

"Or all the guards are dead," said Audrey.

"Yes, there's that cheerful possibility," said Rivera. "So, what do you think? Shotguns and stab-resistant vests?"

"Nah, this ain't gonna be no battle, Inspector." Minty Fresh held up a finger as if testing the wind. "Anyone else hear that?"

There was a whirring sound, above the crash of the surf, the wind, and the traffic on the bridge, like the spooling up of an enormous jet engine. The others nodded, looked around.

"The fuck is that?" said Minty Fresh.

Audrey pointed up at the bridge, beyond the indirect floodlights that illuminated it and the red aircraft warning lights at the top of the towers, the bridge was beginning to glow, as if streaks of light were playing across its surfaces, someone painting it with moving lasers.

"Y'all seeing that?"

Charlie's phone buzzed. It was a message from Lily: MIKE SAYS THE GHOSTS OF THE BRIDGE ARE COMING UP. GO NOW. He read the message to the others.

"That light must be visible for twenty miles," Audrey said. "Why isn't traffic screeching to a halt on the bridge?"

"Because they can't see or hear it," said Minty Fresh. "Same way they can't see the glow in a soul vessel but we all can."

"I think we need to go now," said Rivera. He led them across the parking lot to the steel gates of the fort. There was a single heavy door in the middle of the gates. It was wide open. Rivera stopped at the edge, looked in, went back against the wall. He could see all the way into the center courtyard of the fortress. The side they were on had been the barracks, more or less just reinforced brick buildings with rooms for quartering and feeding soldiers. The other side of the fort was an arcade, three stories of heavy arches, in which the cannons had once nested, facing out to the bay. But now the spaces were empty of cannons and resembled rows of small theatrical stages. No one was visible from the door: no guards, no rangers, no man in yellow.

The roar of the ghosts of the bridge was less like a jet now and more like an atmosphere, like the low rumble of a huge crowd, ten thousand voices in a small room. Rivera reached down and drew the Glock from his ankle holster.

"I'm going in first. I'll signal when it's clear to follow."

Minty Fresh said, "You got some kind of death wish?"

"Apparently," said Rivera.

"Oh, you can go first," said Minty. "But put your gun away. You don't know there aren't guards in there might take someone sneaking in holding a Glock personally."

"I'll go," said Charlie as he breezed by them.

28
THE TAUNTING OF MINTY

Daddy!" Sophie called when Charlie entered the open courtyard of the fortress. She was standing four floors above him on a concrete gun platform. Lemon Fresh stood next to her. In the arched bay on the level below them, the Morrigan stained the bricks as tattered shadows. Only one of them still stood in three dimensions, cradling an arm with no hand attached. She hissed and Charlie jumped back a little.

"How you doin'?" said Lemon.

"Are you okay, honey?" Charlie said.

"I'm okay," said Sophie. "But it's cold and I haven't had a snack in days." She glared at Lemon. Her dark pigtails whipped around her face in the wind.

"Don't be scared, honey. Daddy is here."

"I'm not scared, Daddy. I just need some crunchy Cheese Newts up in this bitch."

Lemon looked over at Sophie, who, because she stood on the gun mount, was eye level with him, "Where you learn to talk like that, child?" Lemon looked down at Charlie. "What you teachin' this child?"

"She's gifted," Charlie said.

"More important," Lemon said, moving his right hand in a stirring motion, "why ain't you sleeping?"

Charlie looked around. Along the edges of the courtyard—the arcade on Lemon's side, and the colonnade on his side—slept a half-dozen rangers. Not dead or injured: they looked as if they'd simply gotten tired and decided to take a nap. One woman was curled up around her M4 rifle as if it were a body pillow. Amid the whir of the ghosts of the bridge above, Charlie could hear one fellow who was sitting against a column on his side of the courtyard, snoring softly, his face under the cover of his Smokey the Bear hat.

"I guess I'm gifted, too," said Charlie. He gestured for the others to join him. Minty Fresh stepped out of the shadows right behind him. Audrey was a few columns down, checking on a sleeping ranger. Rivera looked out from behind a column.

"New meat," snarled Nemain. "This time you'll stay dead. I'll suck the soul from you while you're still bleeding."

"The fuck, Lemon?" said Minty Fresh. "Control your bitches."

Lemon shrugged—*What you gonna do?* "Y'all act like I brought the ladies to the party, but they come on they own, cuz. A door open up out the Underworld, there they is. It's y'all's fault they here. All y'all let shit get so fucked up here they was drawn here like hoes to coke."

"He took my hand," said Nemain.

"And you said you killed him," said Lemon. "Yet there he is, alive as a motherfucker, wearin' some poor child's pj's." With that, Lemon started to laugh, then bent over and wheezed a little bit, raising a palm to hold his place in the taunting. "Wha'chu wearin', Minty?"

"I'm comfortable," said Minty. "Why don't you send that child down here to her daddy, Lemon. You and me talk this out."

"Nah, she mine now," said Lemon. He reached out to stroke Sophie's cheek and his irises lit up like fire.

Inspector Alphonse Rivera had been a policeman more than twenty-five years, and in all that time, from working a patrol car, to narcotics, to homicide, he had never shot a person. He had drawn his weapon, of course, but he had never had to fire on a human being. He'd always been very good at assessing a situation and acting quickly and appropriately when he needed to, as if his mind could prepare dozens of if/then triggers that would put him in motion without hesitating. When Lemon Fresh touched Sophie's cheek, one of those trigger's fired. In a single motion, Rivera went to one knee, drew the Glock from his ankle holster, aimed, and fired four shots in quick succession. Everyone including the Morrigan jumped at the sound of gunfire.

Four copper-jacketed bullets hung in the air—stopped—about two inches from Lemon's face. All could have fit in the space of a tennis ball. Rivera had never shot a person, but Nick Cavuto had been a bit of a handgun enthusiast, so the partners had spent a lot of hours together practicing at the range.

"Hooo-weeee," said Lemon Fresh. He looked all around the bullets, getting a view from different angles. "This motherfucker can shoot."

Nemain screeched and leapt out of the arch where she had been standing across the open courtyard toward Rivera, the claws of her only remaining hand extended. Rivera fired four times again, adjusting aim with each shot, catching her in the collarbone once and in the face three times, spattering bits of black, feathery goo into the air. She landed face-first on the concrete floor and slid several feet until she was only inches from Rivera, who held aim on her. As they watched she melted to an inky shadow and flowed backward, up the arches, until she joined her sisters as another tattered sillouette against the red bricks.

"Well, that didn't work," said Nemain.

"Told you," said Babd.

"When we get the souls, he's the first to go," said Macha.

Rivera ejected the spent clip and snapped a full one from his jacket into the gun.

"Sho can shoot," said Lemon. He made a fist and the bullets hanging before him dropped out of the air with a thud and clatter. "Yo standard-issue Negro wouldn't stand a chance, but I am what . . . ?" He deferred with a bow to Sophie.

"A dookie face," she said.

"That's right," said Lemon, winking at her, "a Magical Negro." He looked to Rivera. "And because I am only interested in nonviolence and harmony among all creatures, I am going to put you to sleep rather than crush you like a motherfucking bug." Lemon waved his palm at Rivera like a hypnotist putting a subject to sleep. Rivera adjusted his aim for the movement, but otherwise did not move. Lemon repeated the sleep gesture. Nothing. He searched the courtyard until he found Audrey, who was checking the pulse of another downed ranger, and tried the sleep gesture on her.

"Yeah, nothing," said Audrey.

"What, did y'all stop at Starbuck's on the way here? Well, I tried. Ladies, I think you gonna need to go get you some breakfast. Go get him."

With that, the Morrigan slithered out of their archway, up the wall, over the roof of the fortress, and away. Sophie ran to the edge of the wall to follow their progress then came back to Lemon's side.

"They're silly."

"You don't never be lyin', peanut," said Lemon.

Charlie was caught between being horrified and relieved that his darling little girl was discussing the silliness of a trio of Celtic death goddesses with a vengeful Buddhist deity dressed like a citrus fruit.

"Lemon, enough of this nonsense," said Minty Fresh. "You need to send that little girl down here now. Me and you'll work this out."

"Can't do that, cuz. I need her for what I'ma do. You do know she the Big D, right?"

Minty Fresh looked around at his companions. If Lemon didn't know Sophie had lost her powers, he didn't think it good strategy to tell him now.

"There they go." Lemon turned and looked at the bridge. Three dark streaks were making their way up the concrete pylons toward the steel cables and arches, which were glowing with the neon flow of mad ghosts.

"They just need to move one more obstacle out of my way and we'll all be done here. All them poor souls will be released and whatever bullshit y'all have been perpetratin' here will be over. Everything will be copacetic. In order. Bitches just need to shred them a Ghost Thief. I expect by the time they find him, they be plenty strong enough. Going to cost some souls, bless their hearts."

Charlie felt his phone buzz in his pocket and checked it: *Lily*. "Hold that thought," he said. "I have to take this."

Lily said, "Asher, I'm on the hard line with Mike Sullivan. He says the ghosts on the bridge are out of control and there's some dark force moving on them."

"That's the Morrigan."

"Well, stop them."

"They're kind of out of range."

Charlie looked back over his shoulder. The dark streaks of shadows that were the Morrigan were almost to the steel arch above them. The ghosts, or the light, or the ghost light seemed to be moving toward them, as if to meet them, swarming along the arch above the fort.

"Lemon says that they are going to shred the Ghost Thief. Tell Mike."

Charlie could hear Lily in the background talking on her headset. "I told him," she said.

"What did he say?"

"He said that was weird."

They all watched as the dark streaks that were the Morrigan took shape as a cloud of black birds, then morphed into their human woman forms. The Morrigan stood on the girders of the arch above them, but the dark tide of ghosts continued to swell toward them until the Morrigan's dark edges began to glow, then pulsate, brighter and brighter. Finally, the three of them popped like soap bubbles, black confetti or tiny feathers burst into three distinct bursts, like negative fireworks made of darkness. An elliptical lens opened in the sky beneath the bridge—a trick of light. The Morrigan confetti fell into it and the lens closed.

"Mike says it's okay now," Lily said. She disconnected.

When Charlie turned back around, Lemon Fresh was bent over laughing again. "That shit is funny. You see that? They went sucked up and bust like balloons. Like we used to feel when yo' mama made hush puppies, Minty. That woman could fry her some hush puppies, rest her soul."

"Don't act like you planned that, Lemon," said Minty Fresh.

"I *did* plan that, cuz. Them bitches was crazy. I told you, I am here to see all them poor, lost souls released from that bridge. All them souls y'all got in jars and golf clubs and I-don't-know-what, that ain't right. That ain't the right way of things."

Audrey moved to Minty Fresh's side. "He did save me from them. And he didn't hurt any of these guards. He hasn't harmed Sophie. He may just be making way for a new order, a new path. There's always chaos when systems are realigning. Yama is a god of death, but he was made protector of Buddhism, protector of the way."

"That's right, Minty, I'm protector of the way. I don't judge, like y'all do. The Morrigan was a different thing. They all about war. Me, I'm all about love."

"Uh-huh," said Minty, unconvinced.

"I'm going to get my daughter," Charlie said. He started up one of the four flights of stairs on their side of the fortresses.

"She fine right here," said Lemon. "Once I'm done with my business, y'all can take her home."

"All right," said Minty Fresh. "I'll wait up there, then." He started for the staircases on the side of the courtyard opposite where Charlie had gone up. Once they got to the top, they'd be closing on Lemon from either side.

Rivera joined Audrey in the edge of the courtyard, the Glock hanging at his side. "You believe what you just said?"

She shook out her hair. "I did when I said it."

Minty came around the roof of the fortress on the left, Charlie on the right.

"Ya'll can stop right there," said Lemon. "I need peanut here for my business."

Sophie jumped down from the gun platform and ran toward Charlie. "Daddy!"

Lemon dropped his hand and Sophie stopped in her tracks. Charlie drew the sword from his cane. "Let her go."

Lemon raised his hand toward Charlie, who stopped and struggled, as if his feet were stuck to the cement. Minty Fresh was only twenty feet away from Lemon when the yellow fellow turned and stopped him with the same gesture. "Not now, cuz. Let me get to this."

"Lemon, I'm gonna bust your ass I get hold of you," said Minty. Under his breath he said, "Anubis, you going to give me some mojo, now would be a good time."

Lemon moved until he was standing directly over Sophie. She screamed. He turned toward the bridge with his arms raised high in invitation. "C'mon y'all. Come on here."

The ghosts of the bridge swirled and stormed, the light moving out now, away from the structure, the streams of ghosts arching toward Lemon. "Come on, my babies. Daddy gonna take you home."

"I burned up your Buick," said Rivera from below in the courtyard.

Lemon tried not to, but looked over his shoulder at the cop. "What you say?"

"This morning. After everyone else left the tunnel at Fort Mason, I went back and threw a highway flare in the backseat of your Buick."

"You did not," said Lemon.

"Let him go," Audrey said. "He's trying to free those souls."

"I got out of there before it blew up, but it did blow up. Like a blast furnace in there," said Rivera. "I'm in a bit of trouble over it, but on the bright side, your Buick is nothing but frame and warm lug nuts now."

"You a dead five-oh," Lemon said. He turned toward Rivera and lost whatever concentration he had on the bridge. The ghosts resumed their frenzied trip back up the metal frame and cables. Lemon raised an arm as if winding up a baseball pitch, and before he could come down, a dark figure appeared behind him.

"*AIIIIIIIIIEEEEEEEEEEEE*," shrieked the banshee, and she touched the stun gun to Lemon's neck. ZZZZZZZZZT!

As Lemon turned to face his attacker, the banshee ducked under his arm, grabbed Sophie's hand, and pulled her away from him. "Hello, love," said the banshee, pulling the child into her skirts.

"You smell like barbecue," Sophie said.

Lemon rubbed the back of his neck as if he'd smacked a particularly annoying mosquito, the stun gun no more than a minor annoyance. "You'll not do that again," he said, his voice sounding different now, not the smooth and amused Lemon.

"The Buick was in the tunnel?" Minty Fresh asked Rivera. "How did the Buick get in that tunnel?"

"Same way the Morrigan got out, I guess," said Rivera.

"Oh, for fuck's sake, you great dog-headed ninny, what are you waiting for?" said the banshee.

Lemon turned to her and froze her as she backed away with Sophie.

"You too, banshee, when I'm finished," said Lemon, still in a voice that was very un-Lemony. He raised his arms and began drawing down the ghosts of the bridge again, their light arching toward him. Above, on the steel arch of the bridge, stood a lone figure wearing painter's coveralls.

"Let him do it," Audrey said. "Yama is the guardian. He's bringing on the new order."

"He's not Yama, you twit," said the banshee. "He's bloody Set, lord of darkness and betrayal and general fuckery, isn't he? He's not releasing these souls to become part of the bloody universe, he's trying to absorb them. They'll become part of his great twatty ego, and good luck then."

"Oops," said Audrey.

Lemon spun on the banshee and made to strike her, but his hand passed right through her. "*AHHHHHHHIEEEEEEEEEEE!*" she shrieked at him.

"The Buick was in the tunnel," Minty said. "Oh. I see."

"Yes, love," said the banshee. "Set has been opening portals into the

Underworld to get around, as any proper demigod would. Do you need a diagram?"

"I knew we needed a diagram," Charlie said. "Thumbtacks and string, right?"

Minty Fresh's golden eyes began to glow like Lemon's now and he smiled.

The portal opened in the tunnel under Fort Mason Green and the hellhounds emerged. They were creatures of fire and force with the scent of their prey in their noses and they entered the world above at a full run, their paws throwing up bits of burned Buick as they crashed through the wooden barrier at the end of the tunnel in a shower of splinters and they made for Fort Point. There were few people out at that hour, and those who saw them thought them a trick of the light, shadows thrown by a spotlight from Alcatraz perhaps, because nothing real could be moving that fast that far away from the road.

They stayed close to the shore, leaping fences or parked cars when necessary, tearing through hedges like cannonballs through lace curtains. Past the Marina green, where children flew kites and played soccer during the day, past Crissy Field, where thousands gathered to watch fireworks or boat races, past the St. Francis Yacht Club, the old fort warehouses, now businesses, down the old battery trail, their paws kicking back gravel with enough force to chip a windshield. A snowflake flurry pattern spattered in the windscreen of Rivera's Ford as they raced through the Fort Point parking lot.

They were creatures of spirit and elation and they hadn't seen him in well over a year, yet they knew his scent, his essence, even though he wore a new body. They came through the fort gates frisking like lambs, slobbering and whining in great doggie joy, bounded up the stairs, and fell upon Charlie, soaking him with hellish dog spit.

"Goggies!" called Sophie, with a little girl yodel of a laugh.

Frozen in place by Lemon's magic, Charlie endured the great hounds' affection as best he could, bending here and there as they rubbed their faces on him, licked him, and finally made him the center of an enormous welcome-home double-dog hump, a mighty black pyramid of doggie delight, red rocket dog dinguses thrusting at him like slippery spears.

"The goggies love to dance with Daddy," Sophie said, offhand, to Lemon, whose eyes had gone wide at the sight of the great hounds. "They missed him."

"Help!" Charlie called. "Help, I'm being humped to death!"

"Aye, love," said the banshee. "But it's a dry hump."

"Not him," said Minty Fresh, his voice now filled with the booming resonance of Anubis.

"No, goggies!" called Sophie. "Down! Down!"

The hounds looked over to Sophie, dropped Charlie like a drooly tennis ball, then bounded over to her. Lemon forgot completely what he was doing, forgot he was drawing down the power of thousands of souls, forgot that when he finished he would rule over the realms of light *and* darkness, and turned to run. The stream of ghosts that he had been pulling down to him snapped back to the bridge.

Lemon threw his hands apart as if pushing soapsuds off the surface of a washbasin, and a portal opened in the fortress courtyard—shimmering like a black mirror. He took a step back to gather speed to leap the four floors when Alvin's jaws clamped down on his arm, jerking him back like a rag doll. His yellow homburg hat fluttered from his head and disappeared into the Underworld.

Alvin shook him twice before Mohammed caught his other arm.

"Hold," said Minty Fresh, who was Anubis. The hellhounds stopped, held Lemon, and growled like idling Ferraris. Minty stepped from where he'd been frozen in place and stood before Lemon, who was Set, once Egyptian lord of the Underworld.

"Hey, Lemon, how you like the goggies?" Minty spoke in his own voice now.

"I ain't gonna lie, cuz," said Lemon. "I do not care for them."

"You done here. You know that, right?"

Lemon hung limp between the two hounds, defeated for a second, then he grinned. "That was gonna be some big-ass consciousness, though, once I become the Luminatus. Some muthafuckin' world-burnin' will."

"Yeah, that ain't never going to happen. Here's what going to happen. These goggies are going to take you to a pit where Ammut has been waiting for your tender ass for thousands of years. Now, I know he can't end you, but he going to chew you up and shit you out in little pieces. And if you ever get your shit together, because that happens with our peoples, these two hellhounds will be waiting on you, Lemon. You can slow them up, but you can't stop them. They will follow you to the ends of the world and the ends of the Underworld, they will never give up and they will never die. You can't control them, and you can't kill them, and they ain't but one person can ever call them off, and she standing right there." Minty pointed.

"'Sup?" said Sophie.

"There is no kryptonite for these motherfuckers, Lemon, do you feel me?"

"You a hard man, Minty Fresh," said Lemon.

"Go!" said Minty.

The hellhounds leapt off the arcade with Lemon between them and fell the four stories into the portal to the Underworld, which closed behind them with the sound of a lightbulb popping.

"Bye, goggies," said Sophie.

Minty Fresh looked up to the lone figure standing on the bridge above them, amid the maelstrom of ghosts, and waved. Mike Sullivan waved back and disappeared into the flow.

29

SO THAT HAPPENED

risis Center, this is Lily. What's your name?"

"Lily, this is Mike."

"Mike, what's going on? Asher said it's over. What's over?"

"I found out, Lily. I found out why I listened to all those stories, what I'm doing here. I'm supposed to lead them. I'm the Ghost Thief."

"That's great, Mike, I have no idea what that means."

"I'm supposed to lead them all off the bridge, show them where they're supposed to go. All the souls stuck here with unresolved lives, they just need to live another life, learn the lesson. That's what the Ghost Thief was supposed to do. Steal the ghosts from the bridge."

"Why you?"

"Evidently I'm an ascended soul—or I will be."

"Which is?"

"It means I'm finished having lives. I move on now."

"What about Concepción? Did you find her?"

"She's here, with me now."

"Well, she might have told you."

"She didn't know. She just knew we had to find the Ghost Thief. We didn't know who it was, what it was. I had to hear the stories of the ghosts of the bridge, become aware of what they were and what we were—what we *are*. She's an ascended soul, too."

"How is that possible, she's been stuck on the bridge, well, in the Golden Gate for what? Two hundred years?"

"She was waiting for me. I guess I had lives to live to catch up to her."

"Well, really, a smart girl would have been wasted on you."

"I wanted you to know, Lily. I'm moving on. And after hundreds of years waiting, Concepción is moving on, too. We're going together."

"To where? Because I've been to Marin and it's not that great."

"Can you envision two beings, people, meant for each other, the elation of being in love—completely aware of your connection to that person, like you are part of them, and they are part of you, inseparable?"

"That's a thing? That's what you have with Concepción?"

"Yes, but an ascended soul feels that way toward everything, is that way with everything. That's where we're going. Sort of everywhere."

"Well, you'll want to take a jacket."

"I wanted to say thanks, Lily."

"You're welcome."

"And good-bye."

"Bye, Mike. I'll be here if shit gets weird."

"We wouldn't want that," said Mike.

Then he showed them the way, those souls that had been lost at the Golden Gate for years, decades, centuries, mad as bedbugs, they came to themselves, and those who had lessons to learn, returned to new bodies, new lives, to take a turn on the wheel of life and death once again, and those like Mike and Concepción, who were the compilation of dozens of lives, who had found the way, become aware, ascended together in loving kindness, to hold each other and all things, one with the universe, complete.

Rivera was leading the Emperor and his men out of the kennel at the department of animal control when she appeared.

"AHHHHHHHIEEEEEEEEEE!" cried the banshee.

Rivera didn't even jump, although Bummer and Lazarus saw to it that the sooty wraith got a good barking-at before the Emperor distracted them with a beef jerky Rivera had brought for just such an emergency.

"So this is going to continue?" Rivera said. He was very tired and still had to get two dogs and a lunatic across town to the utility closet where they lived before he rested.

"No, love. The doom is done. I'm just popping by to ask if I can keep this." She held up the stun gun and gave it a buzz. "The wee box of lightning adds spice to the task."

"Sure, keep it," said Rivera. "What now?"

"I thought I'd go shriek at someone. I quite enjoy that."

"Yes, you do. Be careful with that thing."

"Not a worry, I'll only use it on those who aren't properly surprised by the shrieking. By the by, love, when you get back to your store, I think you'll want to have a look in your death book. Surprises, don't you know."

"Thanks, I will."

"Ta," she said, and in a wisp of smoke, she was gone.

"That's somewhat disturbing," said the Emperor. The men frisked at his sides, hopeful eyes searching for another beef jerky.

"She does that," said Rivera. He led them to the brown Ford and opened the rear door for them. "Did you get your journal?" he asked.

"In the recycle bin," said the Emperor. "Its purpose has been served. I'm going to turn my attentions to the living citizens of my city. They need me."

"Of course they do," said Rivera. The Emperor and his men tumbled into the Ford and Rivera drove them to North Beach, where he installed them in their closet with a large sausage pizza, several bottles of water, and two new wool blankets, before he went home and fell into a sleep as deep as the dead.

Religion in Chinatown, as in most places, is based less on a cogent theology and more on a collection of random fears, superstitions, prejudices, forgotten customs, vestigial animism, and social control. Mrs. Ling, while a professed Buddhist of the Pure Land tradition, also kept waving cat charms, lucky coins, and put great faith in the good fortune of the color red. She gave gifts of money on the Chinese New Year, threw *I-Ching* coins for guidance, believed in the comfort of ghost brides for old men who died alone, and was very much in favor of any tradition, superstition, or ritual that involved fireworks, including New Year's, Independence Day, and the end of the Giants' season. She followed the Chinese zodiac with a stubborn devotion, and because she was born in the year of the dragon, she thought them the luckiest of all creatures. Which was why her friend Vladlena Korjev found her in the state she did when she returned home from the hospital.

Having not encountered her friend in the hallways after two days home, and hearing strange noises at Mrs. Ling's door, Mrs. Korjev did as they had agreed ("In case we fall, and break hip, like bear") and used her key to let herself into Mrs. Ling's apartment. She found her friend seated at one end of the sofa, watching her stories on the Chinese channel, while at the other end of the sofa sat Wiggly Charlie. Each was joyfully eating a mozzarella stick, and Mrs. Ling, who was mildly lactose intolerant, let fly with a diminutive *"bffffrat"* of gas every thirty seconds or so, at which both she and Wiggly Charlie would snicker until they wheezed.

"He lucky dlagon," explained Mrs. Ling. Wiggly Charlie had avoided the braised fate of a prior, and less chatty, Squirrel Person when, after being roughly yanked from his cat carrier by his feet, he asked the petite matron for a cheese, thereby establishing his lucky-magic-dragon-ness. Mrs. Ling agreed that if Mrs. Korjev would keep the secret, she could share in the dragon's luck, and the three spent many a pleasant afternoon sitting on the sofa, dragon in the middle, grandmother on either end, watching stories, eating cheese sticks, and gleefully giggling at Mrs. Ling's delicate condition.

Some mornings, Mrs. Ling would put Wiggly Charlie in the cat carrier and take him for a ride around the neighborhood in her cart, feeling very special and blessed among the multitudes in North Beach and Chinatown, for she alone rolled with a dragon. Other mornings Wiggly Charlie spent with Mrs. Korjev, who would stand him on her counter and drill him like a Cossack sergeant major:

"Need a cheez," Wiggly Charlie would say.

"How you need cheese?" Mrs. Korjev would inquire.

"Like bear," the lucky dragon would reply.

And thus a cheese would be bestowed upon the long-donged dragon.

The care and feeding of their lucky dragon, as well as the leap in credibility engendered by his very existence, helped the two grandmothers better adjust to the condition of their Sophie, who now had not two, but *three* mommies, and to the fact that the sneaky, usurping drug fiend Mike Sullivan was, in fact, Charlie Asher.

Once you accept you have a miniature talking dragon in your midst, the idea that your former landlord has changed bodies and has taken a Buddhist nun as a bride is a minor leap of faith. Audrey left her resident position at the Buddhist Center and moved in with Charlie despite some objections from Sophie ("Really, Dad, the *shiksa* booty nun?") and they, with the help of two loving aunties, and the two rental grandmothers, set about raising the little girl who would possibly grow up to be Death.

"Maybe she has always had the powers, but just didn't want to hurt anyone," said Audrey.

"So you think my daughter may still be Death, but she's broken?" Charlie said.

"Not broken," Audrey said, "just not finished yet."

"I'm telling you, that child is not normal," said Minty Fresh, who had seen her through the eyes of Anubis and knew. "For one thing, she got a mouth on her like a sailor."

"Her auntie Jane is very proud of that," said Charlie.

After a time, their suspicions about Sophie's future were confirmed when the hellhounds returned and remained Sophie's constant companions everywhere but at school, where they waited patiently outside as she instructed until they could escort her home in the afternoon. The goggies were quite happy and fairly well behaved, only occasionally sneaking down to a North Beach sidewalk café where one would eat a comfort dog off the lap of some self-indulgent diner, only to return looking innocent but for the leash hanging out of the corner of his mouth. To atone, Charlie encouraged San Francisco's animal control people to put the hellhounds down, and at Sophie's instruction, they would go away in the back of a truck, only to return a few hours later, justice done, somewhat stoned on whatever poison they'd been given, to resume spinning bags of kibble into great steaming spools of stool.

When Inspector Alphonse Rivera returned to his bookstore and opened his copy of the *Great Big Book of Death*, he found the entire text had been changed to the following:

"Congratulations, you were one of the select few chosen to act as Death. It was a dirty job, but someone had to do it. A new order has been established and your services will no longer be required. Feel free to keep the calendar and the number two pencils for your own personal use. Best of luck in all your future endeavors."

Rivera called the other Death Merchants that he knew to confirm that their copies of the *Big Book* had changed as well, which they had. For a moment, he considered putting a price tag on his copy of the *Big Book* and offering it for sale in his shop, but after contemplating how sneaky and ever-changing the universe appeared to be, he decided instead to keep it in his personal collection, just for reference, in case things got weird.

He also decided, having served twenty-five years as a policeman and survived the reset of the Wheel of Life and Death still never having shot a human being, nor having been shot, that he would take a second retirement and become a bookseller full-time, despite the precarious prospects of that profession.

On his second day of his second retirement, Rivera called Lily Severo's mother, Elizabeth, and invited her to join him for coffee. The two found they quite liked each other, and started dating regularly. What began as gratitude for being rescued from loneliness developed into love; they reveled in sharing who they were and how they had come to this place in their lives, and everything was made that much sweeter by how much their relationship annoyed Lily.

Lily, having served nobly as oracle to the bridge, found the specialness she felt by having been chosen remained, even after the ghosts moved on. She comported herself, at least outwardly, with less cynicism and hostility toward the world, and at times, with humility and style, if only because she knew secretly how much it annoyed everyone who had known her before.

"So," Charlie Asher said to her, "I'm going to reopen the shop. I mean, it was a successful business for my family for thirty years before I became Death, there's no reason why it can't be again. And the pizza oven is still in there. So I thought we might go into *business* together."

"So it would be Asher's Random Used Crap and Artisanal Pizza?"

"No. Not necessarily. You could put your name on the sign, too."

"Thanks, Charlie, but I don't think so. I'm going to stay at the Crisis Center and go back to school. Get a degree in counseling, maybe even become a psychologist."

"That's horrifying," Charlie said. "I mean, I'm happy for you. I'm proud of you, but your poor patients."

"Hey, blow me, Asher. Those crazy fucks will be lucky to have me."

"That's what I meant," he said.

"I have a knack with the damaged," Lily said. "It's my thing. Speaking of which, I'm supposed to go see M."

The Mint One, his duty as a demigod done for now, returned to Fresh Music and resumed his business to great success. Despite the lack of any supernatural stimulus, the current horde of elitist music enthusiasts with money that were infesting the city, each looking for anything more obscure and/or arcane than his contemporaries, had created a booming market for worthless crap that Minty Fresh had long ago relegated to the realm of unsellable, and the buyback market, fueled by their mercurial smartphone-crippled attention spans, was whipped into a light and frothy profit.

He was adding up the day's receipts, and *Bitches Brew* was playing in the background when Lily came into the shop.

"Look," she said, "you are not *the* love of my life, but you are definitely *a* love in my life, so if you're okay with that, I'd love to spend some more time with you, but if I break your heart, I warned you, so it's fair."

"I'd like that," said Minty Fresh. "But you're not going to break my heart. I am the human presence of an ancient Egyptian god of death, girl."

"Sure, throw that in my face. But I got my thing, too. And besides, you cried on my voice mail." She made as if to draw her phone out and play the proof. "You *want* me to break your heart, that's not healthy."

"I do not want that. I am not the blues, I am jazz. I want to be present in the moment, not wallow in it. Do you feel me?"

"About that; how is it you're all erudite and nerdy some of the time, and other times you're all smooth and badass and black?"

"I'm black as I need to be. I use the language that serves what I have to say. You cool with that?"

"Are you cool with me thinking that Miles Davis sounds like he's smothering squirrels?"

Minty Fresh feigned taking an arrow to the heart, then shook it off.

"I guess Miles don't work for everybody."

"And *Pizazz* was a stupid name for a restaurant."

"Well, I don't—"

"Admit it!"

"All right, *Pizzaz* was a stupid name for a restaurant."

"Good, I win," she said, moving close enough to the counter so he could kiss her when the time came. "Now we can play for fun."

When the ghosts of the bridge rose to find their places in the universe, so, too, did all the souls in all the soul vessels around the world. The souls of the surviving Squirrel People, who had turned to neo-druids since the attack of the Morrigan, and who had built a miniature Stonehenge from stolen hotel mini-fridges in their amphitheater beneath the Buddhist Center, also found their way back onto the Wheel of Life and Death, most moving on to live new lives as humans, except for Bob (who was Theeb), whose soul would be reincarnated twice as a woodchuck and once as hedgehog to present to him the lesson of humility, because the universe thought he had been kind of a dick.

When the ghosts of the bridge rose to find their places in the universe, Jean-Pierre Baptiste just happened to be cradling the cat person who had been his patient and friend, Helen. She went limp in his arms and he could see the red glow of her soul in her chest ascend and pass through the ceiling. Baptiste knew he would have some difficulty breaking the habit of being kind to Helen, and would have to console himself by being actively kind to other patients, as did most of the people of his calling.

Not coincidentally, halfway around the world, in Paris, on the four-hundred-year-old stone bridge over the Seine called the Pont Neuf, a craftsman named Jacques was repairing one of the carved marble faces that decorated the fascia of the bridge when a ghost appeared sitting on the railing above him. She wore the midcalf tweed skirt and crisp white blouse of a college girl from the midtwentieth century on her semester abroad in Paris. She wore her hair shoulder length and curled under in the style of Katharine Hepburn's in *Bringing Up Baby*, Kate being her idol.

"Bonjour, monsieur," she said to Jacques. *"Je suis Helen."* And she proceeded to outline, in French with a heavy American accent, what would be required of him. And different ghosts, each more charming than the last, appeared to people on bridges all over the world, and thus was established the new turn of the Wheel of Life and Death, so that each soul on its journey between bodies, would pause in a place between places, and then continue on toward its proper place as part of the universe.

ACKNOWLEDGMENTS

The author gratefully acknowledges the help of the following in the research of *Secondhand Souls*:

Michael Tucker, who helped me locate Concepción Arguella and Count Nikolai Rezanov's love story, prompted only by a very vague memory of a book I read twenty years ago.

Eileen Hirst, for the lowdown on cop funerals and city politics, much of which I blissfully ignored.

Mike Krukow and Duane Kuiper, the intrepid San Francisco Giants TV announcers, to whom I owe credit for all the baseball lingo I know, except the profanities, which they would never, ever use.

Monique Motil, whose brilliant "sartorial creatures" sculptures were the inspiration for the Squirrel People.

Ryan, Piper, and Presley Pombrio, for the lowdown on princesses and little ponies.

And Charlee Gina Michelle Hieronymus Carnitas Tremble Moss Moore, for insight on her hospice work, as well as her patience, tolerance, and generosity, without which, this book would have never been finished.

ABOUT THE AUTHOR

Christopher Moore is the author of fourteen previous novels, including *Lamb*, *The Stupidest Angel*, *A Dirty Job*, *Fool*, *Sacré Bleu*, and *The Serpent of Venice*. He lives in San Francisco, California.